SHAW'S WAR

Antony Melville-Ross

SPHERE BOOKS LIMITED

SPHERE BOOKS LTD

Published by the Penguin Group
27 Wrights Lane, London w8 5tz, England
Viking Penguin Inc., 40 West 23rd Street, New York, New York 10010, USA
Penguin Books Australia Ltd, Ringwood, Victoria, Australia
Penguin Books Canada Ltd, 2801 John Street, Markham, Ontario, Canada l3r 1b4
Penguin Books (NZ) Ltd, 182–190 Wairau Road, Auckland 10, New Zealand

Penguin Books Ltd, Registered Offices: Harmondsworth, Middlesex, England

First published in Great Britain by Michael Joseph Ltd 1988
Published by Sphere Books Ltd 1989
1 3 5 7 9 10 8 6 4 2

Printed and bound in Great Britain by
Richard Clay Ltd, Bungay, Suffolk

They were on their second brandy when Shaw said, 'Now you're in virtual charge, will you be making any changes in Ulster?'

Brigg shrugged. 'I could hardly tell *you* if I were, Harry, but the answer's no, because there are no logical changes to *be* made. We simply have to keep plugging away. The only other option involves an Eastern Bloc scenario; bringing half the Rhine Army home, using tanks and strike aircraft, literally occupying the bloody place and taking it apart. You know perfectly well that that would be a totally self-defeating exercise . . .' He sighed and added, 'Harry, remind me to put you on a charge of something or other. I don't know what yet, but reducing your senior officer to a condition in which he mouths truisms must be to the prejudice of good order and military discipline.'

Shaw grasped the opportunity. 'You'll have to hurry, sir,' he said. 'I've decided to resign.'

'You said that as though you meant it.'

'I do mean it.'

'Want to tell me about it?'

'Killing people seems to have lost its charm,' Shaw said.

For Rupert, James and Emma

I

The curtains of water falling from the heavy overcast added their quota of cheerlessness to the glum little village from which the inhabitants appeared to have fled. Nothing moved in its single street except for the surface of puddles stippled by raindrops until a solitary figure emerged from the woodland at its end, advancing cautiously like an explorer entering a hostile environment. No lights glowed to greet him or to challenge the approaching dusk, not even from the sullen bar of the single inn. There *was* life there, but only a resentful existence, a waiting. Men drank their dark beer as though they hated it and from behind the counter the landlord, squinting against the smoke rising from the cigarette in his mouth, watched them without friendliness. A peat fire smouldered apathetically as if it were dying of boredom, and a black Labrador bitch lay motionless in front of it as though she already had.

The Labrador opened one red eye and growled when the street door opened to admit a man wearing a brown plastic jacket slick with rain, but the other occupants of the room only glanced at him. They knew who he was, but had no wish to make that knowledge evident. The man flicked water from his dark hair, looked around him, then walked to the counter.

'Who's them two strangers, Leo?' He had spoken very quietly.

The landlord took a shot glass from the shelf behind him, slopped whiskey into it and pushed it across the bar-top to the speaker, then just as quietly replied, 'A couple of ravin' German queens from that electronics plant at Enniskillen.'

'Staying here?'

1

'Yeah. Fishin' holiday.'

'Sharing a room, are they?'

'Now, boy,' the landlord said, 'you know I'd not be allowin' that, but only one bed gets used much. I heard one of them creepin' along the passage last night and the pair of them gigglin' 'til all hours. Holy Mother of God! If you don't believe me will you be lookin' at them now?'

Angling his head to gain a view of the couple in the long mirror behind the bar and finding it impossible, the man turned, setting the small of his back against the counter and stared openly, offensively, at the seated figures, but they had eyes only for each other. The elder was dark, saturnine. The younger blond, baby-faced. Both wore belted green tweed sports jackets, knee-breeches, long woollen socks and brogues. Faces close, almost touching, they talked in whispers, the exchange punctuated by the younger's soft treble laugh. Beneath the table their little fingers were linked.

Turning again, the man in the plastic jacket muttered, 'Jesus,' then asked, 'You quite sure they're Jerries?'

'Sure and I'm sure. "Can I for my friend a glass of orange have, and for myself a small glass of bitter, *bitte*?"' The landlord repeated 'a small glass of bitter, *bitte*', and sniffed in disgust.

'Anyody could say that, Leo.'

'No, no, boy. They're Jerries all right. Look at their clothes for a start. They've got German passports, their fishin' tackle is German, and so are their books. I looked in their rooms. They talk Kraut together all the time too, and one of them had a letter waitin' for him here. From Frankfurt it was.'

'All right then,' the other said. 'Hit me with that whiskey again, and let's be having a little light in here.'

The strangers rose and left the bar forty minutes later, turning towards the inn's small dining-room. The Labrador, interested only in the door from the street, ignored them, but the landlord watched them go with distaste clear on his face.

He watched them again as they left the inn the next morning from the barn where he was milking his cows. Rubber boots had replaced their brogues, but the rest of their clothes were the ones they had worn the evening before. Both carried fishing-rods and canvas shoulder-bags, and each clasped the disengaged hand of the other as though sure of their privacy in the early light of dawn, a dawn from which the night's rain had vanished. Now there were only tendrils of mist the sun was not yet high enough to dispel, floating like ectoplasm in the woodland at each end of the village street. The blond man's inane giggle reached his ears as he saw them turn left towards the lake to be lost to sight amongst the mist-shrouded trees. He spat on the floor of the barn, then grasped the cow's udders lightly, unaware that the couple had changed direction, half circling the village to approach the stream separating it from the Republic of Ireland.

The landlord was listening to the metallic tinkle of milk jets striking the side of a newly emptied bucket when the greater sound came, a distant rippling snarl which froze the movement of his hands, but electrified his legs so that he was up and running clear of the barn before full understanding caught up with him.

'Daniel! Sean!' he shouted at the empty village street. 'Come quick! The meetin's been hit!' And suddenly the street wasn't empty anymore. Men seemed to flow from doorways, some armed, some not, some dressed, some struggling into their trousers. 'What?' 'Who?' 'Where?' Then they were surging after him and, because he was no longer young, overtaking him too, urged forward by his violently gesturing arm.

They found the look-out first, lying at the base of the tree he had climbed, a thrown knife protruding from his back. He had a broken neck as well, but whether as a result of his fall or from any other cause they didn't stop to establish. Then they reached the meeting site.

The man who had worn the brown plastic jacket the evening before was still wearing it, but it was pock-marked with a score of bullet holes now and his lower jaw had been shot away. Two other bodies lay near him, one on its side, one face down.

'Flannigan and Quinn! Who's that one?'

Somebody rolled the prostrate figure on to its back and said, 'Oh, Jesus! Isn't this Macnamara?'

'It is so, the Blessed Virgin help us.' Shock and grief in the

3

words. More sharply, 'You with guns! Spread out and search south and west!' The speaker stooped, picked up one of the spent cartridge cases littering the ground and added, 'This is Heckler & Koch calibre, so remember who you're up against. Nobody else uses it. The rest of you –'

His words ceased abruptly at the engine noise which seemed to come out of nowhere. Then a helicopter clattered across the small clearing, almost touching the tops of the trees.

'It's a pick-up! Follow it, and run like hell! We'll get the bastards yet!'

But they had only reached the top of a small rise when the helicopter sagged towards a field more than a mile away. They stood panting, watching disconsolately as four soldiers dropped from it before it had touched down and crouched, rifles covering different sections of the wood. The whirling rotors dispersed the remnants of mist as though they had never been, giving them all a clear view of two figures dressed in green tweed sprinting across the open ground separating them from safety. Somebody spat out a stream of vicious obscenities and someone else fired a single shot from his gun, but the helicopter was already rising, racing nose-down across the meadow with the legs of the last man to board it still dangling from the entry port.

His baby-face creased with concentration as he cleaned his Heckler & Koch machine pistol, the blond man asked, 'Do people normally milk cows at dawn? I thought that happened at night. You know, "The curfew tolls the knell of passing day/The lowing herd wind slowly o'er the lea," and all that.' He had spoken in a near shout to make his words audible above the roar of the helicopter's engine and the buffeting of the man-made gale at the open ports.

Captain Henry Shaw, Special Air Service Regiment, experienced a now familiar start of surprise at his sergeant's ability both to conjure analytical thought out of tension eased only minutes before and to quote from Gray's *Elegy* by way of illustration. Not that it was always Gray; it could be anybody from Shakespeare to the President of the World Bank if the latter ever said anything memorable.

Long self-trained in not showing surprise for any reason, he kept his saturnine features immobile and said, 'It's "parting day", not "passing day", Bill.'

'So it's "parting day". So what about the cows, Harry?' Sergeant William Townsend insisted.

'It's perfectly normal,' Shaw told him. 'They milk around five or six in the morning and again in the afternoon. Sometimes three milkings are possible, depending on the season and the grazing.' He gave his own Heckler & Koch machine pistol a final wipe, put it into his fisherman's canvas shoulder-bag and added, 'But you're quite right. Our host at the inn was the second look-out. I'd have done it anyway, but seeing him squatting on his stool left us no option but to set off in the wrong direction. He could observe the whole village street from that barn.'

Townsend nodded. 'Three times a day, eh? Poor bloody cows.' For a moment he stared absently at the four Armalite 180 rifles they had taken from the men they had killed, then went on, 'You know, I never thought we'd get away with that "fairy" ploy. German or any other kind.'

'The betting was much better than evens,' Shaw said. 'Offend against people's sensitivities strongly enough and they'll believe anything. The chief risk was your terrible German, but the likelihood of some bog-trotting Mick spotting that was small.' He smiled faintly when Townsend mouthed the words '*Ich liebe dich*' with lips formed into a Marylin Monroe pout, then leaned back and closed his eyes.

The sergeant watched him for a moment, glanced round at the other occupants of the cabin, noticing for the first time that they were Scots Guards, then settled back himself feeling glad that he was not of their number. He liked the SAS. He liked it for its swift lethal efficiency when killing was called for, and its capacity for infinite patience when the role required of it was observation without detection. He liked it for its rigid discipline, a discipline almost entirely self-imposed through pride of regiment, and its informality when there was nothing formal about the occasion. He liked Harry Shaw too and, more importantly, trusted him completely and knew that he was trusted in return. That trust had been forged in the

Falkland Islands and had lasted ever since, which was why Townsend thought of Shaw as *his* officer.

He let his mind drift back over the years to the South Atlantic with its mists, gales and snow, remembering raids on the islands by both helicopter and boat. Some of those had been like taking candy from kids, but others had not, because there had been nothing childlike about the troops they had encountered then. There had been endless days as well, lying in shallow camouflaged slits in the freezing ground within rifle shot of an enemy unaware of their presence. That had been alternately boring and frightening and always extremely unpleasant physically, but it had ensured that the conventional forces had an almost complete picture of the Argentine dispositions when the main landings were made.

Once, they had gone further than the islands, Harry and he and the others, in a submarine with the Royal Marines' Special Boat Service to attack an airfield on the mainland and leave a lot of Dagger fighter planes in no condition to do anybody any harm. The Argentines had kept quiet about it, so had the press in Britain and, after a period of mild resentment, Townsend had come to accept the reason for that.

His mind continued to drift back in time to the flight out to Ascension Island and the Royal Fleet Auxiliary he had joined there for the long voyage south, and that reminded him of a song the Marines and Paratroopers on board had sung. Silently he sang it to himself:

> I'm going on a holiday
> To land on a distant shore
> And kill me a Spick or two,
> Or maybe three or more.

'Spicks' then and 'Micks' now, he thought. There wasn't a lot of difference to it except that the 'Micks' hit back harder.

Sergeant William Townsend's mind drifted even further and he slept.

The six men from Belfast arrived at the village two hours after the helicopter had taken off and parked their car outside the inn. All were wearing black knitted helmets which left only their eyes and mouths exposed. A similar number of local residents going about their business disappeared into whichever house was nearest to them, leaving the street as deserted as it had been the evening before.

Without haste, five of the men got out of the car and filed into the inn, moving faster once they were inside it, two of them vaulting the bar counter to stand either side of the landlord. The Labrador growled.

'We hear the Germans have landed at last, Leo.'

The landlord stared at the speaker, the smallest of the three men ranged across the doorway, his suddenly grey face making the distended blood vessels in his nose and cheeks look like a miniature road map. He tried to speak, but no words came.

'Fooled you, didn't they, Leo? The fucking SAS fooled you proper, and that's a shame, indeed it is, when all you had to do was phone Enniskillen and ask for them at the factory there. At least then you would have known what they were not and we would have known what they were. Isn't that right, Leo?'

From somewhere the landlord found his voice. 'I did. It was the obvious thing to do. The factory confirmed their bookin' and told me their arrival time. You can check easy.'

'Ah, the cunning bastards,' the small man said. 'Covered themselves at that end too did they? Well now that's a little better, Leo. In fact, you just saved your life. Now all we need do is discipline you a little to remind you that eternal vigilance is the watchword. Grab him, boys.'

He struggled fiercely, but it wasn't any use and all resistance seemed to run out of him when, holding him by the arms and legs, they bent him backwards across his own bar. He didn't speak, just looked with horrified eyes at the gun in the small man's hand.

'This,' the man told him, 'is for lack of vigilance in the great struggle for a free and united Ireland which cost the lives of four of your comrades-in-arms.'

The sound of the unsilenced gunshot was deafening in the confined space, carrying its message to every house in the village. The Labrador yelped and slunk under a table. The landlord's whole body jerked as the bullet smashed through his left kneecap. For countable seconds there was silence until

7

the anaesthetic of shock receded from him and he began to emit a wild keening sound which grew into a pulsing shriek of agony.

'And this is for one of them being the great Macnamara,' the man with the gun said, when he began to quieten, and shot him through the right knee.

The landlord lay unconscious on the floor and there was only the agitated calling of birds disturbed by the firing to be heard when the five men left the inn.

2

'I'm deeply disturbed by this whole affair,' the youngish man in the grey chalk-stripe suit said. 'No, I go further. I'm distressed and shocked! To sink to such depths can do nothing but bring well-deserved opprobrium down on our heads!'

'The cunning old bugger,' the brigadier thought, a description directed not at the newly-appointed junior minister for Northern Ireland sitting opposite him, but at the major-general, his immediate superior, who had discovered some compelling reason to attend at the Ministry of Defence during this particular visitor's fact-finding mission to Belfast. He raised his eyebrows and waited, not speaking.

'Have you nothing to say?'

'I didn't hear you ask me a question, Minister,' the brigadier replied. 'You were being disturbed – I mean distressed and shocked. If you want me to agree that these are distressing and shocking times in Ulster I will certainly do so. They have been, in this latest phase, ever since 1969 when you hadn't been long out of school. But don't expect me to share your emotions about this particular operation which was cleverly planned and most effectively executed.'

'Planned by whom?'

'By the two men who carried it out. Two men who would have faced certain torture and death had they been apprehended by the Provisional IRA. Macnamara was one of the most important men in that organisation, if not *the* most important. We've been trying to get at him for six years and now we have. Why cavil at success?'

'Because,' the minister said, 'such means defile the ends they were designed to attain, and that cannot be permitted when we are engaged in attempting to win over the minds and hearts of the people.'

'That's your job, Minister. A few years ago it might have been mine too, in the days when the troops could mingle with the local population, but murderous bastards like Macnamara put an end to that. The Army's in no position to deal in hazy abstractions anymore. We're dealing with Ulster nihilism and my brief is to make it as difficult as possible for them to carry that philosophy to the ultimate conclusion of mutual genocide. The elimination of Macnamara will make the task that much easier.'

'And the only way of achieving that was to send in two screaming Yahoos in civilian clothes to gun the unsuspecting man down?'

The question induced instant rage in the brigadier, a rage quickly suppressed and reduced first to contempt and then sadness. He had served with the SAS in Oman and might have been with them still had not the financial demands of an increasing family obliged him to seek promotion outside the regiment. He knew them for what they were, a military force of such diverse abilities as to have no equal, no counterpart, in any army in the world. He knew them as free-fall parachutists, experts in foreign weapons as well as their own, strong swimmers, skilled drivers, adept at unarmed combat, demolition and sabotage. They had linguistic abilities too, covering many tongues from German through Arabic to Thai. Their expertise in such disparate techniques as counter-insurgency and aircraft anti-hijack procedures had been requested by and provided to numerous foreign governments across half the globe. If any body of men could claim to be Jacks of all trades and masters of many, the SAS was that body.

For a moment, the brigadier was tempted to explain all that and more to the minister, concluded that it would be a waste of time and asked a question of his own.

'Do you know who the SAS are, Minister?'

'The glory boys who out-commando the Commandos, and do a little moonlighting in the field of assassination if this recent episode is anything to go by.'

10

'I'm afraid you've been misinformed,' the brigadier said. 'They're neither glory boys nor Commandos. Nor, for that matter, are they Yahoos, screaming or otherwise. They're very highly-trained mobile infantry who act, when the situation demands, as armed extensions of both MI5 and MI6. As it was in one of those capacities that two of their number acted in Armagh recently, I suggest that you voice your objections to your colleagues at the Home Office or the Foreign and Commonwealth Office, not to me.' As if to prevent further argument he added angrily, 'What the blazes do you think they were doing at the Iranian Embassy siege in Princes Gate in 1980 if they weren't supporting Special Branch?'

But the questioning hadn't stopped there and it was over two hours later when, with carefully concealed relief, the brigadier escorted the minister to his helicopter. Within a week he received notification of his promotion to major-general with immediate effect. That both pleased and surprised him. What surprised him more was a covering letter from an officer who shared his new rank. It stated that an unbiased observer had assisted his superiors in arriving at their decision to offer him his new post by reporting favourably on his grasp of the local situation and the function of the forces at his disposal.

'The cunning young bugger,' the ex-brigadier said.

On 15 April 1986, eleven days after the killing of Macnamara, United States Air Force F1-11 bombers based in Britain and aircraft of the US Sixth Fleet in the Mediterranean attacked selected targets at Tripoli and Benghazi on the coast of Libya.

Captain Henry Shaw and Sergeant William Townsend heard of the raid on the same BBC newscast. Both of them had been immediately removed from Ulster as marked men following their incursion into the bandit country of Armagh. Shaw listened to it in his apartment off Kensington High Street, Townsend at his father's house in Blackheath. Shaw switched off his bedside radio and got up, looking pensive. Townsend left his on, turned over and went back to sleep, only to be awakened again ten minutes later by a hammering on his bedroom door and his father calling, 'Phone for you, son. Bloke called Harry.'

'Oh for Christ's sake, dad. It's the middle of the bloody night. Harry who?'

'It's gone eight in the morning, you lazy little sod, and I don't know Harry who. He didn't say, but he sounds like a toff.'

'Oh, *that* Harry,' Townsend said. 'Coming!'

Townsend joined Shaw for lunch at a pub near Marble Arch. They ordered beer and cheese with pickle sandwiches.

'What's up, Harry?' Townsend asked.

'Nothing really. I just thought you might like a beer or two.'

'Well, thanks very much. What do you think the Yanks are trying to do?'

'They're not *trying* to do anything,' Shaw said. 'They're succeeding.'

'At what, for Pete's sake?'

'At over-reacting,' Shaw told him, then asked, 'When are you due to report back at Hereford?'

Townsend filled his mouth with sandwich to give himself a moment to think. 'Nothing really' Shaw had said when asked for a reason for the sudden invitation to lunch, and 'Nothing really' equalled 'something' in Townsend's language. Then had come the indifferent dismissal of what could prove to be the news story of the year in favour of establishing the date of his return to SAS headquarters. Shaw's face, he noted, was as impassive as usual, but he had taken a spent match from the ashtray and was absently excavating beneath his finger-nails with it. It was unlike him to do a thing like that.

'Tomorrow,' he said.

'They got a job for you?'

'Yeah. Running a ten-day survival course in the west of Scotland for some new recruits. Christ! How I hate worms!'

'There's no need to be like the Marines and eat the damned things boiled whole,' Shaw said. 'Bake them and crumble them into water. You retain all the protein that way and avoid optical and tactile revulsion.'

And that was strange too, Townsend thought. It was unlike Shaw to tell him things he knew to be known already.

'What's on your mind, Harry?' he asked.

Shaw examined his manicure for blemishes, then discarded

the match before saying, 'I'm thinking of resigning my commission.'

'Shit! What the hell for? You'll be a major before you know it!'

'There's a job I'm pretty sure I have to do, Bill, and it's a lot more important than being a major.'

'Like what?'

'I can't tell you yet.'

'But it has something to do with the date of my return to Hereford,' Townsend said. It wasn't a question.

'Indirectly. Your time's nearly up, isn't it? Are you going to sign on again?'

'Yes, to the first. I finish in August, as you bloody well know. It was yes to the second too, before this crazy conversation began. The only skills I have are staying alive so I can kill other people, and that's something else you know.'

Shaw nodded and asked, 'Will you do something for me? Will you postpone signing on again until you have to? I need a few weeks. After that, I may be in a position to offer you a job. It could get us both killed but, if I figure it right, it could make us a lot of money.'

'Well, it would need to do that if we're to give up our careers for it, wouldn't it?' Townsend said. 'All right, Harry, I'll wait to hear from you.'

The pub began to fill with office workers released from their desks for their lunch-time breaks and Shaw went quickly to the bar for more beer before the growing crowd made it unapproachable. He was grateful to Townsend for not pressing questions on him, but not surprised. It had been a long time since the sergeant had disagreed with anything he did, even if he didn't know why he was doing it or even what it was. They spent another hour and drank two more beers together, talking of other things, then Townsend rose to his feet.

'Here I stand. I cannot do otherwise. God help me. Amen,' he said.

Shaw looked up at him resignedly. 'So what's that a quote from?'

'It's Martin Luther refusing to retract his teachings before the Diet of Worms, Germany, AD 1521. He and I have a lot in common.'

13

'Powdering them into acorn coffee helps disguise the taste,' Shaw said. 'Now piss off, Bill. I've got some thinking to do.'

Shaw walked through Hyde Park, ignoring the pathways. Striding across damp grass which needed cutting so badly that it soaked the bottoms of his trousers and ignoring that too, his mind strove to encompass a plan long dormant in it. The plan was stirring now, prodded into restlessness by the voice of a news presenter heard six hours earlier. It was still formless, probably hopeless, certainly madness but, his mind assured him, infinitely worth attempting if the means could be found. Means meant money, a lot of money. The plan didn't need form for that to be obvious. Means meant men too, not a lot of them, but men with specialised skills. He possessed many of those skills and so did Townsend which was the reason why, almost as a reflex to what his ears had heard, he had contacted him. Part of the reason, Shaw corrected himself. The other part was that they were a team and a bloody good one, with something close to the telepathic about their combined reaction to an emergency.

For a moment Shaw let his thoughts dwell on Townsend: a man limited by family background to no more than a secondary education, an education which had totally failed to limit *him* until he had chosen to limit himself. He could have held a commission in most regiments of the British Army, had been made aware of that fact by a number of people, including Shaw, but elected to stay where he was. Being a sergeant in the élite body which was the SAS rated higher in Townsend's scale of things than being an officer anywhere else. Such an attitude was by no means uncommon within the regiment and neither Shaw nor Townsend's other advisers pressed him unduly to change his mind. He had done well by his country and if that was the extent of his ambition so be it.

Shaw and a sudden, bad-tempered squall of rain arrived at the Serpentine at the same moment. He paused briefly, watching the surface of the water turn from glass into beaten pewter and the few boats make for the Lido, then resumed his striding, crossed the bridge and followed the curve of the lake towards the north. When he reached the Peter Pan statue he stopped again and stared at it sombrely, wondering if his intentions indicated that he shared arrested development with the fictional whimsy the little figure represented.

'Hello, Harry. Mourning your lost innocence?' It was a familiar voice.

'Nothing so nostalgic,' Shaw replied. 'I'm conducting a technical appraisal into the possibilities of free-fall parachuting without a parachute. This chap knew how it was done.' He turned towards the speaker and added, 'Hello, sir. What are you doing in London?'

The other looked momentarily embarrassed, then shrugged and said, 'I was called to the War House for a briefing. They've just pushed me up a notch.'

'Major-General?'

'Yes.'

Shaw smiled. 'That must be something of a relief, sir. Congratulations.'

'A pleasant surprise, certainly, but why a relief?' the new major-general asked, shaking the hand offered to him.

'Just that brigadier must have been an unfortunate rank for you personally. My sergeant used to refer to you as "Brig Brigg, the double jeopardy". He'll have to stop that now.'

Realising that the chance encounter had presented him with an opportunity both to bolster his resolve by committing himself further to his plan and to pre-empt, at least to a degree, the inevitable official questions which would follow his decision to leave the Army, Shaw added, 'Look, unless you're tied up with affairs of state, why not come and have a drink to celebrate?'

'Nice idea, but the bars are just closing.'

'Mine isn't, sir,' Shaw said. 'I've got a flat just off Ken High. We could walk there within a few minutes.'

Surrendering his raincoat to Shaw, Major-General Brigg looked round at the second-floor apartment, feeling surprise and mild envy that a captain could afford such elegant accommodation.

'What a very pleasant flat. I've always wanted an L-shaped room. Is there much more of it?'

'Bedroom, kitchen and bathroom, plus a studio on the floor

above, up the stairs behind that curtain. My father left me the place. I think he brought his women here. Coffee and brandy suit you, sir?'

'Admirably, thanks.'

They were on their second brandy when Shaw said, 'Now you're in virtual charge, will you be making any changes in Ulster?'

Brigg shrugged. 'I could hardly tell *you* if I were, Harry, but the answer's no, because there are no logical changes to *be* made. We simply have to keep plugging away. The only other option involves an Eastern Bloc scenario; bringing half the Rhine Army home, using tanks and strike aircraft, literally occupying the bloody place and taking it apart. You know perfectly well that that would be a totally self-defeating exercise. It wouldn't get us anywhere, except right down the tubes of world opinion. Our function is to prevent civil war and . . .' He stopped talking, looked at the glass in his hand, sighed and added, 'Harry, remind me to put you on a charge of something or other. I don't know what yet, but reducing your senior officer to a condition in which he mouths truisms must be to the prejudice of good order and military discipline.'

Shaw grasped the opportunity. 'You'll have to hurry, sir,' he said. 'I've decided to resign.'

'You said that as though you meant it.'

'I do mean it.'

Brigg studied the dark face opposite him, but there was nothing to read in its flat planes, its grey eyes beneath intensely black brows, its long slit of a mouth. He felt no surprise because Shaw had appeared inscrutable for all the years he had known him, except for those occasions when he smiled. The cast of the features indicated that if a smile ever came it would be sardonic, but it was not so. It produced a rather sweet expression and Brigg liked that as it made Shaw human.

'Want to tell me about it?'

'Killing people seems to have lost its charm,' Shaw said.

'Balls, Harry! It never had any charm for you, or for any sane man. You can't lose something that never existed. You're a good officer who's done an excellent job over a long period

16

of time and you have medals to prove it, so tell me either what's bugging you or to mind my own business.'

The gentle smile came, then slowly faded before Shaw spoke. 'I can't really accept that, sir,' he said. 'I used to find it quite incredibly charming when I neutralised some Argentine yob or bad-tempered Omani tribesman who had been trying to blow my head off. Still, I know what you mean, but disaffection struck during this last tour in Northern Ireland. It was the first time I ever felt that I was acting illegally.' The lie came as readily as the smile had done.

'The Macnamara business?'

'Yes.'

'Well, now I've heard everything.' Brigg said. 'They had me vetted recently by a chap from the Northern Ireland Office who banged away on the morality drum, but not even *he* mentioned legality. Macnamara was serving eight life sentences for murder when he escaped from the Maze prison six years ago and he was responsible for many more deaths than that afterwards. Claimed them publicly. He was a very good terrorist, if that isn't a contradiction in terms, and he was also a raving psychopath. I see nothing illegal in mounting a search-and-destroy mission to remove a menace like him. Anyway, you suggested the operation yourself.'

Shaw was silent for long second before saying, 'As a matter of fact Sergeant Townsend had the original idea. I went along with it, and I'm regretting that now.' For a further second he considered adding the word 'bitterly', decided against it as being altogether too theatrical, but allowed sadness to shade his voice when he went on. 'We had to kill three other men to get at Macnamara. Who can say if they were guilty of anything meriting a sentence of death? I was trained as a soldier, not a hitman. When one can no longer make that distinction it's time to stop.'

The look on the general's face, a blend of concern and embarrassment, told Shaw that enough was enough. The seed of doubt about him had been sown and there was nothing to be gained by hammering it into the ground. He changed the subject.

'A little more brandy, sir?'

17

'No thanks, Harry,' Brigg replied. 'I'd better be getting along.'

Shaw was helping him on with his raincoat when Brigg said, 'Harry?'

'Sir?'

'Are you doing anything this evening?'

'Nothing in particular, sir. Why?'

'Would you care to dine with me? I'm taking my niece to the Ritz. We'd love to have you join us.'

Enter girl briefed by uncle to find out what's got into me, Shaw thought. Aloud he said, 'That's kind of you, but no thanks. It's a cardinal rule of mine never to go on blind dates.'

'I'm not offering you a date,' the general told him, his voice testy. 'I'm offering you dinner, but had it been a date, blind or otherwise, you'd be a darned fool to pass it up. Sarah's rather . . .' He stopped talking and looked around him as though there might be some clue in the room as to what his niece rather was, then added almost defensively, 'She's rather thrilling.' For a moment he looked taken aback at his choice of word, then nodded emphatically as though determined to stand by it.

Shaw's face remained as impassive as always, but he was disconcerted, firstly by his unmannerly remark about blind dates and secondly by the reaction and description it had produced. He now found himself in a dilemma of his own making, as to stand by his refusal would be churlish and to accept the invitation would imply that he had been tempted by Brigg's assessment of the girl.

Irritation at his own pettiness won and he let his smile show when he said, 'You've talked me into it, sir. I'd be delighted to join you both.'

Watching the general's retreating back from the street door of the flat it occurred to Shaw that his superior's obviously intended inquisition by proxy could be nothing more than a kindly attempt to obtain sufficient information for him to argue a brother officer out of ending his career, but he didn't believe it. Brigg was concerned about security, security placed at risk by the inexplicable attitude Shaw had so suddenly adopted.

He shrugged and turned his thoughts towards the girl he

was to meet. 'She's rather thrilling,' Brigg had said, and that was a very peculiar way for an uncle to describe his niece. It was a strange way for any man to describe any woman to anybody.

Finding himself staring along the street from which Brigg's figure had vanished, Shaw muttered, 'Well, don't get paranoid about it,' and climbed the stairs to his apartment.

3

Shaw had a headache, something he was not used to having. He thought it probably had its origin in drinking beer with Townsend and brandy with the general in the middle of the day. It was a satisfactory enough explanation for his small malaise and hid its true cause from him. That lay in the genie for so long imprisoned in the bottle of his mind and released that day with such suddenness when the United States Navy and Air Force had withdrawn the cork. He overlooked, too, the three hours it had taken him, crouched over his desk, to set the genie's message down on paper. More used to covering great distances across difficult terrain with almost inhuman rapidity, the sedentary exercise and the concentration demanded by it had tired him. The result of his efforts was not long, but it had been necessary to write it all out four times because he had no intention of allowing any part of it to be read by the operator of a photocopying machine. After he had looked for aspirin in the bathroom cabinet and failed to find any, he settled back in an armchair to read what he had written for the final time.

'The Ulster problem,' he read, 'particularly in the form it has taken since 1969, is virtually incapable of solution locally by any civilised means and growing more difficult with every passing day. There is no need to record here the conflicting claims of the Protestant majority and the Catholic minority. They are too well known to bear repetition. Nor is it necessary to make out a case for the British presence in the Province. Apart from the undisputed fact that the Army is there at the request and insistence of the majority of the population, and is

20

entrusted with the duty of preventing civil war, it has every right to be where it is, even though it would greatly prefer to be somewhere else. The right is historical and has far greater validity than, for example, the American presence in California and other territories taken from Mexico by force of arms as late as the middle of the last century. Our right of tenure in Ulster predates that by more than 150 years.'

At that point it occurred to Shaw that it really was rather silly to state that there was no need to make a case and then immediately make one but, having no desire to write the whole thing out again, he grunted and read on.

'What *is* necessary is to look at what has happened and is still happening. Since 1969 over 2,000 people, civilians, police and military, have been killed and 26,000 maimed. This pointless tragedy, the continuance of which is reported almost daily by the media, has now become self-perpetuating, an entire generation having grown up accepting it as a natural way of life. Indoctrination of whichever flavour begins in the family, continues in schools and *Na Fianna Eirann* until the budding terrorist is old enough to be inducted into the Provisional IRA and the Irish National Liberation Army on the one hand, or organisations like the Ulster Volunteer Force on the other.'

Shaw got up, went to his desk and wrote 'Boy Scouts' above *Na Fianna Eirann* on each copy of his notes then returned to his chair.

'This applies only to a small percentage of the population,' the note continued, 'but it is a large enough group to ensure a constant supply of misinformed individuals wedded through brain-washing to ideals totally unacceptable to the great mass of their fellow countrymen. Such people are to be pitied, but they also have to be stopped and the only way to stop them is to deprive them of their source of military hardware, money and moral support. Some small part of these things originates in the Eastern Bloc and Libya, but the bulk comes from the USA and often a proportion reaching Ireland from other sources is channelled through the States. These are established facts from which it follows automatically that the British Army is currently being required to kill the wrong people, because the real enemy is based in Boston, New York and other American cities.

'I recall seeing, a few years back, a photograph published by one of our daily tabloids of a group of Irish-Americans taken in Ireland. They were all members of the organisation known as NORAID, devoted to the arming of the IRA. The picture's caption read: "Say hello to your friends from Murder Inc." That was and remains an apt description, and it is they, not the misguided Irish visionaries they support, who should be attacked. That fact has been apparent for a very long time and is supported, if any support were necessary, by the Senate's inexcusable refusal to ratify the relevant extradition treaty between our two countries.'

Reading that last sentence again Shaw wished he hadn't written it because he had strayed into the field of jurisprudence, a discipline about which he knew next to nothing, but lethargy and his headache persuaded him to let it stand. The last paragraph made his case and his intentions clear enough.

That stated: 'For some time past the President has been claiming the right to take retaliatory action against countries which export terrorism. Today that "right" was exercised by means of air strikes on the two main cities of Libya. That action, and our agreement to it, has written a new chapter in international law. I now intend to apply that law against certain selected targets in the United States of America from which terrorism is also exported in the hope that recognition by the American people of their own double standards will make a solution of the Ulster problem a possibility. This action seems not in the least unreasonable by any standard of moral philosophy. If one equates five American deaths with an air assault on a nation which, however unpleasant its ruler may be, might well be guiltless, what price should be paid by those certainly guilty by proxy of so very many of the casualties suffered in Northern Ireland?'

Back at his desk Shaw addressed four envelopes, put a copy of his signed note into each and stuck down the flaps. He put the envelopes into a larger one, stapled it shut, then wrote on it: 'To be opened and the contents mailed to the addressees only on my instructions or in the event of my death.' Then he scribbled a covering letter to his lawyer and prepared the whole package for the post.

His head was aching quite badly now and he wished that he didn't have to go to the Ritz to eat, be thrilled, or anything else, but he couldn't back out of the engagement at such a late stage even had he known where to contact Major-General Brigg.

'Certainly, sir,' the waiter said when Shaw asked for aspirins, and presented them to him with a glass of water on a tray as though he were serving a champagne cocktail. That had been fifteen minutes ago, the pills had had no effect and now Shaw was ambling up and down a stretch of the familiar Ritz Aubusson carpet wondering, without much interest, how many miles of it the hotel group had had to buy to keep it looking always the same, wondering too what had become of his host.

'Hello. I'm Sarah Cheyney. Please forgive us for being so late. Uncle John's still trying to find a parking space. I told him we should come by taxi, but he wouldn't because he's so pleased with his new car.'

Somewhere between pretty and beautiful, Shaw thought, as he took the hand held out to him. Plain white coat and skirt, white high-heeled boots, light brown eyes and very white teeth, startling against the black skin of her face. It was very easy to let the smile come, headache or no headache.

'How did you pick me out in this crowd?' Shaw asked.

'Voodoo,' she said. 'Thanks for not looking surprised. I know Uncle John didn't warn you. He never does. Actually, it wasn't difficult. His description was a tall, slim Prince of Denmark type. You're the only one around at the moment. Shall we go and have a drink while he's playing with his Jaguar?'

Shaw followed her up the short flight of shallow steps to the bar area thinking about a jaguar, but his mind was on the way she moved, not a car. Long, tapering legs, narrow hips and waist, wide shoulders. An athlete's body. Apprehension flickered in him and he hoped that Brigg would join them quickly, because he felt in no condition to parry questions from such a girl.

'Do I call you Henry or Harry?'

'Harry, please.'

'Oh good. Henry's such a pompous name.'

They ordered vodka martinis.

'Do you often have migraines?'

Voodoo!

'I've never had one in my life,' Shaw said.

'Well, you've got one now, but don't worry. I won't let the evening drag on.'

The drinks and the general arrived together.

Combating an unpleasant combination of trepidation, pain and excitement, Shaw had little awareness of what he was saying or eating during dinner until, towards the end of it, the general was handed a message.

'Damn it,' he said, 'I've got to go to the War House. Sorry, Harry, but you know how it is. Panics are always scheduled at anti-social hours. Sarah, you take the Jag. After all that searching I finally managed to park it right by the side entrance. Here you are. They've sent a car for me.'

Brigg handed her the keys, called for the bill, signed it and departed. Shaw watched him go, suspicion hardening into certainty. It was laughably transparent, but he had never felt less like laughing.

'Right. Let's get you and your migraine home.'

He remonstrated feebly, then bowed to the inevitable, trying to persuade himself that if he was to blunt this weapon it was best to do it immediately. They were three-quarters of the way along the expensive carpeting leading to the side exit of the hotel before the thought came to him that there was no problem. All he had to do was capitalise on his condition and refuse to communicate during the short drive to Kensington High Street. The blunting could wait at least until he felt up to it if he hadn't the wit to avoid the necessity for it in the future.

Neither spoke after he had told her where he lived and Shaw spent the time taking furtive glances at a profile that was almost as European in outline as its colouring was African. Despite the agony inside his skull he found the combination devastating.

With the car parked outside his apartment building he had his thanks interrupted by Sarah Cheyney saying, 'You lead the way, and don't panic. I'm not going to lay you.' He did as he was told and continued to do so until, dressed only in pyjama trousers, he was lying face down on his bed.

She came into the bedroom at his call, straddled his body and began to knead the muscles where his neck and shoulders joined. Her fingers were strong and hurt him, but it was a good pain.

'Dear God,' she said. 'What *do* you do with yourself? You're as knotted as an old oak tree.'

After minutes of that, her fingers moved to his temples, their touch as light as first it had been fierce.

'OK, you can turn over now.'

The light flicked off as he did so and he could see only the whiteness of her clothes, then that was gone and he was watching the faint shine of a pair of boots seemingly moving about by themselves. That vanished too and the bed creaked as she lay down beside him. It was like a mother suckling an infant when she drew his head to her.

'Go to sleep,' she said.

'If you get any more turns like that you can reach me at this number,' the message written in lipstick on Shaw's shaving mirror read. He went to his desk in the living-room and wrote the number down, but left the message where it was.

He had slept instantly and deeply, awakening at two thirty when she left as silently as a ghost, only because any movement his subconscious could not explain invariably woke him. For fear of worrying her further, he had remained motionless, feigning sleep and finding it again as soon as the door closed behind her.

Now he was rested, free from pain and in a turmoil of emotions, the strongest of which was resentment amounting almost to fury against both Sarah Cheyney and himself. Still failing to recognise that a declaration of war by an individual on the United States of America was likely to impose somewhat excessive strains on that person, he felt the exasperation of a man whose work required it of him to be always in peak condition when total fitness temporarily deserted him. That his debility should have been immediately obvious to an attractive stranger but not, apparently, to his superior officer, only made it worse because he was always at such pains to conceal his thoughts and feelings. To have been so instantly read he found alarming.

But all that paled into insignificance beside the girl's assumption and exercise of control over him, a control he had made not the slightest effort to resist. Why that should be of any importance to him he had no idea, but knew only that it was. When he finally abandoned the attempt to nurse his male pride back to health, he turned his resentment on her very existence because now, of all times, he could not afford the complication to his plans she represented.

The acknowledgement of that factor brought Shaw to a mental halt as a chain might stop a leaping dog, for it implied an intention to see her again, to use the telephone number she had left for him, and that was completely at variance with his hazily remembered caution of the evening before. He recalled his suspicion of the invitation to dinner and of Brigg's unexpected departure. He recalled, too, his determination to communicate nothing to the girl, a determination never put to the test, and here he was holding a piece of paper bearing a number copied from his bathroom mirror.

A migraine sufferer could have told Shaw that his weakness of the previous night was unremarkable, and an intelligent observer that he was one step away from falling seriously in love, but neither was there to help him. He picked up the phone and stabbed out the number sequence, telling himself that the least he could do was to offer his apologies and thanks as a means of ending a brief acquaintanceship.

Shaw listened to an unknown female voice saying, 'Doctor Cheyney's surgery. Can I help you?'

Replacing the receiver carefully, not speaking, he stood looking down at it for a moment. 'So that's what they mean by alternative medicine,' he said to the silent room.

No longer experiencing resentment at her domination because her being a doctor somehow made that acceptable, Shaw found himself feeling extremely touched and very grateful. Flowers, he thought. Flowers, but no note, then he would put her out of his mind and get on with the organisation of the mission he had entrusted himself with. He was still standing there, feeling touched and grateful when the telephone began its series of double purrs.

'Shaw,' he said.

'Are you all right this morning, Harry?'

Rather thrilling, the voice. Rather thrilling, all of her. *Rather?* What a stupid Britishism!

'Yes, I'm absolutely fine. How very kind of you to call.'

'Oh, I always check on my patients.'

'You were very sweet to me last night, Sarah,' Shaw said. 'I . . . I'm . . .'

She helped him. 'Hurts like hell, a migraine, doesn't it?'

'Yes, it does. I couldn't even think straight.'

'That's typical of the condition,' Sarah Cheyney told him. 'You'd better go and see your doctor. A head scan would be useful and he could do something about that muscle tenseness. Uncle John told me that you'd been through a bad patch in Ireland, so that's probably all that's wrong, but it's best to be sure.'

'All right. I'll do that as soon as I get back to the regiment in a week or two.'

'Haven't you got a London doctor?'

'No.'

'Then I suggest you let me handle it. We can't have a repeat performance of yesterday.'

'Oh look, Sarah,' Shaw said, 'I really can't impose on your kindness any further. You were –'

'I've got patients waiting,' she broke in. 'Come and have a drink at six thirty and at least talk about it. 198 Wimpole Street. Won't you please do that?'

'Yes,' Shaw replied. 'I'll do that.' Short of downright discourtesy and ingratitude there was nothing else he could say.

It was at their third meeting that they went to bed together for the second time and made love for the first. There was nothing dominating about her then; just a joyously eager response. Entwined in slender black limbs, Shaw said 'Rather thrilling,' to himself and laughed out loud.

'What's funny, darling?'

'Nothing,' he said. 'I'm just so happy, that's all.'

4

Shaw saw a doctor shortly after a stiffly formal meeting with an SAS colonel at Hereford, but the appointment had nothing to do with his solitary migraine or the tenseness of his muscles, a tenseness which had melted away under Sarah Cheyney's various ministrations.

'It was good of you to come and see me,' the Royal Army Medical Corps major said.

'No it wasn't,' Shaw replied. 'I came because the CO told me to. What do you want me to do? Sign one of those waivers saying I won't hold the Army responsible for any medical condition I may develop in the future?'

'I want to ask you a few questions about your letter of resignation.'

'Why? Did I get the spelling wrong?'

'Don't be difficult, Shaw. We like to look after our people. We also like to know where we went wrong, if we did. It's the revulsion thing you wrote of that interests us. Are you a Born Again Christian or something?'

'No,' Shaw said. 'I'm not a Born Again Christian, or any other sort of Christian for that matter, but I think I'm something. You know, *Cogito, ergo sum* and all that. Or if you don't know, that means "I think, therefore I am". Don't feel too badly if that's new to you. I had an educated sergeant who taught me the essence of Descartes' philosophy.'

The major looked suddenly alert, as though he were on to an interesting clue, and asked, 'Why are you so hostile?'

'There's nothing personal about it. I just don't like psychiatrists, Major.'

'So you don't like psychiatrists and you don't like Christianity.'

'You need a hearing aid,' Shaw said. 'I said that I wasn't a Christian, not that I didn't like Christianity but, as it happens, I don't. It may be a wonderful palliative for a lot of people, but it has killed far too many others for my liking – all the way from the Crusades, through the Spanish Inquisition to Northern Ireland. That's a high price to pay for the biggest con ever perpetrated on gullible mankind.'

The major glared at Shaw for several seconds before saying, 'That's an unforgivable remark! I'm not going to listen to heresy!'

Shaw stood up. 'Very well, I'll go. I didn't ask to come here, but you give up on your job rather easily, don't you? I thought it was to find out what makes people tick, not to strike attitudes.'

'Sit down, Shaw, and tell me why you think it's a con.'

'Well, if you're into miracles you might try listening to the views of the Bishop of Durham on those.' Shaw had spoken more quietly than before and when the major made no comment he went on. 'There are many good things about it of course, but you and the padre together couldn't persuade me that a lot of it wasn't designed to keep the lower orders in their place.'

'In what way?'

'By telling them that the meek shall inherit the earth,' Shaw said, 'and that it's easier for a camel to pass through the eye of a needle than for a rich man to enter the Kingdom of Heaven. Terrific propaganda, isn't it? Add a little post-hypnotic suggestion with chants, holy water and incense and you've got the peasants content with their lot. I can't think of a better recipe for a "them" and "us" society.'

'Ah! So you have communist leanings, do you?'

'Not so you'd notice,' Shaw replied evenly. 'My father left me rather well off. I'm happy about that and hope that it stays that way. It's another reason for my resignation. I'd like to live to enjoy it.'

He appeared to have lost interest in communism and there was distress in his voice when the major said, 'I'm sorry for you. I don't think I could bear it if I didn't believe in God.'

'There you go again,' Shaw told him. 'We weren't talking about God and I never said I didn't believe in God. I refuse to say "Him" because I haven't the remotest idea what form God takes, except that it can't be an anthropomorphic one. That was just another part of the con to give the peasants something to relate to.'

'But you accept that God takes some form?'

'For want of a better description, yes I do.'

'Why?'

'In addition to a hearing aid, you also need some lessons in physics and chemistry,' Shaw said, 'then you could look around you and be suitably awed without recourse to dogma. The world we live in is incredible enough to make meaningless propositions unnecessary.'

'So awe me, Captain Shaw.'

Shaw shrugged. 'I'll give you some facts and ask you some questions. If you know the answers to any of the questions, feel free to interrupt me and inform the scientific community immediately. They've been searching unsuccessfully for them for a very long time. All right?'

'I'm listening, but I hope you aren't going right back to the creation of the universe.'

'I said the world, just the world. Logic, supported by comparison with other planets, suggests that it should be an extremely hostile environment, but it isn't. Why is that?' Shaw paused then, expecting no reply and getting none, went on. 'The atmosphere can't exist because it's an unstable, extremely combustible mixture of gases with, very roughly, an eighty/twenty percentage of nitrogen and oxygen which should have combined to form stable nitrates leaving us no air to breathe, but it does exist. Why is that? You don't know the answer and neither does anybody else. Nor do they know why the ratio remains remarkably constant when it shouldn't for a number of reasons, but they're very glad it does. Lower the oxygen by a few percentage points and we die from asphyxiation. Raise them and the world bursts into flames. Why don't these things happen? Why does the temperature of the earth stay inside the very narrow limits which will support life, when the sun is such an erratic source of power? There's a great deal more of it, all ending in a question mark. They're your *real* miracles. Do you want me to go on?'

'I *can* give you an answer to that,' the major said. 'It's "no". Are you suggesting that some force is arranging the impossible for our benefit?'

'Or to see what happens,' Shaw replied. 'May I go now, or do you want to talk about my sex life?'

'I got him on to politics after that, sir,' the major told the colonel, 'but there was nothing there. Says he votes Conservative when he can be bothered to vote at all and has no interest in any of the Ulster factions. He sees the Army's role as an extension of the police.'

'All right, doc,' the colonel said. 'What's your overall assessment?'

'A very controlled man, sir, but without a trace of evasion in him. He's abrasive, sarcastic, intelligent, well informed on a variety of subjects, and articulate. There may be a degree of hubris there, but that could have been put on for my benefit. He was angry at being sent to me.'

The colonel nodded. 'I know he was. So, no religious leanings or scruples, no political bias and no nervous condition, correct?'

'Correct, sir.'

'Money problems?'

'Apparently none. Says he's well heeled.'

'All of which gets us precisely nowhere.'

'I'm sorry, sir.'

'Oh hell, doc,' the colonel said. 'It isn't your fault. I'm grateful for your help.'

When the major had gone the colonel walked to his adjutant's office.

'Bob, get on to Security and ask them to put a day and night watch on Harry Shaw. I want to know where he goes, what he does and who he talks to.'

'They'll want a reason, Colonel.'

'I haven't got a reason,' the colonel said, 'just a feeling. This

31

resignation of his is entirely out of character and with a man like him that makes me wonder. Tell them a week should do it.'

Six hours did it.

Shaw rose from his chair and waved when Sarah Cheyney came in through the street door of Jules' Bar on Jermyn Street. The shock of pleasure he experienced at every meeting was familiar now, but no less strong for that, because reality never failed to improve on memory. She smiled and waved back, then approached his table with her jaguar walk.

'I'm sorry I'm late, darling. I had a patient in a state of total despair because all her tests were negative which leaves her with nothing to tell her friends about. It took me ten minutes to get rid of her.' White teeth flashed at him.

'Will you marry me?' Shaw asked.

'Certainly not. It would be cruelty to dumb animals. You haven't seen me in one of my moods yet.'

'Oh well, in that case you'd better sit down and have some lunch.'

'Jolly good,' Sarah said. 'Are you an ex-officer now?'

'Not quite. Some of the jobs I've been involved in could make me a security risk, so they're doing a little probing. The colonel even made me see the local trick-cyclist. I offended against his beliefs and then blinded him with science. You'd have been proud of me. Have a Bloody Mary.'

When they had finished their lunch, Shaw said, 'Sarah, I'd like you to leave before me. There's something I have to do.'

'Like that blonde at the bar with the excessive pectoral development? There's no need to go overboard at once just because I declined your offer of marriage.'

'I'm being followed.'

'Pooh, that's nothing. I'm always being followed,' Sarah said, but she didn't smile.

'They've set a man to watching my flat, he followed me here and now he's pretending to read a newspaper across the street. I never know why they almost always do that. It's about the most conspicuous thing imaginable.'

'Who are "they"?'

'That's what I intend to find out.'

'Oh great. What are you going to do? Pick him up by the throat in a London street and shake him until his teeth rattle? Point him out to me through the glass.'

When she had seen the newspaper reader, Sarah said, 'You leave this to me, my lad. Give me ten seconds, then follow and we'll play it by ear.' She had gone before he could comment.

Shaw gave her the grace she had asked for before crossing the street towards the couple, a rather small man, blushing now, looking agitatedly around him, then up at the tall black girl.

In a strong West Indian accent she was saying, 'Don't be shy, lover. Ah can show you things you never dreamed of, and don't you go telling me that you don't want that. Nobody loiters here *without* intent!'

Shaw stifled a smile at the words and her provocative stance, legs astride, a hand resting on an out-thrust hip. The man had begun to speak in low, hurried tones when Shaw joined them.

'Is this man bothering you, madam?' he asked.

'Yes. He seems to have got it into his head that I'm a prostitute and won't leave me alone. He's been making the most disgusting suggestions!'

'Right. I'll hold him here while you fetch a policeman.'

With tired resignation the small man said, 'Let it go, Captain Shaw. I know when I'm being set up. This is the lady that joined you for lunch, isn't it? I only saw her back when she went in. I'm Sergeant Fenner.' He held out a police warrant card in support of the statement before adding, 'I told them it was useless trying to keep a member of the SAS under observation with anything less than a full surveillance team, but we're short on manpower at the moment. I'll be getting along.'

They watched him go, then Sarah took hold of Shaw's arm. 'Why, man, Ah never knew you was in the Ess Ay Ess!'

'We're not supposed to advertise the fact.'

'Does you dress up in black with a hood 'n' all, and swing through windows on the end of a rope like Ah seen on TV?'

'Practically every day. Incidentally, you're wonderful.'

'I know,' Sarah Cheyney said in her normal voice and grinned at him.

*

33

'It didn't work, sir,' the adjutant said. 'Shaw was on to them at once.'

The colonel nodded, unsurprised. 'I thought he might be. They probably couldn't spare enough men with all this excitement about possible Libyan reprisals for the air attack. It's going to get even more difficult for•them with the royal wedding coming up in July. We'd better forget it.'

The adjutant turned towards the door, then back again.

'Oh, there was one thing, sir. He had a smashing black girl in tow. Would it be an idea to check her out?'

'No,' the colonel said. 'She's Brigadier Brigg's niece. Beg his pardon. Major-General Brigg, I mean. His sister married a black American doctor and that girl's the result. I hear she's quite something.'

His final sentence didn't seem to cheer the colonel at all and a worried frown settled on his face as the adjutant left the room.

5

Any lessening of purpose Shaw experienced as a result of Sarah Cheyney's entry into his life was offset by the almost daily quota of tragedy inflicted by the people of Ulster on each other, and on the forces of order trying to stop them doing it. There had been no recent attacks on mainland Britain, but he had no doubts that they would come again in the form of the viciously mindless murder of soldiers and civilians alike. It had happened too often before to allow hope that sanity could somehow be miraculously injected into the programmed brains of the Provisional IRA and their like. Experiencing an illogical and unaccustomed shiver of apprehension on a day when Sarah announced her intention of shopping at Harrods only hardened his resolve. At that moment his crusade acquired a personal stimulus born of the memory of the bomb attack on that great store coupled to fear for the safety of a new love.

Shaw wished that there was someone he could discuss his plans with and wished particularly that that someone could be Bill Townsend, but he had no intention of approaching the sergeant again until he was satisfied that Special Branch had lost interest in himself. There had been no further sign of the man called Fenner, nor had he expected that there would be, but a full surveillance team operating both in cars and on foot would be infinitely more difficult to detect. He took infinite pains to detect it and the fact that he failed to do so over a period of days did nothing to decrease his vigilance. If Shaw was one thing more than another, he was a professional survivor.

What he was not was rich. As he had told the army psychiatrist, he was not short of money. That was true as far as it went, but it hardly went far enough to reimburse Townsend for the loss of his career or, if it came to that, his family for his life, let alone mount a military-style operation however small. That he would need a backer had been a conclusion easily arrived at, but he had no ready solution to how one could be obtained. The knowledge that he would be swindling any benefactor, because there was not the slightest possibility of being truthful about what he needed the money for didn't trouble Shaw at all. 'Confidence trickster' would be the least of the charges on his crime sheet if he were caught.

A new charity with a military connection seemed to be something he might understandably be interested in, and controls in charities were notoriously bad with, as was often the case, authority unwisely delegated to one or two people even for major transactions. That, he knew, applied from the parochial to the international where, in different ways and to different degrees, such organisations were milked of significant proportions of their funds with nobody being any the wiser.

A conversation with his accountant, ostensibly about his own funds, provided Shaw with the information that the abolition of exchange control, now some years old, meant that very large sums could be transferred from one account to another, one currency to another and one country to another, without arousing official interest of any noticeable degree. The fact that such transfers were simplest of all between the United Kingdom and the United States pleased him particularly as that meant that he could set up his bogus charity on his own home ground.

What pleased him less was the amount of time which would inevitably be consumed in preparation before action could be taken and he toyed briefly with the idea of a more direct form of robbery, or an attack on a more readily accessible target. The latter would become available to him in August when a group of NORAID members made their now annual visit to Ireland to dispense blood-money and visit what they described as 'the battlefields'. He, Townsend and two others at the most could annihilate that group. It was a tempting prospect if for no better reason than that their leader and spokesman was an intensely objectionable individual who had ranted and raved like some latter-day Hitler, shouting his interviewer down when he had appeared on television. Shaw set that temptation aside because it would not provide the money Townsend was going to need and because he had some faint hope of doing the job he had set himself without killing anybody. It was a very faint hope indeed, but he kept it in the forefront of his mind while the plan grew there like some slowly developing film. The notion of direct robbery he also discarded, as it represented too great a risk too early in the venture.

Long hours in libraries and newspaper offices followed with Shaw examining *Who's Who*, *The Directory of Directors*, the financial press and anything else which would give him a picture of where the big money lay. He need not have bothered. Without having the slightest idea of what she was doing, Sarah Cheyney pointed him simultaneously towards a source of finance and a cover plan.

They slept together as a matter of course now, at his apartment or at hers above the surgery on Wimpole Street, as convenience or mood dictated. Each kept changes of clothing at both places and treated them equally as home.

It was nine thirty in the morning when the phone purred in the Wimpole Street flat. With Sarah long since at work and Shaw making leisurely preparations for another day at the library, he looked suspiciously at the instrument, feeling that it might be an embarrassment to her if he were to answer it. It purred relentlessly on and eventually he lifted the receiver to his ear, not speaking.

Her soft laugh came to him and then the words, 'It's only me, darling, but thank you anyway. It's just a house phone when the green button is pressed down.'

'I love you,' he said.

'In that case will you do something for me?'

'Of course. Do you want a patient ejected?'

'No, I want one kept here. A nice old boy called Sir Soloman Gold. He's in the smaller waiting-room now. I'm half an hour behind schedule and he's terribly nervous because he's got to have a tiny op. The sight of a needle makes him go all wobbly and I had an awful time persuading him to come at all.'

37

'Oh. What do you want me to do? Sit on his head?'

'No, you fool,' Sarah said. 'Pretend you're the patient after him and try to cheer him up. Tell him that awful fib about you always insisting on a general anaesthetic for a haircut. Anything.' The line went dead.

'All right, Solly. Up you get and let's see if you're sober. Careful. There we are. Now walk up and down a bit. Hold on to me if you want to.'

'I should always want to do that, my dear,' Sir Soloman Gold said.

Sarah nodded. 'I know. You only come to me because you think I'm sexy. March!'

A minute later, 'You're OK. Is your chauffeur outside?'

'Yes he is. I like that young man of yours, Sarah.'

'Oh? Which young man is that?'

The elderly man smiled. 'The one you sent in to calm me down. He had a quite horrifying list of maladies. I saw you walking down Bond Street arm-in-arm with him the other day and he didn't appear to be suffering at all then, so his physical condition must have deteriorated extremely rapidly. He is your chap, isn't he?'

Sarah nodded again, emphatically this time. 'Yes, he's my chap.'

'Bring him to dinner on Tuesday if you've nothing better to do.'

'Oh Solly, I'd love to,' Sarah said and kissed his cheek.

'Gadaffi's won that round hands down without lifting a finger,' the other male dinner guest said. 'He's imposed virtually a total air and sea blockade on the eastern seaboard of the States if this tourist panic is anything to go by. What's the matter with those Yanks?'

The women had left the table and the men to their port. Shaw would have joined them gladly as he didn't like port and didn't like his fellow guest much either. Jacob or Joseph Stein, he was called. He couldn't remember which and didn't care. Other than being a rabid Zionist he did not know who the man was or what he did and he didn't care about that either, wishing only that he had a tenth of the charm of his host.

Preparing to be bored by a topic the entire nation seemed to find irresistible, Shaw concentrated on not absentmindedly drinking his port and listened to Sir Soloman Gold saying, 'I think that's a little sweeping, Joe. Nobody that I know deliberately goes on holiday with the intention of becoming a dead hero. They're probably worried about the fall-out from the Chernobyl disaster too. Then there's the weakness of the dollar making this country an expensive resort for them. But don't worry. The Americans will be back.'

So his name is Joseph, not Jacob, Shaw noted and turned his thoughts to Sarah in the next room. By her own admission she spent hours straightening her luxuriant raven hair into soft waves that fell to her shoulders, but this day she had reversed the process. Now she possessed a cascade of tightly plaited individually bejewelled strands almost as long, held back from her face by a gold band round her forehead. 'Tuesday night is ethnic night,' she had told him and the memory made him smile.

'Whatever you may think, young man, it isn't funny!'

Shaw looked at Stein. 'I'm sorry? You were saying?'

'I was saying that having succeeded in screwing up our world, the Americans are content to cower at home and leave us to stew in the juice they've made. All that and the mission wasn't even successful. We'd have nailed Gadaffi if we'd sent our boys in!'

'But *we* didn't, Mr Stein,' Shaw said. 'They sent *their* boys in and whether or not the mission was a success, or even necessary, it doesn't do us much credit to sit on the sidelines and criticise what was at the very least a remarkable technicological achievement.'

'Directed at killing babies?'

'Oh, come now, Joe,' Gold broke in. 'That really is going a bit far. It wasn't directed at anything of the sort and you know it.'

Stein nodded. 'Sorry, Solly. You're right, of course, but my contention is that however technicologically remarkable an air strike may be it can never be totally selective. Troops can be much more so. Specialised troops anyway. Haven't the Americans got any of those?'

'Yes, Mr Stein, they've got some of those,' Shaw said. 'A hell of a lot more than we have as a matter of fact, and they've some pretty impressive hardware too.'

'Like what? I've never heard of them.'

'Do you want a list?'

'If you have one.'

Iritation and embarrassment touched Shaw and he glanced apologetically at his host, but Gold just looked at him benignly over the tops of his glasses, so he turned back to Stein and began to speak slowly.

'There's Delta Force, Mr Stein, Green Berets and Rangers, about 10,000 of them at Fort Bragg, North Carolina, and Fort Benning, Georgia. You've heard of the Green Berets and Rangers surely. Their tactical support helicopters include CH-47 Chinooks, Hughes 500-MD and OH-6s, Blackhawks and – oh never mind. That's the Army and Marines. The Navy has about 1,800 SEALS, the equivalent to our Special Boat Service, with Seafox underwater craft. The Air Force has its Special Operations Wing too. They operate with AC-130 Spectre Gunships, MC-130 Talon cargo planes and – oh look, they're big, they're *really* big.'

'Those names and numbers don't mean anything to me. What are you? A military analyst?'

Shaw ignored the question. 'You asked for a list, Mr Stein. I gave you an abbreviated one.'

Stein grunted. 'Very well. So why didn't they use some of their bigness to mount a logical operation instead of spraying Tripoli and Benghazi with bombs and rockets? Landing those SEALS you spoke of from a submarine or something.'

Irritation took a firmer hold on Shaw, but he kept it out of his voice when he said, 'I don't know. I'm not attached to the Pentagon. It was obviously a decision taken at the highest level and . . .' He paused, a thoughtful expression on his normally expressionless face, then went on. 'Possibly it was because their Special Operations forces don't have a very impressive track record, perhaps due to lack of integration brought about by inter-service rivalry. I hope they'll look into that. It can't be anything to do with the men themselves.'

'For example?'

'Well, they did make a monumental fiasco out of their attempt to rescue the Iranian hostages, and they didn't do all that well during the invasion of Grenada either. Thirteen out of nineteen American fatalities were Rangers or Green Berets. They tried to attack the airfield there in daylight, God knows why. The Falklands campaign should have shown them the value of night operations. On the other hand, the US Air Force has always been first class on its own, so I suppose they entrusted it with the job. It would have meant fewer casualties for them too.'

A dismissive wave of his hand seemed to indicate Stein's lack of interest in casualties, then he said, 'You have a lot of information at your fingertips, Shaw.'

'He's an army officer, Joe,' Gold told Stein.

'Oh, is he? Then perhaps he'd like to tell us how we would have handled the situation. Personally, I'd have sent in the SAS. They'd have gone into Tripoli like smoke, done the job cleanly and vanished the way they came.'

Shaw didn't enjoy being referred to in the third person, but he kept his voice level.

'You have a considerably over-glamourised view of the SAS, Mr Stein. They're not supermen.'

Stein nodded as though he had just received confirmation of a long-held belief before saying, 'Yes, I'd heard that the rest of the Army viewed them with envy. What's your regiment, Shaw?'

It was irresistible and, because he would soon be out of it, the admission could do no harm.

'The SAS,' Shaw said, 'and do call me Harry.'

The following weekend he received a telephone call from Stein asking him to come to his office to listen to a proposition which might interest him. For no better reason than that Stein smelt of money Shaw agreed to go. After revealing what he was, he had told Stein and Gold of his impending retirement and it followed that the summons indicated that an ex-SAS officer continued to possess some value in the market-place. He wondered briefly what that value was and what he might be asked to do, then set conjecture aside as an unprofitable exercise.

The meeting was not cordial, Stein's opening remark rekindling the dislike Shaw had felt for him at the dinner party.

'So I have an overly glamourised view of the SAS, do I, young man?'

'Let's just say that you don't rate very highly as a military tactician in my books,' Shaw answered mildly.

As though he hadn't spoken Stein said, 'I've had you checked out. You've got a DSO and two MCs for services in Oman and the Falklands.'

'So what?'

Again he might not have spoken. 'You were also,' Stein told him, 'responsible for the killing of Macnamara in County Armagh recently.'

There was a long pause before Shaw said, 'Be very careful, Mr Stein. You're on extremely dangerous ground and I suggest that you back off it before you force me to take action.'

Stein shrugged. 'I don't know what action you have in mind, but perhaps I can save you the trouble of taking it if I tell you that I have my sources within MI5. It was they who provided you with the intelligence for that operation and it was you and another man who carried it out. I gather that it was done with ruthless efficiency and I am prepared to pay highly for that commodity. I'm talking about six-figure jobs. That is the proposition I'm making you.'

Shaw stood motionless, not speaking.

'Well?'

'I'm waiting to hear your proposition,' Shaw said. 'You talk of jobs without specifying what they are and mention six figures. I suppose that relates to money, but there's a big difference between 100,000 and 999,999, and in Italian Lira neither sum amounts to a hill of beans.'

'Look at this, Captain Shaw.'

Stein took a sheet of paper from his desk and held it out. Shaw looked at it, not touching it, and read a list of seven names in alphabetical order. The first two had an entry of a quarter of a million pounds sterling listed against them. They were Arafat and Gadaffi.

Taking a diary from his pocket Shaw wrote: 'I'll call you within a week.' He held the page towards Stein and waited for his nod before saying, 'You must be out of your mind!' Then he turned and walked from the room.

6

Back from the survival course in Scotland, Townsend took the call in the sergeants' mess at Hereford, applied for a weekend pass and caught a train to London. There he travelled by tube to Sloane Square as Shaw had instructed him to do. He guessed that station had been chosen because it was a small one easily kept under observation, and he waited without impatience while three trains passed through, glancing occasionally at Shaw standing at the opposite end of the platform. Shaw boarded the fourth train and Townsend followed suit with several coaches separating them. At St James's Park Shaw sat down next to him and began to talk.

In the constantly fluctuating volume of passenger traffic there were long periods during which Shaw halted his monologue, not even trusting the train's racketing progress through the tunnels to blanket his words in the crush of people, and they were three-quarters of the way round the Circle Line before he had finished what he had to say.

Speaking for the first time, Townsend said, 'You missed a bit out. Where does the pretty lady fit into all this?'

Shaw almost frowned. 'How'd you come to know about that?'

'From a sergeant in the colonel's office first, but everybody at Hereford's talking. They think you've gone soft in the head over her and that's why you're resigning.'

'Do you think that?'

'No, but I'd like to hear that she isn't this man Stein's MI5 contact, or anything else to do with Security.'

'Security was my initial thought,' Shaw said, 'but it isn't so. I'd just told Brigg a sad story about why I was leaving the

44

Army and he invited me to dinner with them both. She's his niece. He'll have reported our conversation to Hereford as a matter of course, which was why I spun him the yarn about developing scruples to prepare the ground. Introducing me to Sarah was just his way of cheering me up and, possibly, trying to make me change my mind.'

'That kind of cheering up I could always use,' Townsend told him, then added, 'This is *some* caper you've thought of.'

'Are you interested, Bill?'

'Of course I'm interested.'

'You'll be risking your life.'

'So what's new?' Townsend said. 'The going rate for the job sounds a lot better than I'm getting now and I particularly like the idea of your old pal Stein picking up the tab when he thinks he's paying for something entirely different. He won't even be able to complain when he finds out.' He paused for a moment, his baby-face thoughtful, before going on, 'In fact I like it so much that it makes me more than a little suspicious. It's all a bit pat, isn't it? The happenstance of that dinner party at Sir What's-his-name's and Stein's talk of MI5 links?'

'I don't think so,' Shaw replied. 'The meeting was pure chance. Nobody knew what I was until I told them, except for Sarah, and she wouldn't have mentioned it. Anyway, you know as well as I that quite a number of people who leave the regiment are enlisted by extremely dubious employers and end up as anything from mercenaries to arms or drug runners. Stein will have been well aware of that fact. There's another point we shouldn't overlook too.'

'Yes?'

'The possibility that this is an MI5 or MI6 operation with Stein being used as a cut-out.'

'You're a suspicious bastard, Harry,' Townsend said, 'but you're right. Still, they won't be able to complain either if it's their funds we misappropriate.'

When the train stopped at the Edgware Road Station, a man in jeans and a dirty white T-shirt got into their carriage. He left it at Bayswater in favour of the one adjoining it and watched them surreptitiously through the glass of the communicating doors. Neither Shaw nor Townsend noticed him.

45

They got out at Westminster and walked along the Victoria Embankment, Horse Guards Avenue and into Whitehall. Abreast of the Admiralty building Townsend said, '"There's a porpoise close behind us and it's treading on my tail."'

'How long has it been doing that?'

'Since the tube station.'

'Description?'

'White T-Shirt with nothing funny on it except soup stains, jeans and a pair of diabolical orange shoes. Haven't looked at his face.'

'Good. We'll make a clockwise circuit of Trafalgar Square. If he does the same with all that traffic-dodging we'll know for sure. Try to look like a tourist while I show you Nelson's Column, the National Gallery and all that.'

'Then what?'

'I don't know,' Shaw said. 'I doubt we'd succeed in pulling a switch on him and following him home. We could try to have a word with him, but that won't be easy with all these people around. If Sarah was here we might nail him, although from your description he doesn't quite sound like her meat.'

'What are you talking about, Harry?'

'Oh, that's another part of the story I missed out,' Shaw replied. 'Tell you later.'

The man was still behind them when they turned left into the Strand and took cover in a doorway. When, seconds later, he passed their position they fell in behind him, closing in on him as he halted, searching for them in the throng of pedestrians. At the clutch of Shaw's hand on his shoulder he twisted away and sprinted, zig-zagging through the crowd.

'I've seen that chap before,' Shaw said and Townsend added, 'So have I. In that crummy Irish bar.'

'It was the two what murdered Macnamara,' the man in the dirty T-shirt said into the telephone. 'I only seen them the once in the pub, the day before they done it that was, but I'm sure. Apart I might have missed them, but seeing them together like that there's no doubt at all. Not a smidgen of doubt in all the world.'

The telephone didn't say anything to him and the man drew

in a long tremulous breath before going on, 'I done what I could, Mr Connolly, honest I did, but they –'

'Shut up! I'm thinking!' the receiver told him, and he waited, sweating, until it said, 'All right. Now we know they're in England we'll set watch at Hereford. There's no point in looking for them amongst ten million other fucking people in London.'

'You want me to go up there?'

'At once! You'll be joined by others who know them by sight as soon as I can get them across from Armagh. Report to me on arrival. Understood?'

'Understood, Mr Connolly,' the man said. He replaced the handset on its rest and eased his clammy T-shirt away from his skin.

Two hours later and two miles to the west in Shaw's apartment, Townsend said, 'Yes, sir. Thank you, sir,' and also placed a phone back on its rest. For most of those two hours he and Shaw had watched the entrance to the apartment building from separate vantage points until they were satisfied that it was safe to go in. Then, on Shaw's instructions, he had called Hereford and given the duty officer an edited description of what had happened.

'I'm to stay way until further orders,' he told Shaw, 'in case the Provos send an action squad there. Like you said, I didn't mention that we were together, so he'll be calling you in a minute to tell you the same thing.'

'Who's "he"?'

'Lieutenant Chadwick.'

Shaw only had time to nod before the phone summoned him. After listening to it for thirty seconds, he said, 'All right, James, I get the point. Any news of my release coming through? Not yet? Ah well, keep in touch.'

He poured drinks for them both then and handed one to Townsend before saying, 'I'm going to get Stein along here now.'

'You're not wasting any time, Harry.'

'Sarah's at some medical symposium in Edinburgh. It makes things easier. That's one of the reasons why I wanted you here this weekend.'

47

'Doctor?'

Shaw nodded again and went to the telephone while Townsend sat, looking at the drink in his hand, but seeing only the photograph of the lovely black girl he had noticed in the bedroom when Shaw had shown him round the flat.

'I wish I was ill,' he said, but Shaw was already talking into the phone and that made him instantly alert. He had heard Shaw sounding hard before, but not this hard. It seemed very much as though Shaw neither liked Stein nor was prepared to brook any opposition from him. A happy grin formed on Townsend's face.

Forty-five minutes had gone by when Townsend spoke from his position at the window of the darkened room.

'There's a big silver Roller with this year's registration trying to park between a Mini and a Ford Grenada outside.'

Shaw moved to his side and they watched a man get out of the chauffeur-driven Rolls-Royce.

'That's Stein,' Shaw said. 'Draw the curtains and switch the light on, Bill.'

When Stein, greying, dapper of dress, austere of feature, came in he showed no surprise at Townsend's presence, but asked, 'Who's this?'

Ignoring the question, Shaw said, 'Take your jacket off please.'

At that, Stein looked more startled than surprised and a hand slid inside his coat. With movements too quick to follow Townsend hit him on both biceps, kicked his feet from under him so that he fell face down, placed a foot behind his knee and drew his lower leg upwards. Stein screamed as his tendons stretched and Townsend eased the pressure, watching Shaw move towards the doorway and stop two feet to the side of it.

'Are you just going to stand there while this man tries to kill me, Shaw?' The words came out gaspingly.

'He's not trying to kill you,' Shaw told him. 'You'd be dead by now if he was. Shut up for a minute. I have a feeling that you wedged the street door open.'

The sound of feet pounding on the stairs followed his words, the chauffeur burst into the flat and Shaw hit him behind the ear. When he had lowered the unconscious figure into an

48

armchair he searched it, picked up a fallen automatic and nodded at Townsend.

'Upsadaisy,' Townsend said, releasing the foot he was holding and pulling Stein upright by the collar. Then he added, 'If you'd done what you were asked to do, we needn't have gone through all that horseplay. Now, do you want to take your jacket off, or shall I do it for you?'

'I can't. My arms are paralysed.'

'Oh yeah. I forgot.'

Townsend unbuttoned the jacket and took it off him, revealing the miniature transmitter taped to Stein's shirt with its battery lodged in the waistband of his trousers. He removed those too, then muttered crossly, 'What a lot of fuss over nothing. I thought he was going for a gun.'

Shaw said, 'Check him for a tape recorder. I expect that's in the Rolls, but we'd better be sure.'

There was no tape recorder and staggering slightly, favouring his damaged knee, Stein made his way to a chair, subsided into it and began to flex his fingers, working life back into his arms.

After a moment he gave a barking laugh and said, 'By God! You don't mess around!'

'You wouldn't want us to, would you?'

He shook his head at Shaw's question and asked for a drink, but couldn't grip the glass when it was handed to him and Shaw had to hold it to his lips.

'Thank you. Is my chauffeur all right?'

As though he had heard himself referred to, the man said, 'Fuck it!' and jerked upright in his chair.

'Go back to the car, Barker, and wait there, will you?'

'Yes sir. Fuck it!' the chauffeur replied.

With the door closed again, Stein addressed himself to Shaw.

'We seem to be at something of an impasse. You suspected, correctly, that my office was wired, and now you've taken my transmitter from me. It would hardly be reasonable of you to expect me to discuss anything with you here and be recorded myself.'

Shaw shrugged. 'Then book any hotel room you like for the

night and we'll talk there, if that would make you feel happier. You can search us both when we get there, but it would be a pointless exercise.'

'Why?'

'Because,' Shaw said, 'I haven't the slightest intention of leaving incriminating tapes lying around, whatever source they come from. It would be the worst possible form of security. Think about it.'

'Very well, but I warn you that if you try to double-cross me you'll live to rue the day.'

'If you do as much to us, *you won't*,' Shaw told him. 'I've taken out a suspended contract on you already.' The lie came out quite easily and he added, 'Activating it would be the last thing you do.'

'I think I made a good choice in you, Captain Shaw.'

'Bully for me,' Shaw said. 'If that completes the preliminaries, shall we talk?'

They talked for three hours with Townsend a silent listener. When Stein had gone, Shaw made up a bed for the sergeant in the studio, left him with beer and sandwiches and retired thankfully to his own room. Tired as he was, sleep evaded him, something as rare in his life as his solitary migraine had been. The reason, he knew, lay not in the day's events, but in Sarah Cheyney's absence from his side for the first time since the start of their affair. Turning the light on he smiled at her photograph, then stared at the ceiling as though it bore a record of his conversation with Stein which he needed to check for anomalies.

The planning session had fallen logically into three parts – the target, the operational base and finance. Shaw had dealt with the first and second, Stein the third. There had been little argument. By coincidence of alphabet and geographical location the top two names on Stein's list automatically offered themselves. Arafat based indefinitely in Tunisia and Gadaffi in Libya were reachable. The remainder, in Syria and Iran, were not. Shaw had barely begun his explanation of why the Americans had chosen the soft option before he was cut off by the single word 'Agreed'.

His choice of the Untied States as the best place in which to

50

equip his force, as arms of many types were available for the asking, had been met with less enthusiasm on the grounds of its distance from the Mediterranean. When he had countered that by saying that the Canary Islands would be the final springboard he was met by disbelief which grew when an atlas was produced and examined.

'Let me see if I've got this right,' Stein said. 'Some of you fly into Las Palmas as tourists, but you and others travel by sea with the arms and supplies, and rendezvous somewhere off the Canaries. You then proceed to the coast of Morocco, scuttle whatever vessel you have used and *walk* to Tunisia! You're out of your mind! That's some of the most inhospitable country in the world!'

'I rather hope that camels will do the walking,' Shaw told him. 'It's the best part of 1,500 miles, but I don't have a submarine at my beck and call for a sea trip, and passing unobserved through a radar net all the way from Gibraltar to the target area in any other kind of vessel is something I haven't figured out how to do yet.' He spoke harshly, maintaining his hard image, but softened his voice when he went on. 'Listen, Mr Stein. Apart from the Arctic and Mountain Warfare Cadre, who have other preoccupations, most of us cut our teeth in the Omani desert. That sort of country is home to us. Even if we don't have the right dialect we still speak the language and, if we have to, we can live off the sand for a time. There's water in it, even in the Sahara.'

Shaw reached for the pencil and pad by the telephone and began to sketch saying, 'You dig a conical hole like this, about three yards in diameter and three feet deep, put a can or whatever in the bottom, cover the hole with transparent plastic and weight it in the middle so it sags towards the can.'

His pencil moved as he spoke, completing the diagram, then clattered briefly on the table when he discarded it before going on, 'You leave it like that all day and the heat of the sun through the plastic is so intense that it vapourises the moisture locked even in Saharan sand. That will condense on the underside of the plastic and trickle down into the can. If you can find some cactus flesh and chuck it into the hole, that's even better because the moisture will be vapourised out of that

51

too. Travelling by night and lying up by day to avoid the worst of the heat, plus wearing Arab dress to reduce evaporation from the body helps more than somewhat as well.'

Making a gesture of apology with his hands Shaw added, 'End of lecture. We shall be travelling with fully loaded camels from oasis to oasis and I doubt that any of that stuff will be necessary. I only told you to convince you that we know what we're doing.'

Stein conceded that they appeared to know what they were doing and, when he immediately turned to the subject of financing the project, it did not escape Shaw's notice that no mention was made of how the group, or what remained of it, would extricate itself from the situation it would create. Lying on his bed, still staring at the ceiling, Shaw decided that the omission, apart from strengthening his growing conviction that Stein was not really very clever, was of little significance. Having spent two days preparing, and ninety minutes presenting, a plan he had no intention of carrying out, the fact that it had been accepted was all that mattered to Shaw for the time being.

It intrigued him to find that their thought processes had followed similar lines when Stein announced that a charity would be the most suitable vehicle for the transfer of funds to the States. He and his associates, he told Shaw, would buy a building or part of a building in New York to be used as a hostel for some purpose to be decided. Shaw would be placed in charge of it with full authority delegated to him. He could then sell the property and abscond with the proceeds. If asked for a reason for the sale so soon after purchase, he could explain that market changes indicated that the charity and its dependants would benefit from the speculative transaction in the property, followed by later investment in another. It made good enough sense to Shaw, particularly in that Stein and his colleagues in International Zionism would, whatever happened, be seen to have acted with perfect propriety.

Towards dawn he fell asleep with the light still burning.

7

'You're not in this for the money, are you, Harry?' Townsend said. It was more statement than question.

Shaw was feeling tired after a night of too little sleep, but enjoying the omelette Townsend had prepared. The sergeant really was a very good cook and he wondered if even his purée of worms might not have been almost palatable. He put the last piece of the fluffy concoction in his mouth before asking, 'What makes you say that?'

'This set-up you've got here, your car, your lifestyle. What I've seen of it anyway. It all spells quiet wealth to me.'

'So?'

'"Idealism is born of the heart, not of the wits and, so being, is forsooth witless,"' Townsend intoned.

'All right, Bill. Who said that?'

'I did,' Townsend told him and grinned. 'Not bad for breakfast time, eh?'

'Oh Christ!' Shaw said. 'Listen, you're right about the money, but don't imagine that I'm off on some idealistic trip. This is an intensely practical venture as far as I'm concerned and I would never have asked you to involve yourself in it just to bolster my ego.' He picked up the coffee-pot and tilted it over Townsend's cup, but it was empty and he put it down again before saying, 'Let's reverse the coin and look at the purely selfish side, forgetting all about the people of Ulster, shall we?'

'Let's do that.'

'OK, we're both still in the Army. Imagine that we're sent back to Armagh tomorrow to do another job involving a

53

helicopter pick-up, but this time NORAID has succeeded in supplying the Provos with American M82 machine-guns. As you well know they're accurate over 2,000 yards. Worse still, suppose they've got "Stinger" shoulder-held anti-aircraft missiles through to them. Where would we be?'

'I love answering rhetorical questions,' Townsend said. 'We'd be spread all over the landscape, that's where we'd be. Oh what a gooey mess! I doubt if we could be reconstituted by all the King's horses and all the King's men, even with the help of your Doctor Sarah. I'd hate to be *that* ill. Anyway, I take your point, and I'm glad I'll be working for a realist, not an idealist.'

'Working "with", not "for".'

Townsend shook his head. 'No, Harry. You'll have to run this thing like a military operation. That can't be done by committee. I shouldn't have to tell *you* that.'

As though he hadn't heard, Shaw stood up and took the coffee-pot to the kitchen. When he returned he filled both their cups before saying, 'You're right as far as operations go, but I want you to act as Devil's Advocate during the planning phase. Two heads and all that. I've listened to myself doing a lot of pontificating recently and I may need pulling up short.'

Townsend raised enquiring eyebrows at him and Shaw went on, 'I gave the doctor I saw at Hereford a long lecture on religion, physics and chemistry for no particular reason other than to annoy him. Then Stein got an earful from me about military hardware and tactics. Doesn't mean much probably, but it wasn't like me.'

'Did you mean what you were saying to them?'

'Oh, certainly.'

'Then I don't see much wrong in that,' Townsend said.

'What's wrong in that is that I could be getting big-headed.'

'So what's new?' Townsend asked, but the reappearance of his grin robbed the question of offence. Then he added, 'Don't worry. I'll be your egomania barometer, but one way and another it looks as though I'm going to be overworked.'

'Meaning what?'

'Meaning that, apart from whatever other onerous duties you impose on me, I'm supposed to contact you this weekend

54

and try to find out the real reason for your resignation. Apart from the Doctor Cheyney theory that is. Hereford reckons that with us being a team I had as good a chance as anybody of doing that.'

Shaw shrugged and after a moment Townsend said, 'Your surprise rating has never been very high, but it just sank below the bottom of the graph. How did you know?'

'It was Chadwick telling us both to stay away,' Shaw told him. 'That made no sense at all. What's wrong with using a closed van to get us inside and letting us get on with our work? There's plenty to do which doesn't involve us showing ourselves in the streets of Hereford. The inference was that somebody was being given more time to do something the Army was prepared to pay for. You checking me out, for example. I suppose listening to me in the tube, the brush with that inquisitive Mick, and last night's conversation with Stein made you forget to tell me before.'

'You took the words right out of my mouth, Harry.'

'Don't ever forget again.'

Shaw had spoken quietly, but his tone had been cold.

Townsend nodded and said, 'I told you we couldn't run this thing by committee.' He hadn't minded the rebuke. It was infinitely preferable to the distrust his revelation would have engendered in anyone other than Shaw.

Stein's working breakfast was more formal, the gathering larger, city-suited and older. Shaw, had he known, would have been pleased that Sir Soloman Gold was not present. He liked Gold.

'The question of trust doesn't come into it,' Stein was saying. 'This is a high-risk venture with human avarice our sole safeguard, and that we certainly have. Shaw insisted on half a million for either Yasser Arafat or Gadaffi, that sum to be a flat payment for services rendered, with the funding of the operation dealt with separately. We are looking at something in the region of one million pounds sterling.'

'And you agreed to that?'

The speaker was an enormously fat man, the only one of the group of seven still eating, doing it stolidly and without apparent enjoyment, as though performing a duty to his vast frame.

'I agreed to that.'

'You're very free with our money, Joseph.'

Arms crossed, Stein massaged his biceps with his thumbs. The bruised muscles were aching and so was his knee, constant reminders of the indignities he had undergone. He felt tired and put upon, and that made his voice sound petulant when he said, 'My dear Arthur, here are we planning to change the face of the Middle East and all you can contribute is cheese-paring over a sum I don't doubt you yourself could write a cheque for on your current account. I thought we were all agreed that money was no object.'

'Maybe so,' the fat man replied, 'but then I've never before entered into a business negotiation with nothing but human avarice as security. The two strike me as being mutually exclusive.'

'It's all the security you can hope for when dealing with mercenaries.'

'And if these particular mercenaries default, what then?'

'I told Shaw,' Stein said, 'that he would live to rue the day if he stepped out of line.'

'And how did he react to that enigmatic and somewhat nebulous warning?'

'By threatening my life if I did the same.'

'Well, at least that's specific. Couldn't you have done as much for him? We have the necessary resources to make good the threat.'

'And spend what little time would remain to me in a futile attempt at evading his colleagues? No, I don't think so. I consider myself to be an excellent judge of character and have no reason to suspect my instinct to be at fault in this case. Anyway, there's no merit in presupposing failure.' Stein paused before adding, 'As the front man in this, it is I who am exposed to danger, so I would ask that you be satisfied with what I have already said at this stage.'

Throughout the Sunday of that weekend, Shaw and Townsend took turns as look-outs at the bedroom window of the apartment.

They watched the buildings opposite, they watched the pedestrians, they watched the traffic. Nobody watched for them in return. Of that they were as certain as it was possible to be. There were no loiterers, no occupied parked cars or cars which reappeared without reason, no suspicious appearances at windows, no flashes of reflected light from binoculars or periscopes. They assumed that they were not under observation, and were right.

Throughout that same Sunday, five men from County Armagh kept watch in Hereford for the faces of two men whose names they did not know. Their task was next to impossible, for the area they had to cover was too great and faces passing in vehicles not readily identifiable, but they agreed that it was improbable that their quarry was in the locality. One of them, who had changed from his dirty T-shirt into a dirty denim jacket, expressed this view by telephone to a Mr Connolly in London. The illogicality of his opinion was dismissed in scatological terms and he was ordered to maintain surveillance, but he too was right.

Throughout the evening preceding that Sunday and most of its early morning Lieutenant Harvey Bergquist of the New York Police Department's Seventeenth Precinct had his already heavy workload increased by three homicides, an attempted bank robbery, a successful supermarket hold-up, six muggings, a case of suspected arson, three non-fatal stabbings in a pool hall and a kidnapping. There was also a bomb hoax in the subway and two deaths initially classified as suicides about which he remained unconvinced.

Looking through the glass wall of his office at a throng of pimps, prostitutes, drunks and social castaways arguing or pleading with his officers and, in one case, attempting to assault them, he concluded sombrely that things could only get worse. He was an intelligent man and recognised that tiredness was the cause of his gloomy forebodings, but the passage of time was to prove *him* right as well.

Townsend left Shaw's apartment an hour before dawn to go to his father's home in Blackheath. Five hundred yards behind, Shaw followed him for a mile then, satisfied that they were not followed, he retraced his steps.

The morning post brought him a letter from Sarah Cheyney. It took him some time to establish that fact, but he was eventually persuaded by the Edinburgh postmark and the row of Xs denoting kisses beneath a signature as illegible as the rest of the words on the single sheet of paper. With a gentle smile on his lips, he sat puzzling over handwriting as spiky as she herself was curved, trying to establish some pattern which might enable him to decipher the contents. After five minutes he had got little further than reaching the conclusion that if British policemen were as wonderful as foreigners insisted, then British postmen were possessed of second sight. The envelope was, he conceded, marginally easier to read. He had, after all, distinguished his own name and could now make out part of his address, but the absence of any postal code, which would have helped them enormously, only served to raise his admiration for the Post Office's employees higher. Using the envelope as a key to the rest of the script he obtained confirmation that she was returning to London that day, something he was already aware of, and that she loved him. He was aware of that too, or at least believed it to be the case. The successfully decoded statement made him very happy and he abandoned his study of the remaining hieroglyphics.

'Beast!' his telephone receiver said to him four hours later.

'Darling! Where are you?' Shaw asked.

'Back at Wimpole Street and no thanks to you either! Didn't you get my letter? You must have! I posted it on Saturday and asked you to meet me at Heathrow because I was going to be loaded down with luggage and – well, almost loaded down. I had an airline bag *and* a briefcase! Oh pooh! I just wanted to see you, that's all.'

Happiness washed over Shaw again like a warm wave.

'I got your letter,' he said, 'but I couldn't read it. Honestly, I tried like anything, but –'

'Whitey, you're an illiterate slob! It's just what I might have expected of the Army! The drug dispensers at the pharmacies don't have any trouble with my writing, so why should you? Don't you know anything about doctors? We're trained to write that way!'

'I'll work on it,' Shaw told her, 'but, until I graduate, there's some chap called Alexander Graham Bell who has just invented the telephone. Could you use that as a back-up for your messages? You know, as a sort of fail-safe system?'

'Hmm. Excuses, excuses.'

'May I take you out to lunch?'

'No, you may not,' Sarah Cheyney said. 'I've got rows of patients waiting for me, but if you don't take me somewhere extremely expensive for dinner I shall probably never speak to you again.'

Shaw did not take her out to dinner that night. 'We're going to be late,' he said idiotically, when she opened the front door of the Wimpole Street house in answer to his ring, then took the martini she held out to him. Turning away wordlessly, she crossed the hall and went up the stairs. He closed the street door and followed, using the tarty pair of high-heeled ankle-strap shoes she had on as a point of focus. She wasn't wearing anything else and he didn't want to spill his drink.

Townsend called Hereford from his father's flat and informed Lieutenant Chadwick that he'd made contact with Captain Shaw and learned that he was considering some business venture abroad. Shaw had declined to be more specific on grounds of superstition, in that it might be bad luck to talk about it with his release from the Army still not officially approved.

Townsend was told that it now had been, but the information was for his ears alone as Shaw would be advised officially in writing and should not hear about it from his sergeant. Meanwhile, there was to be no return to Hereford as unidentified men, possibly Irish, had been observed repeatedly passing the gates of the base. When Shaw was aware of his civilian status he might be more willing to talk and . . .

'Yes, sir. I understand, sir,' Townsend had said and changed into a tracksuit and trainers. It began to rain heavily as soon as he left the building, but he ran on through the downpour, intent on covering ten miles. He had decided, philosophically, that as there was little likelihood of his enjoying his days in London as much as Shaw would be doing, he might as well be fitter than his officer, which would make the first time since they had come together all those years ago.

'Shouldn't be too difficult now, everything considered,' he announced to nobody in particular and two pedestrians turned to watch the grinning jogging figure for a moment before shrugging at each other.

Townsend made his rapid way towards the River Thames, jogging for fifty seconds and sprinting for ten in every minute. It would have intrigued him to have been told how surprisingly accurate his mental clock was, but he was thinking neither of mental clocks nor running. There were much more interesting things to consider, things Shaw had spoken of during the long hours when one or other of them had kept vigil at the apartment window.

Townsend knew nothing about Boston, except that some angry Americans had thrown a lot of tea into the harbour there back in seventeen hundred and something, so he thought about New York City instead. He didn't know that place either, but felt that he did because he had watched dozens of hours of *Kojak* on television. That had started out of genuine interest and, when the novelty waned, had continued in the hope that the detective might get shot, even slightly shot. The hope proved a vain one and Townsend wasted a hundred yards of his run wondering if he had missed an episode or two, then brought himself back to the present. Shaw had some surprises in store for *Kojak*, whose real name Townsend didn't know was Lieutenant Harvey Bergquist, and the first step in the preparation of those surprises was the recruitment of 'Logo'.

His real name was Arthur Parry, but everybody called him Logo because a ricocheting Argentine bullet had struck him almost exactly in the centre of his forehead on Tumbledown Mountain in the Falklands. It was necessary to squint only slightly at the healed wound to see that it closely resembled the rearing horse Lloyds Bank uses as its insignia, even if it was white instead of black. That bullet had put Logo into hospital and paid to his army career. By the time he was discharged ten months after the incident, Logo's occupational therapy had progressed from model-making through putting ships into bottles to putting very small ships into very small bottles. Towards the end of his convalescence he was mending people's watches for them, and some of the hospital equipment too.

This ability intrigued his fellow patients and amazed his doctors because the wound had reduced his mental age by more than half of his twenty-three years and the work he was doing was more suited to a Japanese girl than a fifteen-stone Englishman with spatulate fingers and ungainly hands. They would have been even more intrigued and amazed had they seen how far he had advanced in the intervening four years. There was nothing unique about his micro-miniaturisation work. He was just extremely good at it and totally uninterested in anything else.

Townsend had first met the big man by chance in hospital while he was visiting one of his troop who had damaged a knee during a practise parachute drop into rough country. He had found him in the Physiotherapy Department about to have ultra-sonic treatment on the injured joint. As he approached the bed the nurse sitting on the side of it said, 'Damn, this thing's on the blink.'

'Logo'll fix it.'

He had looked round as the speaker clambered off the static exercise bicycle in the middle of the room, then watched him take the black and silver instrument from the nurse, unplug it and put it on the bedside cabinet. He had continued to watch while the man with the indentation in his forehead took a cloth-roll of jeweller's implements from his pocket, selected a probe and dismantled the ultra-sonic transmitter. Less than two minutes later it was re-assembled.

'It's OK now. Little loose wire is all.'

The nurse had smiled at him. 'Well, thank you, Logo!'

'No problem,' Logo had said and got back on the bicycle. He wasn't in need of physiotherapy, he just liked to sit there peddling hard and, provided the machine wasn't needed by anybody else, the hospital staff were happy to let him do it.

It was at the end of his second visit that Logo attached himself to Townsend.

'Come and see my boats.'

Townsend had been fascinated by the things, perfect scale models of galleons, windjammers and ocean liners, some a foot in length, others little larger than a thumbnail. He hadn't realised how long he had spent looking at them and having

61

them explained to him until a passing orderly had told him he must leave as visiting hours were long over. An undemanding friendship had developed from that point and continued after Logo was discharged from the hospital and the Army. The latter provided him with a disability pension and Townsend found him rooms in Hackney because Logo thought he had once lived there. He did have some distant relatives, his Army records showed that, but he became distressed whenever they were mentioned and Townsend made no attempt to communicate with them. His occasional visits appeared to be all the social contact that Logo needed and he put that down to two things. Firstly, his completely genuine admiration for what the mentally crippled man had achieved and, secondly, his own boyish features. It was careful thought, rather than sudden insight, which led him to the conclusion that his face was something the now near-juvenile Logo could relate to.

Townsend went to see Logo whenever he could, partly because it gave the man obvious pleasure and partly because his admiration for him continued to grow. He was looking forward to this coming visit particularly as it was two months since his last and there would be a lot of new things to look at. 1.00 a.m. would, he thought, be about right. For reasons he had never enquired into, Logo did his chores in the morning, slept during the afternoon and evening, then worked all night.

Sudden worry that Logo might be too set in his ways now to alter them struck Townsend, but he brushed the thought aside and ran on through the rain.

8

There were only two rooms. The smaller was Logo's workshop and the larger had to act as everything else except bathroom and lavatory. Those were on the landing outside and he shared them with three other tenants. The combination living-room, bedroom and kitchen looked like a disaster area; the workroom was immaculate. A bench stood at the centre with three powerful anglepoise lamps set on it. There was a tiny vice too, an old brass microscope and soldering equipment. Tools, precisely graded, lay on three levels of a wheeled trolley beside the adjustable typist's chair on which Logo sat in front of the bench.

"Lo, Bill. Beer in the fridge. Must finish this.'

'Hi, Logo,' Townsend said and went back into the living-room for a can of beer. There were always six of them on the top shelf of the refrigerator and he knew that five would be those he had seen last time, with the one he had drunk then replaced. Logo drank Pepsi-Cola himself, kept the beer for him and offered nothing to anybody else. He took the left-hand can from the back row, read 'Best before end Dec 1985' stamped on it, smiled and opened it anyway. Then he went back to the workroom, moving quietly, not speaking.

Most of the wall-space was shelved, the spotless surfaces bearing tools, materials and objects Logo had made, the purpose of many of which Townsend was unable to discern. The model ships had been relegated to a corner, but still stood in tidy rows. There were reference books on subjects ranging from metallurgy to electronics. Those and piles of strip-cartoon magazines for children constituted the entire spectrum of

63

Logo's reading, except for an occasional copy of *Vogue*. The back of the door, covered with pictures of women, showed the reason for that addition. All of them were pretty, all fully clothed and all had been chosen for their compassionate expressions. There wasn't a typically arrogant mannequin's face amongst them. It hadn't taken Townsend long to realise that the montage constituted a composite of the mother Logo had either lost or never known.

'Done it,' Logo said. 'Test it later.'

'What is it, Logo?'

'Fibre-optic thing for seeing through cracks. Round corners, too.'

'Who wants that?'

'Chap I know. Crook probably. Can't think who else wants to look through walls. Never mind, he gives me good money.'

'You short of money?' Townsend asked.

'Sometimes. Anyway, I need a decent microscope. A binocular one. Not this old thing.'

Townsend drank some of his beer before saying, 'If you'd like to do some work for me I'd see that you got a lot more than a microscope. It would mean going abroad though. With me and another chap.'

'What other chap?'

'My best friend after you.'

'Oh, that's all right then,' Logo said. 'Where'd we go?'

'New York.'

'That's near the Falklands, isn't it?'

Always careful never to draw attention to Logo's splintered memory, Townsend told him, 'Somewhere to the west of here certainly. Let's take a look at the map.'

There was a school atlas amongst the reference books. He took it down and, after an unnecessary search, pointed to New York.

'There it is.'

'No problem,' Logo said. 'When do we go?'

'You told me that you had contacts within MI5, Mr Stein.'

Stein looked defensive but, after a moment, he nodded.

'Good,' Shaw said. 'That being the case you'll be able to use their good offices in enlisting the help of their friends in MI6. Well, sometimes they're friends.'

'For what purpose?'

'For up-to-the-minute reports on the whereabouts of my targets for you to radio to me during the closing stages of my approach, of course. You don't imagine that I'm going to wander into Tripoli and ask if anybody's seen Colonel Gadaffi recently, do you?'

'What would you do if it was impossible to provide you with that information?'

'Bloody hell, man! I'd abort the mission,' Shaw replied. 'You aren't paying me to shoot up a collection of Bedouin camp-followers, are you?'

'No.'

'So?'

'It can be done.'

'You'd better change that to "it will be done", or the deal's off.'

'Very well. You may depend on it.'

'Good,' Shaw said. 'We'll arrange transmission schedules later, after I've made some enquiries about local reception conditions. They vary enormously in the desert depending on the time of day, the season of the year and, the boffins tell me, whether or not there are large concentrations of iron-bearing rock in the vicinity.' He was thankful for the opportunity of further underlining his desert wisdom. It was an outlet for his relief at not having had his bluff called. More importantly, it demonstrated an intelligent attention to detail, an attitude of mind it was essential he maintain, however imaginary its need. He had another card to play and proceeded to play it.

'You'd better cover the movements of Abu Nidal as well,' he told Stein. 'He was on that list you showed me and I may need a fall-back target if Gadaffi and Arafat are abroad when I'm in position. He's reported as often being in Libya. I take it he'd be an acceptable prize for you.'

'Eminently so.'

'Then I needn't detain you any longer,' Shaw said and walked to the door of his apartment to let his guest out.

'One minute, Captain Shaw.'

Shaw turned. 'It isn't Captain any longer. My release has come through.'

Ignoring the statement, Stein said, 'You appear to have undergone a change of heart.'

'Meaning what?'

'My sources have now informed me that your wish to leave the Army was based on a matter of conscience in that you objected to the assassination of Macnamara. How do you reconcile that with your willingness to kill these Arabs?'

Speaking slowly, both for emphasis and to give himself time to think, Shaw said, 'The preferred procedure in cases like Macnamara's is a snatch. You try to lift them out and put them back in gaol. Only if they offer armed resistance are they killed. The situation in Armagh that day left me no option but to kill him and that involved the deaths of three others. I didn't like that.' He paused, then went on, 'Let me put it this way, Stein. If I'm going to play at being God, I'll make my own judgements. I'll also listen to the views of the Son and the Holy Ghost, but I won't take orders from them anymore. Your religion doesn't subscribe to the Holy Trinity theory, but I expect you'll see what I mean.'

'Yes, I see what you mean,' Stein told him and, not being absolutely certain what he meant himself, Shaw was relieved about that. It was only after Stein had left that he conceded that his statement had contained a degree of rationality.

For a while he sat, eyes unfocused, staring at nothing, wondering what it was Stein thought he was trying to do. The real problem was the Arab–Israeli conflict and that was very unlikely to be solved by the removal of individuals. There would always be others to replace them and those others could well be more intransigent than their predecessors. He didn't believe that the Americans could have overlooked that elementary fact before their knee-jerk reaction of attacking Tripoli and Benghazi. That had been done to make them feel good about themselves as, he suspected, had their invasion of Grenada. Not that he begrudged them either action. Such things were necessary from time to time in a many-cultured society scattered across a vast continent if cohesion was to be maintained. Nor was he surprised at their choice of Libya as the point on which to apply pressure despite the seeming illogicality of the decision. Any thought of seducing Israel away from its stubborn stand on the West Bank question would founder on the rocks of the Jewish vote before it was fully formed, Iran was virtually unreachable, and an assault on a Moscow-buttressed Syria would involve risks so grave as to make them totally unacceptable.

Shaw was wondering cynically if the Reagan Administration planned a second raid on Libya as a public relations prelude to the November mid-term elections when he realised how far his mind had wandered off the point of Stein's motives. He supposed that the answer could be as simple as a desire at least to do *something* about an intractable problem and left it at that. The man's sources of information were of more immediate concern to him. Stein claimed to have MI5 contacts and probably did, but Shaw no longer believed in the suggestion he had made to Townsend that Stein was being used by that organisation or its sister service, because they couldn't be that stupid. Neither did he believe that the information he had asked for on the location of his three supposed targets would be provided by British government agencies. Israeli Intelligence was a much more likely source for Stein to be able to tap.

'All of which is pretty damned irrelevant in the long term as far as I'm concerned,' Shaw informed the empty room, then went to the kitchen to prepare his lunch.

'I've got to go to the States for a month or so,' Shaw said.

'I'll divorce you if you do,' Sarah Cheyney told him.

'Oh good. That means we'll have to get married so you can. Will you marry me?'

'No, but you can't go anyway. I'm going to have a baby.'

'Congratulations. When's it due?'

'Tomorrow, I think, but to hell with you,' Sarah said. 'Your chin was supposed to drop when I said that. It's a woman's last resort, even when it's a lie.'

'How can it drop when it's resting on your – er – pectoral development?'

'Yes, I suppose you're right. Take it off, then the top of your head won't keep moving up and down in that ridiculous way when you talk. Now, what's all this about the States?'

Shaw pushed himself into a sitting position, the silly, brittle exchange which had followed his announcement seeming to repeat itself like a flawed gramophone disc, confusing his thought processes. It kept him silent long enough for her to say, 'Is this your way of saying goodbye, Harry? If so, you'd better go at once! Go on! Go!'

More stunned now than simply confused he sought miserably for words, then suddenly everything was all right again, long slender arms of surprising strength pulling his head down on to her shoulder.

'Aah,' Sarah said, and it was a happy sound.

'What happened, Sarah?' Shaw asked.

'You gave me an ordinary piece of information, we both made smart-ass noises, and I went into one of the mean moods I warned you about. Sometimes I get mad-dog mean. Well, mad-bitch mean actually.'

'The mood passed quickly enough. What made it do that?'

'You did. It was the most touching thing.'

Shaw didn't say anything and, after a moment, Sarah went on, 'You've got the most immobile face I've ever seen, darling. It's a nice face, but it's only got two speeds – stop and smile. That is, it had until just now when you looked frightened. I didn't know you *could* look frightened and I hadn't realised quite how much I meant to you.' She rolled on top of him then and added, 'Tell me about the States in the morning.'

The suspected IRA watch on Bradbury Lines in Hereford was observed to have been withdrawn and Townsend was recalled. He spent his last few weeks in the Army as an instructor at the Close Quarter Battle House, known familiarly as the 'Killing House'. He was very good at it, moving swiftly from room to room, firing short controlled bursts into every dummy terrorist he encountered. It was always a burst of fire because solitary shots could be a fatally false economy. It was also essential to be exceptionally precise in the placing of those bullets as the 'hostages' present were, as likely as not, live officers of the regiment. Townsend was glad that he was not an officer and required to prove his courage in that way.

Having demonstrated the technique, he set those in his

charge to the task. It required instant appreciation of a situation which was never twice the same, cat-like reflexes and total accuracy. 'There's a good little Sassman,' he would say when somebody showed particular aptitude. None of them minded the condescension. Coming from Sergeant Townsend it was as good as a guarantee that, thus far, their place within the regiment was secure. There were many other hurdles for them to clear involving battlefield medicine, the use of knives and crossbows for silent killing, parachuting, communications, languages, demolition, mountaineering and a host of other things, but Townsend's hurdle was high and a good one to leave behind until it was time to do it all again in semi-darkness and smoke, amidst the blast of stun-grenades emitting CS gas while the sergeant watched their every move.

Lieutenant Chadwick had sent for Townsend immediately on his return and been told that Shaw's revulsion to what he had done in the past had decided him to take up charity work, initially in North America as he would feel safer there until the Macnamara affair faded in the memories of the IRA. Chadwick had said 'Christ', Townsend had said 'Yessir', and that had appeared to be the end of the matter.

Shaw had flown to New York as a tourist on a five-day reconnaissance mission, found the city he hadn't visited for a decade hot, humid and tiring beneath the July sun, but had returned satisfied with what he had seen and learned. The patrolmen on the streets were, if anything, rather more edgy than he remembered them. Most took a step back and put a hand on their gun when asked for directions. One said, 'What do you think I am, mac? An information bureau?' There was little resemblance between them and a London policeman and Shaw took note of the fact, but was not dismayed by it because nervousness was what he hoped to engender throughout the population. There were uniformed armed guards in the banks too, a detail he had forgotten, but that didn't dismay him either for, except with Stein's collusion, banks did not number amongst his intended victims. Apart from that, he had found security measures in general to be no more stringent than they were in London and therein lay his contentment. Now he was sitting in Logo's workshop, knowing himself to be honoured by the presence of a can of beer in his hand.

'You're Bill Townsend's second best friend, you know.'

Shaw looked at the big man. 'Oh, am I?' he said. 'I'm glad about that. I know you're his best friend. He told me so.'

'Well, don't worry about it. Bill says he wants me to make some good old bang machines in New York for him and you. Lot of Argies there, are there?'

'The place is full of them.'

'Bastards get everywhere,' Logo said. 'They tried to take the Falklands, you know. Bill and me stopped all that nonsense.'

'Yes, I remember about that. They say you did very well.'

'Got shot a bit. Didn't make no difference though. I'm ready for them any old time. I'll start packing.'

'Hold on, Logo,' Shaw said. 'We have to wait for Bill to get out of the Army.'

'Oh, sure. I forgot. I forget things, you know.'

Shaw nodded. 'So do I, and that reminds me of something. While we're waiting for him could you make a couple of the things we need, just to test the timing mechanism? I've brought the specifications and rough drawings for you.'

Logo took the proffered papers and began to study them. They weren't extensive, but he took forty minutes over it, silently mouthing words and numbers. Five times he got up and took technical books from the shelves. Shaw watched him without impatience, not speaking.

After the fifth visit to the shelves Logo asked, 'Making these here is OK by Bill, is it?'

'Yes, it was his idea. Once we're certain they work we can go to New York and make a lot of them. We can't make them all here and take them with us because we'd never get them through airport security.'

'Ah.'

'What do you think, Logo?'

'Go off with a hell of a bang, these will. Shake those bloody Argies rigid.'

'Yes, but can you make them?'

'No problem,' Logo said.

*

It took Logo fifteen days to manufacture the first device, under eighteen hours to complete the second, and he told Shaw that he could improve on the latter time now that he knew what he was doing. That was one of the things Shaw had needed to establish and he was encouraged by the news, but a little concerned at the weight of the cassette-like objects. It was sufficient to pull the shoulder of a jacket down and he had intended to carry one in his breast pocket. But after a moment the pettiness of the problem compared with what Logo had overcome made him smile. There was no such thing as light lead screening and there were other ways of transporting a bomb to its destination. He carried the prototypes home in a briefcase still, after the passage of weeks, alert for the presence of followers, of watchers. There were none.

The contents of the flat boxes were familiar to Shaw now, but he still studied them with wonderment as they lay open on the breakfast counter in his kitchen. A thin lead lining was itself lined with putty to represent the plastic explosive of an operational model. Where the twin-detonators were inserted into the charge he could no longer see because they were covered by a small Long-Life battery, two tiny spools of wire, two dials graduated in hours and minutes and a printed-circuit card hardly bigger than a postage stamp. The mercury tilt activator and the mechanical attachment to the magnetic clamps on the back of the casings were invisible too.

In plain view was the penny-sized amplifier grid set into the lid of each box and, on the inner side, a pair of prongs like needles for connecting the spools to the amplifier when the lid was replaced. Firm thumb-pressure on the grid was all that was then necessary to set the timing mechanism in action, Shaw knew, and when time had run its course the spools would be activated and turn for a further forty seconds before detonation occurred. He knew too that those forty seconds of grace would start immediately if the device was tilted or had its magnetic contact broken. Logo had demonstrated that, but he wanted to do it for himself.

With a fine probe Shaw set the dials of one bomb to twenty-five hours and eleven minutes, replaced the lid and tightened the two retaining screws, screws which would not exist on the operational versions. Logo had not yet decided on the most effective method of achieving a permanent seal without damage to the contents, but seemed to be favouring a solvent-resistant super-glue. Shaw was content to leave the problem to him. Never having had any doubts about his own and Townsend's ability to manufacture explosive devices, he was perfectly well aware that neither of them could have achieved anything remotely resembling the sophistication of the objects lying before him now. Picking up the one he had made ready he attached it to the back of the refrigerator. The magnetic clamps clicked sharply as they gripped. Shaw checked the time by his watch, then depressed the amplifier grid.

The timer of the second he set to five minutes, screwed the lid in place, stuck the bomb to the front of the refrigerator, depressed the grid, and pulled. The refrigerator door opened. Shaw said, 'Bugger,' closed the door, held it shut with his knee, and jerked the bomb free, breaking the magnetic contact. Immediately the tinny sound of Elaine Paige's voice singing 'Memory' from the musical *Cats* flowed into the room from the tiny amplifier and continued to do so for precisely forty seconds. Then it cut off abruptly in mid-word.

'Bang,' Shaw said. He took the lid off, wound the spool back and reset the timer. Replacing the cover, he depressed the grid once more and tilted the metal box ten degrees to the left. Elaine Paige began to sing again.

Twenty-five hours and nine minutes later she sang for the third time, doing it from behind the refrigerator. Shaw noted the two-minute discrepancy, decided that it was remarkably and quite acceptably small, then listened to the voice, still pretty despite its tinniness, telling Argentina not to cry for her. He had used her numbers on the minute recorders simply because he enjoyed listening to them and well before he had become aware of Logo's fixation about blowing up Argentinians.

The coincidence brought a smile to his face, but the knowledge that the amplifiers would broadcast a very different message in the United States wiped it off again.

9

It had been an indifferent August and continued to be now
that the month was nearly over, clouds heavy with rain chasing
each other across the London sky.

'No, Harry, I don't want to be driven home. I'll get a taxi
on Ken High. It's hardly raining at all. Better to say goodbye
now and get it over with, otherwise I'd probably howl. Good
luck with your charity, my dear.'

She had been wearing a white plastic raincoat when she left,
its upturned collar framing her hair and face, making her look
like a bar of candy he desperately wanted to unwrap and never
let go of. Standing at the street door of the apartment building
it had taken an enormous effort of will for him not to call out
to her as he watched her getting further and further away.
Come back, jaguar in a white coat. I'm not going anywhere.
He might have done it had she turned to wave at the end of
the street, but she had not. Deeply disturbed, he had climbed
the stairs to his apartment.

It had been an indifferent August too for reasons other than
the weather and it was remembering that which restored
Shaw's sense of proportion and purpose. Earlier in the year he
had been mildly encouraged by the US Senate's eventual rati-
fication of the extradition treaty relating to terrorists wanted
for questioning by the British authorities, but since then the
situation had continued to deteriorate as far as Anglo–American co-operation was concerned. Arms despatched by mail
from the States, destined for the IRA, were intercepted by the
police of the Irish Republic. Amongst them was the M82
machine-gun of which Shaw had spoken to Townsend. That

such a risky method of delivery indicated a degree of desperation on the part of both NORAID and the IRA Shaw saw as a very minor consolation.

Very much less covertly, NORAID and the Irish–American Caucus continued their efforts to demonstrate their belief that Ulster could not, or should not, be allowed to continue to function as an economically viable part of the United Kingdom. American money was donated to the main party representing the Province's Irish Nationalists to the fury of the Unionist majority, comparisons with the situation in Ulster and the apartheid system in South Africa were publicly drawn in the States, and a contingent of the New York police force announced its intention to parade through Bundoran in County Donegal in support of the IRA. This was the third consecutive year in which it had happened adding to the insult, and the fact that the village was only nine miles from where Lord Mountbatten had been murdered by the people they were supporting made it worse because there was nothing coincidental about the choice of location for the march.

Such things, Shaw knew, were little more than ripples on the tide of events which strengthened his long-held conviction that he was witnessing the perpetuation of grave interference by foreigners in the internal affairs of a sovereign state. He mentally amended that to two sovereign states because, at least since the signing of the Anglo–Irish Agreement, the government of the Irish Republic was as opposed to outside pressures as the British. It was ironic, he thought, that one faction in the United States should seek to support that agreement with both funds and encouragement, while another sought to destroy it with funds, arms and propaganda amounting to incitement to murder. To equate the latter with American organised crime had become customary with him, but he doubted very much if more than a microscopic percentage of the forty million Americans claiming some form of Irish ancestry had either strong retrospective feelings of patriotism or Mafia-style leanings, and that made him wonder if NORAID had Russian paymasters.

August had been a bad month in Ulster too with the IRA issuing its civilian 'hit list'. 'Legitimate Murder Targets' was the expression used by them. The targets included anybody

74

providing services for the security forces from vending-machine suppliers to cleaners, from builders to garbage collectors and from caterers to electricians. A grim touch was added by the threat of death to employees of British Telecom, for it was they who had the responsibility and the means to pass on to the authorities the warnings of imminent bomb explosions which the IRA sometimes gave. The family homes of members of the Royal Ulster Constabulary came under attack whether or not the officers themselves were in residence, intimidation spilled over into the factories and shipyards, and random sectarian killings increased, for now the Protestant population, frightened by the Anglo–Irish Agreement, was taking up arms in increasing numbers. It was all very complicated and becoming more so as the tragedy dragged remorselessly on, but one thing was very clear to Shaw. Be it American or Russian, the brain of the octopus was in the United States and must be attacked there.

Shaking his mental cocktail had started his adrenalin flowing again and he felt less despondent about his separation from Sarah Cheyney. Whether or not he would ever see her again was something he refused to think about at all.

'Doesn't look much like the Falklands to me,' Logo said.

Through the cab window, Townsend continued to watch the towers of Manhattan, painted pink by the setting sun, rising like some magic island-city above the haze of heat. He nodded.

'Not a lot, does it?'

'People don't look like Argies either.'

'How can you tell, Logo?'

'Argies wear funny pointed woollen hats with ear-flaps.'

'It's a bit hot for those at this time of year.'

'Then how're we going to know them when we see them?' Logo asked.

The driver was watching them curiously in his mirror. Townsend drooped an eyelid at him and the driver winked back.

'Harry'll know,' Townsend said. 'He arrives tomorrow.'

Logo grunted, as though doubtful about Shaw's ability to identify the hidden enemy, then began to examine his passport as he had done repeatedly during the flight across the Atlantic. Having always been provided with transport by the Army, the Navy, or the RAF, he had never had one before and it was almost virgin. He liked the blue, red and green of his United States visa which took up most of a page, but wished they hadn't stapled the immigration form over it. That had spoiled the appearance of the little book, but Bill had said it had to stay there until they went home so he resisted the temptation to detach it.

'Tunnel or bridge, mister? Tunnel's cheaper for where you're going.'

Townsend met the driver's enquiring regard in the mirror. 'Let's take the scenic route. We've never been here before.'

'That right? OK, you've got it,' the driver said, and began to point out the tall buildings of the city, naming and describing them like a tour guide. He had no way of knowing that he was carrying history in his cab.

'Wait here', the sign read, and Shaw waited, his feet on the line drawn on the ground at Kennedy Airport, while the passenger ahead of him in the queue went to the immigration desk. There were several queues and several desks. Shaw had chosen a line approaching a desk with a middle-aged man seated behind it, because middle-aged men were less inclined to be officious than their juniors. Or women. When the man beckoned to him he walked forward, placed his flight bag on the desk and surrendered his passport with the immigration form he had completed inside it.

'Sir, I'm afraid you'll have to fill this out again. You didn't press hard enough for it to show on the carbon copy.'

'Bloody fool.'

The man looked up at him sharply and Shaw said, 'I was talking to myself, not you. I must be practising to be a brain surgeon.'

Smiling faintly, the man handed him a new form and Shaw retired behind the line. It took him twenty minutes to reach the head of the queue again.

'I put some muscle into it this time.'

'Oh, it's you,' the immigration official said. 'Yeah, that's better.'

Shaw watched the slip of paper being stapled into his passport and unzipped his flight bag.

'How long will you be in the States, Mr Shaw?'

'That rather depends on the lawyers and accountants. I've come to set up a charitable organisation.'

'Sorry I had to delay you with the formalities. Enjoy your stay. Next, please.'

Moving a pace to his left Shaw put his bag back on the desk, zipped it shut, then walked out of immigration with the badly completed form the man had pushed aside adhering to a piece of chewing-gum on the bag's bottom. He had a spare entry slip now which, with a little doctoring, would make him at least apparently legal should he need to leave the country and then return by some unorthodox route. It wasn't something he envisaged having to do, but he didn't intend to miss any tricks.

On his instructions his taxi followed the route taken by Townsend and Logo the previous day, but the silent driver gave him no guided tour. The only words the man spoke were 'Have a nice day' when Shaw paid him outside the Plaza Hotel on Fifth Avenue at Central Park South. Shaw walked into the hotel wondering how many billion times a week that injunction was given across the States, but it immediately became a nice day when the clerk at the reception desk handed him a letter with his room key.

The spiky writing was more familiar to him now, even decipherable in places, and the fact that Sarah Cheyney had taken the trouble to write to him a week before their parting made him very happy. So did the bits he could read. They also persuaded him to be more positive in his approach to her. Before refusing, she had wavered when he had suggested that she join him in New York for two weeks early in his stay in the city and she would have agreed to do so, he felt now, had he been less diffident about his invitation. It would have been the perfect time, with Logo and Townsend hard at their illegal work in the top-floor apartment of an old building on West 14th Street which Stein had rented for them, while he himself would be engaged on the initially innocuous task of organising the imaginary charity on which the bulk of their funds would depend. She had seemed awfully down in the mouth during their last night together, as though still unconvinced that he was not leaving her for ever. Without even unpacking, Shaw sat down at the desk in his suite and began to write.

The girl the hotel's secretarial service sent up in answer to his request was carrying a stenographer's notebook.

'You won't need that,' Shaw said. 'I've written it out, but you'd better read it to make sure it's clear. Then I'd be grateful if you would type it out for me. Make it look important, will you?'

She took the pages from him, a puzzled expression forming on her face as soon as she started reading.

'I'm not really insane,' he told her defensively, then added, 'It's to my girl.'

Nodding, she read on, giggled, then giggled again. 'She's a lucky lady, Mr Shaw.'

Shaw smiled at her. 'Would you be a darling and ask the desk to arrange for that plane ticket? Open dates Concorde return?'

'My pleasure, Mr Shaw,' she replied and returned his smile, pleased to be part of a small conspiracy. 'Is her writing really so terrible.'

Wordlessly he held Sarah's letter towards her.

'Oh, gee! I see what you mean,' the girl said and giggled for the third time.

Sarah Cheyney giggled too.

'The man's quite, quite mad,' she said.

Major-General Brigg had spent the night at his niece's apartment and now he looked at her across the breakfast table.

'What man?'

'Harry Shaw. He wants me to go to New York for a couple of weeks.'

'Will you go?'

'He makes it very difficult to refuse, and I don't want to refuse. Betty March owes me a locum.'

There was a crushed square of chocolate mint paper-clipped to the letter. She took it out of its little envelope and put it in her mouth.

'Yum.'

'What's that, for heaven's sake?'

'Cyanide. Just in case,' she said. 'But I might as well take it now and get it over with.' She got to her feet and added, 'I must dress and get down to my patients. Here you are. Read all about it.'

Brigg stood while she left the room, sat down again, looked first at the British Airways ticket, then at the letter.

FEDERAL SECURITY AGENCY
Bureau of Cryptography
Washington DC 99930

Dr Sarah Cheyney   September 1, 1986
198 Wimpole Street
London, England.

Madam,

As a result of our routine inspection of selected private mail, a procedure authorized under Sec. 2213 (j)(4)(B)(2) of the US Code and now employed on a regular basis as a result of the Walker espionage case, my operatives have brought to my attention a handwritten note from you to a certain Henry J. Shaw dated August 23, 1986, and addressed to him at the Plaza Hotel, New York City. While we cannot definitely say that it is a love letter as we have been unable to read it, we suspect that this may be the case from the row of Xs beneath the illegible signature. Indeed, had it not been for the return address sticker on the back of the envelope we should never have been able to identify the sender.

The point of this communication is that we believe, given your co-operation, that we are on the threshold of the greatest discovery in cryptography since the invention of the reciprocal heptomasic encryptograph machine as your handwriting absolutely defies decoding. Even if an individual letter is identified in one place it is never duplicated elsewhere and, therefore, eludes all known theory and practice.

The Germans having broken our triple encyphered Navajo code, and the Russians our double acrostic Zulu sandwiched in laminated vellum, your cursive may well prove to be the last resort open to us in the realm of national security. As you possess dual nationality we would now call on your sense of allegiance to the land of your birth and request that you proceed immediately to New York and, over a period of two weeks, explain your system in full to Mr Shaw who, we assume, already has some slight knowledge of its workings. On arrival you will be given your own fall-out shelter with all amenities, and transport will also be provided.

We enclose an airline ticket and a cyanide pill.

Respectfully yours,

Hiram D. Johnson.

Brigadier-General, United States Army (ret'd)
Chief of Bureau

At the bottom of the typed letter Shaw had written the single word 'Please!'

Brigg smiled and put the letter and airline ticket back in the envelope. He felt that even if the humour was a little laboured, a little contrived, it was good to see it as it wasn't something that Shaw exhibited very often. Not that Shaw ever displayed anything much, but the man and his niece were obviously good for each other and he hoped that they would marry soon.

The morning Concorde from Heathrow to Kennedy cleared the west coast of England and accelerated, brushing the sound barrier aside with a faint disdainful shudder. Sarah Cheyney hugged herself, watching the sky turn from blue to indigo, seeing for the first time the curvature of the earth, imagining she could make out the pin-points of stars in the daytime heavens, but not being sure about that yet. It was all very exciting with the 'machmeter' climbing from 1.3 to 1.9, then to 2.0 and 2.1 before seeming to decide that enough was enough and settling back on 1.9 again.

There were the people to watch too. An actor she could name, a Member of Parliament she could not, although she had seen him often on television, and two men who might have been American Senators, or big-business executives, or something. Each was led in turn to where the pilots were. She thought it would be wonderful to be important enough to see that place.

'Dr Cheyney?'

She looked up at the face of the flight attendant, noting the girl's expression, half amused, half rueful.

'Yes?'

'The captain wonders if you'd like to visit what he calls "where the work is done".'

'I'd love to,' she said thinking, without a trace of conceit, that it really was rather nice to have things happen, which you wanted to happen, just because you were pretty.

As Sarah Cheyney stepped on to the flight deck, separated from her by a distance which was decreasing at over twenty miles a minute, Logo was placing his fifth bomb under the floor-boards of the apartment on West 14th Street. They were complete except for the plastic explosive, and Bill Townsend was in Mexico getting that.

When he had replaced the carpet, Logo arranged the parts of a tiny model locomotive he had made on his workbench in case anybody came in to find out what it was he did. 'Fool the Argies,' he said, then lay on his bed to read comics until it was time for the local supermarket to open. There was an all-night one quite close, but he preferred to stick to his London routine.

At the moment Sarah Cheyney fastened her seat-belt for the landing at Kennedy Airport, Townsend lowered the window of the rented Buick as it edged forward in the queue for the immigration checkpoint at Nogales on the Mexican border. He gestured at a group of young people standing hopefully at the roadside. One of them was holding up a sign with the legend TUCSON on it in magic marker.

'Americans?'

'Yeah.'

'OK. I can take five of you. Pile in.'

'Oh, great! Thanks, mister!'

Three girls and two boys, students he guessed, got into the car, chattering.

'You sound British.'

'That's right.'

'This is real nice of you.'

'No problem,' Townsend said and supposed he had caught that from Logo.

Three minutes later the car reached the checkpoint.

'You all Americans?'

'Five Americans and one Brit,' Townsend said and held out his passport. The uniformed man took it, glanced at it and handed it back.

'Have a nice day.'

'You too.'

It was a relief to pass through on to American soil with his innocent cover. Much better than doing it as a lone driver with a lot of plastic explosive flattened into a thin sheet and hidden under the carpet of the car. There had been no sniffer dogs on duty. He had kept all the checkpoints, northbound and southbound on both sides of the border, under observation for hours to make certain of that, but he was still grateful to have had his disarming passengers with him. There had been little difficulty in obtaining the explosive. Shaw had said that there wouldn't be, provided that enough dollars were offered and, as usual, he had been right.

As Sarah Cheyney passed through the barrier on to the concourse at Kennedy Airport Shaw began to run. She ran too and people smiled as the couple met and clung to each other.

10

Yes, they were at the University of Arizona at Tucson, his
passengers told Townsend, all of them except the oldest girl.
She didn't tell him anything, but just sat silently in the back
watching him in the mirror as though wondering what he was
and not being particularly interested in the answer. He found
her blankly fixed stare disconcerting. She was attractive without being pretty and would have been much more so, he
thought, had her expression not stated so clearly that the world
and everything in it bored her immeasurably.

At Tucson he went a little out of his way and drove the four
right on to the university campus which seemed to please them
enormously and they got out of the car making friendly, grateful
noises. Townsend decided that he liked American college kids.

'Want me to share the driving?'

He met the older girl's regard in the mirror.

'Where to?'

'Chicago. It's a helluva long way.'

Townsend turned round at that, facing her.

'Why do you want to go to Chicago?'

'It's a place. You said you were going there. You've got
wheels. I haven't.' Her words carried their own shrug with
them.

'What's your name?'

'Zoë.'

'OK, Zoë, what are you?'

'Tugboat skipper, cocktail waitress, orthodontist, realtor or
none of the above. Place a tick in the box of your choice and
will the real nuclear physicist please stand up,' she said.

'Have you got police trouble?'

'Shit, no!'

Her surprise at the question and her positive reply looked and sounded genuine enough and Townsend began to think quickly. It had been simple to fly from New York to Tucson and hire a car for the short trip into Mexico, but the return journey was a very different matter. The fact that he wasn't going anywhere near Chicago made it even longer and he had no intention of trying to transport his detectable cargo by air. That meant something in the region of three thousand miles of driving and he had not been looking forward to that. The roads were too good and too straight, the nationwide speed limit of 55mph too slow and the car too comfortable to call upon the brain for the prolonged concentration which would be required of it. He had already discovered in himself a tendency to take his accustomed left-hand side of the road when that concentration was broken after he had stopped for petrol or anything else. But with a companion . . .

A long-submerged envy of Shaw with the lovely dark woman he had never met surfaced in him then. It was this day she was due in New York and while the girl watching him enquiringly from the back of his car was no Sarah Cheyney she did seem to be growing more attractive by the second. He would have to drop her off at some point along the way, of course, before his true destination became apparent because he couldn't afford to have her getting under his feet in Manhattan.

'All right,' he said. 'Let's find somewhere to eat, then we'll start motoring.'

Townsend found out what she was when they stopped for the night at a motel outside El Paso in New Mexico, and the discovery exhausted him so much that she had to do most of the next day's driving. The event was repeated in Texas, but he crossed Arkansas unscathed in daylight.

It was in Missouri that she said, 'You're well over halfway to Chicago now. I'm going to split at St Louis.'

'Oh? What made you change your mind?'

'My lover lives there.'

'Jesus! I hope he and I don't meet!'

'You shouldn't have any trouble,' she said. 'You and your

big muscles. How'd you manage to get them with that baby face? It's creepy.' Without waiting for a reply she added, 'Anyway, he's a she.'

Bemused and not a little thankful, Townsend left her at a cab rank in St Louis and crossed the Mississippi into Illinois. New York City was only about one thousand miles away now.

'We're getting negative residential feedback, Mr Shaw,' the bank's vice-president in charge of property acquisition and development said.

'You mean the local people don't want a hostel for "winos" and other drop-outs on their doorsteps?'

'Right. Don't tell me you don't have the same problem in the UK.'

'Of course we do.'

The vice-president moved uncomfortably in his chair, as though embarrassed, before saying, 'It's like this, Mr Shaw. We're delighted to handle Mr Stein's affairs on your behalf, but the parameters he has defined are extremely limiting. Not to put too fine a point on it we're dealing in peanuts. As you know, he has allocated eight hundred thousand pounds sterling to this project. Well now, that's considerably more than a million United States dollars which, on the face of it, sounds like a considerable sum of money, but you only have to look at property values here to realise that that's not the case. Ah, here comes our coffee.'

The girl put a tray on the desk and looked at Shaw.

'Cream and sugar, sir?'

'Just black, please.'

When the door closed behind her the vice-president went on, 'I'm not saying that we can't find you a location, but what worries me is that with a shut-ended deal like this you will be left with too little operating capital to fund the venture from the interest on investments. Not to an acceptable standard anyway, and that's something that local residents have been quick to point out. The police are dubious about it too. Without a level of supervision which is manifestly beyond your means, they feel you might, amongst other things, be inadvertently setting up a handy centre for drug pushers and I don't imagine an establishment repeatedly raided by the drug squad is exactly what Mr Stein has in mind.'

'No, it isn't,' Shaw said. He was hearing much what he had expected and hoped to hear, but managed to look worried about it.

'Is there any possibility of Mr Stein upping the ante to provide you with a viable working margin?'

Shaw shook his head. 'Not at this stage. I'm here to test the temperature of the water and if I find that it's too hot for his budget I'm authorised to transfer the money elsewhere.'

'Yes, I know. Is that now your intention?'

'Oh hell no,' Shaw said. 'Not yet. He'd never give me another assignment if I gave up that easily, but I want that money to earn its keep.'

'The bank would be glad to arrange a portfolio for you.'

Shaw shook his head for the second time. 'Too long term and too speculative with the Dow Jones just having had its biggest one-day fall since 1929 or whenever. I don't want to come out of this showing a loss. Property values appreciate all the time, don't they?'

'Virtually always, but –'

'Look into buying me a fancy apartment on Fifth, or Park Avenue or somewhere, will you? Something that can readily be resold. There could be a quick profit in that. Enough to cover my overheads anyway.'

'You might do better to leave the money on deposit here, Mr Shaw.'

'Well, you would suggest that, wouldn't you?' Shaw answered, but he smiled when he said it.

They talked for a few minutes more, then the vice-president walked to the door with his customer, assuring him that the bank would undertake an immediate study of all the options. He was thinking that philanthropists were very peculiar people with their unworkable pet schemes and their appointment of amateurs to run them, when there were numerous hospitals and properly organised charities which would have been glad of such a sizeable donation.

Shaw, had he known of the man's opinion of his ability, would not have minded in the least. The entire sum was available to him whenever he was ready, but in the meantime he had to be seen to be doing something, however implausible. It had been his fourth visit to the bank and regardless of the temperature of the water he had been glad to find it still satisfactorily muddied. Very soon now there would be no time to mess about with notional charities.

Striding fast, he crossed Fifth, then Madison and Park Avenue, making his way towards Lexington and the Italian restaurant at which he had arranged to meet Sarah Cheyney.

At the same moment as Shaw left the bank, Lieutenant Harvey Bergquist said 'The hell with it,' tossed his salami on rye and carton of coffee into the wastebin, watched them form into a soggy mass at the bottom of it, then walked out of the precinct building. It was nearly three months since he had permitted himself a lunch break and he needed a little time to himself, a little time to think. The time he got, the thinking he found difficult because it was almost impossible to concentrate with his eyes constantly turning towards the ravishing black girl with the English voice at the next table. Her companion didn't register in his memory.

When Townsend safely returned his rented car, with its cargo removed, to Hertz in New York, Miguel Fernandez was having less luck with his new Ford near the town of Caborca in northern Mexico. The road quivered and writhed strangely in his headlights and unfamiliar corners appeared with alarming suddenness. He concluded that his country was being ravaged by yet another earthquake and stamped on the brake pedal. The tyres shrieked their protest and lost traction. The car lost direction, abandoned the blameless road and came to rest in some bushes two hundred metres down a gentle slope. Nothing dramatic happened and Fernandez fell asleep behind the wheel, overburdened by the unaccustomed quantity of whiskey in his stomach and bloodstream.

He awoke in a police cell at ten twenty the following morning, but it was two hours after that before he could give coherent answers to the questions put to him by a bored police sergeant. Having established Fernandez' place of work the policeman went away to make a phone call and returned a quarter of an hour later looking less bored, accompanied by an officer in plain clothes who didn't look bored at all.

Fernandez failed totally in his attempts to convince them that no connection existed between his sudden acquisition of wealth sufficient to buy a large amount of whiskey, let alone a new car, and the inexplicable absence of explosive substances from his employer's store. After they had hit him a few times in the face, stomach and kidneys he admitted responsibility for the theft and told them that he had carried it out at the request of a very young, very wealthy *Americano*. His not having seen the purchaser's vehicle and his belief that anybody with a pale skin, fair hair and indifferent Spanish was automatically an *Americano* did little to advance the investigation. Neither did further beatings.

Death from a ruptured spleen in a Mexican prison hospital made Miguel Fernandez the first casualty in Shaw's war.

Sarah Cheyney took Shaw to the Frick Collection and the Guggenheim Museum, to see the house in Queens where her parents had lived and to the opera, to the zoo in Central Park and on a boat trip round the island of Manhattan.

Shaw took Sarah Cheyney to the theatre on Broadway and to Lord and Taylor where he bought her a dress, to the top of the Empire State Building and to Bergdorf Goodman where he bought her lingerie, to Staten Island so she could see the Statue of Liberty again and to Madison Square Garden. Then he took her to Kennedy International Airport.

'It's been like a wonderful, wonderful honeymoon.'

'Then will you marry me?' It was the third time of asking, but the first in full seriousness.

'Yes please,' Sarah Cheyney said.

The Concorde looked very small, squatting like some ungainly bird at the end of the runway, then the ground shuddered and the blast of the jets hammered at Shaw's eardrums. He hadn't seen one take off before and now no longer felt surprise at the initial fierce opposition to the plane's operation by local residents.

'Take care of her,' he said to it and suddenly the bird wasn't ungainly anymore, but a soaring arrowhead quickly obscured by its own exhaust gases. He watched it reappear as it curved around the sky and continued to watch it until it was swallowed by distance.

Shaw drove slowly back to Manhattan feeling nakedly exposed. He *had* worked at his self-inflicted task during the time Sarah had been in New York, but only at those things which would seem natural to her. 'They tell me I've got negative residential feed-back,' he had said to her at the Italian restaurant and she had replied, 'Well, don't come to me for a second opinion. Fractures of the syntax aren't my field.' The memory made him smile, but only a small smile, and it didn't make him feel any less exposed. Apart from the intense pleasure he experienced in her company, in bed and out, he was aware that he had subconsciously been using her as a shield, a talisman, in that nothing bad could happen while she was there because he could not permit it to do so. But now his talisman was speeding away from him, riding on condensation trails ten miles above the Atlantic, and the point of no return at which every man would become his enemy was fast approaching him in its place.

That he had acted with quite incredible selfishness in encouraging his relationship with Sarah Cheyney to develop, at this of all times, was not something that escaped Shaw's attention. The consoling thought that such situations were commonplace in war lasted only as long as it took him to acknowledge that he was solely responsible for the declaration of hostilities. There was no possible excuse and that left him with the responsibility of staying alive for her sake and he was unable even to accept that, because such thinking would inhibit his course of action and, consequently, his efficiency. 'Who dares wins' was the motto of the regiment to which he had belonged and there was much truth in it, for to dare and act was often much safer than to hesitate.

Shaw's mind side-stepped then, bringing back to him Townsend's version of the motto softly spoken as they crawled towards an enemy position in the Falklands. 'Whisper who dares, Christopher Robin is saying his prayers,' he had said. The recollection cheered him slightly, but he had to think of other things to subdue his feelings of guilt. He thought of military bandsmen tossed like rag dolls from an exploding bandstand in a London park. He thought of dying soldiers and screaming horses which, seconds before, had been a ceremonial parade in a London street. He thought of the carnage amongst police and civilians at Harrods and of the so very nearly successful attempted massacre of the British Cabinet at a Brighton hotel. He thought of a host of other grim incidents too, all of them executed by the Irish Republican or National Liberation Armies, most of them financed by NORAID.

It was all there in the records, in the hospitals and in the graveyards, and it was all totally irrelevant to what he had done to Sarah Cheyney. Even his earlier refuge of concern for her personal safety he knew to be too fragile to support itself. 'You bastard!' Shaw said. Had he glanced in the car's mirror, he would have been surprised to see an expression on his face as grim as his spoken words.

That evening he checked out of the Plaza Hotel.

II

Shaw left his rented apartment in Greenwich Village precisely at noon. Townsend was on time, strolling past the entrance and he fell in beside him.

'Feel like a drink, Bill?'

'No, thanks,' Townsend said. 'Well perhaps, but only a large one.'

'There's a pleasant bar just along here.'

'OK.'

'Logo all right?'

'Same as ever. He's made sixteen of the things now, plus four casings for the larger chemical size you wanted.'

Shaw nodded. 'I want you to fly to London, Bill, then on to Las Palmas.'

'Christ! It's all go, isn't it?' Townsend said. 'You'd better make that two large ones. I haven't recovered from my Mexican trip yet.'

'Try not to get yourself screwed stupid this time.'

'I'll try.'

They went into the bar and stood peering about them in the gloom then, as their eyes adjusted to it, made their way to a table in a far corner. Shaw enjoyed the womb-like quality of New York bars. There could be a heatwave or a blizzard outside, it could be day or night, but the places remained oases of dimly lit calm, unconscious of the roaring city beyond their plush walls.

When the waitress had taken Shaw's order, brought the drinks, smiled at Townsend and departed, Shaw said, 'They all want to mother you, don't they?'

'I'm afraid so. All except Zoë, that is. I'm not really very knowledgeable about such matters, but I don't think she was the mothering kind. I may be doing her an injustice of course, but – What do you want me to do in London, Harry?'

'I had a letter from Stein this morning asking for a progress report on what he calls our African venture to be sent to him by a secure route. You're the secure route. Go and see him, shake him down for recording equipment, take him for a walk in the park and tell him these things. First, if he sets anything else down on paper I'll abort the mission. Second, I've had to change the plans. It's too expensive and there's too much explaining to be done to make buying and crewing a vessel capable of crossing the Atlantic worthwhile. Consequently, the arms have been despatched on a Sealand container ship out of Philadelphia to Algeciras hidden in the cylinders and crankcase of a diesel engine where they'll be onward-shipped to Las Palmas. Third, the assault group consisting of five men has now been recruited, making seven of us in all. I'm paying them fifty thousand pounds each, one third before departure, the remainder on completion. The second payment due to anybody who gets killed is shared by the survivors.'

It's like the Falklands and Ulster again, Townsend thought. Harry Shaw had always given his briefings this way, precisely and without pause.

'Fourth,' Shaw said, 'we shall fly into Las Palmas separately and as tourists, but not quite yet because I'm waiting for the desert to cool down. It will have begun to do that by the end of October. Fifth, from 21 November until the end of the year he's to transmit the position reports of the targets to us daily at these times and on those two frequencies one after the other.'

He handed a piece of paper to Townsend and added, 'Memorise and destroy, Bill,' then went on: 'Sixth, you are proceeding to the Canaries to buy a boat to take us to the African coast, and to take delivery of the diesel engine, plus laying in stores, studying local autumn weather patterns and so forth. Last, give him this book. It's the code he's to use for his transmissions. Have you seen that German movie at the Lincoln Plaza?'

'No,' Townsend said, 'I thought I'd take it in tonight.'

When the approaching waitress had checked on their drinks,

found them to be almost full, smiled at Townsend again and gone away, Townsend asked, 'How does it work?' He hadn't touched the paperback wrapped in transparent plastic lying on the table between them.

Shaw told him and ended by saying, 'I wore gloves when I marked it.'

'I see.'

'Questions?'

'Two. A couple of weeks long enough in the Canaries?'

'Ample. Report to Stein again on your way back through London. Tell him whatever makes sense.'

'OK. Do I talk about your charitable efforts?'

'Yes, if he asks you. I've no doubt he's instructed the bank to tell him everything I do anyway.'

Townsend finished his drink, put the paperback in his pocket, said, 'Be seeing you,' and walked out of the bar. Feeling almost content Shaw watched him go. He hadn't asked him to repeat anything he had told him because that had never been necessary with Townsend.

It was pleasantly mild for early October in London as Townsend sat with Stein on a bench in St James's Park telling his fictional tale. Stein heard him out in silence until Townsend slid the paperback from its covering on to the bench between them and put the plastic into his pocket.

'No finger-prints, eh?' he said.

'I admire you, Mr Stein. I really do. You've got a mind like a steel trap.'

Stein frowned. 'How do you use it?'

'The book starts on page seven. That's day number one, which is 21 November. You'll see – well, look at it, then you might see.'

Stein opened the book.

'There you go,' Townsend said. 'Now, you've got the numbers one to twenty-six listed randomly in the margin, each connected by a ruled line to a letter of the alphabet circled in the text. If you can't find an "X", or a "Z", or something, it means there isn't one on that page, so use a different word which doesn't contain the missing letter. You with me so far?'

'Yes.'

'Separate each single number or twin number with the Morse letter "R", so it comes out like "R" 14 "R" 6 "R" 22 "R", etcetera. Don't indicate gaps between words, keep your messages as short as possible, turn to page eight for your second day's transmission and so on. There are forty-one pages marked, all with random numbers, which takes us to the last day of the year. After that you needn't bother. Either you'll have read about it in the papers, or we'll be dead, or in gaol.'

'Do you consider this code to be secure?'

'You're a real caution, you are, Mr Stein,' Townsend said. 'It's a form of one-time pad, and they're unbreakable. Of course, if somebody happens across a copy of *London Match* by Len Deighton, which has been marked in precisely this way, they'll crack it. We'll try not to leave ours lying around and we'll destroy it before we make the attack. If that's all, I've got a plane to catch tonight.'

'I'll take you to Heathrow.'

'It doesn't leave from Heathrow. It leaves from Gatwick. That's quite a long way.'

'I'll take you to Gatwick,' Stein said.

Townsend stopped himself saying anything else caustic and submitted with good grace. If Stein wanted to make certain that he was going where he had said he was going, that was all right. Indeed it was most satisfactory as it would add credence to his story.

In the car, Stein asked, 'What's Shaw doing now?'

Wondering if Shaw had yet left Manhattan to carry out his reconnaissance of South Boston's Irish section, Townsend said, 'Who's Shaw?'

'There's no recording equipment in this car.'

Townsend shrugged, but didn't speak until nearly an hour later. As they were walking across the bridge between the car-park and the terminal building he said, 'He was planning to take the team on a long trek across the Arizona and New Mexico deserts, simulating the conditions we'll find in North Africa as closely as possible. Sort of dummy run really. I don't know if they've gone there yet.'

Stein nodded. 'An excellent plan. Do you know the area?'

'Yes. Shaw sent me down to take a look at it to establish its suitability for the exercise. It's not as bad as Death Valley between California and Nevada, but it'll do as long as they don't cheat, and Shaw won't allow that.'

'Cheat?'

'They have a thing called a Barrel Cactus,' Townsend said, 'which you don't find in North Africa. It holds a lot of water and it would be cheating to use it.'

Stein nodded again, watched him check in his baggage for the Las Palmas flight and followed him all the way to passport control. There Townsend left him and rode the moving walkways to the departure lounge, feeling grateful to Zoë for having told him about Barrel Cactus and Death Valley.

Townsend spent three days in Las Palmas, familiarising himself with the town and its harbour, the boat yards and the ship's chandlers, memorising the names and prices of sea-going boats for sale or rent. Then, with nothing more he could usefully do, he hired a car and drove south and west, following the coast road to the resort of Puerto Rico half-way round the island. There was less wind and more sun there somebody had told him.

It was not until he had passed through Maspalomas that he was certain that he was being followed. Of the many cars travelling in the same direction, only the metallic bronze Audi remained precisely two hundred yards behind him. He watched it thoughtfully, trying to read the licence plate but, with the dust and the distance and the image reversed in the mirror, could not do so. Approaching somewhere called Playa de Patavalaca he drew into the side of the road, got out of the car and opened the bonnet. The Audi slowed, then accelerated past him. Townsend had the number and the face of the driver imprinted on his memory now. There had been another man and a girl with straight blonde hair in the car too, but their faces had been turned from him.

'Suspicious old sod,' he told the engine and waited for five minutes before driving on. When he entered the outskirts of Puerto Rico the Audi was behind him again.

A drink beside him, Townsend sat at an open-air restaurant gloomily surveying a sea of naked female bosoms stretching from close at hand to the water's edge a hundred yards away. From the voices of their owners he knew that the bosoms were German and knew, too, that most of them were far too large. He was wishing that people wouldn't appear in public like that when the trio came round the corner of the building. The man who had been driving the Audi had a collection of cameras slung from his shoulders, the other carried a silver photographer's case, the blonde girl was unencumbered. She was also extremely striking. In a brown cotton jump-suit, long-sleeved and zipped to the throat, a broad gold belt round her waist matching her high-heeled boots, incongruously she looked almost indecently sensual with only the skin of her hands and face visible amidst the surrounding acres of nude female felsh.

He was admiring the way her straw-coloured hair was cut severely straight just above her shoulders when she turned her head and gave him a cold stare before stalking past with her two acolytes half a pace behind her. Townsend watched her retreating back. There had been no invitation in her stare, but it had been a long cold one. Deciding that he needed mothering again he got to his feet and followed the group. Something had to be done about them sooner or later anyway.

'Have you heard the one about the photographer, the art director and the model looking for a location?'

The three stopped and turned to him.

'*Bitte?*' the girl asked, so he said it again in German.

'OK. I speak English. What you want?'

'It occurred to me,' Townsend said, 'that if you're so interested in where I go, you might as well find out in my car, then these two apes could go away and do whatever it is they're good at, which certainly isn't following anybody.'

The man with the cameras scowled, moved towards him and stopped abruptly when Townsend grasped him by the outside of the upper lip, pinching it between his thumb and the knuckle of his forefinger.

'Whatever you had in mind, don't,' Townsend told him. The man squealed, people turned to look, and the girl snapped, 'Stop this! You go, both!'

'Hurts, doesn't it?' Townsend said. 'And the funny thing is

96

you can't do a damn thing about it without tearing your face off.' He released the man and added, 'Now you go, both, like the lady says.'

When the men had gone, she said, 'Our fashion cover, it was not so good?'

'Oh, Christ,' Townsend murmured, then more loudly, 'Wait here. I'll be back in a minute.'

The curved structure with the public telephone sign on it was close at hand, but he was not back in a minute. It took him twenty of those to gain a place at one of the instruments and another eleven before he heard the voice of a British international operator. He was muttering imprecations about the Spanish telephone system when the connection was finally made.

'Call off your dogs, Mr Stein,' Townsend said. 'They're getting under my feet. I'll keep the bitch.' At the growled words, 'Very well' he replaced the receiver.

The girl was waiting for him patiently, staring out to sea, her hands folded on her lap.

'Don't try to move,' she said. 'It won't get you anywhere.'

Townsend thought about that for a long time, wondering what had happened to her German accent and flawed English, but it was difficult to reach any conclusion with the mist floating inside his head, so he stopped doing it.

'Who wants to move?' he asked her, but no words came, only the taste of rubber.

He was lying on his back on her bed in her room in Las Palmas and he was naked. Fact. Well, that was all right. They'd been lying on her bed naked for hours, but he didn't remember her putting on the plain black shirt and white slacks she was wearing now. She wore fresh make-up too and looked sleekly groomed. Strange, that. Movement always woke him at once, just as it did Harry.

'If you're wondering what happened, I put a knock-out drop in that last drink you had.'

Drink? What drink? Oh, that one. The one he hadn't wanted until she had filled her mouth with it and transferred it to his between her lips. She had done that several times and it had excited him, but he had no recollection of what had happened next.

The mist cleared from his brain then as though a curtain had been drawn aside. Spread-eagled! He could see the straps around his ankles securing them to the brass posts of the bed and knew that his wrists had been treated in the same way although he couldn't see them. The taste of rubber was very strong now and he could feel the strap of the gag flattening his lips and cheeks. Townsend struggled violently as fear surged through him, a bad fear, quite unlike anything he had experienced in the Army.

'It won't get you anywhere,' she said for the second time and he lay still, breathing heavily through his nose, watching her fill a syringe. Twisting his head sideways he could see that there were several of them and some squat vials of liquid arranged on a metal tray on the bedside table.

The girl wound something around his upper left arm and tightened it. He could not see what it was, but knew she was bringing a vein up.

'I'm using lysergic acid and amylobarbitone sodium if you're interested,' she told him, then gave him a brilliant smile and added, 'That's LSD and Amytal to you. When you start off on your little trip I'll take that gag out of your mouth and you can tell me all about everything. Won't that be lovely?'

He winced at the prick of the needle, with fear, not pain. Sounds becoming very loud. Clack! The hypodermic being replaced on the tray. Colours vivid. Her hair shining like a burnished bell. Another prick. Her voice seeming to fill the room saying, 'Don't try to fight it, but don't go away too soon either. I'm feeding it in very, very slowly so we can see how you react.'

Colours less bright, her voice softer, a humming growing inside him, more a sensation than a sound, tension easing into a feeling of release.

'Don't be lazy and nod off,' she said, 'or I'll have to bring you back with Coramine and if we have to do that too often you'll die and everybody will be awfully sad.' A reawakened sense of danger at her words, holding him back from the brink of sleep, fingers working at the back of his neck releasing the strap, a plop as it drew the rubber ball from his mouth.

'Hello. I'm Henrietta. What's your name?'

Caution struggled for recognition in his mind. He'd had courses on interrogation techniques and how to combat them. Hadn't he? *Hadn't he?*

'Fuck you!' he said.

'You did, several times, so don't you think it would be kind to tell me your name?'

Fingers caressing him. Pleasant. Violet eyes watching him. Pretty eyes. Said something.

'Town? That's a funny name. Or is it a place?'

'Town . . .' Careful! '"James, James, Morrison, Morrison said to his mother, said he."' The words spilling out of him. Stop talking!

'That's right, darling. It's A. A. Milne, and it goes on "You must never go down to the end of the town without consulting me." The end of the town is Townsend, isn't it? And that's your name. Not James Morrison at all. And I bet your Christian name is Bill. Am I right?' More Amytal eased into his bloodstream at the pressure of her thumb.

God, that was clever of her to work that out. Clever of her. Clever of her. Why not tell her? Why not tell her? So pretty. Townsend nodded.

'There, see how easy it is to tell me things when you try?'

'Yes,' he said. It was to be some hours before he realised that she had read the name on his driver's licence.

'What's your profession, Bill darling.'

'Sassman, gasman, SAS, Scandinavian Airways.' Oh Christ!

'The Special Air Service?'

'No!'

'Oh, but I'm sure you are. Or were.'

She was right again. Always right. Pointless trying to keep things from her. Feeling of affinity for her growing in him.

'Where's your next operation? Northern Ireland?'

'No.'

'It's North Africa, isn't it?'

So sleepy, so relaxed, so nice to be stroked like that.

'Yes.'

'Tell me about it, then you can sleep for a little before we make love.'

Ramblingly, balanced on the edge of unconsciousness, Townsend began to talk. It was difficult to understand all her questions, but he tried. After what seemed to be a very long time he became aware that someone else had entered the room. He thought he recognised him as the man with the cameras, but wasn't sure about that. The last thing he heard was the girl saying, 'He's slipping away now. I've got all I need. Put his clothes on, then take him out and dump him somewhere.'

The police found Townsend lying in an alleyway near the docks. They took him back to the police station, gave him coffee and a fatherly lecture about English tourists taking too much alcohol and too much sun, then they let him go.

Feeling more ill than he thought it possible to be, with nerves he had not known he possessed screaming at him, Townsend placed a call to New York, praying that Shaw was not away in Boston, praying that he would not collapse. Both his prayers were answered.

'Harry, I've blown the whole flaming thing. They've had me under Amytal and LSD.' He spoke flatly, totally without inflection, but failed to conceal the tremor in his voice.

'Are you fit to travel?'

'Yes.' There was a long pause before the word came.

'Go to London by the first available plane and report direct to Sarah Cheyney at 198 Wimpole Street. Tell her that you got into a drug session and took LSD. That's the dangerous one. I'll call her now and introduce you as an old friend of mine and I'll join you in London. Under no circumstances are you to leave her until I get there. Is that clearly understood?'

'Yes, Harry.'

'What's Sarah's address?'

'Hundred and something Wigmore Street. It's difficult to –'

'Have you got something to write with?'

'Yes.'

'Write it down. Sarah Cheyney, 198 Wimpole Street, London. Get there! That's an order!' Shaw said.

Because of all the tourist traffic, it took Townsend two days to get on a plane. He spent them shivering in the heat.

12

'I see,' Sarah Cheyney said. 'You took LSD on lumps of sugar, did you?'

'Yes, doctor.'

'How many lumps of sugar?'

'I don't remember.'

'Several?'

'Oh yes.'

'Then you dissolved them in something and injected them into your arm below the elbow where the bruising and perforations are. Is that right?'

Townsend didn't speak but, as though he had, Sarah Cheyney shrugged and said, 'No, it doesn't make sense, does it? Particularly as you'd tied yourself up at the time. There are still marks visible around your wrists and ankles. Is that why you're frightened lying there?'

It was Townsend's turn to shrug.

'Why do you get more frightened when I walk towards you?'

She watched his eye movements, his glance darting from point to point around the surgery, and listened to him saying, 'I don't know, I don't know. Perhaps it's because you're so pretty. Nothing personal meant, doctor.' There had been something close to desperation in his voice.

'So it was a girl, was it?'

He nodded, lips compressed as though he were trying not to cry. She watched him gravely for a moment before sitting on the examination couch beside him and taking his hand in hers.

'What else did she use on you, Mr Townsend? Pentobarbitone sodium?'

'Amytal.'

'That figures. Well, it's not up to me to ask what was going on. I expect you work for MI6 and the Russians are building a submarine base on Gran Canaria. Yes, I'm sure that must be it.' She disengaged her hand from his. It made a sound like a pistol shot as she slashed him across the face.

Townsend did cry then.

'Good boy,' Sarah Cheyney said. 'Let it all come out. I'll be back in a little while.'

Tired and deeply worried, Shaw paced up and down the big living-room above the surgery. He had been in London for thirty-six hours, wondering what had become of Townsend, feeling extremely concerned for him, feeling extremely concerned for the whole enterprise. Then he had heard Townsend's voice at the reception desk and hurried to the stairs, but Sarah had appeared in the hall, shaken her head at him and taken her new patient away. That had been nearly four hours ago and he had covered miles of carpet since then. It was a lot more than just a relief when he heard the door to the apartment open.

Sarah Cheyney came into the room, shrugging her white coat from her shoulders and throwing it at a chair. It missed.

'Damn,' she said. 'Make me a drink, will you, darling? I'm bushed.'

'Of course.'

He made the drinks, listening to her moving about, hearing the click of the laundry basket lid as the hospital coat was disposed of and the sound of running water, then she was back in the room.

'Your friend's all right, but he's had a very bad time. Some bitch dosed him heavily with LSD and Amytal while he was under restraint. It was the LSD which worried me most. That stuff can seer the brain right out of your skull, but he's got away with it. There are still after-effects, including a degree of psychic shock, and he's pretty highly stressed, but that'll go.'

'Thank the Lord for that! May I see him, Sarah?'

'No,' she said. 'I've given him a sedative. Orally. He's about as keen on needles as old Solly at the moment. You can probably see him in the morning after I have.'

She said 'Thank you' when he handed her the drink before saying, 'You know, I found that "finding your feet in the commercial world in charity work" stuff pretty hard to swallow, Harry. It just isn't you, somehow. You've switched from SAS to SIS, haven't you?'

'Why should you think that?'

'Why should I think that? Oh for God's sake, Harry! This is the sort of thing that goes on in the Secret Intelligence Service, isn't it? Or have I been reading the wrong books? "Carruthers of MI6" and all that!' Her tone grew in exasperation when she went on. 'You telephone me from New York, wanting me to look after an old buddy of yours who's been on an LSD trip, come rushing across here yourself and spend a day and a half pacing about looking so neutral that it creaks, even for you! Then I find out that he's not some stupid kid after kicks, but a full-grown man who's been under interrogation, for God's sake! Oh, do stop me saying "for God's sake"! If you're not MI6 why did he call you and not his own people?'

'I may have been the only chap he could think of,' Shaw said. 'You see, he was my sergeant in the SAS. We were a team.'

Sarah Cheyney nodded thoughtfully. 'That is possible, considering his condition. Well, I mustn't pry, but the Canary Islands of all places. What in the world can go on there? Their only industries are tourism and cochineal. Give me another drink will you?'

'Just as soon as you've lowered that one below the rim.'

'Oh,' she said vaguely, sipped from her full glass and added, 'Whitey, I think you're holding out on me, but I love you.'

His morning meeting with Townsend shocked Shaw. It was nothing that was said, because Townsend could remember little of what had taken place after the injections had begun other than that he had answered questions put to him by the girl. Of what those questions had been, or his answers to them, he had no recollection whatever. It was his friend's appearance and almost tearful remorse that sent him in search of Sarah Cheyney. He had to wait for over an hour before she could spare him a few minutes between patients and that increased the tension building up in him.

'Don't fuss, darling,' she told him. 'If you'd had a close look at him yesterday you'd know that he's much better this morning. I say, you really are worried, aren't you? I can almost read it in your face.'

'That's not worry. It's a mixture of rage and panic.'

She nodded. 'You're right to feel rage. It was the most murderous thing.'

'Do you mean he might have died?'

'Quite easily. The Amytal alone could have done it if the woman had used too much, unless she had adrenalin and oxygen handy to resuscitate him. The LSD could have turned him into a vegetable. But there's no need to feel panic now. He's over the worst. You can believe me, darling. I do a lot of voluntary work on drug cases and I've done all the right things for Bill Townsend. He's OK.'

Shaw left Wimpole Street then, the panic gone from him, but with the rage glowing like a nuclear furnace. Now he was standing in Stein's office.

'So you don't deny responsibility for the treatment of Townsend?'

'I do not. I have an investment to protect. We knew too little about you and your intentions. We didn't even know his name. The Canary Islands visit provided an excellent opportunity for remedying that situation and I must say that the results were most heartening.'

Shaw blinked at that, then said, 'How were you informed of these results?'

'The – er – interview was taped.'

'You and your goddam recordings! Get it!'

He took Stein down to his car then and listened to the tape's message on the cassette player.

'Don't try to move. It won't get you anywhere.' The woman's voice was clear and confident. 'I put a knock-out drop in that last drink you had . . . I'm using lysergic acid and amylobarbitone sodium if you're interested.'

Shaw felt his skin crawl as though it were Townsend's.

'You can tell me all about everything. Won't that be lovely?' Then the tone changed, sinking into husky intimacy. 'Hello. I'm Henrietta. What's your name?' Townsend tried to evade, to confuse, trying so hard in his hopeless struggle against the drugs stealing his will, his mind. Shaw lived through it with him and remembered saying in New York, 'They all want to mother you, don't they?' while the woman alternated sharp commands and provocative endearments between questions and answers. Poor bastard! Poor bloody bastard!

It was some time after the question 'It's North Africa, isn't it?' that Shaw began to think the woman might have made a mistake by leading Townsend in that direction and to hope that the enterprise might still be alive. 'The results were most heartening,' Stein had said. The statement had amazed him, but listening to Townsend's voice, sometimes quite loud, sometimes little more than a whisper, as he described the planned attacks on Gadaffi, on Yasser Arafat, on Abu Nidal, his spirits rose. They rose further when Townsend's replies became disjointed, inaudible in parts, and the woman's commands became sharper. 'Sink, you poor bugger. Sink right out of it and sleep,' he silently urged the tape, but the voices kept on. There were bad moments after that, moments that tautened his muscles, then the woman ordered, 'Take him out and dump him somewhere,' and it was over.

Shaw took the cassette from the player, opened it, tore out the tape and stuffed the writhing thing into his pocket.

'Never interfere in my operation again,' he said. 'You've placed us all in grave jeopardy by that unwarrantable act.'

Stein looked at him. 'It was not unwarrantable. As a professional you know full well that such precautions are necessary. I can now proceed with a much easier mind but, first, perhaps you would be good enough to explain certain references which are unclear to us. They were made towards the end when that unfortunate young man was sinking fast.'

Shaw's muscles tautened again. 'I'll try.'

'Who is Zoë and what logo was being referred to in connection with bombs?'

'"Zoë" was the code name for the attack in Libya. "Logo" referred to Tunisia. The five men I've picked won't be told their final destinations until we land in Africa, but I've been exercising them in simulated conditions for both places, using those names. I'll have to change them now they've become public knowledge. The bombs are just bombs. We've made them ourselves.'

'I understand. There were also some remarks about something which sounded like "noraid".'

'Yes, I heard that. Townsend was trying to explain why we were attacking overland. What he was saying was that he'd as soon try to pierce NORAD in a plane as sail through the Mediterranean undetected. I explained all that to you. If you don't know what NORAD means it's an acronym describing the North American air defence radar net.'

'Thank you. It seems that we are indeed free to go ahead,' Stein said.

'I shall go ahead on two conditions,' Shaw told him, 'and I shan't take one solitary step forward until you provide me with proof that you have carried them out.'

'What do you want me to do?'

'Pay the sum of one hundred thousand pounds sterling in compensation to William Townsend.'

'And the second thing?'

'Kill the girl,' Shaw said.

With the quality papers' attention on the superpower summit in Reykjavik it was left to the tabloids to proclaim the second fatal casualty in Shaw's war. The one Townsend was looking at had devoted most of its front page to her photograph under the banner headline MODEL MURDERED IN MAYFAIR. That the address at which she had been found strangled was half a mile outside Mayfair had not been enough to persuade the editor to abandon such satisfying alliteration.

'Did you do this, Harry?'

It was three days since Sarah Cheyney had discharged Townsend into Shaw's care, one day before they were due to return to New York, and Shaw had been hoping very much that the news would not break before their departure.

'I ordered that it be done,' he said, without looking up from the suitcase he was packing.

'You did that for me?'

Shaw straightened then and faced Townsend who was

leaning against the frame of the bedroom door with the paper hanging from his hand.

'Partly, but there were other reasons. Security was one. I couldn't afford to have her thinking about what she had heard, maybe something the tape didn't catch, and telling Stein. If he made copies of that tape they won't help him, because you were pretty far gone towards the end, but her memory might have done.'

Townsend nodded and Shaw went on. 'There's the inescapable point, as well, that she didn't deserve to live. Obviously she'd done that sort of thing before and couldn't be allowed to do it again to some other helpless – well, you know what I mean.'

'I know what you mean. And I thought I was being so damned smart seeing off her heavies and keeping her for myself like James Bond's always doing. For all that, it's still a bit eerie seeing the picture of a girl whose bed you've shared plastered all over the front of a newspaper as a murder victim.'

'Whose bed you bloody nearly died on. Didn't Sarah tell you that?'

'Yes,' Townsend said, 'she told me. Now there's one terrific lady. She's like some mythical African princess.' He smiled for the first time since he'd seen the newspaper and added, 'Don't worry, Harry. I get the feeling that she's rather fond of you and, anyway, she's got too much class for me. Er – what am I supposed to do with that bag full of money with my name on it?'

'Put it in a safe-deposit box at your bank. It's all in untraceable notes.'

'You must have leaned on old Stein pretty heavily, what with one thing and another.'

'He took a little persuading,' Shaw said, 'but he saw the logic of my arguments in the end. Now, why don't you go and do what you're supposed to be doing and keep watch from the window?'

Townsend smiled again and went to his post in the next room. There had been no spoken expression of thanks and Shaw was grateful to him for that.

13

Logo really preferred to keep his front door unlocked the way he did in Hackney so that Bill could come in without his having to interrupt whatever he was doing, but that wasn't possible in New York with the Argies all over the place. He was in the middle of a tricky piece of soldering when the bell rang.

'Damn nuisance,' he said. He cleared the parts of the bomb he was working on from the bench and put them under the floor boards. One of them was hot enough to burn his fingers and he sucked at them while he arranged the model locomotive components in their place with his other hand. Then he opened the door.

"Lo, Bill. Beer in the fridge.'

'Thanks, Logo. Everything OK?'

'Burnt my fingers,' Logo said. 'Clumsy. Don't matter, though. I've nearly finished. Twenty smokers and twenty-nine bangers. Working on the last of them now. That's the one that burnt my fingers.' He was going to add, 'when you rang the bell,' but stopped himself because that sounded like criticism. He substituted a question. 'You going to set them all off at once?'

'No. Got to learn to walk before we can run.'

'That's stupid, that is,' Logo said.

Townsend looked at him curiously. 'Why, Logo?'

'They always run first.'

'Who do, Logo?'

'Babies. They stretch their arms out, put their feet wide and run to mummy. Fall on their bottoms if they didn't. Long time after that before they can walk. Stands to reason. Balance, it's called. Don't know why people get it the wrong way round. Never watched, I suppose.'

'I hadn't thought of that,' Townsend said.

It was good to see Logo again and have simple things simply explained by a man who was half simple and half highly skilled technician. It was good, too, to be accepted as somebody who put in an appearance sometimes, with no questions asked. The thought of questions still made him shiver. He shivered.

'You all right, Bill?'

'Caught a bit of a cold. Nothing much.'

'Ought to get out more,' Logo said. 'Or, if you can't, try one of those exercise bicycles. I used to use one somewhere. Work up a good sweat with them.'

'I'll look into that,' Townsend said.

Logo retrieved his bomb casing and began to work on it.

'Logo.'

'Yeah?'

'If we were to hollow out a book and put one of those inside, could you fix it so it goes off when the book's opened?'

'Bit of wire stuck to the cover is all.'

'They might notice the tension or see the wire, Logo.'

'Ah.'

When five minutes had gone by in silence, Townsend got up to fetch the beer he had been offered. He had finished it before Logo said, 'Put a light-meter beside the amplifier. Closing the cover depresses the meter and makes the contact instead of the amplifier. You'll hear it click. Don't open the book again though. If light reaches the meter she's off and running, and you'd better be off and running too before she goes up.'

A strange whinnying sound came from Logo's nose. It was a moment before Townsend identified it. He had never heard him laugh before.

Shaw wasn't laughing, but he was feeling cynically amused. A drawer he hadn't previously opened in the small lumber room of his apartment contained a pile of old newspapers dating back some weeks before he had rented the place. Glancing through them he had come across a small item which informed him that those members of NORAID who normally made an annual pilgrimage to Ireland had cancelled it this year because of the possibility of increased terrorist activity in Europe. It was not so much their fear that amused him as their quite incredible hypocrisy. He shrugged, tossed the papers into the wastebasket and returned to his task of bringing to them at home the terror they had needlessly sought to avoid abroad.

The hollow he had painstakingly made by cutting the centre out of page after page of a book was nearly deep enough to accept Logo's gas canister now. Logo had adapted it in a few hours, employing a light-sensitive trigger in place of thumb pressure on the amplifier grid. There was no time-delay mechanism and the spools of tape should turn as soon as the meter registered light. There was no lead screening either, no magnetic clamps and no tilt activator, but spring-loaded needles were positioned to pierce the phials of chemicals replacing plastic explosive in this model. The rest of the device was the same as the originals, with its battery, circuitry and miniature electric drive, except that vents had been drilled in the casing to permit the gas and smoke to escape.

Shaw had handled it roughly, even dropping it on the floor several times, but had done no damage and the spring-loaded needles had not moved. He was satisfied that it would withstand any mistreatment the postal authorities might give it and its successors. Now he was engaged in the monotonous work of cutting yet more pages from the book with a draftsman's knife, resignedly aware that there were many copies to be similarly treated. Those he had bought singly, going from bookstore to bookstore until his briefcase was full, and then repeating the process.

It was another ten minutes before the canister fitted flush with the first page. Shaw sighed and closed the cover, hearing the click as the glass lens was depressed. Leaving the book where it lay, he took the pile of paper he had removed down to the basement, dropped it into the incinerator and watched it burn. Back in his apartment he tied the book with string, did the same to an undamaged copy and suspended both from either end of a coat hanger. Their weights were similar enough and would, he guessed, be more so when the chemicals were placed in the canister. Only then did he remove the string and lift the cover.

Logo's voice spoke to him. That it was Logo's voice he knew because he had listened to him recording it, but the high-pitched monotone delivery, breaking words into separate syllables, was quite unrecognisable to the normal ear. Logo had enjoyed playing that game. 'That'll fool the Argies,' he had said. Shaw felt only slightly guilty about having used him for the purpose. There was a distinct possibility that a tape would be recovered intact from a successfully dismantled device, and parts of one might survive either explosion or chemical reaction. If that happened, a voice analyst would not be long deceived by the play-acting, but by then Logo would be back in England.

A countdown followed a ten-second preamble, then there was a sharp click as the needles leapt forward. Nothing else happened because there had been nothing for them to pierce, but, had there been, concentrated nitric acid would have come into contact with 'white' phosphorous, producing billowing clouds of smoke. To that would be added the disgusting rotten-egg stench of hydrogen sulphide carried into the air by the convection currents set up by the heat of the chemical reaction. It should, Shaw thought, be a salutary experience for the recipients of the book. A costly one too as the smell of hydrogen sulphide clung to just about everything.

For a few moments, he sat considering the risk of fire, but concluded that it was not great with the reaction confined in a metal box. He sighed again. If there was fire then fire there would be. What worried him more was the dangerous nature of the material Logo was having to handle. 'White' phosphorous was not only very poisonous, but ignited spontaneously when exposed to air at a temperature of 35 degrees Centigrade. There was no chance of such a temperature occurring naturally in New York in October, but he still hoped that Logo would not drop a phial. Then he shook his head irritably, wondering if he was becoming nervous. Logo didn't drop things. Logo had the surest pair of hands of anyone he had ever met.

Shaw looked again at the canister nestling in the book, picturing in his mind the dense white clouds of pentoxide pouring from the vents, knowing that at least they were not

111

harmfully toxic, otherwise any soldier who had ever walked through a smoke screen would have been affected. Burning a piece of phosphorous no larger than a ping-pong ball would blanket half the campus, the professor of chemistry at Sussex University who had given him the stuff and the hydrogen sulphide had told him. Knowing that Shaw did something rather unusual in the Army, he had shown no surprise at being asked for an obnoxious mixture of chemicals to take troops under training unawares.

Thanking the God he didn't believe in for the naïve credulity of an academically brilliant friend, Shaw forced concern away and began to excavate the second book. He had a war to fight.

It was three thirty in the afternoon, but the fat man was still eating. Trying not to feel revulsion, Stein watched out of the corner of his eye as a large bar of fruit and nut chocolate was repeatedly removed from a breast pocket as though it were a wallet, a wallet which was reduced in size before it was replaced. Body heat appeared to have destroyed its tensile strength. The four others present stood together at the far end of the room, talking quietly. Stein wished that the man from Mossad would come. He didn't much like these periodic meetings with Israeli Intelligence but, he thought, almost anything was preferable to watching Arthur eat. The man arrived as he was thinking it.

'Bridenthal,' he said and proffered a passport in support of the claim. Stein compared face and photograph, then introduced him to the group. Bridenthal nodded to each in turn, but didn't offer to shake hands. As they joined Arthur at the small conference table he transferred more chocolate from his pocket to his mouth. Perversely the action pleased Stein because it made the visitor from Jerusalem frown. He was aware that Bridenthal held a very senior position. He was also aware that he disliked him on sight and suspected from the man's expression that the feeling was mutual. Now Arthur had attracted some of the distaste to himself and would doubtless attract more as the chocolate bar wasn't finished yet.

'As you all constitute a major source of finance for the operation we are involved in, I am instructed to give you a short briefing on the situation,' Bridenthal said. He sounded as though he both resented his orders and doubted the wisdom of them. Looking with disbelief at the fat man, he went on, 'The Lebanon remains satisfactorily and totally destabilised and will continued to be so. The practice of holding American, British and French hostages there works to our advantage too, as it maintains a high level of distrust of anything Arab in the Western world.'

Arthur's soft sigh made Bridenthal pause and when he spoke again it was pendantically, like a teacher addressing a backward class. Stein listened to the flat voice saying that Iran's volatile condition was now becoming potentially explosive because the Ayatollah Khomeini had not been heard on Teheran Radio for several weeks and was believed to be very ill. That didn't strike him as being of particular note as Khomeini had been very ill often before and he said as much, but the interjection received less attention than Arthur's sigh had done. The dissertation continued unabated with the information that Khomeini's elected successor and a man little respected, had had his position weakened by the arrest of some of his relatives and aides on charges of treason.

According to Bridenthal that left the road to power open either to the powerful Speaker of the Iranian Parliament or to the Prime Minister who had recently visited East Germany and Hungary. He was saying that the latter leaned markedly to the left when Arthur sighed again, more loudly this time.

That halted the monologue and Bridenthal asked, 'Am I boring you, Mr – er?'

'It distresses me to say so,' Arthur replied, 'but that is indeed the case. You speak of a briefing and then provide us with a summary of the daily news. I find that extremely tedious. As I live in hopes that we shall shortly be adjourning for tea, perhaps you could . . .' He let the rest of the sentence go, substituting urging motions of the hands for it.

Almost hopefully Stein waited for an explosion, but none came. Bridenthal nodded abruptly before saying, 'Then here is some information yet to reach the press which may hold your attention. The Americans have been conducting secret arms deals with Iran in contravention of the embargo placed on them by the Carter Administration in an attempt to obtain the release of their hostages in the Lebanon. We see this as a stratagem designed to influence the outcome of the American mid-term elections in favour of the Republicans. It is also a clear indication that Iran rather than Syria holds the fate of those hostages in their hands.' He paused and glanced at each of the six men in turn before adding, 'It would not be in our best interests to permit such an exchange of hostages for arms to take place. Indeed, it is essential that the hostages be eliminated. That should provoke the American action we are all working towards. They reacted positively enough and with much less reason when they bombed Libya in April.'

'And Mossad will carry out these assassinations?'

'Hardly, Mr Stein,' Bridenthal said, without looking at his questioner. 'I'm sure their hosts will see to that in retaliation for the activities scheduled to take place in Libya shortly. Since the British support for the United States over Gadaffi, and American support for Britain when you broke off diplomatic relations with Syria, the two nations have become very much a single entity in the Arab mind, so by punishing one you punish both. No doubt the British hostages will suffer the same penalty.'

Bridenthal heard Stein's murmured 'Most fortuitous, that Syrian attempt on the El Al jet at Heathrow,' tried unsuccessfully to detect a note of irony about what had been a Mossad deception, and joined a man he had never met called Shaw in thinking that Stein was not very clever. That he merited praise for his courage in acting as the exposed member of the group was not in question, but his past conduct of affairs might be. That questioning, Bridenthal decided, would have to wait until they were alone.

'So there you have it, gentlemen,' he said. 'An Iran quite possibly on the verge of setting Islamic prejudices aside to the extent of moving closer to the Russian sphere of influence, if for no other purpose than achieving a swift end to their war with Iraq, is something that America could not countenance. On top of the situation in Afghanistan that would be a strategic disaster of the first magnitude.'

The statement convulsed the fat man. Bridenthal raised his eyebrows at him.

'You find that amusing, Mr – er?'

'Call me Arthur. Everybody does. I was just thinking that Texas would love it. Push the price of oil up no end if the West was deprived of Iranian supplies. Think of all those poor suffering millionaires in Houston and Dallas. Oh dear me. They'd be so pleased.'

Ignoring the comment Bridenthal went on, 'Add to geopolitical necessity the emotional reaction which the death of their hostages would induce amongst the American people and we have a spark for our tinder box.'

'Is that all? It's pathetically flimsy and accounts for only a fraction of the sums we have provided!'

'No, Arthur, that is not all,' Bridenthal said. 'It's the reason behind the operation on which Mr Stein is currently engaged. That is the psychological trigger, the pulling of which will set in train more practical action. If you can bear to forgo your tea for a further half an hour I'll give you the rest of the scenario.'

While Bridenthal, whom he had never heard of, was unveiling his scenario in London, Shaw was looking at New York City and a lot more. Over seven hundred feet above the street on the observation deck of the Metropolitan Tower he had an unobstructed 35-mile view in every direction. To the south stood the serried ranks of the Manhattan skyscrapers and to the west the Appalachian foothills. Eastwards lay Long Island Sound and when he turned to face north over Central Park he could trace the course of the Hudson River running parallel to the Connecticut border.

It was an imposing prospect and half-way between himself and the ground was the imposing apartment he had bought with a large proportion of Stein's money. What the bank's vice-president in charge of property acquisition and development had meant when he referred to the sum available to the charity as 'peanuts' had been brought home to Shaw by that purchase. The smallest apartments in the newly constructed building cost in excess of $300,000 and he had paid nearly three times that amount. He felt no surprise when the bank insisted on the insertion of a clause in the contract prohibiting resale within a period of three months, because Stein had to protect his investment somehow until after the supposed North African venture had been carried out. Nor did he care. The money was of no interest to him, Bill Townsend was already £100,000 the richer, Logo had been adequately provided for, and there was more for both of them in the working capital reserve Shaw had left in the bank. He was free to withdraw that with no strings attached and decided to do it without further delay. With Stein expecting him to be deep in the North African desert by 21 November when the radio transmissions were scheduled to start, it was nearly time to leave the apartments Stein knew of, to drop out of sight and that he would do as soon as Townsend returned from his second visit to Las Palmas.

Those decisions taken, Shaw spent a few more moments staring past the tall blocks surrounding Rockefeller Plaza and beyond the Empire State Building towards the twin towers of the Trade Center near the island's end. He was doing nothing more constructive than wonder how severely he could shake the great city which reminded him that he had defensive purchases to make for Townsend and himself. The elevator carried him rapidly to street level and a cab downtown.

Shaw took the pair of 12-gauge shot-guns he bought to West 14th Street. It seemed strange not to see Logo crouched over his bench and he missed the familiar greeting of 'Hi, Harry. Beer in the fridge.' Using Logo's abandoned equipment he sawed twelve inches off the barrels of both guns, then hid them and the boxes of ammunition under the floorboards with the bombs. That afternoon he collected his belongings from the apartment in Greenwich Village and made up the bed next to Townsend's for himself.

Logo was glad to be back in Hackney. There were the pictures of the ladies who were his mother to look at and it was good to have fibre optics to work on again because making the things Bill had wanted had got very monotonous. In addition, the food was much better than in that New York place where it had been very monotonous too. The fact that its monotony lay in his refusal to buy anything that didn't bear the identical

116

labels displayed in his supermarket at home had escaped him, as had the reason for its sharp improvement whenever Bill had been there to buy and prepare it. Hackney was a fine place to live, particularly now that he had the modern binocular microscope Harry had given him and money was going to be paid into his bank account every month.

Logo rarely looked at newspapers, but somebody had dropped a copy of the *Daily Express* on the stairs. He read all of that slowly and carefully, but the only item he found of interest was a report stating that the Argies were angry about some fishing exclusion zone around the Falklands. He nodded wisely at that in the knowledge that they were going to be a lot angrier by the time Bill had finished with them.

Wide-eyed, lower lip caught between her teeth, Sarah Cheyney stared at the crystal vase rising like a column of frozen light from the sea of protective shredded plastic surrounding it. 'Steuben – An American Treasure' the sticker stated. The three figures, one upright, menacing, two reclining, the girl protecting the man beneath her from his executioner with her body, so exquisitely etched into the glass that they appeared to be three-dimensional, seemed so much alive that a sound might make them turn their heads. She knew what they represented and whom the costly gift was from before she opened the envelope.

'Dear Doctor Cheyney,' she read, 'I never did make "captain", but you did for me what Pocahontas did for Captain John Smith in the early 1600s. As you both rate as princesses in my book I'd be happy if you would accept this with my grateful thanks. Yours, William Townsend.'

Never having been prone to tears, she was startled to find herself crying.

Townsend spent only long enough in London to settle Logo into his rooms in Hackney and deliver the package to Wimpole Street before flying to Las Palmas. The thought of returning to Gran Canaria made his nerves crawl, but he chided himself for a fool and went because it was vitally necessary that he should do so. Now he was squatting in a lock-up garage he had rented,

117

disembowelling a large and perfectly innocent diesel engine. He had been at it for six hours, fighting and defeating stubborn bolts one after the other, until only the casing remained as a single unit. When he had wrapped the pistons and crank-shaft in sacking, he arranged them on the floor of a hired van, added seven similarly covered lengths of lead piping and some boxes to the load, then drove to a boatyard. He did so slowly and carefully so that the man who had carried the cameras for the girl called Henrietta would have no trouble in following him.

It had been difficult pretending not to notice him at the airport, near the customs warehouse and again along the street from the garage, but Townsend conceded that the man's technique had improved marginally since they had last met. The sensation of eyes watching him was strong while he transferred his collection of useless hardware to a power boat. Far out to sea he dropped it all over the side.

14

Bridenthal pushed the room service trolley out into the corridor on the third floor of the Cumberland Hotel at Marble Arch, closed the door on it and turned to face Stein.

'So you know virtually nothing about Shaw's activities in the States, or his man Townsend's, or of the other five, whoever they are.'

'I've learned to be rather circumspect in my dealings with him,' Stein said. 'The last time I interfered in his arrangements I was –'

'I know! I know! He required you to eliminate that woman! That was badly bungled!'

'In what way was it bungled? He gave me no option.'

'You should have extracted every ounce of information she possessed about that interrogation before having her killed. I suppose you never thought of that, or hadn't the stomach for it. At least you had the sense to copy the tape, but that just leaves us with some unsatisfactorily answered questions, questions Shaw may not have wanted answered, questions which could explain why he wanted her dead. Can't you see that?'

'I can see that you have a lively imagination,' Stein replied. 'I suppose that's a necessity for an Intelligence officer, but I think you're jumping at shadows.' His initial dislike of Bridenthal had grown massively during this late-night meeting, a meeting which had developed into an inquisition, and he was finding it increasingly difficult to keep his voice level.

'As you provide me with no substance I have nothing but shadows to react to,' Bridenthal told him. 'I'm perfectly well aware that shot-guns and sporting rifles are readily available without red tape on a cash-and-carry basis in the States in a way they are not in this country, but he would surely need a much wider inventory than that. In what way is he supposed to have obtained suitable armaments? Federal law forbids the sale of military weapons to civilians.'

Stein nodded. 'I took that point up with him the last time he was here and he asked me why I didn't read the newspapers. I took that to mean the American papers and later looked through back numbers for the appropriate period. I found an item about an attack by four men on a National Guard armoury in New Jersey. A watchman was killed and an assortment of weapons stolen. Those were said to include three machine-guns, two grenade launchers, two recoilless rifles, plus appropriate ammunition and some fragmentation hand-grenades. Oh, he also mentioned that they had manufactured other bombs themselves. I gather the SAS is adept at that.'

Bridenthal stared at Stein incredulously for a long moment before saying, 'You gather the SAS is adept at that, do you? So all you have to go on is his word and an allusion to some newspaper article. I suppose it never occurred to you that he could have drawn your attention to an incident he had read about, but had no hand in, and left you to draw your own conclusions, false conclusions which suit his purpose.'

'Which is?'

'To swindle you out of a sizeable sum of money.'

'Oh, he can't do that,' Stein said, 'and he knows it. I've blocked the resale of the apartment he's bought until the end of January on grounds of probable upward property market trends. The sums he has already spent are really neither here nor there. Anyway, the arms you appear to disbelieve in were transhipped at Las Palmas this morning as I've already told you.'

Sitting down for the first time since he had disposed of the trolley, Bridenthal steepled his fingers. Their tips seemed to absorb him and he was silent for so long that Stein eventually stood up and walked to the table with the drinks on it to refill his glass. The movement brought Bridenthal out of his reverie and he stretched out an arm for the telephone. Stein's head turned sharply towards him at the words 'Bridenthal, Room

317. Book me on the first available flight to New York, please, and have my bill ready.'

'What now, Bridenthal?'

Ignoring the question, Bridenthal replaced the phone on its rest and said, 'I was prepared to believe that a transfer of arms had taken place at Las Palmas until you totally failed to convince me of their existence. All your man there witnessed was objects being removed from a van and placed on board a boat.'

'Objects? What conceivable objects other than arms would Townsend bother to transfer? Anything else would constitute a pointless charade which would bring Shaw no closer to his money.'

'Quite frankly, I don't know,' Bridenthal replied. 'I don't like Shaw's arm's length attitude and I don't like your reluctance to do anything about it, so I'm going to do something about it myself.'

'Then you'd better hurry. Shaw will move any day now.'

'I *am* hurrying,' Bridenthal said. 'If you can cast your mind back a full minute you may remember a telephone call I made at that time. Now, if you'll excuse me, I'll pack my bag.'

Townsend had abandoned his boat at Tenerife and flown to Portugal to avoid further contact with Stein's people either in the Canary Islands or England. When Bridenthal boarded a plane at Heathrow, he was lying on a bed in the Hotel Tivoli on Lisbon's Avenida da Liberdade, with nothing to do until his transatlantic flight the following day.

An old Kojak movie he hadn't seen before was showing on the closed-circuit television. He knew it was old because the girls were wearing mini-skirts and it intrigued him to see again the city locations he had come to know well. It intrigued him even more when, against all precedent, Kojak succeeded in getting himself shot and quite seriously at that. But his pleasure in such an unexpected development was short-lived with the detective out of his hospital bed and back at work before the blood had dried. Feeling cheated, Townsend switched off the set and went to sleep.

*

Dawn was still hours away when Bridenthal's Air India Boeing 747 landed at Kennedy Airport, and the Manhattan skyline was subdued as his cab carried him towards the city. He gave the driver Shaw's address in Greenwich Village. A tousle-haired woman opened the door to him, opening it four inches until it snubbed against its security chain.

'No, I don't know a man called Shaw! What the hell do you think I am, and what the hell are you doing ringing people's door bells at this hour?'

Bridenthal apologised and took another cab to West 14th Street. Nobody answered his ring there, but it took him only seconds to gain access with the help of his skeleton key and a credit card.

Dawn made a belated arrival through a heavily overcast sky and saved Shaw's life. It shone dully on the wetsuit he had left in the closet and on the sawn-off barrel of a shot-gun he had left under the floorboards. He thought he saw some of Logo's bombs lying on the table too, but the light was still very dim and by that time he was already airborne, hurtling feet first towards the man sitting in the only armchair with the gun across his knees. As though everything were happening in slow motion he noted the muzzle of the gun turning towards him, felt bleak satisfaction at the knowledge that its swing was not fast enough and prayed to nobody in particular that it would not be fired at all.

Time speeded up again when his heels struck the man in the chest. The gun did not fire, but it clattered noisily when its holder's outflung arm cast it against the radiator and the thud of the overturned chair was loud. As if in protest at the disturbance a glass fell off the shelf and shattered in the sink as Shaw clubbed the man beneath the ear with the side of his clenched fist. He got to his feet then, picked up the gun and returned to the door of the apartment. Seven seconds had elapsed since he had opened it.

The sound of movement on the floor below reached him and a voice called, 'Quit that goddam racket, will you? What gives up there anyway? There's folks tryin' to sleep!'

122

'My friend was replacing a light bulb and the chair broke under him. Sorry to wake you.'

'Jesus! Send for a goddam electrician next time!' the voice said and retreated, muttering.

With the door shut and bolted, Shaw lifted the unconscious man on to the nearest of the two beds, secured his wrists behind his back with a roll of Logo's insulating tape and stuck a strip of it over his mouth. Then he searched him, wishing that Bill Townsend was at hand to help him before stopping himself because there were very urgent things to think about.

No hand-gun, no police badge. Did the FBI carry badges? Bound to. The CIA? Probably not. Name revealed as Samuel Bernard Bridenthal by contents of wallet. Jewish. One of Stein's men? Israeli passport in hip pocket recording previous twenty-four hours in UK. US Immigration stamp showing arrival New York this same morning. Open date return Air India ticket ex-London. The man's eyes open, watching him. Who are you, Mr Samuel Bernard Bridenthal? Did you come alone? Have you telephoned anybody from here? Well, whoever you are and whatever else you've done you've learned far too much about me. I must get you away from this place, Mr Bridenthal. Christ! I wish you were here, Bill. I wish ... Oh, shut up!

'Don't struggle, or I'll smash you again,' Shaw said. He unbuckled Bridenthal's belt and drew his trousers down to his ankles before adding, 'I'm not after your virtue. I just want to make sure that we walk out of here without any fuss.'

Bridenthal watched with bulging eyes as the shot-gun was pressed against the inside of his left leg, winced as the muzzle moved into contact with his groin, and began to tremble jerkily when Shaw taped it firmly in place. Whimpering sounds came from his nose.

'Be quiet,' Shaw said. He undid the lace of Bridenthal's left shoe, withdrew it from the top pair of eyelets and secured it again at the second row. He cut the cord from the window blind, threaded it through one of the eyelets and tied it to the trigger of the gun, covering the knot with tape to prevent it slipping from the smooth curve of metal. When Bridenthal's trousers were back in place the other end of the cord hung from the waistband.

Moving rapidly, Shaw replaced the wetsuit in the closet and the bombs under the floorboards. Then he took two of them out again, one armed, one not because the supply of plastic explosive had run out. He put them in the side pockets of his jacket and turned back to Bridenthal, releasing his wrists, tearing the tape from his mouth and taking hold of the cord.

'Get up.'

Still trembling and with sweat shining on his face Bridenthal eased himself to the side of the bed and stood up, swaying.

'My car's garaged down the block,' Shaw told him. 'We're going to walk to it now. You can't bend your left knee, so it'll be perfectly natural for me to support you. I don't suppose I have to paint you a picture of what happens if you do anything silly.'

Bridenthal made slight negative motions with his head, but didn't speak.

His right arm around the man's waist, his left hand gripping his belt and the cord, Shaw propelled him towards the stairs. With one leg rigid it was difficult for Bridenthal to negotiate them and, with Shaw supporting much of his weight, their stumbling progress was not silent. The door of the apartment below opened again.

'Now what?'

Shaw looked at the speaker, the sight of the angry, unshaven face bringing to mind his own dark stubble. Well, there was nothing he could do about that.

'Now hospital. A torn cartilage in the knee is my guess.'

'Aw, shit. I didn't realise somebody got hurt. Can I lend a hand?'

It wasn't easy to let the gentle smile come, but Shaw managed it. 'No thanks,' he said. 'We're OK now. The stairs were the hard part.'

There weren't many people in the streets yet and the few there were paid no attention to the two men. Guiding Bridenthal down the ramp to the subterranean car-park Shaw was feeling grateful to the average New Yorker's indifference to what anybody else was doing, and beginning to believe that the comparative safety of the car could be reached before his prisoner fainted completely. Twice he had nearly done so, his body sagging, his head drooping, and Shaw had shaken him back to consciousness saying 'Sober up, you silly bastard!' for the benefit of anyone near.

Then at last the car was there after what Shaw felt to have been the longest walk of his life. He opened the driver's door, pushed Bridenthal in and across to the front passenger seat, transferred the cord to his right hand and drove up into the daylight. They were almost through the Lincoln Tunnel and into New Jersey when Bridenthal spoke for the first time.

'You play very rough, Mr Shaw.'

'I'm not playing,' Shaw said. 'Are you part of Stein's set-up?'

'I know many people called Stein. It's a very common name. Which particular one are you referring to?'

Shaw let it go and asked, 'Are you with Mossad?'

'Who's he?'

'Wrong question, Bridenthal. Every Israeli knows what Mossad is. So you do work for them. What's their interest in me?'

There was silence for a full minute before Bridenthal sighed and said, 'Stein's a fool. For that matter so am I for not checking on him much earlier.'

'Yes?'

The car bumped heavily over some uneven area of paving and when, two hundred yards further on, Bridenthal had said nothing more Shaw glanced at him, noting that his face was drawn and white again, and that the sweat which had dried in the warmth of the car's heater had been replaced by running rivulets.

'Can't you –? Won't you –?' The words came out hoarsely.

Shaw waited, saying nothing.

'The gun! I thought it was going to go off when we went over that bump! I – I – I tested the trigger! It's got a very light action! Oh dear God, I can't take much more of this!'

'I'll try to drive more carefully,' Shaw said. 'What's Mossad's interest in me?'

'Where are you taking me, Mr Shaw?'

'What's Mossad's interest in me, Bridenthal? Let's hear it

before I get annoyed at repeating myself. You wouldn't want me to get annoyed, would you?'

'We're interested in the whole operation. Not just you.'

Mossad – check, and there was more to the operation than his part in it Shaw's mind told him. Well there had to be, didn't there? Check again.

'What made you decide to investigate me?'

'Several things,' Bridenthal said. 'Your refusal to keep Stein informed and your insistence on the killing of Henrietta Lloyd after your very glib explanations of parts of the tape of Townsend's interrogation. Stein took a copy and I've listened to it several times.'

'Bully for both of you. Is that all?'

'No. What really set me thinking was something you said to Stein on a subject he had no knowledge of. You said that for crossing the desert you hoped that the camels would do the walking.'

'So?'

'There are no camels in Morocco, Mr Shaw.'

'Well, fancy that,' Shaw said. 'You learn something new every day.'

'I had you figured as an ordinary con artist until I found all those explosive devices.' Bridenthal sounded resentful, as though he had been deliberately misled by a close colleague. He muttered something that Shaw didn't hear, then asked, 'What use are those sophisticated things to an assault team? How could you transport them to Africa at this late stage when your arms are supposed to have gone already? By air freight?'

'Good questions,' Shaw said.

'What's that completely new wetsuit for? Mining an oasis?'

'That's an idea,' Shaw said.

'You don't intend to go to North Africa at all, do you?'

'Not now you've told me there are no camels in Morocco,' Shaw said.

The resentment in Bridenthal's voice had become irritation, irritation edged with incipient hysteria. Shaw decided to take advantage of that unease, glanced in the mirror and stamped on the brake pedal. The car swerved, pitching on its soft springs. Bridenthal screamed.

Weehawken and Union City on the banks of the Hudson were behind them now, the Passaic River ahead. The river bank somewhere above Little Falls would be the place, Shaw thought.

'You all right, Bridenthal?'

He got no reply and hadn't expected one with the man locked once more in terror, his hands clutching his groin as though they might afford him some protection from the blast of the gun.

'Sorry about that. I've been driving with a stick shift recently and I'm inclined to forget that thing down there is a brake, not the clutch.'

Still his passenger did not speak and Shaw decided that he should not apply that particular demoralising pressure again in case Bridenthal came to realise that the gun was not cocked. He hadn't cocked it because the disinterest of New Yorkers would not have stretched to a noisy and messy disembowelment in the street. So far, fear had served his purpose and it would be best to keep it doing so.

Six minutes and four miles passed before Bridenthal found his voice.

'You're going to kill me, aren't you?'

'That depends.'

'On what?'

'On how much you tell me about the whole operation. The one that involves more than me.'

'Mr Shaw,' Bridenthal said. 'During the last hour I've discovered that I'm a coward, but there are limits to my cowardice.'

Shaw nodded, but made no comment. Although there had been no bravado in the statement, it had sounded like someone trying to convince himself. He did not believe that the man would find the courage to withhold the information for long. Not, Shaw supposed, that that would make any difference to him personally. Time was to prove him wrong on that score.

Nearly twenty miles from New York Shaw parked in woodland, then told Bridenthal to get out. It was very cold after the warmth of the car as they made their way deeper into the wood. Beside a young straight tree he let go of the cord for

127

the first time, swung Bridenthal to the ground, pulled his trousers down for the second time and removed the shot-gun and its securing tapes. With the trousers belted again he doubled Bridenthal's legs back around the sapling's trunk, jamming the instep of each foot behind the calf of the opposing leg. Bridenthal drew air in through clenched teeth. It made a pulsing hissing sound like a steam locomotive.

'Uncomfortable, isn't it?'

Flat on his back Bridenthal stared up at him and whispered 'yes'.

'It's called "grape-vining",' Shaw told him, 'and it gets much worse. Quite agonising, in fact. You can't sit up to release yourself and eventually you die because your circulation is obstructed, but as I don't want to stand here all day I'm going to speed things up.'

It was close to freezing, Shaw thought, but not close enough to prevent moisture dripping from the tangled bare branches above his head. The droplets made a steady pattering, almost loud enough to drown the hum of traffic coming from the distant highway. Apart from that, there was only the occasional flight of a bird and the heavy breathing of the man on the ground to disturb the silence.

'Recognise this?'

Bridenthal's gaze moved from Shaw's to the grey canister in his hand. He nodded and watched the cover removed, the dials set and the cover replaced. Then the thing was placed on his stomach and the little grid pressed inward.

'It's got a tilt mechanism, so if you buck it off you it'll be activated at once,' Shaw said, turned and walked away into the wood. Shaking with cold, pain and fear Bridenthal watched him go until the canister spoke to him and his eyes jerked back to it. He had barely assimilated its message before it began to count, to count downwards.

'Come back!' he shouted. 'For pity's sake come back!' But nobody came and the voice counted remorselessly on. Before it reached zero he had fainted.

A hand shook his shoulder and a voice said, 'Wake up. There was no explosive in it.' His vision cleared to show him Shaw's darkly stubbled face looking down at him.

'But there is in this one,' Shaw said. 'Tell me about the operation, or I'll set it going. You'll have to sweat it out on the time factor because you won't know what delay I've set until the voice starts. After that you've got forty seconds before you disintegrate. If somebody happens by and takes it off you, you both get blown to pieces. Understood?'

Several seconds went by with Bridenthal's lips moving soundlessly before the ability to speak returned to him. After that, the words came pouring out of him. He talked for nearly a quarter of an hour. When his trapped legs were released from the tree it took him almost as long again to walk without falling.

Shaw killed him as he was getting into the car with a chopping blow to the side of the neck and a twist of the head which snapped the spinal cord. It was the most humane method Shaw could think of to dispose of a man who had persuaded himself that he would be allowed to live, but quite obviously could not.

What had seemed to Shaw, that dawn, to have been the longest walk of his life was followed by his longest day sitting, for most of it, with the corpse propped up beside him in the car. He saw few people but, with dusk approaching, surveyed the surrounding area as carefully as if he were carrying out a battlefield reconnaissance. When it was fully dark he slid Bridenthal's body into the Passaic River.

15

'Jesus! You look terrible, Harry.'

Seeing Townsend standing in the doorway made it very easy to smile and almost to relax. Moving past him into the apartment, Shaw said, 'Yes, I forgot to shave.' For a moment he stood looking around him as though he had never seen the place before, then added, 'I'll do that now and take a shower. Could you rustle up some grub and the biggest drink you can think of while I'm doing it?'

'Coming right up.'

'Oh, Bill, take these down to the incinerator first, please.'

Townsend looked curiously at the wallet, passport, travellers' cheques and other papers belonging to a man he had never heard of, nodded and left the flat. When he returned to it he found Shaw asleep in the armchair. He shook him awake.

'That's no way to behave, skipper,' he said. 'Clean yourself up and get something inside you in case Logo's Argies decide to attack. You know the correct procedure. You can sleep after that.'

The use of the term 'skipper' told Shaw that Townsend was worried. He was also absolutely right.

'Yes, sergeant,' he said and made his way tiredly to the bathroom.

Bathed, shaved and fed, Shaw began his story. 'I spent last night checking out the piers and shipping along the Hudson, and establishing where I can get in and out of the river. There's a four- or five-knot current so there won't be a lot of swimming to do. I'll just have to steer the crate of bombs and let the tide do the work. Anyway, I got back here at dawn and . . .' He recounted the events of the day and ended by saying, 'I don't think Bridenthal can have had a companion, or telephoned anybody from here, otherwise the place would be swarming with people by now, but we're getting out tomorrow and going to ground.'

'Why not tonight, Harry? It'd be safer.'

'Because of the man in the flat beneath this. He's curious about me already and he'll be more so if we stagger down the stairs with relays of Logo's stuff at this time of night. We'll do it after he's gone to work in the morning.'

'OK. You turn in. I'll go to the garage and clean any traces of Bridenthal and that wood off your car. You never can tell.'

'Thanks, but I've already done that,' Shaw said.

And that was Harry for you, Townsend thought. He never did things by halves.

Stein opened the Chippendale cabinet on his office wall and poured a small whisky. He didn't usually drink at five o'clock in the afternoon, but had persuaded himself that he was celebrating the telephone call he had taken from the bank in Manhattan a few minutes earlier. He had been informed that Shaw had withdrawn the balance of his working capital and told the bank that he would be out of touch for some weeks. The timing was right as Shaw had said that the desert would have started to cool by the end of October and now November was just in.

His self-persuasion lasting only as long as it took him to close the cabinet, Stein opened it again and doubled the measure of whisky in his glass. The need for consolation had replaced any thoughts of celebration in his mind because of Bridenthal's continued silence. That silence had been increasing his anxiety by the hour and almost twenty-four of those had gone by since the man might reasonably have been expected to telephone him. He was not alone in his concern: an attaché at the Israeli embassy was worried too.

A morgue attendant in Paterson, New Jersey, could have told them both that he was the temporary custodian of the unidentified body of a male Caucasian, aged between forty and fifty, which had been removed from the river it had been deposited in several hours after death by violence, but nobody asked him.

While Stein was drinking his whisky, Mossad's man in London became sufficiently worried to call his opposite number in Washington, DC, only to be told that Bridenthal had not been in contact. A request that an attempt be made to establish if a certain Henry J. Shaw had left the States, probably from an airport in the New York area, during the past day or two, produced an affirmative reply within nine hours. That reply did not include the information that, having flown to Canada, Shaw had walked back into the United States across the 49th Parallel – not the most difficult cross-border penetration he had ever made. Now, the immigration slip removed from his passport on departure and replaced by the one he had purloined weeks before at Kennedy Airport, he was back in New York City and apparently legally so.

As Townsend might have remarked, Shaw never did things by halves.

'Stein's radio messages will be designed to direct us into Libya regardless of where any of the three targets are,' Shaw said, 'but there was never any intention of letting us reach Tripoli. According to Bridenthal, news of a British attempt on Gadaffi's life, and the direction it's coming from, has already been leaked to the Libyan government. Our death or capture, and Libyan yells of outrage, were to be the signal for a bunch of enthusiastic suicidal Shi'ites purporting to be Libyans to attack our listening centre on Cyprus. Apparently they're much better organised than that gang who had a go at the airfield there.'

'"Charge, Muhammet, charge! On, Ali, on!"'

'What?'

'Sir Walter Scott's Arabian brother,' Townsend said.

'Oh, shut up, Bill. This is serious.'

'Sorry. What exactly is it supposed to achieve?'

'Well, it's likely to annoy Her Majesty's Government more than somewhat and it'll make the Americans mad too. The radio intercepts we make there are as important to us and the States as GCHQ at Cheltenham, but the spin-off they are hoping for is the reprisal killings of the Western hostages in

Lebanon. Bridenthal told me that there has been an attempt by the White House to obtain their release by supplying arms to Iran. It was hoped to achieve that before the mid-term elections to bolster the Reagan Administration, but – election day is tomorrow, isn't it?'

'4 November, yes.'

'Then it doesn't appear to have worked, and when the news breaks there are going to be an awful lot of angry people both here and in the Arab world.'

'Will the news break?' Townsend asked.

'It'll be leaked if it doesn't,' Shaw told him. 'The Israelis were the middle-men if Bridenthal was to be believed, so they're in a position to leak it.'

'And why would they want to do that? It's the Americans they depend on, so why spit in their eye? There's no percentage for them in handing the Arabs a propaganda coup.'

Shaw left his chair, walked across the shabby room to the dirty window and stood looking out at the poorer section of So Ho they had chosen as their final base of operations. His eyes showed him the street kids, the drunks, the derelicts, the prostitutes and the litter, but his brain was focused on a dripping wood in New Jersey where a frightened man had talked in a vain bid for life. His voice had been tinged with hysteria, but he had spoken articulately and with a compelling urgency about his fears for the future he was never going to see.

The Americans, he had said, were going through a strange and dangerous aberrational phase in their history, seeing themselves as the moral leaders of mankind and wondering why the rest of the world could not be like them, much as the British had done in the nineteenth century. On a psychological level this had been demonstrated by their unseemly nationalistic euphoria over such trifles as the Grenada invasion, the Olympic Games and the centenary of the Liberty statue.

Feeling a certain sympathy, Shaw had nevertheless grunted impatiently at that, but the sound had served only to increase Bridenthal's vehemence and produce the statement that the United States were slipping back into a womb of self-congratulation and isolationism. He had pleaded with Shaw to

133

open his eyes and look at the world around him, to look at the shift of American interest, population and industry from the east coast to the west, distancing them mentally and physically ever further from the troubles of Europe and the Middle East. Look too, Shaw had been told, at their fears of the election of a Labour government in Britain and the virtually inevitable destruction of NATO which would result. Bridenthal had ended his frantic oration by saying that the American people had had it up to here with foreigners and were ready to stay home with Mom and apple pie in the naïve belief that the third of a million troops they maintained in Europe were there for the protection of the Europeans and not as their first line of defence.

Requested to come to the point, Bridenthal said that such an American ambition had to be thwarted and that was to be achieved by confronting them with a situation they could not turn their backs on. That was when Shaw heard of the Zionist-planned kamikaze-style seaborne attack by Iranian volunteers on one of the American warships normally to be found in the Gulf of Oman. The action, he had been told, would galvanise the States into military retaliation, if the murder of their hostages had failed to do so already. Simple provocation was then to be turned into strategic necessity by the mining of the Strait of Hormuz at one end of the Persian Gulf and an attack by Israeli-supplied elements of the Iranian forces on the oilfields of Kuwait at the other. The latter group would subsequently proceed northwards to take the Iraqi Army facing Iran in the flank, and those two factors would inevitably draw the United States Navy into the Gulf in force. America could afford neither the disruption of a large part of the Western world's oil supplies, nor the gift of warm-water ports to the Russians, should they succeed in undermining the Islamic Fundamentalist regime in Iran.

Half his attention on the woods about him, his ears straining to detect any sound of human movement above the patter of drops of water, it had taken Shaw a moment to register the contradiction of supplying arms to a country you detested, and whose political stability you doubted was capable of with-standing Russian expansionism. When he put the thought into words Bridenthal had replied with quavering anger that any fool could see that the States seemed no longer able to differentiate between expediency born of chauvinism and national security in the longer term.

That the man was by then in considerable pain from his trapped legs Shaw could tell from his trembling thighs and rasping breath. He felt no doubt at all about the truthfulness of the reply he received to his statement that, apart from ensuring a continuance of the American presence in the Middle East, there appeared to be nothing to Israel's advantage in such dangerous machinations.

Bridenthal had said, 'Our political and military analysts are satisfied that with Iraq's forces in action on two fronts Syria will go to the aid of their Iranian friends by attacking Iraq in the rear, in much the same way that Italy attacked France in 1940. When that happens Israel will invade Syria and clear up the whole mess once and for all. That's what it's all about.'

Deep in his own recollections, Shaw had not noticed Townsend's approach, but turned immediately at the sound of his voice.

'Really, Harry! If you're going to spend your afternoons watching tarts in the street you'll leave me no choice but to warn Dr Cheyney.'

Shaw smiled, nodded and told him Bridenthal's tale.

'That's pretty heavy, Harry.'

'It's heavy all right.'

'Who are we going to tell?'

'Nobody yet,' Shaw said. 'Bridenthal has handed us an insurance policy, a bargaining counter if you like, and it's valid until the last day of December. After that, knowing we've failed them, Mossad will think up some other way of setting off the train of events, but we'll have alerted our people before then.'

The thunderstorm rolled across Tel Aviv like a creeping artillery barrage, but the five men in a room secured against sight, sound and electronic surveillance in the sub-basement of a tower block were unaware of it. Four of them were casually dressed in slacks and open-necked shirts. The fifth wore a city suit. It was he who was asking the questions.

'This so-called "Q" ship fitting out at Elath. How is it hoped to get it close enough to an American warship to do any damage?'

'When it is within visual range of the American squadron it will be set on fire, sir,' one of them told him. 'That and distress signals should produce the desired result. When the vessel the Americans send to render assistance is close enough, the cargo will be detonated. There's enough explosive on board to sink or severely damage any ship within two hundred metres.'

The man in the city suit lay back in his chair and said, 'I should have got beyond the stage of feeling surprise at anything these Muslims will do after what has happened on our doorstep, but I haven't. How many of them have elected to be blown to pieces in this enterprise?' Before anybody could reply, he added hastily, 'Don't answer that. I don't really want to know. Is there anything else I *should* know?'

'There's the Bridenthal problem, sir. He seems to have disappeared without trace. We don't know how or why?'

'Oh, balls!'

All heads turned to the new speaker.

'Meaning what, Eli?'

'Meaning don't let's pussyfoot around the obvious. Bridenthal took it upon himself to check on the activities of that ex-SAS fellow Stein hired for Phase One. Name of Short, I think.'

'Shaw.'

'Shaw then. Anyway, he'd made it clear to Stein that he would brook no interference in his part of the operation. He even insisted on the liquidation of that female interrogator when Stein put his oar in. Anybody who would go to those lengths wouldn't have hesitated to kill Bridenthal if he'd got in his way.'

'Just like that? Out of pique?'

'No,' Eli said, 'not out of pique. To cover his tracks, which is something he's insisted on doing all along, and to stamp his seal of authority on that insistence. With my life in the balance I'd have done the same.'

The man in the city suit nodded. It sounded plausible enough for, although Bridenthal had known a great deal, mercenaries

136

were in the business of killing for money, not of extracting information which could have neither relevance for their safety nor beneficial effects on their incomes.

When he left the building the storm was no more than an irritable rumbling far inland. He found himself sharing its apparent emotion because he distrusted plausibility and that left a lot unanswered.

Townsend placed the metal box carefully in the hollow book and closed the cover, hearing the faint click as the light-meter was depressed, arming the device. Then he wrapped the book in brown paper, holding it tightly shut as he did so. With its covering securely taped he added the parcel to the pile beside him and started to work on another. Now that the time had come he was feeling both nervous and exhilarated, and quite enjoying the two sensations which in his army life had so often gone hand in hand.

Similarly occupied on the other side of the table, Shaw completed his final package, stripped off the rubber gloves he was wearing, and asked, 'How about the "Hands Off Ulster Regiment" as our by-line?'

'It's terrible,' Townsend replied. 'Let's use it.'

Shaw wiped the sweat from his hands, put the gloves on again and began sticking postage stamps on the parcel bombs before saying, 'The initials spell "hour".'

'Yeah, I noticed. Want me to recite Churchill's "finest hour" speech?'

'Not a lot.'

'So be like that. It's your loss. I can imitate his voice very well.'

'So can everybody else, Bill. I thought we could put things like "The hour has struck" in the classified ads section of the newspapers when these things have gone off.'

'God, that really *is* terrible,' Townsend said. 'I love it.'

They mailed the packages that night.

16

Senator James Fairbridge stopped the Cadillac at the entrance to the driveway leading to his New Canaan home, lowered the window and reached into the mail box. There were three official letters from Washington DC, one from a friend in Cleveland, two for his wife, another in a mauve envelope inscribed with green ink, the usual pile of junk mail and a package which felt like a book. He dropped them all on to the seat beside him and drove towards the house.

'Nothing for me, dad?'

He glanced in the mirror at his fourteen-year-old son clutching a large nondescript dog on the rear seat. The dog, tongue lolling, looked very content. Mike looked agonised.

'Nope.'

'Oh gee, dad. You'll give me a complex or something. You certain that kinda purple one isn't for me?'

Mike was known by his parents to be deeply involved with an older woman. The older woman was fifteen and lived in Providence, Rhode Island. Fairbridge grinned and handed the envelope back over his shoulder.

'Oh gee! Thanks, dad!'

At the sound of the car his wife and daughter came out of the house and began to take the groceries from the trunk. He let them get on with it, watching, smiling, as his son raced indoors with the dog at his heels. He guessed that the dog was going to have the letter read to it.

'Has Cupid struck again, Jim?'

He kissed his wife over the top of the bulky brown paper

bag she was holding, took it from her and said, 'He sure has. Bring the mail, will you honey?'

It was over half an hour before he had dealt with his correspondence, part on paper, part by telephone, then he picked up the package and ripped it open. Somebody had sent him a copy of *Red Storm Rising* which had been on the bestseller list for months and which he had already read. Curiously, he opened the book to look for an inscription and felt himself freeze instantly.

The flat grey metal box counter-sunk into the pages had a tiny grille set at its centre, with what looked like a photoelectric cell beside it. His eyes recorded those things; his imagination showed him a seering blast of light and heat, his own disintegration and his family crushed beneath a collapsed building. Then his ears heard recorded speech, a high, monotone voice squeaking 'I am a talking bomb. I have now been activated and will detonate in precisely thirty seconds. Twenty-nine seconds. Twenty-eight . . .'

He swung round to hurl the thing through the glass of the closed window of his office, but his daughter was there, riding her bicycle in aimless circles on the gravel of the driveway.

'Twenty-five seconds. Twenty-four . . .'

Horror shook him so violently that he nearly lost his grip on the book. He juggled it desperately, caught it, placed it carefully on the desk and hurled himself through the door into the hallway.

'Twenty-one seconds,' the bomb said, then he was shouting, 'Mike! Mike! Get down here and get out of the house! There's a bomb in it! Run like hell! Marianne? Where are you? *Oh Christ! Where are you?*'

'What's all the yelling about, lover?'

She was standing in the doorway to the kitchen, a pan in one hand. He leapt for her, grasped her wrist, whirled and dragged her towards the front door. She stumbled, almost fell, recovered and ran with him staggeringly. Mike was standing on the bottom step of the stairs.

'What's up, dad?'

'Fourteen seconds,' a tinny voice said from his office.

Fairbridge bellowed, 'Out! Out and run! Beat it!' He propelled the boy along the hallway by the back of his sweater, still gripping his wife's wrist, then flung them both outside. Mike sprawled on the gravel and he saw Marianne lose a shoe and stumble again, then he was sprinting towards the little girl on the bicycle.

'Come with daddy, sweetheart.'

Suddenly inexplicably calm he dodged the advancing machine like a basketball player, snatched the child from the saddle and ran on, a backward glance showing him his wife and son following twenty paces behind. In the middle of the lawn he threw himself at full length on his side, cushioning his daughter from the fall before rolling on top of her. She began to cry, but he barely noticed the sound through the surge of love and pride for his wife which washed over him. Lying beside him now, Marianne was watching him gravely, enquiringly, but not asking questions. She was also sprawled on top of Mike although she was smaller than he. The pan was still in her hand.

'Hold tight, you guys,' Fairbridge said. 'There's going to be a big bang right now.'

There was no bang, but he let a full half-minute go by. Nothing. Nothing but bird song, the distant hum of traffic and the sound of a jet in the distance. Even his daughter was silent. Cautiously he lifted his head and looked over his shoulder towards the house. It stood, just as it had for the eleven years since he had built it except that his office window was completely opaque and smoke was drifting through the open front door.

'Marianne.'

'Yes?'

'Get over to the Bartholomews, will you? Call the fire department and the police. They should rustle up a bomb squad as soon as they can too.'

She got up at once, kicked off her remaining shoe and ran towards the belt of trees separating them from their neighbours. Relieved of his mother's weight Mike sat up. The smoke was billowing now.

'Jeez, dad, what – Oh Jeez! Caliban's in there!'

He was within fifteen yards of the house before Fairbridge brought him down with a flying football tackle.

'Leave the dog, son. We don't know what the hell's going on in there.'

Caliban silenced further protest by appearing through the smoke, wearing his contented expression. At its edge he paused, sneezed twice, then loped towards his master. Mike threw his arms round him, gasped and thrust him away.

'Oh boy! You stink! You really stink! What the heck have you been doing?'

Fairbridge caught the scent then, the smell of hydrogen sulphide, the stench of rotten eggs. It grew stronger as the smoke drifted towards them across the lawn.

Marianne Fairbridge thought drearily that she hadn't seen the driveway so full of automobiles since the poolside party she had given back in the summer. There were four police cars, one of them unmarked, three fire trucks, an ambulance, a high-sided vehicle somebody said was a mobile laboratory, two pick-ups which had brought television crews and another with some people who knew about bombs. The rest, she supposed, all belonged to the press because so many people, men and women, kept sticking microphones under her nose and asking futile questions. The futility, she knew, was largely of her own making because the reporters had their job to do and needed something more from her than the constantly repeated 'no comment' she had been instructed to say to anything of the remotest relevance by the man from the FBI.

'What do you aim to do, Mrs Fairbridge?'

'Send for the National Guard. There's still room for them on the lawn.'

Damn. That sounded so ungrateful to all these people who were trying to salvage something of her ruined home and find out who had ruined it. She had fallen into the pattern because she was very tired now, tired, confused and distressed. Flippant replies were much easier to give than trying to figure out what was remotely relevant to anything.

'I'm sorry,' she said. 'Our friends the Bartholomews are giving us beds for the night, which is pretty darned nice of them considering we stink like polecats. After that I don't know yet.'

As soon as the men from the high-sided truck had agreed with the bomb squad that it was safe, one of the firemen wearing breathing apparatus had fitted her with a set and taken her into the house. It had been a shocking and miserable experience, but she had come out with her jewellery. At least that hadn't been ruined by the fumes as everything else seemed to have been. The drapes, the linen, the carpets, books, clothes, wallpaper. Everything.

Suddenly it was all too much and she began to cry. A man with a TV camera on his shoulder swung it towards her, but one of the objectionable men with a microphone stopped being objectionable and stepped in front of the camera saying, 'Leave it, buster. There's no percentage in that.' Then he took her arm and led her away adding, 'Let's go find the Senator, Mrs Fairbridge. He's over there someplace, talking to the Feds.'

'Thanks. You're nice,' she said.

Fairbridge was standing with a group of five men, alternately shrugging and shaking his head at them as she approached. When she reached his side he put an arm across her shoulders.

'Gentlemen, my wife.'

They said 'Mrs Fairbridge' almost in unison as though they had rehearsed it.

'You OK, honey?'

'Sure.'

He returned his attention to his questioners and said, 'Leaving aside the misuse of the US Mail, I get this feeling that something else makes this a Federal case.'

'It does, Senator,' one of them told him. 'You're the ninth victim so far today. There have been three incidents in New York City, one in Boston, two in Washington DC, one in Maryland, one in New Jersey and you. All of them identical. We're wondering just how many other people are going to come home and open that fucking book.' His eyes flicked to Mrs Fairbridge and he added, 'I beg your pardon, ma'am.'

She nodded, half smiling her forgiveness.

'Have you found a link?'

'No, Senator,' the FBI man said, 'but we're sure as hell going to.'

Of the sixteen people Shaw had identified through the press and the Congressional Record as having pro-IRA leanings, twelve suffered a comparable fate to the Fairbridge family's. So did three others he had known about before he left England. The remaining four experienced greater afflictions. A woman in Boston, running with her husband away from the talking bomb, fell and fractured her pelvis. A lawyer in New York, living in an apartment building, most of which was rendered uninhabitable by the fumes, was beaten up by an infuriated neighbour who blamed him for the disaster. In Westchester County a Congressman had a heart attack which was to prove fatal three days later. His doctors angered the police by refusing to state categorically that it was directly attributable to his experience, as it was his fifth in eighteen months. In Vermont a house, rapidly evacuated, burnt to the ground when an abandoned pan of cooking oil ignited.

Television coverage was extensive and so repetitive that Shaw and Townsend began to feel that they knew their victims personally. When Townsend said that he liked the Fairbridges, who seemed to be a nice-looking gutsy family, Shaw replied tersely that he might have joined him in that but for the nineteen-year-old soldier and his twenty-one-year-old corporal who had had their guts blown all over the border when their truck had been destroyed by a mine remotely controlled from the Irish Republic three days earlier. With little or no attention paid to events in Ulster by the American media, it had become Shaw's custom to buy a London paper whenever he could. That kept his motivation steady and his determination strong. He neither liked nor disliked the Fairbridges. To him they were nothing more or less than part of a cornucopia of death for British soldiers and civilians both in Ulster and England.

A film clip of a big man with a steady face and greying blond hair who said his name was Lieutenant Bergquist was screened every hour on the hour on most channels as the officer warned against suspicious packages received through the mail or by any other means. They were to be left untouched and the police informed immediately. The same message was broadcast regularly on radio as well.

When he had learnt what little there was to learn from watching the four smokey scenes that television crews had been able to reach, Shaw put on his rubber gloves and typed identical messages for publication in newspapers in New York, Boston, Chicago and Washington DC. He added dollar bills to each envelope, then drove to Brooklyn to mail them, wondering if the papers would accept the unsigned cryptic insertion and if anybody would notice it if they did.

They did accept it and, amongst others, Sergeant Alton of Manhattan's 17th Precinct noticed it.

'I guess we're dealing with some kinda crazy nut, Lieutenant.'

Lieutenant Harvey Bergquist looked sombrely at the speaker and said, 'As an intelligent observation, Ace, that leaves quite a bit to be desired.'

Detective 'Ace' Diamond blinked at him and Bergquist went on, 'We have no idea whether we're dealing with a nut or a whole bunch of nuts, or whether he, she or they is or are nuts. Anyway, "crazy nut" is tautology, and don't ask me what tautology is. Look it up in the goddam dictionary. Now, anybody got any ideas about this book? It's the same darned book in each case so the Feds tell me, and we've seen the remains of three of them ourselves.' He looked at Diamond again and added, 'I'll probably crucify whoever suggests that we're up against commie agitators or Soviet spies just because it's called *Red Storm Rising*.'

'It has the right dimensions and about the appropriate weight with the pages hollowed out to accommodate the smoke bomb without arousing suspicion, Lieutenant. The title's irrelevant.'

Bergquist nodded at the speaker, then looked round at the group.

'Lieutenant.'

He turned his regard to the plain stocky girl with dyed blonde hair and thin lips.

'Yeah?'

'That book was used in quantity and it may have been bought in quantity from a single source. I think we should check the sources. Scribners, Doubleday, everyplace. It sounds pretty dumb, but the buyer may have charged them, or paid by check or credit card. People do dumb things. On the other hand, the store clerk might remember a sizeable cash sale to an individual. That could get us a description.'

'Nice going, sergeant. Get on to it.'

'There's something else. Well, maybe there is. It struck me as strange that nobody has claimed responsibility for all this. They nearly always do, otherwise there's no point, so I looked in the paper. Here.'

Bergquist took the folded copy of *The New York Times* from her, looked at the small box she had marked with yellow highlighter, and read aloud, 'The HOUR has struck faintly and will continue to do so with increasing clarity.' He looked round at the group again before saying, 'Now you all know why Sergeant Alton's a sergeant.'

He did not add that the editors of all four newspapers had contacted the FBI on receipt of the note and been requested to run it in their next editions in an attempt to establish a channel of communication with the perpetrators of the crimes and not to handle the paper any more than they already had. He didn't add that, because Sergeant Alton was a very good cop who deserved the credit for having followed through an intelligent line of thought on top of her already heavy workload. Her example might, he told himself, make even Detective 'Ace' Diamond think.

'Incidentally,' he said, 'the word "hour" is in caps, so it probably stands for something. Anybody got any ideas about that?'

Nobody had.

Refolding the newspaper Bergquist looked at the front page again. The headline proclaiming the gas bombings was as sober as was to be expected of *The New York Times*, but it had nevertheless pushed the Democratic Party gains in the midterm elections off the lead column.

'Ace.'

'Lieutenant?'

'Follow up Alton's line on book sales. You, sergeant, pick yourself a team of three and try to find a common link between the victims. Party affiliations, Vietnam, the anti-nuke lobby, organic vegetables, wife-swapping, any darned thing. Let's see if we can beat the FBI computer to that.'

Mary Alton nodded, stood up and said, 'Meynard, Tyler, Penkala. Let's go.'

Detective Diamond traced eleven people in New York City who had bought *Red Storm Rising* in numbers larger than three, but it got him no further than being offered the loan of a copy by one of them. Sergeant Alton didn't lose her race with the FBI computer, but only because neither she nor it reached a conclusion.

17

The news of the supply of arms by the United States to Iran broke in Beirut on 4 November and dislodged the gas bombings from their prominent position as lead story in New York the following day. Shaw didn't mind. The extraordinary revelation gave added credence to what Bridenthal had told him and he had little doubt that the reports of what he was about to do would receive maximum exposure.

It had been difficult getting into a wetsuit within the confines of a car, but he had managed it and now he was up to his neck in the scummy water of the Hudson River near the end of West 72nd Street. The brilliance of Manhattan cast the area immediately around into deep shadow, which was one of the reasons he had chosen the spot, the other being the comparative ease of access to it from the section of roadway where Townsend had let him out of the car. At two o'clock in the morning the volume of traffic had been light, but it had not been until they approached the place for the fifth time that Shaw judged it to be sufficiently deserted to make the attempt.

Logo's explosive devices, fourteen of them, were in a satchel strapped to his chest. Their tilt mechanisms were disconnected, timers set, recordings wiped clean, their lids sealed and their magnetic clamps screened with insulating tape. Shaw began to transfer them from the satchel to a wooden box surrounded on three sides by what Townsend described as his flower arrangement: a confection of plastic straw, an empty milk carton, a beer can and other apparent flotsam wired loosely together. With the weight gone from him, it was harder to maintain his position against the urging of the current. The water dragged at his body and built up around his face like a small bow wave. He released the cord connecting him to the bank.

An eddy carried Shaw, his bombs and his camouflage far enough out into the river to show him the lights of traffic moving along the West Side Elevated Highway. His flippers working rhythmically he forced himself and his load back towards the bank, grateful for the exercise because cold was to be one of his major enemies this night. Behind him a launch crept upstream close to the New Jersey shore. He could not see it, but its engine became audible to him despite his rubber hood whenever his ears dipped beneath the surface. Ahead, the first main piers of the Port Authority seemed to slide by from right to left as fast as a man would walk, their batteries of overhead arc-lamps dimming the lights of the skyscrapers beyond. Visibility good. Much too good. Waterborne sounds increasing, swamping the audio-sensory faculties. Ships' generators, small craft motors and propellers, winches, a rivet-gun hammering somewhere. Ignore and use eyes. A medium-sized container ship in ballast, riding high in the water, was moored to the next pier to the right. Target! Shaw increased the tempo of his scissoring legs.

The surface of the river between the pier and the ship was a log-jam of floating debris, cartons, bottles, bits of wood, paper and other objects he tried not to think about, but he had expected that and it suited his purpose well enough. Allowing his own collection of garbage to merge with it Shaw secured his box to the vessel's hull with a short length of cord. The magnetic clamp on the end of it clicked sharply as it made contact.

He had just withdrawn his first bomb from beneath the piece of ragged carpeting covering the box when his peripheral vision detected movement above and to his left. Eyes slitted to conceal the only reflective parts of his grease-blackened face he watched the sailor in a pea-jacket light a cigarette, lean on the guard-rail and lose himself in contemplation of the detritus of human consumption below him.

Hanging vertically in the water Shaw continued to watch throughout the life of the cigarette, a life longer than he would have believed possible, then saw its red end curve down to extinction and the sailor move away. Sighing softly he tore the insulating tape from the bomb's magnetic clamps with fingers already clumsy with cold, and drew himself under the ship's stern. The upper pintle connecting the huge rudder to the hull was out of reach above his head, but he didn't want that one, because cushioning water would add to the blast effect of the explosion. Jack-knifing, he drove himself downwards, feeling the increase of pressure on his ears, feeling, too, gratitude now for the blazing arc-lamps far above which enabled him to see what he was doing. There weren't many barnacles or much sea-weed around the bottom pintle and the bomb gripped at once, seeming to jump from Shaw's hands as though eager to do its job. He depressed the amplifier grid and swam upwards. The oil-scented air smelt very good to him when he broke surface with his back against the rudder, within a few feet of his box.

It was also very good to rest where he was with the force of the current holding him motionless against the steel behind him, and he did so for several seconds while he waited for his breathing to return to normal. Rest? He hadn't exerted himself yet and had barely begun what he had set out to do! That realisation brought home to him that the cold was already sapping his strength and jerked him into motion so suddenly that it set the garbage trapped along the ship's side rocking. He cursed silently and paused until he was satisfied that the movement had attracted no attention. Then he detached the box from the hull, drew it clear of the stern and let the current carry him downstream.

Shaw had repeated the manoeuvre six times on an assortment of ships before he bungled one and watched the bomb oscillate down through the murky water until it was lost to vision beyond the depth to which the lights could penetrate. That he had forgotten to remove the masking tape from the magnetic clamps took longer to occur to him than it should have done and that told him his concentration was failing. He had placed his tenth charge and was drifting rapidly, estimating his position as opposite West 30th Street from the bearing of the Empire State Building, when the launch ran him down.

Disorientation total, body rolling slowly somewhere beneath

149

the surface, no indication of which way was up, uncertain whether the pain in his lungs, head or left shoulder was the greater. Telling himself to relax, float, not to burn the residual oxygen in his system. A lesser blackness. Up? Left? Right? Over there anyway. Is that the best you can do with your billions of candle-power, Manhattan? Nothing else to be done, so check it out. It seemed a very long time to Shaw, but it was only seconds before his head lifted clear of the water and he retched a pint of Hudson River back to where it had come from.

The stern light of the launch receding directly ahead of him, his box, almost awash, fifteen yards to his right, most of Townsend's flower arrangement ripped away. Very tiredly, one arm trailing, he swam towards it. His three remaining bombs were still inside and he wasn't sure that he cared overmuch about that, but it was good to have the thing to hold on to. With almost automatic movements of his legs Shaw began to propel it towards the shore and what he knew had to be his last target. When he reached the passenger ferry he was too exhausted to do more than attach the magnetic clamp on the cord to the vessel's rudder, depress the three amplifier grids, and drift away.

There were still four piers to pass before he reached the partially lit one under repair he had chosen as the rendezvous point, and he doubted if he could get that far, even with the river's help. He spent the time wondering, without a great deal of interest, whether the last three bombs in the box would detonate simultaneously, or if one would explode and scatter the other two. Numb with cold and resignation Shaw was within ten yards of the floating wooden platform alongside the pier when he knew with absolute certainty that he wasn't going to make it, but his legs continued their feeble kicking as though that knowledge had yet to reach them from his brain.

'Upsadaisy,' Townsend said.

The hand gripping his right wrist like a vice, lifting him from the water as though he weighed nothing, swinging him on to the platform. Strong little bastard, Townsend. Chattering teeth forced apart and hot liquid running into his mouth and over his chin. Choked, gagged, swallowed. Taste of rum and milk. More. Swallowed straightaway that time. More again.

Swallowed. The sound of the zip at his chest opening, then the glint of a knife and the legs of the wetsuit being sliced from top to bottom and everything being dragged off him. Friction of a coarse towel on his body and wool being drawn up his legs. Agony forcing a yelping cry from him when his left arm was raised to fit the sleeve of a sweater over it. Fingers kneading his shoulder, a voice saying 'Bite on that, skipper.' Something that felt like a glove thrust into his mouth, a foot jammed into his armpit, his arm pulled violently and twisted. The pain was savage and he had fainted before the dislocated joint clicked back into place.

Although he was still shivering uncontrollably when he recovered consciousness, Shaw thought it was rather restful lying there with his shoulder doing nothing more than ache in a distant fashion as though it belonged to somebody else, but he couldn't understand why he was having his wrists tied together in front of him. He was thinking about that when someone shouted 'You! What in hell's going on down there?' and the figure beside him whirled. Steel flashed briefly and a shape like a giant bird dropped in a swallow-dive to thud on to the platform not far away. The man who had been tying his wrists walked to it and jerked free the knife protruding from beneath the body's chin before toppling it into the river.

'Sorry about that, skipper.'

Townsend? Well of course it was Townsend. Very good with a knife, Townsend. But where were they? Belfast? Londonderry?

'Where . . .?'

'Don't try to talk, Harry. You've taken a crack on the side of the head. Dislocated your shoulder as well, but that's fixed now. Just relax while I get you up top.'

All very confusing, but he understood what was happening when Townsend stooped, drew the bound wrists over his head, turned his back and stood upright. Shaw's toes were too cold to register any sensation when their upper sides were dragged across rough wood for the few paces separating them from the iron rungs set in the vertical wall of the pier. Then Townsend climbed and Shaw hung from his neck. Strong little bastard, Townsend. Good Sassman too. The SAS always looked after its own.

Shaw had no recollection of being carried to the car parked between a crane and the deserted customs building. He didn't remember anything much about the next eighteen hours, except that Bill Townsend was there, so everything had to be all right.

High up on the bridge the master of the container ship *Sea Sentinel* out of Felixstowe felt the deck quiver beneath his feet. It had been a barely perceptible movement, but it happened and he looked round angrily to see if one of the New York harbour tugs had butted his command, but both were lying innocently waiting out in the stream. He shrugged and was turning forward again when the telephone beside him shrilled.

'Yes?'

'Cap'n, Chief speaking. Sharp explosion right aft. Made everything down here ring like a bell.'

'I thought I felt something,' the master said. 'You'd better – Just a minute, Chief.'

He glanced over his shoulder in response to an urgent call from the First Officer. There was a telephone in his hand too.

'What is it?'

'Something's blown up below the stern, sir. Soaked the men handling the mooring wires. They don't –'

The thud of a second explosion, unblanketed by the hull, reached their ears clearly from the direction of the Dutch freighter lying alongside the next pier and water soared briefly. A third detonation followed from somewhere further away and a fourth more distant still.

'Close all water-tight doors,' the master said. 'I think the port's under attack.' Then into the telephone, 'Chief, test the steering and the propeller shaft, check for leaks and stand by for rapid orders. I want to get out of here and I shan't be waiting for the tugs.'

'Understood,' his telephone told him.

An unimpressionable man, the master was nevertheless impressed by the speed with which the authorities reacted to whatever it was that was going on. Police materialised as if from nowhere, herding the curious away. The ever-present wail of car sirens increased dramatically in number, seeming to come from all parts of a city until then not fully awake to the new day, their message of urgency converging on the dock area. The tugs moved in closer, ready for whatever might be required of them and a helicopter made its clattering way along the line of piers at little more than masthead height. A policeman and a deck official boarded the ship at the run and climbed to the bridge deck to join him, but he could tell them little until the phone shrilled again and informed him that the rudder was jammed. Then the fire appliances and an ambulance arrived, only to depart as rapidly as they had come on being assured that their services were not needed.

It seemed to be no time at all before the single police helicopter was replaced by a swarm of others with 'Navy' painted on their sides. A similarly marked car drew up at the gangway and a Navy lieutenant joined the group on the bridge. One of the helicopters hovered close to the ship's stern only feet from the water and the black figures of two frogmen dropped backwards into it. The master noted that similar scenes were being enacted near the Dutch vessel and at numerous points beyond that. At the most distant of those, and unknown to him, a passenger ferry lay with her after-deck under water. Three bombs exploding simultaneously by sympathetic detonation had cracked fuel lines and caused arcing in the electrical circuits. The resultant fire was immediately extinguished by the automatic release of carbon dioxide gas, but welded seams had opened in the hull and before sufficient men with breathing apparatus could be assembled to deal with the problem the engine room had flooded.

'What the hell's happening?' the master wondered, and didn't realise that he had done it aloud until the lieutenant said, 'Search me,' left the ship and stood waiting on the dockside. Periodically one or other of the frogmen reappeared through the accumulated garbage, removed his mouthpiece and called up to him. Twenty minutes passed before the Navy officer returned to the bridge.

'Your ship's externally clean, Captain, but you won't be going anyplace until it's been searched right through inboard. After that it's a dock job. Seems like they used a small limpet mine. Anyway, your bottom rudder pintle is cracked and distorted.'

'Who are "they"?'

'Search me,' the lieutenant said for the second time.

Most of the police on the jetty had been replaced by troops in full combat gear now. Having no idea what it was the soldiers thought they could do, the master remained impressed by the rapidity of their deployment. He would have been more so had he been able to see the warships probing the waters of New York Bay with their sonars and their helicopters dipping sonobuoys in the search for an unknown enemy. But he knew nothing of that, nor that similar operations were being mounted off ports from Maine to the Gulf of Mexico and San Diego to Washington State.

Nor was that all. Albeit faintly, the shock-waves from the little quake of which Logo's bombs had been the epicentre reached out to touch the US Fleet on the high seas, the submarines under them, and the Air Force. Even the missile silos felt the tremor. The armed forces of the nation were suddenly very much on the alert, but against what only William Townsend could have told them, and he chose not to.

'We'll let them sweat on it for a while without your newspaper release, Harry,' he told the sleeping figure on the bed as he turned off the television set. 'They're spending a king's ransom every five minutes. Let's keep them doing just that.' Then he turned the set on again, curious to know what emergency the newscasters would think of next.

Frogmen recovered a lot of peculiar things from the bottom of the Hudson River that day, including a small refrigerator so new that the masking tape on its door, and pieces of moulded plastic for protecting its corners during transit, had not been removed. The bomb squad treated it with extreme caution and then to some colourful language when it was found to be precisely what it looked like. Four bodies were found too; three of them in varying stages of decomposition and one newly dead from a wound in the throat. Having more important things to think about than helping the police establish the identities of missing persons, the frogmen left them where they were.

Amongst the things they didn't find was a grey canister lying

154

in similarly coloured mud beneath the keel of one of the damaged ships.

'There's nothing wrong with you that six months in an isolation ward won't fix,' Townsend said.

'Smelt a bit, did I?'

'You could say that. How's your head?'

Shaw put a hand over his left ear and winced before saying, 'Bit sore, but it's stopped aching. Fill me in, Bill.'

'You're causing concern,' Townsend told him. 'Yes, I don't think that's too strong a word. The story goes something like this. New York is virtually closed as a port since you sank one ship and immobilised ten others. All vessels that can sail are leaving as soon as they've been cleared and all incoming shipping is being diverted to other places. That, I imagine, is by mutual consent of the owners and the Port Authority. I wouldn't argue about it anyway. Everybody's interviewing everybody else on TV about what might be going on and there are some pretty wild theories flying around. My favourite was contributed by a visiting fireman from Utah who's beating the Russian drum loudly and reckons that a *Spetsnaz* detachment is responsible. Then there was a "Hand of God" advocate you'd have enjoyed. He looked quite disappointed when it was suggested to him that if the Almighty had been responsible He'd have used His hand to rather more effect. Here you are. Get this inside you.'

Townsend picked up the tray of food he had been preparing, placed it on Shaw's stomach and fetched him a can of Budweiser from the refrigerator. Shaw thanked him and asked if that was all. There was a hint of disappointment in the question and that made Townsend grin.

'Not quite,' he said. 'The Army, or the National Guard, or whoever, is out in force, the sky's full of choppers, the airline schedules are all shot because everybody is getting searched, and there are so many frogmen queuing up to jump in the water that they'll probably have to issue them with tickets soon. It isn't just confined to New York either. There are reports coming in from all over, and people have started

155

sighting everything from submarines to UFOs. As I said, you're causing concern.'

'What about casualties?'

'None that I know of, except the bloke I killed.'

'When was that?'

'When I pulled you out of the river. He turned up just at the wrong moment.'

'Oh yes,' Shaw said. 'I think I remember, but I'm not sure. Something – somebody fell, didn't they?' Without waiting for an answer he added, 'All I'm clear about is feeling pretty desperate because I thought you weren't at the rendezvous. That was a bad few seconds.'

'What were you expecting me to do, Harry? Jump up and down yelling "Come in Number Eight, your time's up"?'

Shaw shook his head. 'Now that you mention it, no. Thanks for the rescue act.'

'My pleasure.'

'Bill.'

'Yeah?'

'You mentioned eleven damaged ships. I wonder what happened to the other three bombs.'

'I've been trying to figure that out,' Townsend said. 'My theory is that you got hit, presumably by a boat, when you'd nearly finished the job. So you switched over to automatic pilot and used up three bombs on your last target in case you foundered with all hands.' He gestured towards the TV set and added, 'If that's right it doesn't make me psychic. They've said several times that the explosion at the ship that sank was much heavier than the others.'

'All I can remember is getting into the water and just before you pulled me out. Nothing in between.'

'Well don't worry about it,' Townsend told Shaw. 'It's a condition called retroactive amnesia and can be self-induced in the comfort of your own home by striking your head with a mallet. It's a technique I employ when I've done something I might regret if I knew what it was. Now, finish your supper and watch some re-runs about yourself while I go out and pick up the newspapers. I didn't want to leave you before.'

The television showed Shaw a ship with its stern under water and a recovery vessel twice the size alongside it. There were a lot of frogmen going calmly about their tasks, brushing aside a man with a microphone who sounded excited enough to be reporting the closing stages of a horse race. The clip, taken in daylight, was obviously hours old and Shaw switched channels to be shown Kennedy, La Guardia and Newark airports, Grand Central and Pennsylvania railroad stations, and the bus terminals. There were soldiers at each place, looking simultaneously stoic and puzzled as if wondering what they were supposed to be doing. The third button he pressed brought him a concert from the Lincoln Center, the fourth a group discussion on AIDS, but with the fifth he was back in business, watching a close-up of the rudder of a ship in dry dock. A pretty girl-reporter wearing a safety helmet as though it were an exotic piece of millinery was pointing to a brightly scarred area of metal with a vertical crack running through it. It seemed to Shaw that the workmen surrounding her were about equally divided between those content for her to stay as long as she liked and others anxious to get on with repairing the damage.

Townsend came in then with a bundle of newspapers under his arm. '"Mad Bombers Strike Again" has it by a short head over "New York Paralysed",' he announced. 'I think the latter's something of an overstatement, but that's the prerogative of editors, isn't it? Like the royal we. But this is the best.'

Shaw took the tabloid from him. In letters a foot high, the front page of the *Daily News* asked 'WHO?'

'Tell them, Bill,' he said.

18

In a country inured to terrorism within its borders on an almost daily basis, the British newspapers gave less prominence to the events in the United States than their New York counterparts, but they still made the front page. Having returned to his headquarters at Hereford from a NATO exercise in Norway only that morning, the SAS colonel read the article surrounding a photograph of a partly sunken ship with interest. According to the paper's Washington correspondent the current rash of outrages could be attributed to anybody from Cubans to Iranians, and Sandinistas to domestic subversive elements, depending on whom he had spoken to last. It was not until he listened to *The World at One* on his office radio that the colonel learned that responsibility had been claimed by an organisation calling itself the 'Hands Off Ulster Regiment'.

It was seven seconds before the appropriate electrical circuits in his brain linked to allow the passage of thought towards his speech centre and form the murmured words 'Bloody hell. I bet that's Shaw.'

Listening to the same broadcast, Sarah Cheyney arrived at conviction five seconds before the colonel's synapses closed on suspicion. She put her hands over her eyes. Half a minute later and a hundred and fifty miles to the west and north of her, the colonel picked up a telephone.

'There's a policeman to see you, doctor. He says he's from Special Branch.'

Sarah Cheyney felt sharp anxiety, but no surprise at all. 'Put him in the little reception room and tell him five minutes, please,' she said to her receptionist.

'Yes, doctor.'

When she had finished writing out her prescriptions she crossed the hall and a small man rose to his feet at her entry.

'It's Sergeant Fenner, isn't it?'

'That's right, doctor. They sent me because we've met before.' He smiled quickly at his own recollection of the occasion and added, 'We're anxious to establish the whereabouts of Captain Shaw and thought perhaps you could help us.'

Sarah Cheyney found herself fingering the stethoscope hanging from her neck, stopped doing it and asked, 'Why? Is he in some sort of trouble?'

'Not that I know of, miss – er, doctor. We just want to know where he is.'

'He's in Canada, travelling around on business.'

'Are you sure about that?'

'It was in his last letter.'

'May I see it?'

'I suppose so,' she said. 'I'll fetch it.'

She went upstairs, took the letter from her desk and brought it to him.

'I'd be grateful if you didn't read the front page. It's rather personal and wouldn't tell you anything more than that we're lovers.'

'Of course.'

Fenner read the back of the letter, then: 'He signs himself "Whitey" – Oh, I see. Yes. Quite.' For a moment he looked as embarrassed as she remembered him doing on Jermyn Street before saying, 'This charity he refers to. Can you tell me anything about it?'

'Yes, he was sent to set up some sort of rehabilitation centre in New York, but found it too pricey. Now he's trying Canada as he says there.'

'He was sent, you say. Do you know by whom?'

It required an almost physical act of will of Sarah Cheyney to prevent herself biting her lip. Why had she said that? Did it matter? Wouldn't they find out anyway through the banks?

'By a philanthropist called Joseph Stein,' she said. 'He's something or other in the City.'

Please God, don't let him ask me about interrogations under drugs, or the Canary Islands, or William Townsend, or why I'm so sure that he's working with you, Harry, even if being given a lovely present bought from the Steuben Glass people in Manhattan is only circumstantial evidence. He's such a close friend of yours that you must surely know that he'd been in the same city. Why did you never mention that, Harry?

'What? Oh no. I'm afraid I don't know Mr Stein's address. Do you want my receptionist to see if it's listed in the phone book?'

'Thank you, doctor, but that won't be necessary. Can you tell me how he and Captain Shaw met?'

Do you remember how pleased we were to be asked out as a couple, Harry? I'm not having them bothering dear old Solly. I refuse to have my patients badgered!

'I've no idea,' Sarah Cheyney said.

Sergeant Fenner didn't ask her anything else, not even if she would let him know when Harry next contacted her, and that made her wonder if her mail and telephone were going to be tampered with.

'I have a built-in distrust of all beautiful women,' Sergeant Fenner said. 'That gets magnified when one of them looks like a black high-fashion model masquerading as a doctor, and it goes right through the roof when she has already made a fool of me, which is why you sent me, I suppose.'

'Very perceptive of you, George. Is this your roundabout way of telling me that you think she's telling the truth?'

'All I'm saying is that I don't think she has any precise idea where Shaw is now. I announced myself to the receptionist as being from the Branch, but the magic words didn't seem to throw our doctor much. She kept me waiting for a few minutes, then walked in looking like – well, I already told you what she looks like, guv. She wasn't exactly calm, but then you'd hardly expect her to be when the law arrives and asks questions about her boyfriend, would you?'

'Maybe she was too calm,' the Inspector said. 'Could be she knows what's going on and had anticipated your visit.'

'Could be. Particularly as Joseph Stein's statement makes our doctor either a very forgetful lady, or a liar. He says he was introduced to Shaw and her at Sir Soloman Gold's earlier in the year. Gold's the banker. Why would she forget that meeting? Want me to run communications surveillance on her?'

'On the basis of the suspicions of an Army colonel and a possible female fib? You must be out of your mind. The Home Secretary would have my guts for garters.'

'Pity you spotted that, guv.' Fenner said. 'I was hoping to get your job.'

The Mossad agent who broke into Shaw's London apartment searched it very thoroughly. When he had failed to find what he was looking for he began all over again. Men always had photographs of themselves somewhere, even if only as one of a group, a school, a team or, in this case, a regiment. Shaw could have told him that he was wasting his time. He had never kept a scrapbook and the SAS was very particular about not getting itself photographed in the first place.

Accepting failure eventually the agent put everything back exactly as he had found it, reset the intruder alarm he had neutralised and left the flat. Fifteen minutes later he was at the Israeli embassy talking by scrambler to the man in Tel Aviv known unofficially as 'The Suit', because he was alleged to be the only government official who habitually wore one.

As soon as the brief exchange was over, the man in the city suit phoned the embassy in Washington DC and ended the conversation by saying, 'We can't wait any longer. Start at the Bridenthal end. I'm more convinced than ever that he stumbled upon something.'

The man who had taken the call took the shuttle to New York and a cab to Greenwich village and the first of the two addresses known to Stein which Shaw had used.

'Yeah?'

He held a photograph of Bridenthal towards the woman who had opened the door at his ring and asked, 'You recognise this guy, lady?'

'You a cop?'

'Private licence.'

'Get lost.'

'There's a reward.'

The door ceased its closing movement.

'Let me see that licence again.'

The licence in one hand and the photograph in the other the Mossad man waited.

'Sure I recognise him,' she said. 'He came here maybe a week back in the middle of the goddam night asking for some guy.'

'Do you remember the name?'

'No.'

'Was it MacGregor?'

'No, it wasn't as long as that.'

'Then it was probably Shaw.'

'You know something?' the woman said. 'That's exactly who he asked for.'

When he had thanked her and written down her name in connection with the imaginary reward he took another cab to West 14th Street. The apartment there was empty, as were most of the others in the building, and he had to wait until people began to return home from their jobs at five thirty in the evening before he could continue with his enquiries. The occupant of the apartment immediately below the one Shaw had rented recognised Bridenthal.

'I only ever saw him the once,' he said. 'Fell off a chair upstairs fixing a light bulb and hurt his knee. The crash woke me. Then I saw him when his friend took him to hospital. This guy in the picture looked real bad, like he was in shock.'

'Did you recognise the friend?'

'Yeah. Tall, dark Limey. He shared the place with the other two.'

'The other two what?'

'Limeys of course.'

'What did they look like?'

'One was a real big feller with a dent in the middle of his forehead. Kinda simple and slow, but he made amazing miniature railroad locomotives. He showed me one. Cutest damn thing, about as long as your finger. It worked too. Battery driven, I guess.'

162

'Sounds like a great hobby,' the man from Mossad said.

'Wasn't no hobby. He was at it, day in day out, until all hours.'

'And the third?'

'Blond kid. Moved like he was an athlete, or a middle-weight fighter, or some such, but he didn't look no more than seventeen. Eighteen maybe.'

'Thanks,' the man from Mossad said. He walked away looking for a public telephone, fighting down the urge to run.

Senator James Fairbridge had intended to move his family into a rented apartment in New York City, or the rooms he had in Washington DC, while the New Canaan house was stripped and redecorated, but the Bartholomews would have none of it. You'll interrupt the kids' schooling, they said. Marianne can keep an eye on the decorators from here and Caliban wouldn't like it in a city. He pointed out to them that by housing him they were making targets of themselves, but the Bartholomews wouldn't have any of that either, simply gesturing towards the policemen stamping their feet in the snow outside, and that was why he was sitting in their living-room talking to Special Agent-in-charge Charles Roetter of the FBI.

'It came in the morning mail,' he said. 'I'm sorry I've fingered it, but you can take my prints if you want to.'

Roetter made a dismissive gesture and took the letter from him. 'That won't be necessary, Senator. They handle everything with gloves. I'll have it checked out of course, but I'll be surprised if anything shows.' He read the typed message before adding. 'They change typewriters between each batch of mail too.'

'Uhuh. Have the others received this communication?'

'Some. We're getting in touch with the remainder, but it's looking like the same circulation as for the gas bombs thus far. What's your reaction to their demand, Senator?'

Fairbridge got up and walked to the window, then stood watching the Bartholomews' maid pouring something from a thermos into plastic cups for the policemen.

'They make a strong case. Two thousand dead and twenty-six thousand other casualties,' he said. 'I hadn't realised it was

163

anything like that bad but, having said that, I'm not about to be bullied into writing an open letter to the press forswearing future support for NORAID. That would be too much for any man. For a United States senator it's unthinkable. Did they send copies of that to the newspapers?'

Roetter nodded. 'Yes, with a complete list of names of the addressees, but we asked them not to publish. Not that that helped much. A couple of Canadian papers have already received and reproduced it and I expect it'll be given wide coverage in Britain and everywhere else. The wire services will see to that.'

'So much for my bid for the presidency.' It had been only a murmur.

'How's that again, Senator?'

'Nothing,' Fairbridge said. Then as though to cover his lapse he added hastily, 'It's a telling point of theirs questioning our right to be in California. I don't believe I had ever thought about it. How does it strike you?'

'Senator, I'm a law enforcement officer. It's not my job to make moral judgements.' When a quarter of a minute had gone by in silence, Roetter went on, 'It sounds like they're getting to you, sir.'

Her thermos empty now, the maid was making her way back to the house. She called something over her shoulder which made the policemen laugh.

'You may be right at that,' Fairbridge said.

Amongst the group of people who had been the targets of the gas bomb attack Senator Fairbridge was not alone in his self-questioning, but he was very much in the minority. The emotions of the greater number ranged from defiance coupled with fury at the suffering already inflicted upon them, to fear of what might follow should they fail to make the public statement the letter demanded of them. The regret expressed by those calling themselves the 'Hands Off Ulster Regiment' that they would be unable to give a guarantee of no further action against the addressees who failed to comply had been explicit enough.

Lieutenant Harvey Bergquist, who had listened to two angry citizens and one frightened one within the space of an hour, assured them that they would continue to receive round-the-clock police protection for the foreseeable future and passed the identical letters they had produced to the FBI, was turning his attention back to routine matters when Sergeant Mary Alton came into his office.

'It better be important,' he said.

'Two things, Lieutenant. Now the Navy divers are through looking for mines they've started bringing up bodies. One of them is the Port Authority watchman "Missing Persons" told us about. He died of a stab wound in the neck and was found near where he was supposed to be. That's at one of the two piers just above West 23rd Street where modernisation work is being done, or being half done. There's some pay dispute or other which has been dragging on for weeks and the union has banned night work. Second thing is they found a wetsuit and flippers nearby. The legs of the suit had been slit open with a knife, like maybe the wearer was injured and that was the easiest way of getting it off.'

'You're telling me that this team, one of them hurt, got out of the river at a pre-selected darkened pier, were seen by the watchman and killed him, right?'

'That's the theory I'm postulating.'

'Postulating,' Bergquist said. 'Christ, how I hate educated cops,' but he smiled when he said it.

'There's more, Lieutenant. The store tag had been cut from the suit, but there was a serial number inside a seam. That gave me the manufacturer and the manufacturer gave me the names of stores here in Manhattan they supply. I struck lucky at the third. Well, nearly lucky.'

'Meaning what?'

'The Feds were there ahead of me, so I just stood around and listened. The suit had been built for someone tall and they were asking the clerk if she remembered making a sale to anybody six foot or more. She told them the usual stuff about half the population being that height and that she sold a lot of the things, then recalled one guy who had stuck in her memory because he was pretty good-looking in a dark way and had a fancy Limey accent. It's little enough to go on, but . . .' Sergeant Alton let the rest of the sentence hang in the air.

'Did the Feds know you were a cop?'

'No, Lieutenant. I was just a woman looking at scuba gear. They didn't so much as glance at me.'

'Oh great. Now when they tell me about it I can say I know already.'

Sergeant Alton's mouth twitched in irritation and she was almost at the doorway when Bergquist said, 'Mary.'

Surprised, she turned back again. He had only once called her that before and that had been on the day she had received her promotion.

'Lieutenant?'

'That was very well done,' Bergquist told her.

'In summation,' 'The Suit' said, 'on a probability factor greatly in excess of a bare hypothesis we are left with little option but to conclude that Shaw killed Bridenthal and that the tribulations currently afflicting the Americans have been unwittingly financed by Stein and masterminded by Shaw, with the big fellow as his bomb maker and the blond man his muscle. Are we agreed?'

Three of the men in the screened room in Tel Aviv nodded. The fourth gave no sign.

'Do you have doubts, Eli?'

'Not really. I was just admiring your blending of grandiloquence with the colloquial and trying to figure out what you meant. I've got it now and, yes, I agree.'

There was no trace of annoyance in the other's voice when he said, 'Very well. In that case it follows that Shaw and his party are not in North Africa, never had any intention of going there to do the job they were hired to do, and that their activities in the Canary Islands were designed to disguise those facts. Suggestions?'

'Well, we can't alert the Americans to what's going on, that's for sure. The last thing we can afford is to have Shaw made to tell what he knows.'

'The Suit' nodded at the speaker before saying, 'Eli?'

'We must contact Gadaffi and suggest that he rigs the destruction of the assault team and produces bodies in evidence. After that, the operation can proceed as planned. It would probably have been much simpler had we followed that course in the first place, but that's hindsight speaking. There was no way of forecasting Shaw's defection.'

'Who will you use as intermediary?'

'Tariq bin Bukhari, I think. Gadaffi trusts him. Goodness knows why, but he does.'

'Do it,' 'The Suit' said, 'and do it as a matter of urgency. It will take time to set up and time is of the essence now. It's imperative that we act before Shaw is taken by the Americans and forced to speak.'

'Will Gadaffi play ball?' The question came from one of the junior men.

'Oh, he'll play all right,' Eli told him. 'He's dying to have another crack at Cyprus and, with his plans so far advanced, he won't let a little thing like the absence of any genuine British provocation stand in his way.'

19

'I've been thinking, Bill.'

Nodding gravely, Townsend said. '"It is a kind of poetry".'

'What is?'

'Thinking is. That's according to Havelock Ellis, psychologist, author and scientist.'

'Does he know anything about electronics?'

Townsend shook his head. 'Not a damn thing. Sex was his strong suit. Anyway, he died in 1939.'

'Do you feel better now?' Shaw asked him.

'Yes, thanks. I'll let you know when I detect the symptoms of another attack coming on. What have you been thinking about?'

'Computers.'

'Oh my God, I should have guessed! I can't even work a pocket calculator and I've never seen you use one either.'

'We could always learn.'

'What for?'

Shaw didn't answer directly. 'One thing I certainly hadn't anticipated,' he said, 'was our inability to locate any central NORAID organisation. I'd pictured an office set-up housing their records of subscribers, their bank accounts, their shopping lists for military hardware and their suppliers. If we could have blown that to bits we'd have set them back years and by then the situation in Ulster would probably have been resolved.'

He fell silent, but Townsend didn't say anything. They'd been over the point weeks earlier, but if Harry wanted to think aloud that was all right by him. Half a minute went by before Shaw began to speak again.

'And there has to be a lot more to it than that, Bill. They must have staff and equipment for forging fraudulent manifests and "end user" certificates for arms. There's likely to be a narcotics store for transactions with members of the armed forces, to avoid the risk of cash being traced back to the buyer. The names of those contacts must be recorded somewhere, together with others with a drug dependency, or who are open to extortion and blackmail for any other reason. Then what about the heavy mobs they use for stealing from arsenals and hijacking military supply trucks? Think what it would have meant to us to disrupt a network like that.'

Still Townsend didn't speak and Shaw said, 'I've talked about all that before, haven't I?'

'Most of it. I hadn't thought about the drug angle. Where do computers come into it, Harry?'

As though he hadn't heard the question Shaw went on, 'It's pathetic! Apart from those people we know by their own admission to be financially supporting the IRA, the only other active participants I've set eyes on are men with collecting cans in Boston bars, for Pete's sake!'

'The computers, Harry.'

'Ah yes, the computers. Well, in my opinion our failure to pinpoint NORAID is a considerable defeat. There are those we could lean on for the information, of course, but at the end of it we'd have to kill them or we'd be blown. Anyway, I draw the line at physical torture. That would be sinking to the level of the IRA, so I've been looking at other targets like the manufacturers of the Stinger missile they want to get their hands on. Have you read any of this stuff?'

Townsend took the newspaper clipping held out to him and began to read it. 'Hackers threaten havoc' the headline proclaimed and the first column told him of a bank swindled out of a considerable sum of money by computer fraud. From the remaining columns he re-read what he already knew of operators falsifying or destroying records, altering computer commands, programming a thing called 'a logic time-bomb' and compounding the resultant confusion by the insertion of 'a computer virus' whereby illicit instructions would regenerate themselves indefinitely and probably permanently. Phrases like 'irreparable damage' and 'catastrophic collapse' were used and it was stated that a number of companies had been forced to cease trading as a result of electronic sabotage.

'I suppose,' Townsend said, 'it was the reference to amateurs having created this sort of shambles that induced your brainstorm.'

'Yes.'

'Marvellous! It says here that the hacker would enter an organisation's computer system at one "node" in order to initiate erroneous commands in another at the receiving end, and that all you need to become a do-it-yourself "node" is a small computer, a telephone line and a mains electricity supply. It doesn't say what you do next, but I suppose you've taken out a subscription for *Happy Hacking Weekly* and know all about that.'

'I've learned enough, Bill. Enough to make it worth trying. I must do more. I must do everything I can. Many lives depend on the outcome of this operation. You don't need me to tell you that.'

'No,' Townsend said, 'and I don't need you to tell me that you've finally flipped either. It must have been that crack on the head you got. Listen, Harry, my experience of officers is that they always want too much. Take one enemy strong-point and they have to have the next. I'm glad I never had a commission, as that spares me that compulsion. When all this started you asked me to act as Devil's Advocate if I felt you were pushing things too far, remember?'

'Of course.'

'Then let me say this. First, you and I are professionals and we've come through a lot together since the Falklands because we never did anything amateurish, which is what you're suggesting we do now. Second, you're expecting too much because, regardless of what Logo may think, this is not Port Stanley and no way are they going to raise a white flag over the White House whatever we do. Are you with me?'

Shaw moved restlessly in his chair. His face was as impassive as ever, but there was irritation in his voice when he said, 'I hear what you say, but I don't think much of your advocacy. On your first point, one doesn't ignore a potentially valuable weapon simply because it's unfamiliar and your second – well, that's daft. We're trying to affect public opinion not, even allowing you some poetic licence, to defeat a nation.'

'You just stated my case for me,' Townsend told him. 'We want what we do to be seen by as many people as possible. Why hide our light under a bushel for a doubtful return? Listen, I know that computer programmers are notoriously lax with their private coding and are inclined to use something easy to remember. That makes the hacker's job quite simple. All he needs to do is feed in every girl's name ever invented, the presidents of the United States, the days of the week, the signs of the Zodiac, plus a few other lists and at the one million and fifteenth combination of letters, bingo! He's got the key.'

'So?'

'So that takes time and as I'm expecting a SWAT squad to burst in here any moment now I doubt we have a lot of that left. Even if the authorities obligingly sit around picking their noses for another month, what would you have got? Half a dozen very worried members of the board of directors of a factory in North Dakota, or wherever, who'll do their utmost to keep the whole thing under wraps. I call that indifferent public relations and a poor return on investment. We're in propaganda, not the Ministry of Economic Warfare, or whatever it was called back in World War Two.'

Shaw said, 'Hmm.' It was a neutral sound, indicating neither acceptance nor disagreement, but he seemed to put the matter beyond doubt when he added, 'You have an offensively insubordinate habit of being right, Sergeant.'

'Cheer up,' Townsend told him. 'Thursday night is railway night. That should be good for a laugh. I'll fix us something to eat before we bugger up the New York subway system.'

Townsend moved towards the cooker and Shaw's eyes followed him, but he was seeing an elegant dark-skinned girl in a shoulderless evening dress of gold, with a matching band of metal around her forehead and her hair plaited into bejewelled strands. 'Tuesday night is ethnic night,' she was saying and the visual and aural memories made him suddenly absurdly happy.

*

They avoided appearing together in public now and Townsend left the tiny apartment first. He boarded an IRT Flushing Line subway train at Times Square and travelled by stages through Queens, changing trains at random points, allowing several to pass before boarding another. At each change his briefcase grew lighter. There were numerous concealed spots in a subway car where their magnetic clamps would hold Logo's devices securely in place and, choosing his moment carefully, Townsend varied the placing as much as possible. The best time, he found, was when passengers were preoccupied with getting on or off.

Halfway back to Manhattan on his return journey he disposed of his last bomb, wondering if any one train now carried two of them, not caring if it did, because that would add to the confusion. With over 7,000 cars in the system a lot of people were going to be very busy searching them all.

Shaw, travelling up and down the island of Manhattan almost at right-angles to Townsend's course, followed a similar procedure. Until now he had avoided using New York's underground transport facilities and felt slightly bemused by the paint-sprayed graffiti which made a surrealistic nightmare of the carriages. A bizzarely decorated southbound train stopped beside him shortly after midnight and he got into an empty car, immediately planted his penultimate bomb and sat back to wait for the next logical stop. That was when two blacks entered the car at opposite ends through the communicating doors. Each carried a knife in his right hand.

The one to Shaw's left was the closer and the first to die. With no lapse of time between realisation and reaction Shaw reached him in five long strides, parried the expected knife-thrust with his briefcase and drove the stiffened fingers of his upturned hand into the mugger's solar-plexus. His central nervous system paralysed, the man folded forward from the waist like a puppet whose strings had been cut, then straightened again abruptly when a knee smashed against the underside of his chin.

Nor was there any break in Shaw's practised movements when he picked up the fallen knife by the blade, whirled around and threw it in a flat trajectory at the man nearing the mid-

172

point of the clattering, rocking car. The knife buried to the handle in his abdomen, the man's fingers clutched at it and the look of amazed horror on his face made a short-lived cliché before he toppled headlong to the floor.

Shaw sighed gustily, a sharp exhalation of breath as though he himself had been struck in the stomach, then moved the bodies together. Not, he knew, that that would fool anybody for very long, but then he didn't need very long. A deserted platform, or a few seconds to blend with a crowd would do. The logical stop was the next one now and he waited tensely by the doors for the brakes to come on.

It was a small eternity until they did so and the station slid into his field of view. People – not many – waiting. The train slowing, stopping. A couple standing, talking, immediately outside, ignoring the train. Deeply shaken, Shaw got off and walked away, not looking back. He was waiting for an outcry, but none came. Ten blocks away he flagged down a taxi, his nerves still taut.

The double killing did not affect him particularly. That had been a matter of self-defence and he felt satisfaction in the proof that there had been no blunting, through disuse, of his finely honed reflexes. What concerned him, and continued to do so, was evidence of the frailty of the foundations of his campaign. Law enforcement agencies of numerous kinds and various nationalities would be interesting themselves not yet in him necessarily but in his activities. So much had not only been certain from the beginning, but had been a necessary part of his strategy, and he still felt that he had time in hand, however clever they might be, before he was finally tracked down amongst the teeming millions of New York City. What he had not catered for was an incident such as that night's when an entirely extraneous and unrelated force had touched him.

Accepting that catering for the unforeseen was a contradiction in itself, and that his SAS training had equipped him better than most to deal with the unexpected, calmed Shaw, but left him angry with himself for succumbing to irrational anxiety. Fear that his nerve might be failing him grew out of the anger and persuaded him finally that Townsend had been right about the use of computers. The sands, be they of courage or circumstance, were beginning to run out and the luxury of prolonged subtleties could not be afforded.

His briefcase under his arm to conceal the knife-slit, Shaw paid off the cab half a mile from the apartment and began to walk. It was bitterly cold and pale phantoms of steam escaped from man-hole covers peopling the night streets.

'I'll be after tellin' you this only the once, so get it right,' Townsend said, using a lilting Irish accent of which he was rather proud, and the man he had been connected with at *The New York Times* replied 'Shoot' in a bored voice.

'The "Hands Off Ulster Regiment" wishes you to know that there's a bomb or two, or maybe fifty, on the New York subway system,' Townsend told him. 'They're set to detonate in about twenty-four hours, but with the shoddy workmanship you get nowadays there's no guaranteein' they'll not explode earlier than that. Be a darlin' man and spread the glad tidin's, will you now?' He paused for a moment before adding, 'If you're a wise little virgin you'd best mention the buses as well. Let's not be forgettin' the buses.'

A voice which was no longer bored was saying something he didn't hear when he replaced the receiver and left the public call box. There were no bombs on the buses yet, but there would be on one of them when he planted it later in the morning. For some reason not yet explained, Harry had brought it back with him from his outing. They had agreed that it should be enough to disrupt that service too because the authorities would have no choice but to search every vehicle.

Eyes watchful, shoulders hunched against the biting wind, Townsend strode back to So Ho picturing the dislocation of the city's transport his phone call would produce. Since the invention of the automobile, the Americans were less inclined to walk anywhere than any other nation on earth and Townsend concluded that several million of them were in for a new experience.

Having more money now than he knew what to do with, Logo had bought himself a large television set because it was easier to watch that than read the newspapers when he wanted to find out how the war was going. He had particularly enjoyed the scenes of what he took to be Special Boat Service frogmen getting in and out of the water blowing up Argie ships, although it puzzled him that they should have allowed the pictures to be taken because the SBS didn't like being photographed any more than the SAS did. It annoyed him a little that all the other really good programmes like *Blue Peter* and *The Muppets* were shown either in the afternoon when he was asleep or early in the morning when he was still at his workbench, but he had solved that problem by buying himself a video recorder so that he could watch his favourites at a reasonable hour and limited his live viewing to the 10.00 p.m. news.

Today that had been encouraging and when it had ended with the reporter saying 'This is Charles Warren, *News at Ten*, New York' he wished that he had taped that too so that he could watch it again.

People, thousands of people, had been shown milling about at the locked entrances to subway stations and the bus terminals while policemen with bull-horns tried to explain to them that no trains or buses were running. Some of the people seemed to accept that, but couldn't get away because of all the pushing and shoving by those who hadn't heard, or didn't believe what they were being told. It was all very entertaining until two women fell down and got trampled on and had to be taken to hospital in an ambulance. Logo was sorry about that because one of them was pretty enough to have been his mother, but he had cheered up again at the sight of cars bumper to bumper, most of them blowing their horns, locked in a solid traffic jam on East River Drive and two men leaving their vehicles and punching each other. The smaller of them appeared to be winning and Logo was silently urging him on when the scene had disappointingly shifted to an important-looking man saying important things about leaving no stone unturned and this being one haystack in which the needle would inevitably be found. That had made him smile because more than 10,000 Argies had tried to find Bill Townsend before, and failed.

Logo programmed his video to record the next morning's *Muppet Show*, then settled down at his workbench.

Lieutenant Commander Eugene Todd, USN retired, had dismantled explosive devices in both Korea and Vietnam and had lost count of the number of times he had done it. He was getting on a bit now and did not feel that being told he was amongst the best in the business was sufficient recompense for having to lie on the floor of a New York subway car to do it again. He had been given the FBI reports on the gas bombs to read and photographs of the damage to shipping sabotaged in the harbour. The first revealed that activation had been caused by a photo-electric cell, and the second that the explosions had been powerful, but almost certainly not strong enough to indicate the use of military-grade material if the canisters had been of the same size as the one he was now looking at. Not, he reminded himself, that that would make the slightest difference to him if the thing blew up where it was, under the seat and within inches of his face.

They'd persuaded him to wear cumbersome protective clothing and a helmet with a toughened plexiglass visor, but he knew that wouldn't help him either. All it did was make his already overweight body that much more difficult to contort in the confined space available to it. He said 'Shit' in a quiet voice, but the microphone at his throat carried the word clearly to the men crouching behind the hastily erected barrier of sandbags down the platform from him.

'You OK, Gene?'

Not bothering to answer the question his earphones had asked him, he removed his helmet and them with it, then took the Polaroids they had taken of the object from his pocket to see if they could tell him anything his eyes could not. Beyond showing him the canister from angles the camera had reached where his head could not follow, they told him nothing. Dropping them on the floor he took out a stethoscope and listened for a long minute, but all he heard was the surge of his own blood.

Todd located the magnetic clamps by sliding a spatula into the tiny space between the bomb and the car. 'So what did you expect? Glue?' he asked and the helmet on the floor beside him twittered something he didn't hear. There was a copper hammer amongst the non-magnetic tools in the long pocket attached to his left thigh. He drew it out and tapped the bomb casing sharply. It produced a dull thud with no resonance at all, but from behind him came the sound of breath sharply drawn in. Turning his head, he looked at the man from the FBI whose name and presence he had completely forgotten.

'Why,' Todd said, 'don't you go the fuck someplace else? You're making me nervous.' Getting only a frown in reply he added, 'Go on. Beat it. I'm not going to do another fucking thing until you're behind those sandbags.'

Watching Special Agent-in-charge Charles Roetter leave the car and walk away along the platform, Todd wondered why he had talked that way, why he had always talked that way. He had done it once to a US Navy vice-admiral which was why he had never got further than lieutenant commander. 'Fuck him too,' he said and turned back to his task, feeling not in the least nervous. Being superstitious about numbers, that emotion had dropped from him after he had dealt successfully with his thirteenth under-water beach obstacle leaving only a sense of dull resignation.

'You guys listening?' he asked and the helmet at his side twittered what he took to be an affirmative.

'OK, so hear this. Looking at this damn thing gives me a big negative, like the X-rays did. The device has magnetic clamps and I'm going to jerk it loose to see what happens. The subway is likely to lose one railcar, but that's just too bad. Could be there's a triggering link to the clamps. Could be it's radio-controlled. Could be it has a rocker firing mechanism. Could be the timing is by acid, or battery-powered clock.' Todd paused before adding, 'Could be any of those things, or all of them. What it is not is magnetic, heat, light, pressure or sound sensitive, and it isn't clockwork either.'

Beside him his helmet was talking urgently. What it was saying he had no idea, but as though he had heard its words he said, 'OK, OK, don't get steamed up. If I ever possessed suicidal tendencies I lost them way back. What I want you to do is build me a hollow square of sandbags, three by three by three feet, ten yards in back of this car. That's away from you, I mean. Do it fast before this thing makes up its own mind to blow up.'

Listening to the sound of voices and the footsteps of people carrying heavy weights along the platform behind him but not bothering to glance in that direction, Todd took a ball of string from a pocket, secured its end around the bomb with a clove hitch and backed out of the railcar, the ball unravelling as he went. The small block-house of sandbags was in position where he had ordered it to be and the men who had built it were sprinting towards the shelter of their own protective wall. He clambered down on to the track, placing the bulk of the car between himself and the position of the bomb and drew the string taut.

'I'm going to try to dislodge it now,' he told his throat mike and wondered cynically if his discarded helmet had received an acknowledgement. Nothing happened when he pulled at the string, so he jerked it savagely and felt it go slack. Without pause he hauled himself on to the platform and went back the way he had come, unaware that he was doing it on the tips of his toes.

The bomb was lying just inside the doorway of the car. 'Twenty-four seconds,' it said. 'Twenty-three seconds.'

Todd picked it up and loped to the square of sandbags while it talked to him in a high-pitched monotone. It was saying 'Fifteen seconds' when he placed it carefully on the ground inside the blast walls.

'OK, OK,' Todd muttered, then turned and ran for his life, his lips silently continuing the countdown. He cleared the protective barrier where the others crouched, arms and legs flailing, landed heavily and said, 'I'm too old for this kinda –'

Concussion. A flat, slamming bellow of sound which seemed to grow as the tunnel tossed it from wall to wall and floor to ceiling like some gigantic bass instrument until the pressure dissipated and there was only the humming of shocked ears, drifting dust and the sight of dislodged masonry falling on to the track. There was sand everywhere.

'Worked real good, didn't it?' Todd said.

Roetter stared at him. 'Jesus! Is that all you found out?'

'No. I found out how it works, and that means I know what

to do now. The guys who made these things are tricky but not nasty. They've given us a break.'

'Like what?'

'Like run like hell. That's what the tape's for, to tell you to beat it. I had to be sure they'd built that warning into these explosive versions as well as into the gas bombs.'

The FBI man continued to stare at Todd for a long moment before saying, 'Oh, that's great. That's really great. So all we have to do is trigger them as we find them, move out of harm's way and watch the roof fall in all over the subway system. Right?'

'You,' Todd said, 'are an asshole. Why don't you go sleuth, or whatever it is we pay the Feds to do?' He turned his back then and spoke to the chief petty officer in charge of the Navy bomb squad.

'Jake.'

'Sir?'

'Figure this through with me and stop me the minute you think I'm talking crap, OK?'

'Sure.'

'OK. That little box was heavy, much heavier than you'd expect, so I guess it was lead-lined. That could be to inhibit X-ray examination of the works, or an attempt to prevent us magnetising them. Perhaps it's just there to act as a tamper and increase the blast effect, but that seems a tad elaborate.' For several seconds Todd massaged the shoulder he had fallen on, then said, 'Doesn't matter anyway. The tape is an integral part of the firing mechanism and that has to be battery-powered and that is the key to the problem. Whether the tape is set in motion by disengaging the magnetic clamps, by a mercury tilt or by a timer is largely irrelevant. If it doesn't run the bomb doesn't detonate, so we stop it running.'

'How?'

Ignoring Roetter's question Todd continued to address the chief petty officer. 'Jake, if we freeze the damn things there'll be zero voltage coming out of the batteries, right?'

'Right, sir?'

'So, OK, I never heard of a tape running on zero voltage, so let's do it. We'll need flasks of liquid nitrogen. Fix it so they can be carried in a back harness or some such, and arrange for them to be issued to all the other teams unless they have a better idea. Not that it matters much but the stuff will also freeze the mercury if there is any. Can do?'

'Sure can,' the chief petty officer said and began to talk into his radio handset.

His job finished, reaction struck Todd. It took the form of extreme tiredness as it always had since he had passed out of the nervous phase ending with his thirteenth device, but he felt he should make an effort, make amends for being gratuitously rude. He turned to Roetter.

'I'm sorry I talked the way I did. I get a little frayed at the edges sometimes.'

Roetter smiled at him. 'Forget it. They tell me you stayed unfrayed long enough to win a Navy Cross in Nam.'

The hint of camaraderie destroyed Todd's good resolution. 'Ah, go puke in your hat,' he said.

20

Apprehension and distrust hung over the city like a shroud. Lieutenant Bergquist could sense it in the precinct building from the overly casual stance of the patrolmen with their thumbs hooked into their belts and in the exaggerated slouching postures of the people in the detectives' room. He could see it in the carefully controlled expressions of television announcers and hear it in the irritable tones of the crowds of pedestrians in the streets, crowds that had grown in size almost beyond belief. He could feel it inside himself.

Not that he was apprehensive for himself. Virtually the only time he experienced that emotion was when confronted by his sister's dog, a small hairy rug of a creature which had developed an ungovernable loathing for his ankles. The source of his disquiet was his in-basket, its contents flowing across his desk in mute evidence of an alarming upsurge in crime of many types. The knowledge that such a manifestation of lawlessness was the inevitable consequence of so many policemen being transferred to anti-terrorist duties, both on their own and in co-operation with the military, was no consolation at all. Nor, he felt, had the President's remarks on nationwide television about not leaving stones unturned and finding needles in haystacks been particularly helpful with their bland assumption of victory over an enemy which continued to remain invisible. They had simply increased the demands for results directed at such as his Captain and himself from the Governor to the Mayor to the Police Commissioner, as well as the media and the public. The District Attorney's office was not helping either.

Such results as there had been were defensive in character. A

Navy officer had swiftly devised a method of neutralising the bombs on the subway and, with so many thousands to be searched, it was hardly his fault that three railcars had been destroyed by explosions when the twenty-four-hour warning expired with some hundred of them still to be examined. The system was believed to be clear now, but the trains would not run again until every yard of tunnel, every maintenance shop and every station had been declared safe. It occurred to Bergquist that that at least freed the police for the time being from the duty of riding the trains as guards against further attack, but he found no consolation in that either.

The buses were a different matter. One city bus had blown up at its terminal, setting fire to four others, but no further bombs had been found and the vehicles, both local and long distance, were being allowed back on the roads after inspection. The fact that they were inspected again at frequent intervals did little to persuade the public to use them. Private cars jammed the streets and taxi drivers charged exorbitant prices.

Immediately after reports of the stalling of the New York City transport system had been broadcast, the man with the Irish voice had spoken to one of the television stations, warning of similar action in Boston, Chicago and Washington DC. So far, nothing to support the threat had been found in those cities but, with the example of New York before them, the authorities there had no choice but to suspend their equivalent services. Somewhat obscurely, bus drivers in Detroit and Cincinnati had come out on strike.

It had been cleverly done, Bergquist thought. First the gas bombs pinpointing individuals and their allegiance to a foreign cause. Next the attack on shipping to ensure international interest. Now the near-crippling of the most famous city in the United States and interspersed between those actions the reason for them explained by mail and phone to victims and the media. Millions of citizens across the country who had never heard of NORAID and, in all probability, would have failed to locate Ulster on the face of the globe, knew what and where they were now. Bleakly he wondered what was going to happen next.

*

Agustin and Luis Campeche happened next, their action a shocking prelude to a spate of telephone hoaxes from many parts of the country threatening airline targets, Amtrak railroad trains, St Patrick's Cathedral on Fifth Avenue and a host of other things from the Pentagon down to Al's Diner somewhere in the Bronx. Because there was no option, each warning was treated seriously with a consequent stretching of manpower resources, but the Campeche brothers gave no warning and they were not hoaxing.

In the basement of their West Side tenement home the nineteen-year-old Puerto Rican twins, excited by the events around them, made their own bombs out of fertiliser, and one of them worked appallingly well.

'You'd better catch this, Lieutenant,' Sergeant Alton said.

She had come into his room and pressed a button on the channel selector on the desk without pause or explanation. A picture leapt into life on the television screen in the corner before the door had closed behind her. It showed the George Washington Bridge seen from a helicopter and the huge structure appeared to be on fire for over a third of its length. A man's voice was saying '. . . and the emergency services estimate that . . .' when she stabbed at the 'mute' button and began talking herself.

'That's a playback, Lieutenant. A gasoline tanker exploded some five or six minutes ago. It's got worse since then. There are some thirty automobiles in that pile-up and – Oh Jesus.'

The last two words were spoken very softly and they both watched the screen in silence while five human figures engulfed in flames detached themselves one after the other from the bridge and fell like dying rockets on the Fourth of July towards the Hudson River far below. They seemed to take a very long time to reach it.

The picture changed to a live one of a man mouthing soundlessly at a camera. There were tears on his face, but that might have been because of the smoke swirling around him.

'They got a ground crew there already,' Bergquist said. 'That was quick.'

Mary Alton nodded emphatically as though he had said

something important. She depressed another button and the man's face, and the smoke, and the fire appliances in back of him, flicked out of existence as the human torches had done when they reached the merciful river.

'Accident?'

'In this of all weeks? You believe in Santa Claus, Sergeant?'

'We shouldn't jump to conclusions.'

'Oh sure. Pull the other one. It plays the "Star-spangled Banner".'

'It's not their – their style, Lieutenant. They haven't gone in for indiscriminate killing. They gave a warning over the subway and so did the bombs. In a crazy off-beat way they've even earned some goodwill in certain quarters. You've read the letters to the papers. Why would they want to throw that away?'

The light on one of Bergquist's phones began to blink. He lifted the receiver, grunted, listened for ten seconds, grunted again and replaced it.

'Somebody agrees with you, Sergeant.'

'Like who?'

'Like them,' Bergquist said. 'They just called the Mayor's office and disclaimed responsibility.'

The Campeche brothers were arrested by security guards inside the perimeter of a New Jersey oil refinery that night while they were attaching a home-made bomb to another tanker. Within two hours they had been arraigned on forty-one counts of first degree murder. It was to be much longer than that before the charred remains of bodies and road vehicles had been cleared from the George Washington Bridge and traffic flowed again.

'That's an outrageous suggestion,' the Home Secretary said, 'and the answer is an unequivocal "no". Where did Special Branch get this from? Defence?'

'Yes, Minister.'

'You tell them that if they think I'm going to authorise passing it, or his name, to the Americans they must be out of their minds. I will not have a British subject hounded on the basis of an Army colonel's brain-storm.' He tapped the photograph of

Shaw lying on his desk with a finger and added, 'Imagine copies of this plastered all over New York while he's fishing in Scotland or whatever. Talk about defamation of character! He could sue for millions and if I were the judge I'd see he got them! I can't imagine what the Branch is thinking of!'

'They agree with you,' the Parliamentary Private Secretary said. 'It's just that, with the situation in the States being so grave, they felt it should be a ministerial decision.'

'Oh, very droll. It's that man Travis trying to put ideas in my head. That's what's going on and I won't wear it. Do we have *any* idea where this fellow Shaw is?'

'He's believed to be in Canada, Minister.'

'Well, there you go,' the Home Secretary said. 'Put this damn thing in the shredder.'

Shaw hadn't needed to hit the bedroom door to tell Townsend that he was deeply distressed. That had been apparent when Shaw switched off the television set and said, 'If you quote me something about emulation being the sincerest form of flattery I'll hurt you, Bill.' It was the use of the word 'hurt' that had made Townsend blink. Anything more extravagant, like killing him, he would have ignored, but the milder word mildly spoken had been a statement of intent. Added confirmation came when Shaw pushed his steak aside untouched. Townsend had gone to a lot of trouble over preparing dinner, as he did with all his cooking, but that hadn't been the point. The point had been that when one wasn't in action one ate, or slept, or cleaned one's weapons, or exercised. If there was time, all those things had to be done, and Harry knew that better than most.

It was while Townsend was thinking about those pointers that Shaw left the table and paused in front of the door to the bedroom before driving his fist through its panelling. For a moment he contemplated the splintered wood, then murmured, 'Sorry about that,' and licked his grazed knuckles.

Townsend didn't say anything and Shaw added, 'Bad show, eh?'

'It's all right for sergeants and below,' Townsend said. 'Not for the upper classes. When officers start getting demonstrative I start getting worried. When you, of all people, do it I get scared. It's like watching the Iron Man developing metal fatigue. What the hell do you want to keep watching that blasted newscast for, anyway? You've seen it five times.'

Shaw muttered something that sounded like 'appalling' and began to wander around the small room, stopping to stare at objects as though he hadn't noticed them before. Townsend followed his aimless shambling with his eyes, eyes so much older than the face in which they were set, the face itself troubled now like that of a youth confused by some question in an examination paper. He sighed gustily and that brought Shaw's head sharply round to meet his gaze.

'Don't you find it appalling, Bill?'

'Difficult not to, but there's no point in working yourself into a lather about it. We've killed too, and there's a bloke in intensive care having bits of subway carriage pulled out of him, but it could have been a lot worse. But for the grace of God we could have had a massacre down there.'

'Grace of nothing,' Shaw said. 'We didn't have a massacre thanks to our warning, precision work by Logo, and an intelligent response by the authorities and the bomb disposal people. In addition, we declared our war, declared it immediately after the gas bombs. They should have listened if they didn't want casualties.' He licked his knuckles again before saying, 'None of which alters the fact that I'm responsible for the carnage on that bridge. I had anticipated the possibility of being copied but not – but not on that scale.'

Shaw's face remained as neutral as ever, but there was something close to dismay in his last sentence. Townsend heard it and heard too, for the second time, the words 'They should have listened if they didn't want casualties' when he replayed them in his mind like one of Logo's tapes. Oh, Harry, you're not making sense. No matter what you do, or how long you stay here doing it, they're not going to raise a white flag over the White House. I've told you that before, or something like it.

He didn't put his thoughts into words, saying only, 'It's time to go home, Harry. You've made your point and done it more positively than I'd have believed possible. Enough's enough.'

'No, it isn't. I haven't finished yet.'

'Well, make up your mind,' Townsend said. 'Either you stop,

or you get emulated some more. You can't have it both ways.'

Half a minute passed before Shaw spoke again. When he did so it was slowly, intensely.

'I want to leave them a longer-lasting, more visible reminder. Something they can all see and think about after we've gone. I *must* do that! You know the kind of visual impact I've got to create!'

'Yeah, I saw the movie. *The Towering Inferno* it was called. Can't remember who was in it, but a bloke called Dante wrote the film script.'

Shaw grunted impatiently, opened the bedroom door and began to pull off the jagged splinters surrounding the hole he had made. Townsend watched him doing it, his expression still troubled. It was so unlike Shaw to put the case for a project already planned, a project already executed to the extent of his having rented office space in a tall block on Sixth Avenue, that he knew that Shaw had been simply talking to reconvince himself of its desirability. If further evidence were needed of the damage the tragedy had done to Shaw's resolve, it was there.

Townsend gathered the dishes and took them to the sink. He had almost finished washing and drying them when, from behind him, Shaw said, 'We'll use a codeword when phoning in further warnings. That way they'll know they're genuine.'

The deaths in the holocaust on the George Washington Bridge had been genuine enough, Townsend thought. He knew what Shaw meant, but found little comfort in his change from fear of emulation to the need to have future events correctly attributed. Hearing himself say 'All right' he added, 'But I still think it's time to go home.'

'You go, Bill. You've done much more than I had any right to expect. Not, come to think of it, that I had any right to expect anything.'

'You mentioned further warnings, Harry. Why the plural? What's to do after we torch the building? We'll be almost out of bombs.'

'Who needs a lot of bombs now?' Shaw said. 'One at a time will be enough to underline each threat. They know we're not kidding.'

Townsend lay sleepless in bed that night, listening to the silence from across the room which meant that Shaw was sleepless too, thinking that about the only noisy thing Harry ever did was sleep. That thought carried him back to the Falklands and slit trenches so close to Argentine positions that he had had frequently and physically to suppress his officer's rumblings. Now there was only the periodic creaking of mattress springs above the subdued night-roar of the city to bear witness to Shaw's presence. Simulating sleep by slow regular breathing, for no better reason than the absurd one that to appear to be awake might be an intrusion on another's private thoughts, Townsend checked his own mental inventory.

He too had been dismayed by the tragic scenes enacted on the bridge, but had not shared Shaw's compulsion to watch them again and again. Why had Harry needed to do that? No answer. Why, after that, the switch from revulsion to a previously unannounced prolongation of the campaign when their final agreed operation had been the firing of the building on Sixth? A knee-jerk reaction countering a show of humanity felt to be weakness? Improbable. The only knee-jerks Harry had ever given were into an opponent's groin. So, no answer again. So, think the consequences of extended action through.

They had agreed from the outset that the likelihood of their being apprehended during the course of the campaign rested on chance to a far greater extent than on whatever the law enforcement agencies might do. It couldn't be otherwise with the initiative always in Harry's hands, the choice of virtually limitless targets and the method and timing of the attacks on the chosen ones his alone. That had always been the strength of the urban terrorist and it had been that strength which had made the campaign possible at all.

The frequently repeated claims of guarded optimism made by the police through the media and the massive presence of the military in the city did not impress Townsend because the authorities had so little to go on. Not for the first time, by any means, he made a short mental list of what that little was. Bombs. They had plenty of those now, both the remains of the gas canisters and intact explosive devices, but forensic tests would have revealed only that they had been manufactured

188

from readily available materials and presumably stolen plastic charges. Books. Identical and untraceable. Tapes. Logo's disguised voice wouldn't help them. Letters. Typed on different machines each time, machines subsequently destroyed, the letters themselves mailed at locations far apart. His own voice. He doubted they had a recording of that with its simulated Irish accent because he never spoke for long and never called the same newspaper or broadcasting station a second time. Then there was the wetsuit that the intense diving activity was almost certain to have recovered by now. So what? With Harry to handle there had been nothing he could have done about that and it wouldn't tell them anything worth knowing. As for the killings of the man on the pier and the two on the subway train, Townsend concluded that they would pass almost unnoticed in a city with a homicide rate as high as that of New York. In New Jersey Harry had ensured Bridenthal's anonymity. So far, so good, but could it last?

It didn't take him very long to decide that the question was as unanswerable as asking it was pointless with chance a random factor which, by definition, could not be quantified. The facelessness granted to them by the teeming millions of New York and the fact that the police and the FBI had so little to work on seemed to indicate that his and Harry's chances were good, but there was that word 'chance' again.

Abandoning his attempt to foretell a precarious future, Townsend asked himself if he still wanted any part of it. The surprising challenge offered to him by Harry he had accepted partly because he found challenges irresistible which was why he had joined the SAS, partly because, like Harry, he found its objective just and the achieving of it a better way of dying than becoming another statistic the IRA could brag about, and partly because it offered a means of making his father financially secure, which an Army career did not.

Townsend was fond of his father, exasperation at his slow-wittedness more than offset by admiration and gratitude for the dogged tenacity with which he had brought up his child after its mother had abandoned them both in favour of the more lucrative pastures offered by the pavements of Piccadilly. Now, with the £100,000 Harry had extorted from Stein he

189

could repay that devotion in practical form. As for Harry's crusade he felt, as he had said, that enough was enough, or would be once the firing of the skyscraper on Sixth Avenue had been achieved.

That left only his own liking for the improbable and that, at least for the time being, was close to satiety. Having faced violent death so often and in so many places he still disliked the thought of it as much as anybody, but had no particular fear of it. For all that, the knowledge was growing in him that he hated the thought of meeting it after the due processes of the law had played out their protracted and gruesome game.

Townsend was thinking that if they left soon that game need never begin when, in a fierce whisper, Shaw said. 'We didn't do it, Sarah! I swear by my love for you that we didn't do it! I beg of you to believe me!' Despite the fierceness of the delivery there had been a depth of entreaty in the words and despair in the long soft sigh which followed them as though Shaw had received an immediate refusal of his plea by telepathy.

Although he had never before known Shaw either to plead or to despair, it was what they represented rather than the acts themselves which brought understanding to Townsend. Without pause, that understanding brought muscle tenseness with it so that it took physical and mental effort on his part to maintain the slow, regular breathing of pretended sleep. Since the aftermath of the Canary Islands episode Shaw had scarcely mentioned Sarah Cheyney, nor had her photograph been in evidence. From that, apart from his own gratitude towards her, Townsend had had her labelled in his mind as his friend's gorgeous black lay and nothing more. Now this sudden revelation of an intensity of feeling which he had not suspected, but no longer doubted was shared, explained Shaw's reaction to the tragedy on the George Washington Bridge and came as a shock to him in its implicit selfishness.

For long minutes he tried to find some small degree of acceptability in the simultaneous admission of a woman into one's life and the placing of that life in jeopardy with no greater thought for her than the need for her body and good opinion. He failed and said, 'Harry Shaw, you really are a complete shit!' but he said it only to himself.

21

'No,' Sarah Cheyney said, 'I will not write you a prescription for an antibiotic, or anything else. All you're suffering from is inertia. Why don't you go away and do something positive like having an affair, or a traffic accident, or finding another doctor, instead of cluttering up my surgery every week? Now, if you'll excuse me . . .'

She barely glanced at the furious woman's retreating back, grateful for once to the mean mood gripping her for giving her the strength to make a break she should have made months earlier. The mood had come to her immediately after the need to protect Shaw from the Special Branch man had gone. It came with the bitter taste of jealousy of a rival she had not known existed and who had proved more seductive than herself. Had the rival been another woman she felt that would have been more understandable and, consequently, less hurtful, although she wasn't certain about the second part. But the rival she saw on her television screen each night and in her newspaper every morning was drama and Harry, she now knew, had been living with the bitch even as they 'honeymooned' in New York.

She watched the affair, such a very public affair, develop with her thoughts in a turmoil of mixed emotions. There was incredulity, and a hint of unwelcome admiration, that two men could create such havoc in a great city. Or had they recruited more? The basic unit in the SAS was a 'stick' or four men, Harry had told her, or was it five? What difference did it make? The result would have been incredible for a battalion, however many that was. There was deep resentment at having been so

191

cynically used by somebody already preparing to throw away his life and bitter-sweet memories of their times together. Overpowering love and overwhelming hate alternated with each other in equal quantities. There was, too, terror that he might be caught and fear that he might not before something really horrible happened.

It happened and it was shown to her in ghastly detail on ITV's *News at Ten* that night. Numb with anguish, unable to take her eyes from the screen, she sat rigidly, her nails digging deeply into the fabric of her chair while a bridge burned. There seemed to be some enormous fire-ball on it, a ball which hurled bright streamers of flame towards cars which slewed and collided and overturned and burned themselves and people too. Some did it thrashing about on the ground, some did it running and others did it falling through the air. When the scene shifted abruptly to a talking face she didn't hear what the face said because she was thinking that the news editor had decided that the public had seen enough, but hadn't decided it soon enough because too much had already been shown. Then it was over and she found herself looking at the results of a car-bomb explosion in Beirut. Compared to the George Washington Bridge it didn't look much of an event.

'Oh Harry,' she whipered and switched off the set.

For a long time after that she just sat and wished that she could cry, but she had never been very good at that and no tears came. Saying 'Oh Harry' again broke the spell binding her and she began to seek for an explanation in a coldly clinical way as though she were a psychiatrist and Shaw a patient she had interviewed that afternoon whose notes she had to bring up to date. Setting herself a scale of plus and minus ten she began to think of the number of times since she had known him that Shaw had deviated markedly from the zero line of total control: controlled movements, controlled emotions, controlled face. She awarded herself a conservative 'plus 5' for his reaction when they were making love and a 'plus 7' that first time when he had laughed aloud and said 'I'm just so happy, that's all.' Most of the rest of their shared experiences came out as pluses too, but not to any extravagant degree above a natural togetherness or gentle amusement.

Only once had he dropped significantly below zero on her private scale. That was when she had flared at him and demanded that he go, but even that hadn't rated more than a 'minus 2', and his concern for Bill Townsend's drugged condition had been only just detectable. So controlled, so very tightly controlled. Too tightly for the tension to sustain itself?

The mean mood had evaporated now as though it had never been, leaving only an infinite sadness. 'Did something snap, Harry?' Sarah Cheyney asked the empty room, nodding as though it had given her an affirmative reply and adding, 'It can't go on, you know. It really can't.' She shook her head as if to emphasise the statement and the action seemed to release the tears at last, just two of them, one spilling from the corner of each eye and tracing a parallel path down either side of her nose. They brought no relief.

There was a period of muddled thinking after that, a snatching at strands and missing them, a grasping of strands which led nowhere, the only certainty being that Harry had to be stopped. Stopped? Stopped how? Sergeant Fenner, this is Dr Cheyney. You remember my telling you that Captain Shaw was in Canada. Well, he isn't, he's in New York doing all these terrible things and somebody must stop him for his own sake and for the sake of those poor people on the bridge, although I don't suppose they care much, because they're dead and ... Stop it! Try again. No, Sergeant Fenner, I haven't heard from him and I haven't any idea what his address is. I just know he's there because – because I know. He's gone berserk, you see, and ... Oh God. When she finally went to bed at one o'clock in the morning Sarah Cheyney took a sleeping pill for the first time in her life. There were her patients to think about later that day.

She was at her surgery desk, not eating the sandwiches she had ordered for lunch, when the house phone rang.

'There's a Mr Steuben Glass calling from New York, doctor.'

Her heart lurched and there was a tremor in her voice when she thanked her receptionist. Then she picked up the other phone and listened to William Townsend saying 'Is that Dr Cheyney?'

'Yes, Mr Glass,' she said. The words calm now, calm and cold.

'Oh, thank goodness. Listen, things are getting a little out of hand over this side. Your boy has run into a Mafia protection racket over his hostel and is determined to fight them himself. It's madness of course. The police can't help much with all this terrorist activity stretching them to the limit and The Mob are putting the screws on, but he doesn't seem to care. I argued with him last night and again this morning, but he won't listen to me, so I thought if you'd come and talk some sense into him we could get him out of here before he gets hurt. Will you do that? He's begun to act irrationally, even recklessly, and it's really very important.'

'The things that happen in sleepy old Canada,' she said.

The phone was saying 'What? Oh, he came back from there last . . .' when she put it back on its rest.

For a full minute she stared at the instrument, thinking dismally of stronger words than 'recklessly', then picked it up and keyed 999. 'Police' she said to the voice which asked her which emergency service she wanted, and to the police, 'This is Dr Cheyney of 198 Wimpole Street. I want to speak urgently to Detective Sergeant Fenner of the Special Branch. He knows who I am.' Sitting, waiting for the connection to be made, she thought it would be nice if she could die before it was.

'Damn it all to hell,' Townsend said, resisting the pointless temptation to jiggle the rest up and down as that had never resurrected a dead line, and replaced the receiver. He knew that Dr Cheyney had hung up on him anyway and that meant she had guessed a very great deal as she was not the sort of person to end what he now understood to have been a strong relationship for anything as minor as lack of communication over a brief period.

While he was gathering up the row of coins he had placed ready on the ledge of the booth, wondering if there *was* such a thing as female intuition and thinking about the significance for Harry and himself of her apparent knowledge, he noticed the message somebody had written on the wall with a felt-tipped pen. 'Brits Out! Support INAC!' it read. Something deep in his memory stirred, but resisted his attempts to identify it, so he went back to thinking of Sarah Cheyney's languidly cold tones and the abrupt end to the conversation. That had been one exchange he had had no intention of telling Harry about, but he knew he would have to now and wasn't looking forward to doing it.

Shaw was at the window when Townsend let himself into the So Ho apartment.

'Seen that one before, Bill?'

Townsend looked down in the direction indicated by Shaw's pointing finger and at the blonde prostitute in the fake fur coat across the street. Every so often she let the coat fall open to reveal an exiguous black latex dress. He thought that she must be in danger of freezing to death.

'No, help yourself,' he said. 'You saw her first.'

Shaw grunted impatiently before saying, 'She's new. If you wanted to set a watch on this place, an inconspicuous watch, how would you do it?'

'Not by dressing a police woman up as a tart, Harry. The other girls would scratch her eyes out for muscling in on their patch. You'd know that if you hadn't led such a sheltered life.'

'I suppose that's so,' Shaw said and turned away from the window.

'Harry.'

'Yes?'

'They aren't using stake-outs. At the first hint of suspicion they're going in like a herd of bull-elephants. It's been reported from all over town. Quite a few innocent citizens have been roughed up. You know all that.'

'Yes,' Shaw said again. 'I know all about that. Mustn't start jumping at shadows, must I?' He paused, then added, 'I wish to hell I knew who they think they're looking for with those raids.'

Townsend wished he did himself, thought of quoting 'They seek him here, they seek him there,' but did not. He was too concerned about Shaw's continued slide into ambivalence for levity. Instead he asked, 'Ever heard of INAC, Harry?'

Shaw raised his shoulders and let them drop again in the nearest thing to a physical manifestation of dejection Townsend had ever seen from him.

'East 194th Street, the Bronx,' Shaw said. 'The initials stand for the Irish Northern Aid Committee. NORAID for short. It's the bloody place I've been looking for from the beginning. I'd never heard of INAC until I saw a paint-spray sign on a billboard yesterday. Would you believe it? Everybody at home thinks of it as NORAID and I – I ought to have a head transplant.'

'Join the club.'

'Well, there's nothing to be done about it now. That's one place they certainly *will* have staked out and I'm not going within a mile of it.'

'I'm delighted to hear it,' Townsend said, 'and that brings me to something which I'm afraid *you're not* going to be delighted to hear.'

Shaw watched him levelly, waiting, and Townsend went on, 'After I'd telephoned the CBS people this evening and given them "Jupiter" as the authentication code for the week I made another call.'

'To Sarah.' Shaw had spoken very quietly and there had been no trace of questioning in the two words. Townsend blinked.

'How did you guess?'

'From the way you've been carrying on at me these past twenty-four hours. I suppose you asked her to come and take me home.'

'Yes.'

'And?'

'She hung up on me, Harry.'

Nodding, Shaw moved back to the window and stood, staring through it. The girl in the latex dress was walking away, arm in arm with a client.

'No, you're right,' he said. 'She wouldn't have been a very effective watcher, would she?'

'What?'

'Nothing, Bill.'

Townsend waited, feeling the silence of the room, a silence made more intense by the sound of the city outside, a subdued background roar of traffic he had long since ceased to notice except when there was nothing else to listen to.

When the stillness, particularly Shaw's, became oppressive,

he broke it by asking, 'Aren't you going to kick my shoulder-blades off or something?'

Shaw didn't look at him, but the slow smile Townsend hadn't seen for so long creased his left profile around his mouth and one visible eye.

'Why should I want to do that?' Shaw said. 'I've been consistently wrong since that bridge massacre. Before that even, when I had that non-starter idea about computers. I must be getting tired, or old, or perhaps I'm losing my marbles.'

'You've had a lot to think about, Harry, and you've done a very great deal.'

As though Townsend hadn't spoken Shaw went on. 'You, on the other hand, have been boringly right, which means that I am no longer competent to command this two-man regiment. It's time to start demobilisation.'

The smile was still on Shaw's face as though painted there and Townsend didn't like that at all. Quietly, not believing his own words, he said, 'So we bomb the building and go home.'

'You go home, Bill. I suggested that yesterday. This time it's an order. We can't run this thing by committee, remember?'

'And you?'

'She hung up on you,' Shaw said. 'I've got nothing to go home for now.'

'Sir John's here, Minister.'

'Ask him to come in,' the Home Secretary said. 'Oh, you already are in, Travis. How's the Security Service today?'

'Secure, thank you. Have you read my note on that man Shaw?' The head of MI5 didn't believe in wasting time.

'I have, and my answer's the same as before. We simply cannot go around pointing the finger at individuals against whom we have not one shred of evidence. Admittedly it's curious that Shaw's mistress and his ex-commanding officer should, unknown to each other, share the same suspicions, but I can't act on coincidence of imagination. You must see that.'

Sir John Travis steepled his fingers and said, 'I wouldn't be here taking up your time if I didn't have something rather more positive to tell you, Secretary of State. There have been two developments since I wrote to you. The first is that Dr

Cheyney has been persuaded of the logic of telling us the identity of the man who informed her of Shaw's whereabouts if, as she claimed, she was anxious that an end be put to Shaw's alleged activities. She was reluctant to do so before on the grounds that her informant was a patient of hers. He is, or was, an SAS sergeant who was very close to Shaw and left the Army shortly after him. The supposition is that they may be working as a team.'

'And the second development?'

'I had lunch with Bendix today and –'

'CIA?'

'Yes. He told me that the FBI had possibly traced the sale of a wetsuit almost certainly used for the attack on shipping in the port to, and I quote, a tall, good-looking saturnine man with a fancy Limey accent. The physical description fits Shaw and he is said to speak with what I imagine the Americans would take to be a fancy Limey accent. It's still extremely tenuous, but with a national emergency across the Atlantic . . .' Travis let the rest of the sentence go and unsteepled his fingers.

'Hmm.'

When fifteen seconds had gone by with the Home Secretary volunteering nothing more, Travis asked, 'What do you think?'

'I think that, before we go any further, Shaw's medical records should be thoroughly checked for any signs of criminal insanity. That's what this is, you know. Apart from destroying the Special Relationship single-handed, what on earth can he hope to achieve? Absolutely nothing!'

'I've already had his records looked into, Minister, and they reveal nothing deleterious. Quite the reverse, in fact. As to your rhetorical question, according to our informants within the Provisional IRA, he is causing that organisation considerable concern for its future. An emissary has already been sent to Libya on a fund-raising mission in case, as seems possible, the US source dries up. I don't call that nothing.'

'You sound almost as though you approve of his activities.'

Travis sighed audibly before saying, 'My brief, as you well know, is to maintain the internal security of the realm. I can

198

scarcely approve, but I'm sure you wouldn't begrudge me a feeling of satisfaction when outside forces assist me in my task. Shaw may prove to have been a godsend but, be that as it may, he can't be allowed to continue.'

'If this conversation is anything to go by, we appear to have lapsed into mutual acceptance of the hypothesis that Shaw is indeed responsible for these outrages,' the Home Secretary said and matched Travis's sigh before adding, 'You'd better provide the Americans with descriptions and full background details of both men. On an entirely informal basis of course. I hope you're not going to ask me for that in writing.'

Sir John Travis shook his head, rose and left the room, walking quickly.

It was as though she had gone back in time to her African origins. The heels of her hands pressed against her eyes, Sarah Cheyney sat on the edge of a chair and rocked back and forth, wailing softly like some lost soul. After a little she took her hands from her face and clutched her body fiercely beneath her breasts, but her eyes stayed closed and she kept on rocking. And wailing. On the floor beside her lay a copy of *The Daily Telegraph*.

She kept up her lament for several minutes, then suddenly sat rigidly still and opened her eyes so wide that the whites were visible all around the irises. As if having to fight some tangible force, she slowly lowered her gaze to the newspaper. It settled on the column about the disaster on the bridge linking New York to New Jersey, and on the very words that had pierced her through. Burned into her mind, there was no need for her to remind herself of them, but they stared up at her accusingly.

'The terrorist organisation calling itself the "Hands Off Ulster Regiment" is reported as having denied any connection with the catastrophe, a claim apparently accepted by the police who have brought charges of mass-murder against two youths of Puerto Rican origin who are said to have been caught in the act of placing a bomb on a second petrol tanker.'

'Oh God, what have I done?' Sarah Cheyney whispered. All the other things she remained convinced Shaw *was* responsible

199

for seemed perfectly acceptable to her now. The urge to start rocking again fingered her, but she brushed its touch aside and walked in misery to the bathroom to wash her face clean of unaccustomed tears.

22

Very much to Lieutenant Bergquist's surprise it wasn't anybody's computer, or Sergeant Alton, but Detective 'Ace' Diamond who noticed that the number of the subway car in which the two muggers had been killed was the same as one of the many in which explosive devices had been found and rendered harmless.

There was no question but that the men had been muggers. If the possession of flick-knives with their prints on them had not been proof enough, credit cards belonging to other people found in their pockets led to the identification of the bodies by their victims. With so very many cases to handle he had been only marginally interested in the manner of the deaths of two such undesirable citizens, but Detective Diamond's discovery had altered all that because it pointed to the possibility that their killer and the man who had placed the bomb in position were one and the same. That it would be 'man' and not 'men' appeared to be a reasonable assumption as single individuals were the mugger's natural prey, and the presence of the bomb in the same car was too much of a coincidence for him to believe that the murderers had been members of a rival gang stupid enough not to have profited financially from their act.

That set him to wondering what talents were required of a train bomber. Nothing much occurred to him except coolness and sufficient knowledge of railcar construction to enable him to locate the steel framework and avoid the much larger areas of light alloy to which the magnetic clamps would not have adhered. To his mind there was no connection at all between those attributes and the ability to break the jaw and neck of one armed assailant and knife the other. Then there was the medical evidence on the Port Authority watchman who had been killed by a knife wound extending from the underside of the jaw to the brain. Reconstruction had proved that the knife had been thrown from below him and that he had then broken various bones in a fall from the pier to the floating platform beside it before being dumped in the river.

Bergquist thought about the river and the attack by frogmen on shipping along the Manhattan shore, of the gas bomb campaign against individuals and the disruption of the transport system with canisters of explosives. There were photographs in his desk drawer of some of those, taken after people whose job he did not envy had made them harmless by freezing and then dismantling them. They were high-quality pictures of quality hand-made devices. He thought, too, of a tall saturnine man with an educated English accent whose alleged purchase of a wetsuit had led to the over-zealous hounding of a lot of tall saturnine men whose accents were unknown until they remonstrated. Another accent was the Irish one of the man who made the phone calls, but two recipients of those calls, at *The Times* and NBC, had been of the opinion that the accent was phoney because the blarney had been overdone. Those voices pointed to the British, but then that had been much more than simply likely ever since the 'Hands Off Ulster Regiment' had announced its existence. On that everybody was agreed. But what British?

Linking his thoughts together as though he were making a chain of paper-clips Bergquist looked at them as he had done so often in recent days. They made a depressingly short chain for encompassing so much clinical efficiency, efficiency which had his city by the throat with no sign of the grip slackening and no visible sign of the hooked fingers. The only fact to emerge with reasonable clarity was that, after the mailing of the gas bombs, New York alone had become the target because threats to other centres of population had been found to be bluffs. With half a million men and women from the military and every law enforcement agency in the land working on the emergency across the nation the fund of available knowledge about what was going on was, he knew, worse than derisory. There simply had to be a break soon.

Bergquist rearranged his mental paper-clips until he had unarmed combat linked to knife-throwing and that linked to under-water sabotage. It didn't add up to a lot, but something was better than nothing at all. Six minutes had gone by since Detective Diamond had told him about the number of the subway car when he picked up the telephone.

'Charles, I have this idea we could be dealing with British Special Forces. One of my men has just noticed that –'

'What took you so long?' Special Agent-in-charge Charles Roetter broke in.

Tiredness close to exhaustion blossomed into fury. 'God damn you!' Bergquist shouted. 'When will you mother-fucking Feds learn not to operate behind closed doors? How long have you known?'

The line chuckled at him. 'About ten minutes, Harv. We just got pix of two of them from the CIA, courtesy of British Security. At least, there's reason to believe they could be two of the guys we're looking for. Copies and full physical descriptions on their way to you of Captain Henry Jardine Shaw and Sergeant William Arthur Townsend, late of the SAS. I recommend you tell your patrolmen not to get cute if they find them. That could mean trouble, and I mean trouble.'

The beginnings of hope stirring in Bergquist stifled resentment of the patronisingly gratuitous advice. 'We don't have any cute patrolmen at this precinct,' he said and replaced the receiver.

During Bergquist's brief exchange with Roetter, Shaw walked into the rented office on the sixteenth floor of the building on Sixth Avenue for the last time and locked the door behind him. He was thankful that it was the last time because he did not know what Sarah Cheyney might have felt compelled to do once she had deduced his responsibility for the events in the United States, and he no longer felt safe on the streets. There had been a sense of anonymity to be found amongst the hordes of pedestrians on the sidewalks, hordes that his actions had placed there, but not anymore. With his identity possibly no longer just a matter for media conjecture, the police and National Guardsmen standing at street corners and in so many doorways, once a symbol of his own success, were menacing now. His emotions a confusing mixture of apathy and urgency, he took the tools he needed from a drawer.

While Shaw knelt on the carpet, cutting the vent of the air-conditioning system out of the wall, an elderly Bedouin moved restlessly in his tent thirty miles to the south of Tripoli, Libya. The long journey north from Sebha in the Fezzan had tired him, but his worry about the unmarked helicopter was keeping sleep at bay. Half an hour before sunset it had flown over his camel caravan low enough for the down-draught to disturb the gravel-specked sand of the desert floor and then hovered just above the horizon, as though watching him, until darkness came. He wondered if he was breaking some law.

At the moment when he prodded his number two wife awake with his foot so that she might share his wakefulness, two hundred Rangers from the 2nd Marine Division at Camp Lejeune, North Carolina, were put on one hour's notice to fly to New Jersey in response to expected developments in New York City. They began to recheck weapons already checked many times and mechanics did the same to the CH 53 helicopters which would carry the élite assault force to its target.

'That's that,' Shaw told Townsend when he had closed the door of the So Ho apartment behind him.

'So where did you place them?'

Townsend asked the question as though it was expected of him, but without any real interest in the answer. Shaw noticed the tone of indifference and felt first saddened, then resentful and finally irritated with himself for indulging in emotions for which there was no justification because Townsend had made his views perfectly clear.

'The three smoke bombs are in the ventilation duct,' he said. 'That should give every part of the building a fair share. The duct is non-ferrous, so I glued the canisters in position. The explosives are in the office, the cleaner's room across the passage and in the lavatories of the two floors above. Oh, and I blocked every sprinkler I could get at.'

'And you set the timers for 1530 hours, right?'

'The smoke, yes. The explosives for 1545. I want the maximum confusion before the balloon goes up, but the people out of the building too.'

Townsend looked at his watch and said, 'Twenty-one minutes. OK. I'll call the *Wall Street Journal* from along the street and then get out to the airport.' He picked up his suitcase before adding, 'One last time. Won't you come with me?'

'You know I can't, Bill. We've been over all that. I simply have to have some feedback before I pack it in. Just something to tell me it's been worth doing.'

'Feedback? You've driven a whole collection of small companies into bankruptcy with all this disruption, the Dow Jones has gone into free-fall, wiping billions off the value of shares, and the dollar's way down against the pound and the mark and the yen. You also have the avid attention of the world's press. What the hell's that if it isn't feedback?'

Stubbornly, Shaw said, 'I must know about NORAID. I must know about Ulster.'

'Then you'd better telephone General Brigg and ask him if he's finding life any easier over there.'

Shaw didn't bother to reply to that and Townsend shrugged before saying, ''Bye, Harry. Take care.'

''Bye, Bill. Er, Bill.'

'Yeah?'

'Thanks for everything. We go well together, you and I.'

'Like assault and battery,' Townsend said and let himself out of the apartment. He hadn't smiled.

Standing alone at the centre of the room Shaw felt the clutch of migraine inside his skull. It was only the second attack in his life, but the knowledge that this time there were no magic black fingers to make it go away was worse than the pain.

He switched on the television, but the light and the sound combined to channel additional agony from outside to a focal point of incandescence behind his forehead and he pressed the 'standby' button. It didn't matter. Townsend wouldn't have made his call yet and it would be minutes after that before they had cameras in position to cover mid-town Sixth Avenue. Shaw covered his face with his hands and tried to concentrate on wondering why only the street signs called it the Avenue of the Americas, but the migraine swamped the pointless specu-

205

lation. Grimly, he switched the set on again, muted it, and sat watching the screen through slitted eyes.

People streaming from the main doors of the building, some chattering and laughing in nervous relief at reaching the open air, some tight-faced and glancing back over their shoulders, some rubber-legged after the long descent of the fire stairs from up to thirty storeys above the street because they had been forbidden to use the potential death-traps the elevators had become. National Guards and firemen making violent sweeping motions with their arms as though that might assist the people towards the safety of the barriers set up on all approach roads. Sirens wailing and dying as military vehicles, fire appliances, heavy-rescue squads, ambulances and police cars got as close to the barriers as they could through the growing crowds, crowds deaf to the urgent bull-horn appeals to disperse. The last of the people coming from the building holding handkerchiefs to their faces, followed by tendrils of smoke and the smell of rotten eggs.

Lieutenant Bergquist caught the sickly scent as soon as he got out of his car a block and a half away. He wrinkled his nose in disgust and hoped bleakly that the gas would be more effective at moving the mass of onlookers than the police had been. It irritated him that his force should have been relegated to the tasks of crowd and traffic control in a major incident in his city and the knowledge that that had been inevitable once the Governor had declared a state of emergency and called out the National Guard did nothing to lessen his irritation.

Even had it not been the centre of intense activity and the focus of all eyes, it would still have been immediately apparent which the target building was. Row upon row of its windows were white, sightless, like the irises of trachoma sufferers, and the tendrils at the doors had become billows as the smoke sought an escape route from the climate-controlled edifice. It seemed to Bergquist that the whole structure quivered as he forced his way towards the barrier, splitting vertically from top to bottom, the two halves forming a widening letter 'V', its arm toppling towards the throng below. He grunted with impatience and stamped firmly on his imagination. Not even a nuclear device could produce that effect. He ducked under the barrier.

'Hold it right there, bud!'

'Take it easy, son.'

The National Guard private glanced at the gold badge, lowered his rifle and said, 'Sorry, Lieutenant.'

Bergquist moved on towards the building and the firemen with their hoses, axes, breathing equipment and thermal cameras which could see through smoke. A helicopter rattled overhead, circling, a television camera aimed from its doorway. Near the entrance but clear of the smoke, the State Governor and the Mayor stood, heads tilted in concentration listening to a fire chief. Bergquist wondered how the two politicians had got to the scene so quickly, then remembered the press conference on the emergency at the Hilton Hotel close by. He thought of requesting them to back off on the grounds that they hadn't been elected to have a building fall on them, but did not.

A line of firemen emerged from the smoke like ghosts solidifying and one of them ran towards the fire chief, taking off the mask covering his mouth and nose and calling 'All floors vacated as far as we can tell.' Brave, very brave, Bergquist thought, for the warning given by the Irish-sounding voice and circulated to all concerned had been explicit about the danger of going above the fourteenth.

The explosions, when they came, were flat, unemphatic, lost immediately in the high air. The building didn't so much as tremble, let alone split and fall, but in a number of places halfway to the summit the white smoke found new outlets. For an instant the sun glinted on hurtling shards of glass as if a vast swarm of golden bees had been released from a giant hive. The bees fell to earth and stung and people screamed.

'Let's go,' the fire chief said.

High above the street the white smoke darkened to greyish black and increased in volume. Licking tongues of orange fire followed it as plastic and paint and rubber began to burn. Dusk came early to mid-town Manhattan that day.

Dawn raced from Egypt across the Libyan desert as the Bedouin left his tent. He frowned quickly, nervously. The helicopter was still there, hovering to the east of him, black against the harsh light of the nail-paring of sun showing above the horizon. *Still* there? That seemed hardly possible, but perhaps it had gone away and then come back. Perhaps it had landed for the night and taken off with the coming of day. Perhaps it was a different machine. Frowning again he set his family to their various tasks in preparation for the last stage of the journey to Tripoli. They still hadn't completed them when the jets came, two Libyan Airforce MiG-23s diving silently out of the northern sky, outpacing the sound of their engines, then slamming overhead with a thunder-clap which stunned the senses.

It took him countable seconds to recover his wits and clear his eyes of sand. During those seconds he gradually became aware of the frightened wailing of the women above the ringing in his ears and then of the quiet cursing of his brothers and cousins. Returning vision showed him the bolting camels and the one aluminium-framed tent not yet dismantled toppling over and over like tumbleweed. The jets were far to the south, climbing vertically as though driven upwards by the columns of their condensation trails. Almost as soon as the climb ended he knew that they were coming back. Watching them as though mesmerised, he saw them growing in size, but the brightness of a sun clear of the horizon now hid the sparkle of cannon fire from him. The first he knew of that was small explosions stitching towards him across the sand.

The old man had time to wonder what law he had broken, and in what way he had offended Allah, before he died. He died very quickly, his body lifted and torn apart by the projectiles, and was fortunate to do so because he was spared the sight of the MiGs' third pass and the swiftly rolling fire of napalm engulfing his wounded family.

When the flames had subsided, the helicopter moved in and landed near to the charred bodies.

The Search Co-ordination Committee decided to give the foot patrols of the National Guard and the police twenty-four hours to locate the area occupied by the terrorists with the help of the photographs. By doing so it was hoped to establish their approximate whereabouts without alerting them until the Special Forces were in position. It was agreed that the chances of success were slim, given the vast area covered by New York City, but the tactical advantage which would come from complete surprise made the prospect tempting, and almost unlimited manpower made it at least possible to achieve. If it failed, pictures of two of the men wanted for questioning broadcast on television, printed in every newspaper and posted in every street, would turn the entire population into hunters and deprive the bombers of their mobility. It did not fail.

Sergeant Mary Alton was tired and her feet were hurting her.

'OK, Ace,' she said. 'Let's get on with it. Only eight more blocks for us. You take this side and I'll – No, the other way around. Those are hookers over there. It'll look more natural if you're seen talking to them.'

Detective Diamond nodded, crossed the street and for the two hundred and eleventh time said, 'You seen either of these guys any place?' He knew it was the two hundred and eleventh time of asking because he had been keeping count for something to do.

The blonde girl knew the voice of officialdom when she heard it and closed her fur coat quickly to conceal her black rubber dress. Then she looked at the photographs and the badge cupped in his palm.

'Sure. They live right here. I seen them going in and out often. At the window too. The fair one's real cute.'

She was starting to point as she spoke, but Diamond stopped the motion with his hand and drew her arm under his saying, 'Lady, you just found yourself a customer, so let's stroll along real natural.'

'Where are you –?'

'Shut up and walk.'

Not until they had rounded the corner of the block did Detective Diamond take a radio from his pocket and say, 'I have a positive ID on both men.'

The CH 53 helicopters looked like a line of migrating birds as they dropped towards the New Jersey marshes across the

Hudson River from mid-town Manhattan. When they touched down, armed Rangers in full combat gear flowed from them only to vanish again into unmarked covered trucks. The rotors of the helicopters were barely still before the vehicles moved off preceded by a single police car, its lights flashing, its siren silent. As convoy and escort entered the Holland Tunnel linking New Jersey to New York, traffic lights along a selected route across the island of Manhattan turned red and stayed at that colour.

23

Shaw's migraine had gone, but it left him drained, not rested as it had after Sarah Cheyney's ministrations, and that added to his lethargy. That there was nothing basically physical about that condition he was perfectly well aware. He hadn't been getting the exercise he was accustomed to and he hadn't been eating well either, but he knew those factors to be irrelevant. One didn't get exercise or proper food when lying in cover for days on end watching the movements of an enemy, and he had done that often enough around the world without any ill effects. He knew, too, that the symptom had its root in resignation and nothing else.

Exactly when he had reached the decision that he must continue with his campaign until he ran out of resources, even at the cost of being taken alive, he was uncertain. The notion had first formed in his mind with the realisation that he was getting altogether too little intelligence about what effect his actions were having on the provision of funds to the IRA. There *had* been letters to the press condemning NORAID, a politician or two had spoken out against the organisation and, the day before, the media had reported that the building in the Bronx housing its offices had been vacated as a precautionary measure. The last, Shaw felt, might or might not be true and didn't amount to much anyway as its records and supplies could already be in use again almost anywhere. Cynically asking himself if he had expected a presidential citation or a vote of confidence published in the Congressional Record had done nothing to assuage his sense of failure but, failure being something he was unaccustomed to, it had hardened his resolve.

He did not attempt to deny that Sarah Cheyney's abrupt termination of Townsend's telephone call had been a major factor in what was more than likely to prove a suicidal resolution, but it was not the only one. He had been, and remained, sickened by the murderous cruelty of a small group of mindless people in Ireland, and it continued to amaze him that those people should be actively supported by citizens of a great nation who were not mindless at all, but simply imbued with the concept that revolution was automatically right because it was deeply ingrained in their history. Whether or not he had done enough to show them that the terrorism by proxy in which they indulged could reap an alarming harvest for themselves, was the unanswered question riding his back like a monkey. It was that lack of an answer which had led him to wonder if his own trial might not prove to be the best platform from which to publicise even further the views he had already made clear with violence and bulletins to the media.

He knew that Townsend guessed that something of the sort was in his mind and that he disapproved strongly. There had been neither a handshake when they parted, nor a quotation from anybody, and that meant that Townsend was as reproachful as he was capable of being. Shaw sighed and began to consider the possibility that he would not be granted a trial, that he would be made to disappear, then pushed the worry away. The international furore he had created would guarantee him a hearing.

Shaw sighed again, his gaze roaming the room sightlessly, then focusing on the window. The resident pigeon stood on the ledge outside, head cocked, watching him. He got to his feet and went to the kitchen to fetch a piece of bread for it, his thoughts on the relative merits of shifting his scene of operations to South Boston with its large Irish population, or to Philadelphia which, after New York, was the largest source of funds for NORAID. It was when he opened the window with one hand, crumbling a stale crust with the other, that he guessed with near certainty that he wouldn't be going to either of those places.

The sound had been coming to him for about half a minute, he realised, but his brain had failed to register it. It recognised it now – the swelling cacophony of a multitude of car horns borne into the room on the freezing air. He spread his handful of crumbs along the ledge, closed the window and watched the pigeon settle and begin to peck. Only then did he look down at the street.

It seemed much as usual except for the presence of two men in civilian clothes on the opposite side, positioned so that they had the front door bracketed. They were rising up and down on their toes and turning their heads from side to side as though searching for vacant cabs. A vacant cab drove by, but was not flagged down. Shaw thought that they were probably part of a military reconnaissance unit and that there would be more of them outside his field of view. Telling himself that he was being fanciful occupied him for only a second or two because they looked like soldiers despite their civilian clothes and they were trying too obviously to be inconspicuous. Not, he admitted to himself, that he would have noticed them had it not been for the car horns blaring across the city. Somebody with a Hollywood mentality had cleared a path for cross-town traffic by setting the north- and south-bound lights at red. He could see them and the impatiently waiting traffic at the end of the street, and it required little imagination to guess what the traffic was being made to wait for. It required even less imagination to guess that some military commander would now be blazingly angry with whatever fool had sacrificed his cloak of silence for unnecessary speed, and wondering what the blunder was going to cost him in dead men. Shaw's mouth twitched at that last notion as he pictured his armoury of two shot-guns and the few that remained of Logo's bombs resting on top of the old-fashioned wardrobe in the bedroom, but the embryo smile failed to mature.

'Oh, Sarah,' he said, and there was both sadness and understanding in the words.

The trucks arrived then, blocking the end of the street he could see, and soldiers poured from them. He had no doubt that similar scenes were being enacted at the other end of the block and on surrounding streets. He could hear shouted commands now and the clatter of a helicopter somewhere overhead. So much noise and the use of so many men surprised

213

him because both were diametrically opposite to everything the SAS had taught him about limited urban operations.

Civilians being hustled away, trucks moving forward, soldiers loping on their far side using them as cover, carrying everything from automatic weapons to grenade launchers to recoilless rifles, a helicopter gun-ship hovering in full view. Shaw moved away from the window and lay face down on the floor beside it for, guessing what would happen next, it was the safest place to be.

Nothing did happen for long minutes and he spent them trying to feel thankful that he had been given enough time to fire the building on Sixth Avenue. It had hardly been the towering inferno Townsend had spoken of, the Fire Department and the sprinkler system had seen to that, but he had provided New Yorkers with a spectacle, and the badly flame-scarred outer walls would remind them of it for days to come. He was remembering the dramatic pictures of the event his television screen had shown him and wondering if the house he was now in was already on camera when the window disintegrated and bullets pock-marked the opposite wall.

Shaw lay where he was, cringing in anticipation of the gas grenades which would come next, but all that came through the empty frame was cold air and the roar of a bull-horn.

'Captain Henry J. Shaw!'

He stood up and approached the window, glass crunching beneath his feet. There were riflemen on the roofs and in the windows of the buildings opposite now, some aiming at him, some at other parts of the house.

'Yes?'

'You are completely surrounded and hopelessly outnumbered! You are ordered to lay down your arms and leave the building by the door directly below you at fifteen-second intervals with your hands above your heads! Anyone leaving by any other exit will be shot! Move!'

'All right,' Shaw said and crunched his way to the door of the apartment, bracing himself for the shock of violent bodily contact as soon as he passed through it. There was no shock. The passageway outside was deserted, the doors of the other apartments prudently closed, and he glanced suspiciously around and behind him as he walked down the single flight of stairs because, according to the book, there should have been soldiers on every level by now. Just before he reached the bottom he reminded himself that it was a different book, a book a general had explained on the way to the Falklands. The Americans favoured the sledge-hammer frontal assault, he had said. It followed that the American-trained Argentinian Army would be preparing for such an attack on Port Stanley, which was why the main British landing force would be going in through the back door at San Carlos. The general had been proved right and Shaw decided that he was witnessing the employment of American tactics now. There certainly was a sledge-hammer waiting outside, but he couldn't see that as any substitute for infiltrating the building.

It was like a double hammer blow too when a Ranger slammed into him from either side the instant he reached the open air as though they were blocking a football player. Winded, he felt himself hurled face down on to the sidewalk.

Hands dragged his arms behind his back and there was the bite of leather as his wrists were secured with a self-locking strap. That procedure he *was* familiar with. Then a hood was drawn over his head and he was being dragged along with his toe-caps bouncing on the pavement. Disorientation was complete when he was lifted bodily, dropped heavily, and the hood snatched off. The world steadied around him.

'So you're one of these "Hands Off Ulster Regiment" bastards, are you?'

He was lying on the floor of a large command vehicle, with radio sets and television screens along one side, and the officers standing over him all held levelled hand-guns. The speaker wore the insignia of a lieutenant-colonel.

'No,' Shaw said. 'I'm all of them. You'd better put me back inside if you want me to come out at fifteen-second intervals.'

The colonel watched him expressionlessly for a moment before saying, 'Very funny,' and turning to look at one of the television screens. Following the direction of his gaze, Shaw saw that it showed the front door of the apartment house with a Ranger crouching either side of it. There was no movement and he looked at the other screens. They seemed to have most

215

of the rest of the house and adjacent streets covered. There was no movement there either.

'Gas, Colonel?'

'Not yet, Hank,' the colonel said. 'They're not going any place, and I'd like to avoid damage to public property if possible. There's been enough of that.' He looked down at Shaw then and added, 'Let's hear from you, buddy, and don't give me any more of that crap about you being a one-man band. That way you get your teeth kicked in. So where are they?'

'Hank's right, Colonel,' Shaw told him. 'You should use gas. While you've been poncing around out here staging your military parade my men have taken over the house and are holding the occupants of the other five apartments hostage. They've probably wired them all up with explosives by now. You'll be receiving a demand for a chopper to take them out to Kennedy shortly and –' he stopped talking, his nose forced sideways by the muzzle of the colonel's automatic.

'And you just walked out because you didn't want any part of that. Right, Shaw?'

'Right, Colonel.'

'May you be forgiven, son,' the colonel said. 'Men from the recce squad went into that building through the roof access a quarter-hour before we shot your windows out. Nobody came out of your apartment but you, thermal sensors tell us there's nobody in the main room shown on the builder's plan, but we can't get at the others from inside to check them out. Now, I may be old-fashioned but I have this rooted objection to losing any of my boys to some booby-trap you may have fixed up, or to gunfire from any kamikaze bastards you may have walked out on, so make it easier for yourself and tell me the truth.'

The muzzle of the gun was pressing against Shaw's upper lip now, forcing it up against his nose, baring his teeth. It was painful and made talking difficult, but he managed to say, 'As you don't believe anything I tell you you'll have to figure it out for yourself.' Incongruously, he felt fleeting satisfaction that they had got it right, that they *had* infiltrated the building, because not to have done so would have been professionally offensive to him. The condescension in the thought passed him by. He just liked to see things done properly.

216

'Where's your pal Townsend? Sergeant William A. Townsend. This guy.'

A photograph of Townsend was held in front of his eyes, the pressure of the gun increased and there was the taste of blood in his mouth as his lip split.

'In the bar of the Hotel Pierre,' Shaw said. 'He always goes there for the happy hour.' It came out lispingly.

They seemed to lose interest in him then, the hood was replaced on his head, his ankles were strapped together, and he felt himself being lifted again. A brief period of cold told him that he was in the open, then he was lying on something yielding in another vehicle and more straps tightened around his chest and thighs. He was glad he had made Bill Townsend go home.

The Pan Am 747 broke into sunlight above the uniform layer of nimbostratus stretching eastwards across the Atlantic just as photographs of Shaw and Townsend began to be distributed at Kennedy International Airport a hundred miles behind the plane, but Townsend was unaware of either event. Normally, he enjoyed the almost instant transition from gloom to brilliance, but this day he had no eyes for it, nor for the red-headed hostess who wanted to mother him and whose expression made it clear that she was prepared to continue the process after arrival at Heathrow. He drank with indifference, ate hardly at all and then tried to sleep, but could not. Trying not to think about Shaw didn't work either, except for the ten minutes he spent inventing his own dialogue for the film he was watching without headphones on. When that distraction palled he went back to thinking about Shaw again and continued to do so for five hours with nothing to reward him for the mental activity other than heightened concern. It was a relief when increasing pressure made his ears hurt as the big jet dropped joltingly down through the cloud cover on its approach to London.

During the long tube journey from Heathrow to the East End, Townsend changed trains four times, more out of ingrained caution than from any belief that he might be being followed yet, and then walked the last mile to Hackney. His mood remained bleak, his conviction that he had somehow failed a friend strong, although in what way he had done that he was unsure. Then he climbed a flight of stairs, opened a door and depression lifted.

"'Lo, Bill,' Logo said. 'Beer in the fridge.'

As always, there were six cans there and he selected the oldest. It bore the legend 'Best before end Jul 1986'. He opened it, sipped at the contents, then leaned in the doorway of the workroom watching Logo at his bench. What the object was being held up to the light in the big hands and being carefully examined by its maker he had no idea, but it was so good to find that some things were still to be relied upon in a frenetic world, that some situations did not change by the minute.

'Nice fire you got going there, Bill. Argies running about all over the place like when you kick an ant-hill. Was you, wasn't it? Big building. They've put it out now, worse luck. It's recorded on video if you want to watch.'

'Thanks, I'd like to. I've been in a plane for the last few hours, so I missed that.' Townsend sipped from his can again, then asked, 'Could I stay here for a bit, Logo?'

'Bastards after you, are they?'

'Could be.'

'No problem,' Logo said. 'Stay as long as you like.'

Recognition was slow in coming, but when it arrived Sarah Cheyney bit her lip, released the security chain on her front door, gestured wordlessly towards the stairs, then followed the bald man up them.

In the flat she asked, 'Are you here to kill me?' The question had sounded as though she had little interest in the answer.

'Don't be fatuous, doctor,' Townsend said. 'I needed to talk to you and I thought you might hang up on me again if I phoned.'

He looked at the lovely dark-skinned woman, then around him at the elegant room, thinking that they suited each other to perfection, then quickly back at her at the words 'I'm afraid I smashed it. I got into one of my mean moods and smashed it to smithereens. I'm so sorry. So very sorry.'

'You smashed what?'

'Your wonderful glass vase from Steuben of course. It was

the most beautiful thing I've ever owned so – so I smashed it.'
She gave an emphatic nod of her head as though underlining
the logic of cause and effect contained in the statements, before
adding, 'I've never known a case of alopecia to progress so
rapidly. There were no signs of it when I examined you – after
you came back from the Canary Islands. Perhaps you're
radioactive. Harry did promise me a fall-out shelter when he
wrote me a funny letter before I went to New York and –'
Very white teeth clamping again on to her lower lip stopped
the flow of nonsensical words.

Grasping at the first fairly understandable statement Sarah
Cheyney had made, Townsend said, 'I dyed my hair and eyebrows black yesterday. It made me look exactly like me wearing a wig, so I shaved the hair off and left the eyebrows. Well,
a friend did it for me actually, and I don't look so much like
me now, do I, doctor?'

She shook her head as emphatically as she had nodded,
before saying, 'I did it to punish myself, you know.'

'Did what?'

'Smashed the vase. You see, I thought you and Harry had
killed all those poor people on the George Washington Bridge.
That's why I talked to Special Branch and when I'd done that I
learned that you hadn't had anything to do with it and I wanted
to die and –'

'It's all right,' Townsend interrupted her. 'I know, and so
does Harry. I heard him talking to himself during the night.
Well, he was talking to you really. I was going to tell you
when I called, but you rang off.'

'Oh God, ' Sarah Cheyney said and the abject misery in the
softly spoken words made Townsend curl his toes in an agony
of embarrassed sympathy. His mind groped for something to
say but made no contact, and that left him nothing to do but
meet the gaze of eyes like headlamps staring at him. They had
a hypnotic quality which deprived him of the power to look
away, to stop reading the appeal in them, and that dismayed
him because he didn't know what to do. Women, as Shaw had
remarked, had always wanted to mother him, which usually
meant seduce him too, or in one instance, he reminded himself
ruefully, drug and interrogate him. Whatever they wanted they

had been perfectly clear what it was, but that didn't apply in this case. Now he was confronted by a woman totally lost, and the fact that she had once genuinely mothered him made the knowledge that she was asking him for something which neither he nor she could define very hard to bear. Her being the most glamorously exotic creature he had ever encountered didn't help him either, because he had always equated female beauty with self-sufficiency and was flustered by having his naïvety held up for his own inspection.

She broke the spell by saying, 'They've arrested Harry!' as though to startle him out of his immobility.

It had been reported on every television and radio newscast and in every newspaper. It was a major topic of national conversation. It was no longer news.

'Yes,' he said. 'Would it be all right if I took my coat off?'

The question sounded absurd to his ears, but it introduced a degree of normality between them with his coat taken from him with hurried apologies about bad hostessses, the unnecessary re-arrangement of cushions and the offer of a drink if he didn't hate her too much to accept one. Townsend sank thankfully down amongst the cushions with a glass of Scotch and water without ice in his hand. He rarely drank Scotch without ice and never with water, but Harry did and that made him feel obscurely privileged because she hadn't asked him how he liked it.

'You said you needed to talk to me.' Sarah Cheyney had control of herself now.

'Yes, doctor. I –'

'Sarah please.'

'Thank you. I'm Bill.' Townsend took an envelope from his pocket and put it on the sofa beside him, then said, 'Before Harry started all this he wrote a letter. That was a few hours before you two met for the first time. There are four copies of it in existence lodged with his solicitor addressed to the Prime Minister, *The Times*, the BBC and ITV. Well, there are five now actually, because he made another copy for you from memory the other day. This is it and he hopes . . .' Townsend breathed in deeply, murmured 'Oh hell,' then went on, 'He says he knows you can never forgive him for carrying on with his plan after you had fallen in love with each other, but hopes you may understand a little because it's something he feels terribly strongly about. I am also to tell you that he tried to write you a letter, but couldn't do it because he feels – because he feels degraded.'

Her unblinking gaze was on him again, her eyes huge. He moved uncomfortably then, with an almost physical effort, broke the visual contact, picked up the envelope and held it towards her.

'Here.'

She said 'Thank you' like a polite child accepting a gift it was unsure of and sighed shudderingly before taking the sheets of paper from the envelope and beginning to read. She spoke only once to whisper 'So many dead. So many injured. I had no idea. No idea at all,' then silence returned to the room until she had finished and dispelled it with another long sigh.

'Oh dear.'

'Oh dear what, Sarah?'

'Just "oh dear". I'd workd a bit of it out for myself from your statements to the American media, but this is a much more explicit and telling document than anything they saw fit to print. What bastards they are over there.'

'No, that's wrong,' Townsend said. 'They're very nice people. The ones I met anyway. They're a bit inclined to go overboard for revolutions because they think they invented them, and if there isn't a good one going somewhere they're likely to invent it, like in Nicaragua. We've done it ourselves often enough when it suited our purpose.'

'But what reason can they possibly have for interfering in Ireland?'

'Ties of blood, memories of British repression and an Arcadian idea of the place which never had any basis in fact. Not since the leprechauns migrated back to Alpha Centauri anyway.'

'Yes, I see,' Sarah Cheyney said. 'At least I don't see, but I'm sorry for saying what I did about them.' She paused before adding, 'If *only* there was some way of letting him know.'

'Letting who know what?' Townsend asked her, puzzled by the *non sequitur*.

'Harry, of course. Letting him know that I *do* understand and that he mustn't feel degraded, but I don't suppose there'll ever be a chance of that now.'

Quiet contentment flowed over Townsend with the knowledge that Harry Shaw still had a great deal to live for, if he were allowed to live at all.

Suppressing the second part of the thought he said, 'There just might be. Not now and not soon, but sometime. I can't tell you how or why, and it's a very slender chance anyway, but it's there.'

He stood then, afraid of the questions she might ask, but none came. Sarah Cheyney rose too and put her hands on his shoulders and her cheek against his before saying, 'You keep giving me lovely presents. If the time ever comes to unwrap this one I promise not to smash it.'

24

The fast-moving motorised convoy with the military ambulance at its centre turned off the New Jersey Turnpike at Exit 9 and slowed, following a minor roadway through the night until it ended abruptly at the still waters of a swamp. Briefly, the headlights illuminated a shallow-draught boat, then they were switched off and a loaded stretcher was transferred from ambulance to boat in total darkness. As though overawed by the eerie remoteness of the desolate place men spoke in whispers or not at all, and the boat burbled quietly as if matching their mood when it moved off through the reeds with its new cargo. A mile away banks closed in on it, banks which joined overhead to become a low cave. The boat stopped and behind it a camouflaged solid steel door sighed downwards from the roof like a portcullis, cutting off the world, then the lights came on. The National Security Agency's Command, Data and Interrogation Centre code-named 'Maple Anchor' had taken Henry J. Shaw into its care.

When they took the strap from Shaw's ankles, the hood from his head and stood him upright, he swayed for a moment, seeking balance, and blinking in the bright light of a small windowless room. It was empty except for television 'eyes' high up near the ceiling at each corner and two Marines standing with their backs to either end-wall. One of them was stuffing the hood inside his tunic. They watched him, their faces wooden, and he didn't say anything because he knew he wouldn't get a reply. He was wondering why his wrists were still strapped behind his back when the door opened and a short broad-shouldered man came in. There were gloves on his hands. The Marines moved forward and grasped Shaw by the upper arms, holding him motionless.

The short man said, 'We have a whole raft of ways of extracting information here, Shaw, but right now we're in a hurry, so this is to persaude you not to give us any more horse shit about the Hotel Pierre, or the Taj Mahal, or any other darned place when you're asked where the rest of your guys are. No hard feelings mind.'

He hit Shaw in the stomach then, a hard, clubbing right-handed blow which drove him against the wall and the Marines with him. Shaw noticed no lessening of impact when a left followed the right. It was after the fifth punch that he slumped and, using the Marines' grip as a fulcrum and the wall for purchase, jack-knifed and drove his legs horizontally forward. One shoe took the man in the groin, the other under the heart, and there was the soft crunch of ribs fracturing.

Shaw found himself flat on his face for the second time that day, one Marine's knee grinding into the small of his back, the other's hands gripping his ankles. There was the taste of bile in his throat and the smell of leather in his nostrils, but he couldn't see with his eyes pressed against the short man's outflung gloved hand. 'No hard feelings at all,' he said and the act of speaking brought the waiting vomit welling from his mouth. Then there were people everywhere, lifting him to his feet, wiping the mess from his clothes, carrying the short man from the room.

'That wasn't so smart, Shaw.'

The speaker was tall, angular, prematurely grey. Everybody else had gone, except for the two Marines gripping his arms again.

'And you can get fucked too,' Shaw told him and retched, but nothing came up.

The grey-haired man chuckled as though pleased by a piece of sparkling repartee and said, 'Let's have a couple of chairs in here.'

The door opened at once and two upright wooden chairs were carried in. The Marines forced Shaw down on to one of them and secured his strapped wrists to its back, then stepped away. His face still creased in the smile the chuckle had implanted on it, the grey-haired man swung the other chair in a great arc and smashed it down on Shaw's head and left shoulder. Pain exploded in him, then faded as the room greyed into blackness. The words 'That was for talking dirty' welcomed him back to consciousness, a ringing inside his skull, and a deep pulsing ache in his shoulder and left arm. He had no vision in his left eye and didn't know then that that was because it was full of blood from a scalp wound. The other showed him bits of chair scattered over the floor.

'My name's Homer.'

The statement seemed to boom and echo off the walls. Shaw shook his head in an effort to clear his ears, but the movement hurt him and he stopped doing it. Homer. Townsend would have done something with that, he thought. A quotation from *The Odyssey* probably, if there were any memorable lines in it, but all he could manage was, 'Code, given, or surname?'

The chuckle came again and Homer said, 'You're a wit, Shaw. You know that? I like wit in a man, but right now there's no time for badinage. I need to know where the rest of your Brit wits are, if they are all Brits, and I still need to know where they are if they're not. Where are they?'

'Some Marine colonel wanted to know that too,' Shaw replied. 'I told him the truth which is that there's only me, but he was so interested in seeing how far his gun would go up my nose that he probably forgot.'

'Shaw.'

'Yes, Homer?'

'I appeal to you not to do this to yourself. What they'll decide to do with you eventually I don't know. Maybe you'll go to the chair or the gas chamber. Maybe they'll hang you or put you in solitary confinement for about three hundred years. Like I say, I don't know, but between now and then you could save yourself a whole lot of grief by being sensible. Do you know what's next on the agenda if you continue to act stubborn?'

'You'll shoot me full of drugs, and you'll be wasting your time. I can't tell you about people who don't exist.'

Shaw was thinking drearily what nonsense that was and wondering how deeply he would be forced to implicate

Townsend and Logo when the man who called himself Homer said, 'No, it won't be like that. It takes too long and a hard man like you seem to be can sometimes blur information at the edges for a while. We wouldn't like that with a bunch of terrorists either heading for the hills or running around New York City planting more bombs. No, we wouldn't like that at all, so what happens next is you get the "Three Tees". Know of it?'

Shaw knew of it. They system had been used in the Argentine in the days of the military *junta*, still was in Chile and a lot of other countries, and was believed to be employed by the IRA. He didn't speak.

'The "Three Tees",' Homer told him, 'means we wire your tongue, tits and testicles to a hand-generator and crank the handle. Man, you'll go through the roof! When you've done that a few times you'll go mad, but you'll have talked first. Now, I'd guess that was the kind of unpleasantness you could do without. Who made your bombs?'

The sudden shift in direction caught Shaw unawares and his right eye blinked rapidly. His left, sticky with congealing blood, did not.

'The bombs, Shaw. Who made them?'

'I did. We're trained to handle explosives.'

'I know what the SAS is trained to do, Shaw. It's trained to make the best possible use of available materials, not produce sophisticated gadgets like you've been using. Their high-tech equipment comes with the rations.'

'It's not my fault I'm clever with my hands,' Shaw said.

'Where's Townsend?'

'I wish I knew. God, how I wish I knew!'

'Explain that.'

'Next to getting out of here,' Shaw said slowly, 'the thing I'll do my best praying for is an hour alone with Townsend. I wouldn't bother with any "Three Tees", I'd just break his bones one by one. He's the little bastard who blew the whistle on me.'

'Meaning what?'

'Meaning that we were friends. Meaning that he was the only person alive who knew what I was doing. Meaning that

226

he came to New York to talk me out of it. Meaning that he failed, promised to keep his mouth shut and broke his word. There's no other explanation for your identifying and locating me amongst ten million people. I was shopped, probably for the good of my soul. He's some sort of religious freak and I hope he burns in hell!'

'Sure, sure,' Homer said. 'There's one little lady of the streets who plies her trade near your apartment and confirms he was with you for quite a while trying to make you mend your ways. Christ, you really are a terrible liar, Shaw. Next you'll be telling me he left his shot-gun behind in case yours got lonely. I'm afraid we don't have any more time to waste on that kind of stuff, so we'll have to see what a little electric shock-therapy can do for your memory.'

He jerked his head at the Marines, added, 'Bring him along,' and turned to the door. It opened at his approach and, as he passed through, Shaw heard a voice say, 'You better read this first, Homer.'

There was a long pause with the Marines standing uncertainly beside Shaw and Shaw himself feeling nausea expanding in his stomach like a balloon inflated by fear, then Homer was back with a green plastic folder open in his hands.

'You're dead, Shaw,' he said and there was intense curiosity in his voice. 'You died from gunshot wounds and napalm burns. So did Townsend. The rest of your party were too cooked to identify. If it's any consolation you downed a Libyan Airforce chopper before they finished you off. Now isn't that interesting?'

Shaw's mind was filled with visions of seering agony in his mouth, chest and groin, and it was several moments before the words formed into a comprehensible pattern. When they had done so he let his head drop forward and whispered something inaudible.

'How's that again?'

'I said it's begun. It's ahead of schedule too.'

'What's begun?'

Raising his head, feeling his nerves quieten as he regained control of his imagination, Shaw said, 'Get these Marines out of here and don't have anybody without top security clearance

227

listening outside. When you've done that I'll tell you one thing and one thing only. After that I want the British Ambassador here, or at least his military attaché, when I may or may not tell you and him the rest of it. Hurry!' The orders came out with sharp authority.

Homer neither spoke nor moved until a disembodied amplified voice came from the direction of one of the television 'eyes'.

'Do what the man says, Homer. There's some interesting satellite intelligence coming in, but we'll hold back on the Brits.'

The door opened then and the Marines left to be replaced by three men in civilian clothes. They stood with Homer in a semi-circle around Shaw. One of them kicked a piece of the broken chair out of the way.

'Well? Let's hear this one thing you're prepared to tell us.'

Ignoring the speaker, keeping his regard on the more familiar face of Homer, Shaw said, 'I suppose I was making an attempt on the life of the Leader, but the alert Guardians of the Revolution thwarted it.'

Homer nodded. 'That's pretty close to what Tripoli Radio said.'

'Hmm. I always thought we were intended to be sacrificial goats, but it never occurred to me that they'd be stupid enough to use our names when they killed substitutes for us. With us still alive it's so easy to disprove. Still, that's the Libyans for you.'

'Who's "us", Shaw?'

'Townsend and me. We were hired to assemble an assault group and knock off Gadaffi, Yasser Arafat or Abu Nidal as opportunity offered, or as we were directed by radio. I never had any intention of doing anything of the sort. I sold them the idea of the States as my jump-off point because you can lay your hands on a lot of weapons here. Well, you can in Arizona anyway. Then I misappropriated the funds I had been given in order to finance my campaign against NORAID. That's why Townsend got so mad and walked out on me, whether or not you believe that.'

It seemed to have been tacitly accepted that Homer was

Shaw's chosen channel of communication, because it was he who said, 'Never mind what we believe or don't believe. Where's your so-called assault group now, Shaw? The guys you turned into urban terrorists.'

'I keep telling you there's only me.'

'And we don't believe you.'

'That's your problem,' Shaw said. 'You just told me not to worry about what you believe. Your other problem is forestalling the war in the Middle East my supposed attempt on Gadaffi is designed to trigger.'

'Like how?'

'Search me. Ask the Pentagon. They probably have a desk somewhere with a sign on it reading "War forestalling handled here".'

'You're getting just a little cute,' Homer said. 'That's not a good thing to be around this place. I meant, how is your supposed attempt on Gadaffi's life intended to spark a war?'

'That's the part I may decide to share with you and the British,' Shaw told him. 'You won't get it alone.'

Homer turned to the one new arrival to have spoken and raised his eyebrows. 'Electrodes?'

The other shook his head. 'No, I don't think so. We don't want to confront the Brits with a gibbering idiot. You'd better get on to Washington and ask their embassy if they'd like to do what this man wants. What's the time in London now? 3.30 a.m. about?'

'Right.'

'Too late to set it up for tonight.'

'Set what up?'

'Oh, this background material we've been given on Shaw mentions a Dr Sarah Cheyney of Wimpole Street, London, England. If he stays intractable he can listen to her screaming over the trans-Atlantic line at this time tomorrow.'

Four pairs of eyes were staring at Shaw now. He could feel them as though their contact was physical, but he continued to look only at Homer. Years of practice kept his expression neutral, but did nothing to prevent the balloon of fear expanding again in his stomach, expanding so strongly that it deprived him of speech. While trying to regain that faculty he thought quickly, asking himself if they could, if they would, and getting an affirmative reply to both questions. Gaining access to the house would be simplicity itself. Two men, one taken ill, the other ringing the bell of the house with the doctor's shingle on it, as had most of the houses in Wimpole Street and Harley Street. They would be admitted automatically, the call would be placed and the pain applied.

It was then that Shaw realised they had got it wrong and the balloon in his stomach collapsed. Only minutes earlier their desire for information on the New York bombings had been urgent, but that need had been replaced, at least for the time being, by the necessity to find out more about whatever was written in the green folder regarding his alleged activities in Libya. For that purpose, psychological pressure on him over a period of twenty-four hours had been deemed preferable to physical torture, but by then it would all be over one way or another. It followed that Sarah Cheyney was in no danger, a conclusion he intended to keep to himself.

For the first time Shaw looked from face to face, his right eye wide as though with shock. 'You stinking, slimy, sadistic bastards!' he shouted, hoping his words conveyed the sense of horror he no longer felt.

Two rooms away, three men and a woman sat silently at a console watching the images and print-outs produced by the row of grey machines in front of them, machines electronically linked to the metal-studded strap around Shaw's wrists and the wired back of his chair. They appeared frozen into immobility until, with economical movements, the woman broke the tableau by placing a cigarette between her lips. A cat's tongue of flame from her lighter lived briefly and smoke rose almost vertically in the still air until the extractor fans dissipated it at ceiling height. A very large blond young man stood behind them. He had the appearance of the archetypal college football player he had recently been, but not of the holder of a doctorate in the human behavioural sciences which he had become. Apart from his size, the most noticeable thing about him was his regard. It could remain fixed on its object for long periods of total absorption, or flick from point to point with an intensity which always indicated purpose. His eyes seemed never simply to wander and they snapped towards Homer as he came through the doorway.

'What do you know, Zach?' Homer asked him.

'A very controlled man,' Zach said, echoing the words of a British Army doctor spoken months before and thousands of miles away, adding, 'The two things don't often go together, but he has fast physical reflexes as well. What's his background?'

'Never mind about that. Just tell me what you've got.'

'Not as much as I would have done with efficient skin contacts,' Zach grumbled, 'and not a darned thing from his face on the tube here. Nothing genuine, that is. Do you want it from the top line down?'

'Yes.'

'OK. Pulse fractionally above what I guess to be normal for him at the outset. Understandable. He wasn't impressed too much with that guy who hit him in the stomach and – and this is interesting – I detected no trace of increased neural activity when he took him out with his feet. That was a programmed reaction, not a premeditated one involving thought. The conclusion is he's probably combat trained. OK?'

'Keep going, Zach.'

'Nothing to say about when you busted him over the head with a chair. Reaction was that of somebody being busted over the head with a chair. In fact, there wasn't a lot of anything which, considering his circumstances, is also interesting, until you mentioned the "Three Tees". That scared him, and it scared him before you spelt out what it meant. Draw your own conclusions. Next, he's lying about having made the bombs himself and he's covering up for this guy Townsend. He over-played that bit badly. All very British, don't you know? But you figured that for yourself. Could be Townsend made the bombs, huh?'

'Skip the conjecture and stay with what you know,' Homer said. 'What was his reaction when I gave him the Libyan bit?'

'Relief. Big relief, after he'd gotten over thinking about having his balls fried. That was when he started yelling orders, remember?' Without waiting for a reply Zach went on,

'Nothing strange there. The change of subject must have been very welcome at that point in time. Why didn't you pursue it, like asking who had hired him for the assassination attempt? I could have built up a better picture, given more material.'

'Because, Zach, we were already straying outside the parameters of the original enquiry about the New York City bombings and I wanted to check with you on that before the situation got any more confused. But first I need to know your reading of his reaction to the threat to the woman Cheyney. The boss threw that in as a shot in the dark. Her name only came up at all because we asked the Brits about his known contacts. She was the only female listed, but it doesn't follow that she means anything to him.'

'That's another interesting thing,' Zach said, took his eyes from Homer's for the first time and ripped a length of stylo-marked paper from one of the grey machines. He tore two sections from it, wrote 'Subject' and 'Girl' respectively on them and handed the strips to Homer saying, 'These are the torture threats to him and the girl. Very similar peaks indicating extreme agitation, with the girl's a tad higher than his own, but not sustained for so long. Not being a mind reader I can't tell you why. Possibly he kidded himself that the boss was kidding him. His outburst at the end doesn't register worth a damn, but his initial reaction is clear enough, so maybe he persuaded himself that we wouldn't dare touch her in the UK. Whatever the reason, you have a lever there.'

'Thanks, Zach. Now for the bottom line. How do you read his claim to have been operating alone?'

'It's a lie. Townsend was working with him. I already told you that.'

'Yeah, so you did, but are you suggesting that just the two of them caused all this chaos? That there are *no* others?'

'Suggesting? Yes. I can't put it more strongly than that. My discipline isn't a precise one.'

The statements seemed to perplex Homer. He worked his chin from side to side as though testing the elasticity of the jaw muscles, then muttered, 'I suppose it's possible.' More loudly he added, 'You're not often wrong.'

Zach shrugged.

'Immigration reports that Townsend has left the country,' Homer told him. 'He took a Pan Am flight to London before we slammed the door.'

Zach shrugged again and said, 'Then my guess is you don't have a bombing campaign anymore, but don't quote me on that.'

Able to see out of his left eye again after the blood had been washed from his face, with a light meal inside him and his wrists free at last, Shaw sat on another upright chair in another room facing a long trestle table with twenty-three men ranged along its far side. The scene made him think of a witness facing a congressional committee of enquiry. Homer was there. So was the man who had threatened Sarah Cheyney and who seemed to be in overall charge of the proceedings and whom he had heard addressed as Maxton. The remainder he had never seen before. There were four doors to the room, each with a mirror set in it, and he knew that he was being observed through the devices, probably by armed Marines. Lethargy, close to indifference, had hold of him and that interested him. It also worried him when he could find the energy to allow it to do that.

'Identify yourself for the record.'

Shaw looked at Maxton, ignored the command and said, 'Which are the British?' He thought he had identified one of them: a slender, immaculately dressed man with a clipped military-style moustache and a languid appearance. He was wrong.

A short tubby figure, with tufts of hair above each ear bracketing his bald head like quotation marks, moved slightly on his chair and jerked a thumb to either side of him.

'Three of you?'

'Yes.'

'Who are you, please?'

'Major-General Purbright, British Military Attaché to Washington.'

'Who won the county cricket championship this year, General?'

Purbright blinked, half smiled and said, 'Essex, I think. Yes, it was Essex.'

'Where did you go to school, sir?'

Before the general could reply Maxton asked angrily, 'What the hell's going on?'

Purbright looked along the table at him. 'He's trying to put my nationality beyond question to ensure that his own country is not deprived of information in his possession by your possible use of American actors to impersonate us, for example. I think you'll agree that that is prudent of him.' He turned back to Shaw and said, 'Harrow.'

'What's an "Oppidan"?'

'That's Eton, not Harrow, but the word describes a student at Eton whose accommodation is in the town, not in the College itself.'

'Thank you, sir,' Shaw said. 'You're British.' Then, for the record, he identified himself, doing it precisely, pedantically, as a curb to a mind showing a tendency to wander. After that the questions began, but Shaw ignored them, outlining instead his recruitment and his imaginary plans for carrying out the tasks assigned to him, declining to name his contact on the grounds that that was a matter for the British alone which he would reveal only to General Purbright. Why he did that he was unsure, knowing only that it had something to do with maintaining control of the meeting and preventing it developing into an inquisition, at least until the clouds of mist floating like a television weather-map projection inside his skull dispersed. That was when he realised why the mist was there.

Maxton asked something about the reason for it all.

'What?'

'Get hold of yourself, Shaw. Earlier you talked of war in the Middle East resulting from what you were supposed to have done. What's the connection as you see it?'

'The hostages,' Shaw said. 'The hostages in Lebanon.'

'What about them?'

'The assassination of Gadaffi or one of the others at the hands of the British was expected to result in an anti-Western backlash and the killing of the hostages.' Shaw looked vaguely along the line of men until his eyes settled on General Purbright. It was more comforting talking to him, almost like being back in the Army again. 'It was intended to produce a gung-ho mood in the States, sir,' he said, and almost to himself added, 'I hope they're all right. This wasn't supposed to have happened for some days yet.'

'Is that all?'

Maxton had spoken, but Shaw kept looking at Purbright.

'No, it's not all. There are to be retaliatory attacks from Libya, or Lebanon, or both, on British installations in Cyprus. I believe the targets to be the RAF airfields at Dhekelia and Akrotiri-Episkopi, and the 9th Signals Regiment's radio intercept station at Ayios Nikolaos. I have no knowledge of the strength or type of the forces to be employed.'

The statements brought no reaction at all until Purbright asked, 'Do you have access to news in any form here, Shaw?'

'Not so far, sir,' Shaw told him. 'They talk to me occasionally, beat me up from time to time, and feed me, but that's the full extent of the entertainment on offer. Except for putting thymoleptic drugs in my food that is. I've just worked that bit out.'

'What sort of drugs?'

'Greek derivation,' Shaw said. '"Thymos" means "mind" or "spirit", and "Lepsis" is "breakdown", I think. I once had an educated sergeant who taught me that.' For a moment Shaw stared blankly in front of him trying to remember the context in which he had made a similar remark about Townsend, but his memory failed him and he went on, 'Librium, Valium, one of those things. I think they're all called Diazepam back home now in a general way and – well, never mind about that. If I start talking a lot of balls you'll know the reason for it. Where was I?'

'Shaw.'

Shaw looked at Maxton. 'Yes?'

'Are you all through with your reminiscences?'

'Yes.'

'Well now, that's just dandy because you may be interested to hear that sea and air raids were launched against British bases in Cyprus following your supposed attempt on Gadaffi. The fact that the attacking forces were cut to pieces in no way reduces the value of the intelligence you appear to have available to you, and we'd be very interested in hearing the rest of it.'

'I'm sure you would. It's an interesting story,' Shaw said and seemed to lose himself in contemplation of the red marks left by the strap around his wrists.

'So tell it.'

'I might, if the price is right.'

'Price? What price?'

'I can't expect you to let me go,' Shaw said, 'so I'll settle for your word, in front of these British witnesses, that I'll be taken out of here and given a public trial. This is the sort of place people disappear in, having unexpectedly succumbed to a terminal attack of galloping dandruff. I don't need that. There's still a lot I have to say to the American people about Ulster.'

'The United States of America make no deals with terrorists, Shaw.'

'Well, you would say that, wouldn't you?' Shaw replied. 'No doubt it explains why the District of Colombia isn't a State, because from the way the White House has been carrying on with the Ayatollah Khomeini it can't be governed by the same rules. Still, we'll let that go.' He turned to General Purbright then and added, 'Sir, would you please note that by implication I have been refused a trial?'

Purbright raised his eyebrows fractionally, but didn't speak and, for twenty seconds, neither did anybody else. Shaw spent them trying to probe through the mists in his mind for something, anything he might have overlooked, which he could turn to his own advantage, but the drug circulating in his bloodstream finally persuaded him that it was all too much of an effort. His eyelids began to droop.

'Let's hear it, Shaw. You know we can drag it out of you if we have to.'

'You'd probably be too late,' Shaw said and made a gesture like a poker player discarding his hand. 'All right, I came to the States in an attempt to save lives, so I might as well be consistent about it.' The statement sounded affected to his ears and that annoyed him because the sentiment he had expressed had been genuine and as logically arrived at as his clouded thinking permitted.

Staring fixedly at Maxton he went on, 'Get an immediate signal off to all your warships and any other vessels you have in the Gulf to Oman and the western part of the Indian Ocean. They should treat all requests for assistance from unidentified ships claiming to be in distress with the utmost suspicion, and if they come across one that appears to be on fire they shouldn't approach within bloody miles of it. You too, General. Warn our frigates and whatever else we have out there. The sucker punch is intended for the Americans, but there might be a case of mistaken identity.'

His message delivered to his own hazy satisfaction, the incongruity of his issuing orders to the USN and the RN struck Shaw. For a few moments he sat enjoying the thought then, realising that nobody had moved, that nobody had said anything, he shouted, 'Do it! Don't just sit there like a bunch of stuffed dummies!'

Almost kindly Maxton said, 'Take it easy, son. This room is wired for sound and you have a bigger audience than the people in it. The Navy guys outside will be enciphering signals right now, so why don't you just keep talking?'

Shaw kept talking. He talked of the Q-ship with its holds crammed with high-explosives and of its Iranian crew members. He talked of the intended firing of barrels of combustible materials concealed in the superstructure to lure a victim near and of the suicidally murderous blow which would be struck when that had been achieved. He talked, too, of the intended mining of the Strait of Hormuz, but it was not until his rambling account touched haphazardly on the fitting-out of the Q-ship in the Israeli port of Elath that he obtained a startled reaction from his listeners.

'*What?*' It was an incredulous bark from Maxton.

'Yes, that's right,' Shaw told him. 'The whole thing is Israeli-inspired, or Mossad-inspired anyway, which isn't necessarily the same thing, but looks like it in this case. The object is twofold. First to ensure the continuation of an American military presence in Europe and the Middle East. They're nervous about your possible abandonment of international obligations in favour of a "Fortress America" scenario, and they believe that a sharp kick in your national pride will result in an increased presence instead of a withdrawal. The second factor is Syria.'

'In what way, Shaw?'

'They – the plan is . . .' Shaw shook his head violently and said, 'Somebody bring me some coffee. A big mug of it. Black and sweet. And you Marines peering through those mirrors, take your itchy fingers off your triggers. I'm going to get up and walk around to work some of this drug out of my system.'

He stood up and began to stride back and forth parallel to the long table. Nobody shot him. Nobody tried to stop him. A woman came in with the coffee and he thanked her politely.

'You're welcome.'

'Have a nice day,' Shaw said.

It was several minutes before he sat down, looked at Maxton and asked, 'Have you been getting any satellite intelligence on new Iranian military build-ups south of Abadan on the Shatt al Arab?'

Maxton returned his stare, not speaking.

'Well, have you or haven't you?'

'Yes, we have. They're preparing to mount a new attack on Basra.'

'No they're not,' Shaw said. 'They're going to invade Kuwait, destroy the oilfields there, then turn north to take the Iraqis in the flank. It's a much more logical line of approach to the battle for Basra than fighting through all those marshes. They have just about everything going for them too. They're Israeli-trained and supplied, and they already have a Fifth Column of Persian-speaking Shia Muslims in Kuwait, descendants of Iranian immigrants who've been there for decades. They'll probably do most of the demolition work, leaving part of the Army free to set up a military government while the rest moves into Iraq. In one stroke they'll have turned the Iraqi flank, increased world dependence on Iranian oil and destroyed Iraq's main financial backer. The Israeli theory is that that will bring you people running and keep you there. Us too, probably. Neat, isn't it?'

'You spoke of Syria, Shaw.'

'So I did. That's the bottom line for the Israelis. They have it worked out that with Iraq engaged on two fronts Syria will move on Baghdad in support of their Iranian chums. When the

Syrians are fully committed Israel will take Damascus and clear up the whole Syria–Lebanon mess.'

Maxton turned his head to the left and looked enquiringly at the languid man with the clipped moustache.

'Only whispers pointing to 1988, and very low-grade material at that,' the man said. 'Not enough to even analyse, let alone act on.'

'Shaw.'

'Yes?'

'How come you are in possession of hard intelligence while the CIA has heard only whispers?'

'I found a folder in a phone booth,' Shaw told Maxton. 'It's funny how people always leave them there.'

25

The missile frigate USS *Tallahassee* heard the SOS on the five hundred kilocycle distress frequency, reversed course and increased to flank speed, spray exploding with metronomic regularity as her stem sliced through the short steep seas of the Gulf of Oman.

'Must be that coaster flying the Saudi flag we passed an hour back,' the executive officer said and the captain nodded his agreement. Neither spoke again until the radar's probing electronic finger found the stricken vessel at the same moment that a smudge of smoke lifted above the northern horizon.

'Dead ahead, Cap'n.'

'I see it. Get the chopper airborne.'

By the time the machine had clattered away to the north the smoke had thickened, forming a black zigzag shape against the pale grey winter sky. Then decreasing distance flattened the earth's curve and showed them the burning ship.

'Cap'n sir, the chopper reports three individual fires. Bow, midships and stern, about equally spaced.'

The captain glanced at the sailor with the earphones on his head and the microphone on his chest, nodded again and said to nobody in particular, 'Now I wonder how in hell they managed to do that?'

'Chopper says they have hoses rigged, but nothing much coming out of them, sir. About a dozen men on deck waving.'

'OK.'

'Fire and boat crews, Cap'n?' The executive officer's question came out like a gentle reminder.

'No, not yet,' the captain said. 'Sound General Quarters.

The missile crews can stand down, but I want the Phalanx manned. The 76mm too.'

The executive officer relayed the orders, wondering what his superior proposed to do with two systems, one light and one heavy, which could fire 3,000 and 90 rounds a minute respectively. The frigate's intercom chanted metallically and for long moments feet pounded on steel, then there were only the sounds of the wind and the sea and a waiting which seemed audible too.

'Reduce speed to fifteen knots.'

'Fifteen knots, aye aye.'

The wind and the sea quietened.

As though he had heard the executive officer's unspoken question the captain said, 'I don't like any of this. I don't like those three spaced fires, I don't like the coincidence of them breaking out just after we went by, I don't like their radio dying right after they got their message away and I don't like dry hoses. Maybe the fires killed the radio and the pumps. Maybe they have a missile or a gun aboard that tub. Maybe we're being suckered, and maybe I'm nuts. Tell the chopper to stand off and watch for anything unusual, and reduce our speed to five knots. We'll take this very slowly.'

Less than a thousand yards separated the two ships now and a shift in the direction of the wind linked them with smoke from the fires.

'Come twenty degrees left and keep me clear of this stuff. I need to see.'

'Twenty left, aye aye.'

With the *Tallahassee* out of the smoke, their binoculars showed them men capering wildly, their arms flailing.

'The lifeboat's alight back aft,' the executive officer said and added unnecessarily, 'That's why they're not abandoning ship.' There was reproof in the words. The captain heard it, but didn't speak until two figures ran to the side of the coaster, scrambled over the rail and dropped into the sea. With the range down to five hundred yards nobody aboard the frigate needed binoculars to witness that.

'OK, let's go see –' The phone beside the captain shrilled. He stopped talking and snatched it from its cradle.

241

'Captain speaking.'

For six seconds he listened, then in a calm, almost fatherly voice he said, 'All ahead emergency. Full left rudder. Men in exposed positions lie down on the deck.'

Vibration building rapidly throughout the length of the hull, spray bursting at the bows again as the speed increased, the ship heeling as it began to swing to port. The turn was less than half completed when the coaster vanished in a blaze of seering light, light which lessened in intensity to form a writhing ball of fire, a ball which expanded and rose as though forced upwards by the gigantic column of water beneath it.

Then the shock-wave hit the frigate, making it reverberate like a gong and throwing men and loose objects about. One of the men was the captain, standing, watching, in disobedience of his own order. He fell heavily, his head striking the side of the bridge so violently that he was unaware of the sound of the explosion, of the brief blast of heat, or of the rain of metal fragments which struck his ship. When he staggered to his feet the fire-ball had formed into a mushroom cloud and the pillar of water had gone.

In the same calm voice, he said, 'Get me a radiation count and a casualty and damage report.'

In seconds they told him that radiation was normal and, in minutes, that there was extensive damage to piping and electrical circuits, but little that the crew could not repair. Finally he was told that there were two dead men aboard, another seriously injured and eleven with fractures or lesser injuries.

'That doesn't include you, sir.'

He looked at the ensign who had reported the casualty situation to him, then down at his own right forearm. His sleeve did not disguise the fact that the arm was no longer straight.

'Sure, sure,' he said. 'Tell the Exec I'll be visiting the wounded as soon as the medics have time to fix this, that I want a detailed list of all damage on my desk in one hour and that a service for the dead will be held at sunset.'

The captain started towards his cabin to prepare a report on the incident for transmission, but was intercepted by a sailor with two radio signals for him. The first repeated what he had already been told by telephone about the possible existence of a Q-ship. The second instructed him to rendezvous with a carrier group proceeding at speed from the Diego Garcia base in the Indian Ocean to the vicinity of Kuwait at the far end of the Persian Gulf.

'What the hell's going on now?'

'Sir?'

'Nothing, son,' he told the sailor. 'I shouldn't have gotten out of my bunk this morning is all.'

Townsend was deeply worried and struggling with his conscience to a degree which had never been required of him before. The news of the Libyan attempt on the Cyprus bases had seen to that and the photograph of the remains of a Libyan airforce Ilyushin bomber scattered along the Nikosia–Limassol road staring accusingly up at him from the front page of the *Daily Express* ensured that there was no lessening in the conflict between his loyalty to Shaw and to his country.

Earlier he had been intrigued by the status of folk-hero bestowed on Shaw by the tabloid press and interested to read of his own and Shaw's death in the Libyan desert, although the picture of the helicopter they were supposed to have destroyed, standing on its nose near a group of charred bodies rather spoiled the effect for him. The machine's tail section was out of the frame, but the shadow on the ground of the crane holding it in its tilted position was clear enough. That had been mildly amusing, but there was nothing amusing at all about the start of a sequence of events ahead of a schedule he believed only he and Shaw and some others in the Western world, all of them outside the law, knew about.

That the Americans would have had the whole story out of Shaw by now, Townsend accepted as a distinct possibility. They would, after all, be many times more efficient than the girl called Henrietta, the memory of whose ministrations still made him sweat, but there was no guarantee of that because you never could tell with Harry. Never being able to tell with Harry left Townsend bouncing from horn to horn of a dilemma which demanded speech from him on the one hand, or at least an anonymous letter to authority, and silence on the other lest he destroy Shaw's only bargaining counters.

While Townsend agonised, others, better informed than he, were taking action. In the Indian Ocean, American warships sped towards the Gulf of Oman to join more of their kind. In the Gulf itself a British destroyer, a frigate and a support vessel awaited their arrival with the mine hunters which would offer the combined fleet a safer passage through the Straits of Hormuz. Over the Mediterranean, RAF Tornado fighters flew east below the speed of sound, were suckled twice by airborne tankers, went supersonic over Saudi Arabia and howled down on to the runways of Kuwait. Behind them lumbered the Hercules transports with their cargoes of men from the Parachute Regiment and the Royal Marine Commandos. In Cyprus, the RAF, still clearing up after the abortive Libyan attack, stood by to receive additional numbers of aircraft of various types, both British and American, in case their presence should be required in the Persian Gulf.

Nor did it end there. At various Israeli embassies the ambassadors received urgent summonses to present themselves before senior officials of the governments to which they were accredited. In all cases but one they professed genuine ignorance of the activities for which it was diplomatically suggested that their country might be responsible. The sole exception was that of the ambassador to Washington who said with some heat, 'Of course we are supplying arms to Iran, Mr Secretary. They are mostly your arms, delivered at your request. You can't hold us responsible for the use they are put to!'

In Brussels, guarded orders were issued to senior NATO commanders to prepare for certain contingencies. In Tel Aviv, the man known as 'The Suit' made a helpless gesture with his hands and commented to his group on the irony of his country having no option but to afford over-flying rights to the RAF at the request of the British and Kuwaiti governments. In London, Joseph Stein completed the destruction of his records relating to the affair half an hour before Special Branch relieved him of his passport and took all the rest of his papers away for examination.

Of those and other activities Townsend knew nothing yet, and he continued to walk miserably up and down Logo's all-purpose living-room trying to catalogue the various pressures

244

to which Shaw would now be subjected. Then, halting in mid-stride as though he had encountered some obstruction, he said, 'They wouldn't!' He frowned and added, 'They bloody might!' Snatching his coat from the hook on the door he called out, 'Back later, Logo!' and left the flat at a run.

He had covered a mile before he saw a vacant taxi, flagged it down and asked to be taken to Wimpole Street. As soon as the cab turned into it he knew that they not only might but would.

They were using an ambulance and a mail van to bracket the house and that, he thought, was clever of them. Nobody would question the right of an ambulance to be parked in Wimpole Street of all places, and nobody looked twice at a mail van parked anywhere. Townsend might not have looked again so readily had he not been suspicious of everything, particularly a mail van with an aerial on it. Ambulances, yes. Mail vans, no. That wasn't so clever of them and this one had two men crouched in the back. He could see their dark shapes through the driver's window.

'What number, Guv?'

'I've changed my mind,' Townsend told the cabbie. 'Head back towards Hackney, please, and let me off at an electrical appliance shop near there.'

Two hours later Logo accepted the gift of a new refrigerator with some bewilderment as there wasn't anything wrong with the one he already had, but he admired the stout crate it had been delivered in with the bulldog wearing a Union Jack waistcoat and the words 'Made in Great Britain' in red, white and blue lettering on it.

Two hours later, Sarah Cheyney was admiring the same crate in her own kitchen while she levered the top off with a screwdriver.

'You look like a bald girl rising out of a cake at a stag party,' she said.

Townsend swung himself out of the crate admiring not it but her: admiring her for being so beautiful, admiring her for being so quick on the uptake when a Mr Steuben Glass had said cryptic things to her on the telephone, and admiring her most of all for not asking questions now.

He said, 'Please go to your drawing-room window and tell

me if you can see an ambulance and a mail van parked opposite in the street below, about twenty yards to the right and left of your front door.'

Following her into the big room he saw her go to the window, glance down, turn immediately away from it and nod wordlessly as though anything she said might reach the ears of the watchers.

'OK. You've just got yourself a lodger. I don't think Harry will mind.'

Sarah Cheyney nodded again and asked her first question. 'Who are they, Bill?'

'Search me. Not our people. They'd have come straight in. If you want an uninformed guess I think they're probably Yanks, and I think they may want to use you to put the frighteners on Harry. I don't know how, but I'd like to be here if they try.'

'I'd like that too.'

Townsend nodded in his turn and said, 'Look, I'm sorry about the jack-in-the-box bit. These eyebrows and my shaven head work well enough. I hung around outside my father's place and he looked right through me when he came out, but with trained observers actually looking for me I thought that –'

'You're a bit prettier than the original, but it's a jolly good Kojak impersonation,' Sarah Cheyney broke in. 'Still, you thought absolutely right. Now, why don't you stop explaining the obvious, and tell me what you want me to do if those men come here?'

Wishing that there had been time to find a gun somewhere, shrugging mentally and substituting thankfulness for the presence of the two throwing-knives inside his socks, with their points embedded in the heels of his shoes, Townsend told her. 'Do whatever they say. I'll see that the situation doesn't get out of hand.' He hoped that he had sounded more certain about that than he felt.

He was in yet another room, small and featureless. The British had gone and so had most of the Americans because there were only three people in front of him now. For a moment he tried to remember what the British had wanted, but could not, so he let his mind settle again on his important discovery.

'Long time,' Shaw said.

'What is, Shaw?'

Shaw looked at Homer out of red-rimmed eyes, then he looked at Maxton. When he'd finished doing that he looked at a big fair-haired youngish man whose name was Mac or Zach or something, as far as he could remember. There was nothing else to look at except the needles taped to his forearms and the tubes hanging from them, so he just sat and let the sense of cunning grow in him, enjoying the secret knowledge he had acquired. His training had ingrained in him the vital necessity of always being able to place himself in relation to some known point, and he had been faithful to it. He knew precisely where he was now. He was below ground, that was where he was! They had brought him here in a road vehicle, then a boat. Certainly in a boat because it had tilted when they lifted him in and again when they lifted him out. There had been the smell of muddy water too which the hood over his head hadn't concealed. After that his feet had dropped below his head which meant he was being carried down steps and, as he hadn't been carried up any, it followed that having started at water level —

'What's a long time, Shaw?'

'A million years,' Shaw said.

That should hold the bastards. He had no intention of letting on that he knew where he was and, even with his watch taken from him, how long he'd been there.

'Two million is longer,' he added helpfully.

'Shaw!'

'Why do you keep saying that? Shaw, Shaw, Shaw. If you've got an identity crisis that's too bad. I haven't, and I know who I am.'

'We have to know where you got your intelligence, Shaw.'

'From my parents, I suppose. They were called Shaw too.'

Steady, don't bring the old folks into this, whatever it is. Oh, it's all right, they're dead, but don't talk so much. Name, rank and number, that's all. Says so in the Geneva Convention.

'Says so in the Geneva Convention,' Shaw said.

'What are you talking about, man? We simply want to know

who gave you your information about the Middle East problem. You and they are heroes. Amongst other things you saved an American warship from destruction. There could be a medal in it for you.'

There was probably something wrong with what he had said and Shaw worried about that because he might have given the impression that it stated in the Geneva Convention that his parents were called Shaw, but he wasn't certain because he couldn't remember which words he had spoken and which he had only thought.

As if to cover an embarrassing lapse Shaw said, 'Thank you, but I've already got some medals.'

'Think about it for a minute, son. That's one alternative. The other is you spend the rest of your life in a psychiatric prison. There'll be no problem proving you're insane and you sure as hell won't get that trial you were asking for.'

'The Queen was very pleasant when she gave me them,' Shaw said. 'Talked to me for nearly five minutes.'

'Homer.'

Homer looked at Zach. 'Yeah?'

'You'd best skip it. He's not resisting, he's just too far gone.'

'Can't you bring him back?'

'I can,' Zach said, 'but I don't advise it. There could be brain damage. He was exhausted before we even started this session and now he's wandering off on some track of his own. I warned you that could happen. Is the girl option still open?'

'Yes. The Agency reports that she's alone in the house and as it's around ten in the evening over there she isn't likely to go out now, but it means taking a big, big risk.'

Zach shrugged his wide shoulders. 'Not my problem. I'm not in the political assessment business. I'm here to recommend the quickest way of obtaining accurate answers to that raft of questions you have. That recommendation is that you let this guy sleep for two hours and then have him listen while they work the girl over. His reaction was very strong when Maxton threatened her until, like I told you, he somehow rationalised the threat. He's a soldier, not a raving Islamic fundamentalist, and I think he'll talk fast enough.'

Homer sat silent, thinking, until Maxton said, 'We'll do as

Zach suggests. There's been another bombing in New York City.'

Shaw sat silent too, secured to his heavy chair, his wrists and elbows strapped to its arms. He was feeling annoyed because he remembered having worked out his location and now could not recall where that was.

Special Branch had put a large surveillance team on to keeping track of Townsend from the moment of his arival at Heathrow. Its members looked like business executives with umbrellas and students with Swedish flags on their back-packs, like labourers and elderly ladies, like young mothers clutching plastic bags of groceries and like old men with canes. The visual image they presented constantly changed and they had no difficulty in countering his evasive actions without detection all the way to Hackney. Nor, with a minimum of three cars always at their disposal, had they lost him since then.

His suddenly bald head and his first visit to Dr Cheyney had been noted with interest. So had the events leading up to his purchase of a refrigerator and the strange course its crate had followed before arriving at 198 Wimpole Street. The reason for that had become apparent when the presence of a mail van and an ambulance, one or the other of which occasionally drove away but always returned to approximately the same spot, was also noted. It took only seconds for a radio car to link through a local police station to the main road-traffic computer at Hendon and establish that the vehicles were no longer in post office or hospital service.

Over a period of three hours Detective Sergeant Fenner and seven of his team found it necessary to visit in succession a dental surgeon with a practice on the opposite side of the road to No 198, but only five of them came out of the building again. Of those that remained inside, one had taken with him a violin case containing a directional microphone, and it was he who reported that two people, a man and a woman, were still upstairs in Dr Cheyney's house after the staff and patients had left. Fenner and two of his colleagues settled down, as he later wrote in his report, to await developments.

*

Two Marines had had to carry Shaw to bed and then assist him back to the heavy chair after a too short spell of sleep. When they had strapped him into it they left, marching as though on parade. The room was empty of people, but heart-stopping beauty regarded Shaw gravely from the leather-framed photograph on the table in front of him. Maxton's dimly remembered words about listening to her screaming came into sharp focus like a neon sign in his brain and he began to sweat the cold clammy sweat of fear. He could re-member disregarding the threat, but his reasons for doing so were no longer clear and he struggled to recall whatever thoughts he had had. The greyness of his drug-affected mind failed him and his struggle took on physical form with his muscles bunched and straining against the straps securing him to the chair.

'That's one gorgeous piece of black ass,' Maxton said. 'They found the photo in your apartment and I thought you might like to see her that way one last time before she's rearranged.'

He hadn't heard them come in and was only dimly aware of who the three men were, knowing with certainty only that he hated them with a deadly loathing beyond any emotion he had ever experienced. There was nothing impassive about Shaw's face now. With eyes like slits and his mouth wide in an animal snarl, rumbling sounds came from deep in his chest as he renewed his hopeless battle with his bonds.

'Connecting you with London,' a metallic voice announced from the direction of the ceiling.

It happened just as Shaw had predicted, but Townsend wasn't to know that. Shortly after midnight he watched two men leave the ambulance and walk away in opposite directions. When each had covered a hundred yards they crossed the street, reversed direction and strolled towards each other. Townsend, his face blackened with shoe polish, lowered his balaclava-helmeted head below pavement level and crept swiftly down the steps of the service area. There he waited in deep shadow, listening to the sound of two sets of approaching footsteps. When both were above him he heard a gasping cry, the shuffling of feet and a voice asking, 'What is it?' It was an American voice as was the one which replied, 'Heart, I think.'

'Take it easy, you hear? You picked a good spot. This street's full of doctors. Look, there's one lives right here. Let's get you up these steps.'

More shuffling of feet and the faint ringing of the bell reached his ears from inside the house. Don't hurry, he had told her, you're supposed to be in bed and asleep. She didn't hurry and the bell rang again before the front door was opened. Townsend listened to the explanations, saw the two men admitted and the door close. So it wasn't to be an instant snatch. He was glad about that because he didn't know how many men were still inside the parked vehicles. Two at a time was enough. He went in through the service door, bolted it behind him and made his way silently up to the ground floor with one of the knives in his hand. Peering into the hallway he saw Sarah Cheyney being propelled up the stairs by one of the men. There was a strip of adhesive tape over her mouth and both her arms were twisted up into the small of her back. The second man followed, a gun dangling at his side.

Townsend waited until the figures had disappeared into the living-room, put the chain on the front door to discourage reinforcements, and followed, crouching, keeping to the wall side of the treads where he had found that the stairs didn't creak. The living-room door was ajar and he stood to one side of it and waited again. He had a knife in both hands now.

One of the men picked up the telephone and keyed the number of Saks, Fifth Avenue, as he had been told to do, so that nothing out of the ordinary would appear on the British Telecom computer. The store was closing, but the switchboard was still manned.

'Extension 7890,' the man said.

The extension which had existed for only a few hours linked him at once to an installation in New Jersey, buried underground to avoid detection and subsequent observations by Russian satellites.

'Sophomore One,' he said. 'Thirty seconds from now.'

Peering again around the frame of the door, Townsend saw Sarah Cheyney forced down on to an upright chair and secured to it with a length of cord around her elbows. He saw, too, her dressing-gown and pyjama jacket wrenched down almost to her waist and her breasts spring free. Fury shook him physically so that he had to fight the trembling of his own body, shook him mentally so that he had to fight the violent urge to act at once. That he knew he must not do until their intentions were clear enough for him to swear to, clear enough to forge a card for Harry, for her. But the timing. Oh God, the timing. What were they going to do to her? Try to do to her, he amended and had himself back under control.

'Lady, you're going to send a message to a guy named Henry J. Shaw. You'll save yourself a lot of pain if you make it good and loud the first time.'

The speaker ripped the tape from her mouth and held the phone close to it.

'Identify yourself!'

'I love you, Whitey,' Sarah Cheyney said.

The second man was holding a pair of pliers now and their jaws were closing on her left nipple when Townsend threw his first knife. If it made any sound when it transfixed the heel of the hand gripping the pliers it was drowned out by a yelping cry of shocked surprise.

Townsend moved into the room saying, 'Don't anybody do anything aggressive, like breathing. I've practised and practised, but I never have got the hang of missing with these things.' The hilt of the second knife was resting on his shoulder, the point held between his fingers and thumb. 'You with the phone, just let it hang, and the two of you lie face down on the carpet.'

They did as they were told, the man with four inches of bloodstained steel protruding from the back of his hand staring at it in disbelief, his face very white.

Picking up the dangling phone, Townsend said, 'It's all over, skipper. The doctor's fine and will stay that way, so be of good cheer. I have to ring off now and call the police.'

'Save the price of the call, Mr Townsend. We're already here and would have been sooner if some clown hadn't chained and bolted the doors. We didn't want to make a noise until we'd heard enough, you see, so that held us up. Drop that knife, please.'

Townsend let it fall, turned and faced the three men with levelled guns standing just inside the door. To the short one in the centre he said, 'Do you get the general picture?'

The only reaction he got to his question was an order to put his hands behind his back. He ignored it, crouched and closed the front of Sarah Cheyney's pyjama jacket. Only one button still remained in place, but it was enough.

She stared at him out of eyes unnaturally wide and stammered, 'D-detective Sergeant Fenner d-doesn't know they d-don't charge for emergency c-calls.' Then she began to emit great whoops of laughter and Townsend struck her cheek with his open hand.

Sarah Cheyney sobered at once and said, 'Thanks. That makes us quits. You're a nice man, William Townsend.'

26

'Oh, they'd have got away with it all right,' Sir John Travis said. 'They had passports and air tickets for an early morning flight to New York in their possession and luggage in the ambulance. Obviously they would have had no option but to leave the country at once as Dr Cheyney would have had no difficulty in identifying them from photographs.'

'Who are they, Travis?'

'Charley's Indians.'

'They're *what*?'

'I'm sorry. Silly of me. It's a name my people use for the CIA.'

The Home Secretary said, 'Well, even if they are addicted to giving people ridiculous names they are certainly to be commended for preventing an act of unbelievable savagery. Are we the only civilised nation left?'

It hadn't really been a question, but the head of MI5 frowned and grunted as though impatient with his political master's ingenuousness, and that made the Home Secretary say, 'Surely you aren't telling me that we subscribe to such practices.'

'I'm not telling you anything, Secretary of State, and I shall be grateful if you will refrain from pressing me on the point.' Then, as if suddenly aware of his tacit admission, Travis hurried on, 'Thank you for your commendation but, in this instance, it is undeserved. The fellow Townsend had put a stop to the proceedings before Special Branch arrived. It was he we had under surveillance, not the CIA, and he led us to Dr Cheyney. And them.'

'And he's in custody?'

'Of course.'

'And how many Americans?'

'Five. The two apprehended in the house, plus two drivers and a locksmith taken from the vehicles. Obviously he was there in case they failed to gain access in any other way.'

'Obviously,' the Home Secretary said and glanced at his wrist, but his watch was still lying on his bedside table. 'What's the time, Travis?'

'Four thirty-five.'

'Hmm, I'd better have a word with Number Ten anyway. This has all the makings of the embarrassment of the century. Help yourself to some more coffee.'

Straightening his dressing-gown as though appearances were of the essence for a telephone conversation with the Prime Minister, the Home Secretary walked out of the room. Within three minutes he was back again, looking slightly puzzled.

'The PM sounded rather pleased,' he said.

The three men had left the room abruptly when the connection with London had been cut, leaving Shaw alone, still strapped to his chair. His wrists were raw, his ankles chafed, his shoulder muscles ached and he was shaking. He couldn't remember ever having been happier. 'I love you, Whitey,' she had said.

Then had come a gasp like some grim prelude to a crescendo of pain and his body had locked rigid in awful anticipation. Shaw supposed that his brain had frozen in sympathy with it because he was unaware of the passage of time before he realised that he had been listening to Bill Townsend's voice for some seconds. Distant at first, it had come closer and finally spoken to him directly. 'It's all over, skipper. The doctor's fine and will stay that way.' That was when the shaking had started in wave upon wave of cathartic release. How he had no idea, but the SAS had looked after its own again.

'You're really causing us a great deal of trouble, Mr Shaw.'

He hadn't heard the woman come in, but he looked up at her now. Squat, fiftyish, grey coat and skirt, motherly face, a pair of spectacles suspended from a cord about her neck resting on her heavy bosom. Not the seduction routine.

'That,' Shaw said, 'was the general idea.'

'Yes, I understand that. How would you react if I suggested an intelligent discussion on your motives?'

'I could take it or leave it, but I'd feel better about it if I wasn't strapped up.'

She walked to him and unbuckled the straps one after the other. Shaw stretched and began to massage his wrists, winced and stopped doing it.

'You're trembling.'

'Full marks for observation,' Shaw said, 'but didn't you mention an intelligent discussion?'

'Yes, because you appear to be an intelligent man. The two things are not mutually exclusive, but I'm interested in establishing how that equates with your immorality.'

'If it's immoral to try to right a wrong I accept your charge. I have noticed since I have been in this country that it's even more difficult to muzzle the American press than it is the British so, I'm glad to say, your media has made it abundantly clear what I consider that wrong to be. No, let me rephrase that. What I *know* that wrong *is*.'

Patiently the woman said, 'We are all aware of the publicity your views have received, Mr Shaw, but perhaps you might care to attempt to justify terrorising a city of innocent people.'

'I did it to teach them that reverential feelings for an idea are no guarantee of its existence as a fact,' Shaw told her. 'That way I hoped that they would put pressure on the less innocent amongst them. Surely that's obvious.'

'But it's not logical. You should have directed your campaign against the Palestine Liberation Organisation, the Red Brigades, Action Directe and the Red Army Faction, all that mess of Middle Eastern and European terrorist outfits which supply the IRA with arms. Not against the USA.'

'I'm glad I didn't have you as my Intelligence officer,' Shaw said.

'Explain that.'

'Because the people you mention are better known for supplying the Irish National Liberation Army, not the IRA. INLA's a small splinter group formed when the IRA once declared a ceasefire. They're even more fanatical, but the IRA is the main threat and it's them I tried to hurt.'

'And are still trying, Mr Shaw.'

'No, Mrs whoever you are. It's finished.'

'But the bombing continues. Your people have attacked the Staten Island ferry.'

It had been such fun taking her on the ferry so that she could see the Statue of Liberty again, such fun taking her anywhere and being taken by her anywhere else. No, not just fun. Thrilling. Even a silly boat ride. Just being near her was thrilling because she was thrilling, exactly as Major-General Brigg had told him all that long time ago. 'I love you, Whitey,' she had said not so very many minutes before. He was sorry somebody had attacked the ferry. It was a form of desecration to have done that. Vaguely he remembered Homer, or had it been Maxton, saying something about another explosion in New York City.

'Not my people,' Shaw said. 'I haven't got any people.'

'Mr Shaw, after we had established your *modus operandi* of issuing warnings to TV stations and newspapers, we made arrangements for all incoming calls to organisations of that kind to be recorded. It took a little time to do that, but the last warning, the one phoned to the *Wall Street Journal*, is on tape. So is the voice of the man who spoke to you from London just now. Our voice analyst assures me that, with or without an Irish accent, they are one and the same. That man was William Townsend, wasn't he?'

The question, which was not a question, brought Shaw down from the high plateau of euphoria he had been inhabiting. The descent stopped his trembling as though a power circuit had been cut and lassitude flowed into him to fill the vacuum the involuntary muscular spasms had left. He could feel it pressing on him like a sudden increase in the earth's gravitational pull, pressing on his arms and legs and head, pressing on his eyelids. Exhaustion, never far from him since his first hours in whatever this place was, had him firmly in its grip. It wasn't an unpleasant feeling, but it deprived him of the ability to think quickly, to decide if what the woman had said was important, if it constituted legal proof of Bill Townsend's involvement and if he could be extradited on those grounds alone. It didn't occur to him to question whether or not she actually had the evidence she claimed. Shaw's critical faculties were failing.

The woman saying something he didn't catch, raising his head to look at her, requiring a physical effort, seeing the glasses on her nose now, big glasses with heavy frames, the cord hanging down either side of her face and disappearing behind her neck like a horse's reins. No, it wasn't a cord, it was a gold chain. He could see the electric light glinting on the tiny individual links and marvelled at the sudden clarity of his vision which made her stand out like a two-dimensional photographic representation of herself. Huge glasses on a flat head. All the better to see you with said the – Concentrate, damn you!

'What?'

'I was saying that your failure to comment on my assertion amounts to an admission. You lied to us about Townsend, Mr Shaw, and you're lying about the Staten Island ferry. Isn't that so? I know you're very tired, so just tell us the truth and then you'll be allowed to rest. Wouldn't that be pleasant?'

'Not really,' Shaw said. 'It's rather interesting here. A moment ago you looked like a cardboard cut-out and now you've gone fuzzy round the edges, so I'm waiting to see if you disappear like the Cheshire Cat.'

There had been no trace of facetiousness in the words and the woman saw that the tired eyes watching her had a look of child-like anticipation in them. She moved then, opening a drawer, pushing his sleeve up, swabbing his arm with alcohol and inserting the needle of a syringe, all with quick, practised motions.

'Don't worry. This won't do you any harm.'

'If you grin, that'll be the last bit of the Cheshire Cat to go,' Shaw said.

'That's right. Now sit quietly for a moment.'

Shaw had shown no interest at all in the injection, keeping his gaze fixed on her face. She returned his regard, waiting for the re-emergence of intelligence. When it came, 'You were telling me about the Staten Island ferry,' she said.

Feeling alert, confident, Shaw told her, 'Oh, that was nothing to do with me. In fact, I didn't know anything had happened to it until you said so. I'd already done my shipping thing, so why repeat that? There are a lot of useful man-holes giving access to several public utilities simultaneously. Gas, electricity, water, telephones, you name it. That was the sort of thing I'd

258

have blown up next, not some old ferry. In fact I was trying to decide which to choose when I got this feeling that I'd be identified soon, so I decided to switch to another city. Then half the United States Army arrived and arrested me before I could move somewhere else.'

It felt so good to have his wits about him again, to be able to explain things rationally, to be back in control. He looked gratefully at the hypodermic syringe lying on the table. Obviously he had begun to doze off and she'd given him a jolt of Coramine, or Megimide, or one of those things, to pull him together.

'Where did you get the SEMTEX, Mr Shaw? It's a Czechoslovakian plastic explosive not normally available in this country.

'Mexico.'

'You collected it personally?'

'How else? You can't obtain it by mail order.'

'Which border crossing point did you use?'

'Tijuana.'

'Now that is strange,' the woman said. 'We have a Mexican police report on all illegal transactions in SEMTEX since your arrival in this country, and the only one that appears to have real relevance occurred near the town of Caborca. It's very close to Nogales which spans the border between Mexico and Arizona. That was the obvious route to use, so why drive many miles in the wrong direction across virtually non-existent roads to come in through California?'

Shaw knew the answer to that. 'Because the SAS never does the obvious thing,' he told her.

'I see, but the sale was made to a seemingly very young man with fair hair bearing a marked resemblance to Mr Townsend.'

Shaw knew the answer to that too. 'Right, but that was before the quarrel we had when I told him we weren't going to North Africa.'

'Yes, that makes sense. That would be about the time you recruited Mr Bridenthal, wouldn't it? We've just received an enquiry on his whereabouts from the Israeli government we'd like to reply to.'

259

Shaw was ahead of her. 'Don't be silly. Bridenthal was a Mossad agent and nothing whatsoever to do with my two-man regiment.'

'Thank you, Mr Shaw,' the woman said.

Watching her retreating back, Shaw felt disconcerted and a little annoyed at the abrupt cessation of the discussion. They had barely touched on the subject of his motives and he had wanted to tell her about the letter he had written and mailed to his solicitor for safe keeping. That would have explained everything clearly. He began to think about the points he had been able to make, replaying the exchange as though a tape of it existed inside his head. The tape was very clear and so, when he approached the end of it, was the realisation of the damning things he had said, the damning things he had admitted while he thought he was being so clever.

Shaw withdrew into himself, willing the darkness to come and shut out the world. The darkness obliged him and he toppled forward from his chair, thudding on to the floor, and lying there his muscles rigid, cataleptic.

'That about wraps it up,' the woman said. 'There were just the two of them. Him and Townsend. His brain went out of control at the end and I don't think he was capable of logical lying by then. Agree, Zach?'

'Yes.'

'What about the bomb maker?'

The woman looked at Maxton and shrugged. 'Shaw's probably good for another forty years, so you've got plenty of time to wring that out of him. The urgent questions are answered. The attempt on the ferry was emulation, like the George Washington Bridge. That was always possible as you said yourself because dynamite was used, not SEMTEX. I suggest you recommend to the Governor that he stand down the National Guard and that the rest of them go home too. It's over.'

'And the Middle East connection?'

'Well really, what do you expect me to say? That Israeli enquiry gave us the name of a known and highly placed Intelligence operative. You heard Shaw recognise Bridenthal's name and state correctly what he was. If you prefer my inferences to your own I figure that Bridenthal went after Shaw and got himself questioned and killed for his pains. It's the only explanation for Shaw being in possession of that kind of information. What puzzles me is, with Bridenthal missing for so long, why it took the Israelis until now to ask about him.'

'They didn't dare ask before,' Maxton told her. 'We could have back-tracked and tied him in with Shaw, maybe through the guy in London he told Purbright about. That would have alerted us to Shaw's existence, and with them suspecting how much Shaw might have learned the last thing they wanted was to hand him to us.'

'And now?'

'And now it doesn't matter. Their plan's blown and they're trying to get back into our good books by persuading us that the whole darned Middle East thing was Mossad-inspired and executed without either official government backing or knowledge. It's nonsense of course.'

'Oh, I don't know. Ever hear of the CIA?'

Maxton smiled, shook an admonitory finger at her and said, 'Not even the CIA would consider invading Syria.'

Townsend's incarceration was not rigorous and he put that down to the fact that nobody seemed to have any very clear idea of what to charge him with. Whatever he might or might not have done appeared to have been done or not done outside the jurisdiction of the British courts. The excessive use of force through the throwing of a potentially lethal weapon while preventing grievous bodily harm to a fellow citizen was all Detective Sergeant Fenner had come up with and he had chuckled throatily when he said it.

For all that, they had put Townsend handcuffed into the back of a windowless van with two men who didn't say anything at all during the ninety-minute drive out of London to a large country house standing at the centre of ten acres of land, all of it surrounded by a twelve-foot stone wall. As it was still dark when he was let out of the van he knew nothing of the mansion's setting until some hours later when he concluded that it was one of those places spies were taken to for interrogation, or defectors for debriefing. He also concluded that it was out of season for both spies and defectors for, apart from his guards, he appeared to be the only occupant.

Townsend was glad to have the handcuffs removed and be led to a pleasant enough bedroom with a bathroom next to it. There were bars on the windows but not, apparently, to confine him, because somebody spoke at last to tell him that breakfast was 8.30 and that he was free to wander where he liked provided that he did not go within twenty yards of a wall surrounding the property. The man went away then, leaving the door unlocked.

There were toilet articles in the bathroom and clothes of his size in the closet. Townsend brushed his teeth, put on pyjamas and got into bed nodding goodnight to the closed-circuit television 'eyes' watching him from the corners of the room. Sleep evaded him and two hours later TV 'eyes' set in the corridors watched him leave the house dressed in a tracksuit and trainers. More of them followed his progress from the trees as he jogged down the drive towards the main gate in the early light of dawn and then make ten circuits of the small estate keeping well inside the forbidden area near the wall. The grass was brittle with frost and his feet were soaking when he returned to the house, but he forgot the small discomfort when from a room to the left of the front door a man's voice called, 'Come and look at this.'

He went into the room and stood by the man's chair, watching the television screen, hearing a newscaster say '. . . at the request of the Government of Kuwait', seeing the RAF Tornado fighters dropping out of a vividly blue sky, their tyres creating bursts of the smoke of friction as they touched down. Then he was looking at paratroopers and Royal Marine Commandos, all in full combat gear, streaming out of Hercules transports and running towards waiting trucks and buses, but he heard very little of what the announcer was saying as his racing mind strived to answer the unanswerable questions of whether Harry had played another of his trump cards, had had it snatched from him, or if information from some totally different souce had triggered the movement of planes and troops to the Persian Gulf.

The scene had shifted to a multi-vehicle pile-up on a motorway near Manchester before Townsend became aware that the man in the chair was talking to him.

'I'm sorry. What did you say?'

'Just asked you what you made of all that Kuwait stuff.'

'Oh, it'll be another of those rapid deployment exercises,' Townsend said. 'They did one last summer to Oman. Operation "Swift Sword" it was called.'

The other shook his head. 'Doubt it. I was watching you doing your marathon round the grounds on this screen, then when I could see you coming back up the drive through the window I switched to the news. They're tying it in with some attempt to blow up an American warship which the US Navy has just announced. Could be we've got trouble. The Iranians are making noises about Western imperialistic aggression.'

'So what's new? Tell me, what would have happened if I *had* gone within twenty yards of that wall?'

'I wouldn't try to find out if I were you,' the man said.

Townsend nodded and went upstairs to change out of his wet shoes and socks.

By the end of the day he had established several things. He had discovered that there were six men in the big building apart from himself, quiet men without any particularly noticeable characteristics, or accents indicating class or regional origins, quiet men with little to do but be there and watch him without appearing to do so. One seemed to be in charge, but only to the extent of handing an envelope to the leather-clad motorcycle messenger who came at noon and departed again immediately, while the others were left with the chore of unloading groceries from an unmarked van which arrived an hour later.

He had established that there were two cars, a Volvo and a Jaguar, in the big garage at the back of the house and that the rotor arms had been removed from both of them. Inclining his head towards a watching TV 'eye' in acknowledgement of that precaution, he had returned to the room by the front door and asked the watcher why he was being held, where he was being held and for how long he was likely to be there. The man had given him a weak smile, but no reply.

He had established, as well, that the cooking was terrible. His offer to take on the task for all their sakes and to give himself something to do had been met with indifferent acquiescence, and the results with the nearest thing to animation he had encountered in an all-pervading atmosphere so negative as to seem tangible. Never unfriendly, the men became more companionable, prepared to talk on any subject other than those that affected Townsend personally. But it was not a friendliness he welcomed, making him think of the solicitude of warders keeping vigil with a condemned man during the night before his execution. In the hope both of inconveniencing them and ridding himself of fanciful notions he went jogging in the dark. Townsend failed in both those aspirations, but the events of the next thirty-six hours drove away his gloomy forebodings.

The television warned him of the developing drama in the Persian Gulf first, and the newspapers delivered by the grocery van on its second visit confirmed what it had told him. They fleshed out the bare bones too with the views of foreign correspondents, special correspondents, military correspondents, retired service chiefs and veterans of the Falklands War served up in a mix of conjecture and fact.

Satellite observation revealed a formidable build-up of Iranian troops and vessels a few miles from the borders of what all the papers referred to with a single-minded lack of originality as the 'oil-rich' State of Kuwait, and that the Emir had appealed to his old friends the British for protection against this potential threat. They had given it before when Iraq had shown signs of expansionism, Townsend read, and he thought he remembered something about that from his childhood, and had given it again now being geographically the best placed of Kuwait's supporters to do so.

That was all clear enough, but what was not clear at all was what the Iranians thought they were doing in launching an atttack on Kuwait at battalion strength in two ships each carrying some 500 men, with an escort of two gunboats and without air-cover. Theory, supported by a rapidly mounted Intelligence operation, had it that the threat to Kuwait was real and presumably intended as an extension of the war with

Iraq. Conjecture suggested that the sudden arrival of British air and ground forces had given the Iranian military command pause, that dissension had followed discussion and that excitable undisciplined elements of the Revolutionary Guards had decided to act on their own initiative.

Conjecture lost its immediacy when the small convoy entered Kuwaiti waters and fired upon the three gunboats which intercepted it. With the warships locked in battle, the two freighters loaded with wildly cheering teenage soldiers proceeded on their way towards the port of Mina al Ahmadi. Only then, with firepower in excess of the broadside of a battle-cruiser of a generation before, had the Tornados struck. The survivors lifted from the water by the Kuwaiti Navy seemed pleased with their futile attempt at invasion and happily confirmed that conjecture had been right about the reason for it.

It was not until the following day that Townsend learned from the BBC that that was not the end of the matter. At the Security Council of the United Nations in New York the Russian delegate had made angry demands for the withdrawal of all foreign forces from the Persian Gulf but, it was reported, had seemed not in the least put out by a prompt Anglo-American veto. Those mandatory motions having been gone through and successfully disposed of, attention centred on Tehran where the state-controlled radio maintained a silence so untypical as to be sinister. Conjecture suggested that the British destruction of Iranian ships had stiffened the resolve of the military establishment there, and conjecture was to be proved right again.

The build-up to the south of Abadan, temporarily halted, was resumed and continued until a battle group of mostly American warships, with a 90,000-ton aircraft carrier at its centre, passed through the Straits of Hormuz. It was challenged there by a probe of six Iranian Airforce jets, a challenge contemptuously and lethally brushed aside by Tomcat fighters from the carrier. The fleet sped on towards Kuwait and Iranian resolve suffered a relapse. The Kuwait crisis was over and, with it, the Israeli threat to Syria, but of the seven men following the course of the brief emergency from the big house in Berkshire only Townsend knew both those facts.

For nearly a week he cooked, jogged and grew bored with the diet of mutual admiration served to each other's citizens by the British and American media over the joint handling of the events in the Middle East. He read everything he could find in the house, refrained from asking for more in case that should be taken as a tacit acceptance of a prolonged stay, and found himself reduced to looking through a pile of girly magazines.

Townsend heard the van arrive with the groceries and the newspapers, but ignored it, concentrating instead on trying to decide which of the girls in the photographs he would most like to be mothered by. It was a difficult choice because most of them looked as though they should still be at school, preferably one devoted to the eradication of vacuous expressions, and he had identified only four possibles when a voice murmured, 'Well, well,' paused and added more loudly, 'Well, well, well,' as though underlining an essential part of some carefully constructed argument.

Not bothering to look at the speaker Townsend said, 'You can't blame me for developing a Lolita complex after being locked up with you lot.'

A pile of newspapers dropped on to the magazine he was holding. Most slid from there to the floor, leaving him looking at the front page of the *Daily Express*. 'WHERE ARE THESE MEN?' the headline demanded. It was strange suddenly to meet Harry's level regard again, stranger still to see himself with a full head of hair and that made him run his hand over the bristles on his scalp which had not yet quite attained the status of a crew-cut. The photographs were taken from Army records, he knew, and it wasn't difficult to guess that they had been sent to the States for official reproduction, probably by the thousand, and then copies had been bought or salvaged from a police garbage can by some enterprising reporter. 'WHATEVER HAPPENED TO HABEAS CORPUS?' asked the *Daily Mirror* from the floor at his side.

'I'd like the answers to those two questions myself,' Townsend said and glanced up at the man. It was the one he thought to be in charge.

'We didn't know we were entertaining a celebrity,' the man told him.

'Detective Sergeant Fenner suggested that I keep my name to myself in case you got overheated, what with all the excitement around this dump.'

'Did he indeed?'

'Yes,' Townsend said, 'but don't worry about it. I'll sign a menu for each of you when I leave.'

When the man had gone Townsend read all the papers. It was as though the editors felt that trans-Atlantic amity had been given enough of an airing during the Kuwait affair which had lost its news value anyway, and that now was the time to speak sternly to their American cousins about the fate of two British citizens whose activities and stated aims had, rightly or wrongly, caught the imagination of the British people. Both were assumed to be held in the States; Shaw because the American authorities had announced his arrest, and Townsend because his father had been interviewed and claimed not to have seen his son for months. 'Let them be brought to trial' and 'Innocent until proven guilty' were recurrent themes.

Townsend sighed, tossed the papers back on to the floor and went jogging. He didn't really feel like doing so, but knew that he would be deprived of that simple pleasure once he was extradited. It was several minutes before he was able to rid himself of the illusion that the blank stare of the television 'eyes' in the trees had been replaced by inimical watchfulness.

27

The Ambassador of the United States of America to the Court of St James's was furious, and that distressed him because he was a gifted and highly intelligent man who felt that he should have been above falling prey to such a negative emotion. He was also intensely likeable and his being completely unaware of that fact served only to make him the more so. Not being aware of it made him, between bouts of anger, rather wistful that a number of people appeared not to like him at all at this late stage of his long tenure of office.

Most immediately, his anger was directed against the London Station Head of the CIA for mounting a covert operation involving the terrorising of a respectable member of the British public. That that member *was* respectable and female as well was, he knew, irrelevant, but the facts had heightened his disgust as did the conviction that the terrorising must have involved torture to achieve its object. To add insult to the injury done to his high office, five of those responsible had been taken into custody by the British police, an event witnessed by their back-up team, and the ambassador had rightly guessed that had those men not been arrested he would never have been told of the incident. But they had been arrested and he had been told, because the CIA had no choice but to tell him as it was he who would be called to account by Her Majesty's Government.

His exchange with the Head of Station had been vitriolic and resulted in the latter transmitting a long ciphered message to his superiors at Langley, Virginia. That in turn had brought the ambassador a sharp instruction from the State Department to cool it, an expression he did not appreciate, to deny any knowledge of the event when he was questioned about it, but to promise a full enquiry in the interests of stalling for time. Such petty evasion was anathema to him and his wrath expanded to encompass Washington DC.

But his overriding exasperation on this day was reserved for the British and, as a life-long Anglophile who resented the constant strains placed on his affection, that hurt him the most. He had taken up his appointment in London just before the Argentine invasion of the Falkland Islands and had been saddened by the stubborn British belief that obstruction had been the sole contribution of the United States to the recovery of those territories. When at last they were made aware of the role played by American satellites in relaying vital information from the battle zone to the headquarters of their Commander-in-Chief, Fleet, in the London suburb of Northwood and back again, when they were reminded that American Sidewinder aircraft missiles had done much to ensure the virtual destruction of the Argentine Airforce, when the political considerations the Americans had had to agonise over before openly declaring in favour of Britain were explained to them, the British people had responded with a collective sneer.

Their ability to do that was, the ambassador thought, one of their less endearing traits and one that they were only too ready to direct at Americans. He knew that they did it partly out of jealousy and partly because of the misconception that most Americans were of British descent and should therefore think as they did themselves. The fact that the predominance of those of British extraction amongst the American population had ended more than a century before was lost on them.

Nor, with one exception, had their attitude changed much in recent times. From the Lebanon to Grenada and from Libya to Nicaragua nothing the Americans did, either in aim or execution, was right in the eyes of the British people. Then had come the astonishing events in New York City, made the more astonishing by the barely concealed approval of the less responsible sections of the British press for the activities of the so-called 'Hands Off Ulster Regiment'. The exception had been the mutual esteem generated by the success of the joint action over Kuwait, but that had proved transitory and was now replaced by demands for information on the whereabouts of two terrorists, one of whom he knew to have been apprehended in New York, in terms which fell little short of threatening.

It was against that background and in a mood of infuriated dejection that the ambassador received a request that he attend upon Her Majesty's Principal Secretary of State for Foreign Affairs at his early convenience. The request, amounting to a command, had been formal, but the meeting was not.

The Foreign Secretary poured a drink from a bottle of Bourbon which the ambassador knew was kept especially for him and said, 'Neil, we'd like to have our ball back.'

The ambassador made no pretence of not understanding him. 'Henry Shaw?'

'Yes.'

'Why? The man's a self-confessed terrorist.'

'Agreed, but a strange one. I have no information on the number of deaths he may have caused, if any, but I'll hazard a guess that he has saved many more American lives than he has taken. The crew of the USS *Tallahassee* for a start. Add to that the potential for death among many nations, including yours and mine, had the Iranians invaded Kuwait. He gave us forewarning of that voluntarily, according to our Military Attaché in Washington, not under duress.'

'Oh come on, Jack,' the ambassador said. 'You know as well as I that you can't operate the law like a profit and loss account. The law is what it is and Shaw must answer to it. Anyway, you haven't answered my question. Why do you want him back?'

'Off the record?'

'Certainly not. When I'm summoned to the Foreign Office officially, it is my duty to report accurately on what transpires, adding my own opinions and recommendations. I shouldn't have to tell you that.'

'No, you don't have to tell me,' the Foreign Secretary said. 'I just wanted to be quite sure that what I have to tell you will reach the appropriate ears in Washington. You see, depending on the public opinion polls nearer the date, there's likely to be a general election here next June.'

'So?'

'You've seen the tabloid press. Shaw has become something of a folk-hero, a national institution almost, and the pundits tell us that if the Government is not seen to have done everything possible to ensure his welfare the Conservative vote will be adversely affected. I don't think you will disagree with me when I say that the White House will view the prospect of a Labour administration with considerable disquiet. Yanks go home and take your rockets with you and all that nonsense.'

The ambassador sipped at his Bourbon before saying, 'The White House will also view the prospect of being asked to involve itself in such blatant electioneering with considerable disquiet.' The simmering anger inside him boiled over and he added, 'Perhaps "contempt" would have been a better word!'

'Ah well,' the Foreign Secretary said, 'I thought I'd just test the temperature of the water. It seems a little chilly to me and that leaves us with the question of what we're going to do with your five CIA men. Do you have any suggestions?'

'What five . . .?' The ambassador stopped talking at the sight of an upraised hand.

'Hang on, Neil. We've known each other for years, so don't let's start fencing. GCHQ intercepts at Cheltenham indicated above-average high-priority radio traffic from your embassy on the night of an incident in Wimpole Street involving the CIA some days ago. I imagine that was you asking for instructions. Now, in the normal course of events you would have come to me at once, so I can only suppose that State instructed you to play for time. Huge embassy staff. Boss-man can't possibly know the whereabouts of each and every one of them. CIA didn't tell him. That sort of thing. The question was "why?", and the answer seems to be that Washington is perfectly well aware of the electoral point I have made to you, and realised immediately that we would be suggesting an exchange of personnel once the CIA had tripped over its own feet, but needed longer to extract everything they could from Shaw. Well, we certainly owed you that, but they've had long enough now. That's why I asked you to come and see me today. Have I read it right?'

Neat, the ambassador thought, the bland assumption that

the United States would be prepared to trade wrapped up in a tissue of inferences, but he wasn't about to fall for that one, to commit his country, even if he did feel that the implied solution to the problem would be close enough to the probable outcome.

'You're telling it, not me,' he said. 'May I go now? I have some consulting to do.'

The Foreign Secretary stood at once. 'Of course, my dear chap. I'll walk you to your car. That'll just give me time to explain the Cabinet's view on Shaw's message to the American people.' He took the ambassador by the arm and led him out into the passage saying, 'His activities are naturally condemned out-of-hand, but his motives strike a very sympathetic cord with us. Let me put it this way. The Prime Minister and Gorbachev have developed a certain mutual respect, almost a liking for each other, but that liking does not extend to inviting him to Northern Ireland.'

'What are you talking about, Jack?'

'I'm talking about the mistaken conviction held by many of your countrymen, and by successive administrations, that it would be in the best interests of all if we were to withdraw from Ulster against the wishes of the vast majority of the people there. Leaving aside the inevitable blood-bath which would result, a certainty you people either refute or accept as a natural concomitant of revolutionary aspirations, I am also talking about the equally inevitable reduction of the whole of Ireland to a peasant society. Neil, if we withdrew our massive financial support for the industries in the north their economy would be shot to pieces. They've got nothing, you know. Not even their own coal. Are you with me now?'

The ambassador nodded. 'I take your point, albeit with a pinch of salt. Nature abhors a vacuum. Russian investment, Russian installations, Russian domination. Right?'

'Right, and go easy with the salt. A Cuba both sides of the Atlantic, or another Nicaragua in the making. Try to persuade them back home not just to make life difficult for NORAID. You're already doing that. Make it impossible. You Americans are not exactly famous for allowing yourselves to be pushed around and Shaw's activities could have exactly the opposite effect to the one he intended. That could be disastrous. It would also be a great pity just when he seems to have achieved a degree of success.'

Raising an eyebrow quizzically, the American asked, 'What success? By my tally IRA killings have increased recently if anything.'

'You're right, but their tactics have changed. They are now resorting to shooting policemen in the back at point-blank range in crowded streets, which is a risk they would never have contemplated before. That, coupled with the fact that their use of car bombs and mortar attacks against hardened targets has fallen right away, is considered by the Army and the Intelligence people to indicate a shortage of supplies and growing desperation.'

The Foreign Secretary received only a non-committal grunt in reply, followed by, 'Jack, I don't hear any reference from you to the fifty million dollars in aid Ulster has received from the US since the signing of the Anglo-Irish Agreement.'

'Chicken-feed, Neil, and you're too stretched at this time to give more.'

They had reached the car now, and the chauffeur was holding the door open.

The ambassador said, 'I've just realised why I admire you Brits. It's for your uncanny ability to turn a silk purse into a sow's ear.' He smiled faintly, got into the car and added, 'I'll pass your words along.'

It was only a six-inch column tucked away inside *The New York Times*, but Sergeant Mary Alton noticed it. She read it, frowning, marked it for Lieutenant Bergquist and handed it to the office messenger. Then she sat back, her tasks forgotten, and waited for the explosion.

There was no explosion, but a few moments later Bergquist opened the glass door to his office and called, 'Mary, Ace, come in here, will you?'

They followed him in and stood in front of his desk watching him read the article again. When he had finished, he looked up at them and said, 'I'm sorry, you guys. All that work you did wasted. Well, dammit, I'm telling you you did real good, both of you.'

'I don't think Ace knows about it yet, Lieutenant.'

'Oh, don't you, Ace? The bad news is that they're letting that bastard Shaw go for lack of evidence against him. I wonder what they call being found in possession of explosive devices these days. He's to be deported. The good news is that the Feds are about to round up a bunch of Iranian students now known to have carried out the bombings to distract attention away from their military build-up in the Persian Gulf. It figures, of course.'

'It does?'

Bergquist looked tiredly at Detective Diamond and said, 'Sure, Ace. Students is the key word. They attended at one of those Oxford colleges to learn fancy Limey accents, then they took a course in Irish dialects in Dublin and boned up on NORAID and the history of the troubles in Ireland. After that they came across here and fucked up this city. Very thorough people the Iranians. Now, why don't you –'

Closing his mouth firmly on his sarcasm, Bergquist made a dismissive gesture towards the door.

The announcement of Shaw's impending release was given wide coverage by the British media and brought balm to the soul of Joseph Stein, a soul desperately in need of solace. Harassed by Special Branch and other men whose identity he did not know, but whose authority was unquestioned, and treated for that reason as a leper by his colleagues, he was dejected by the failure of the plan for the subjugation of Syria and close to a breakdown.

To those things was added the knowledge of the extent to which he had been fooled and that he found so intolerable that not even the partial success of the venture in ensuring a continued American presence in the Middle East came as any consolation. The physical and verbal abuse he had suffered at Shaw's and Townsend's hands he had borne stoically enough at the time in the belief that his claim to be a good judge of character was well founded, but the shattering of that belief gave those petty indignities a significance which almost broke his tenuous hold on himself. Then his morning newspaper brought him relief. The man he had thought lost for ever within the confines of the American legal system was to be delivered up to him.

Stein knew what he was going to do before he had finished reading the report and abandoned his breakfast to start doing it. He heard no clicks or echoing sounds when he used his own telephone, but suspected that technology had advanced beyond the stage when bugging, particularly government bugging, would give such tell-tale signs. Putting coins into his pocket he went out to a phone box, called the senior Mossad representative in London and asked two questions. To obtain the answers a file had to be checked and a telephone call to the States made.

'Call me back in two hours,' the Mossad man said.

Stein had done so and been given Shaw's flight arrival time at Heathrow the following day and the telephone number of a Mr Connolly, co-ordinator for IRA activities on the British mainland. Stein used some more of his coins.

'Never mind who I am, Mr Connolly. Do you want to get back at the man who killed Macnamara and earn fifty thousand pounds for IRA funds? If so I'll send you ten thousand in cash this morning through any cut-out you name as a gesture of good faith. You get the balance on completion.'

There was a long pause before Stein's ear-piece said, 'Keep talking.'

'Very well. This is what you do and if you deviate from these instructions in any way you won't see a penny of the extra forty thousand. Is that clear?'

The ear-piece agreed that it was, and Stein talked on for another minute and a half before breaking the connection and making his fourth call of the morning.

'Hello, Solly. It's Joe here.'

'Morning, Joe,' Sir Soloman Gold said. 'What can I do for you?'

'I was wondering if you could tell me if there's any romantic attachment between this chap Shaw all the fuss has been about and that pretty dark girl who brought him to dinner with you back in the spring. Doctor somebody.'

'Why do you want to know that?'

'I don't really. It's just that I know his arrival time at Heathrow tomorrow, if that's of any interest to her.'

'Kind. Most kind,' Sir Soloman Gold said. 'Give me the details and I'll pass them on.'

*

Townsend heard the news on television long before the van with the groceries and the newspapers arrived at noon, and one minute before he was told that he himself was to be released within twenty-four hours. He assumed that a trade had been arranged for the two men in Sarah Cheyney's house, and experienced a bewildering sensation of overwhelming relief and alarm.

'Jesus, skipper,' he whispered, 'don't you go wandering around London without me to watch your back. There's all sorts of bastards who'll have it in for you now. Persuade your lady to set up a practice in Australia or somewhere. She'll probably offer you a job as receptionist if you're no good at anything else.'

'You say something, Townsend?'

He glanced sideways at the guard watching the news with him. 'Just wondering why he's getting preferential treatment.'

'Don't work yourself into a lather about it,' the guard said. 'They're letting you go tomorrow.'

Shaw was handcuffed and hooded for his departure from the establishment codenamed 'Maple Anchor' and remained hooded until the skyline of Manhattan was close across the Hudson River. He remained handcuffed all the way to the departure gate at Kennedy International Airport and even when the cuffs were removed two men stayed with him until the doors of the British Airways Boeing 747 were about to be closed.

'Are you all right, sir?'

'What? Oh, yes thanks. I'm fine.'

The concern on the flight attendant's face was clear to see and his reply had done nothing to remove it.

'Can I bring you a drink or anything?'

'Thank you. A beer would be nice.'

He hadn't noticed the plane take off and, as he watched her walking away, had difficulty in remembering how he had got on board. The ticket he was still clutching told him that he was going to London and his passport, with its United States visa comprehensively cancelled, that he was denied readmit-

276

tance to that country under any circumstances. Sarah Cheyney drifted in and out of his mind like a restless ghost, but she was in a mean mood and wouldn't speak to him. When the girl came back with his beer Shaw had fallen asleep, one leg twitching occasionally like a dreaming dog's.

The waiting man was a terrorist by profession, a marksman by speciality and a sexual deviant by nature. His name was Flannigan.

People moved out of the customs area in a never-ending stream, some purposefully, sure of where they were going, others hesitantly, looking for friends or at the sign boards held up by drivers who had come to take them to their final destinations. Flannigan ignored them because it wasn't time yet and his mind was engaged in assessing the directional flow of pedestrian traffic, the distance to the numerous exits and the availability of practical cover. The police and the men he took to be plain-clothes security he ignored as well for they never stayed in the same place for long enough to make pinpointing them a profitable exercise and he'd lose sight of them in the smoke anyway.

The brown plastic jacket he had on was the twin of the one his brother had been wearing when the SAS murdered him, Macnamara and Quinn. Patrick and he had bought them together in Belfast and he had decided to wear it this day as a talisman and as the most suitable garment for the execution. The gun concealed by it was most suitable too, a KGB assassination weapon designed not only to punish the victim, but relatives, or friends, or anybody else called upon to identify the body.

Flannigan's favourite weapon was his rifle, an old Lee Enfield .303 with a telescopic sight – still, despite its antiquity, amongst the best sniper's rifles at 2,000 yards. He had killed two soldiers of the Parachute Regiment with that, plus a sergeant of the Black Watch and three men of the Royal Ulster Constabulary, but he couldn't very well carry it around Terminal 4 at London's Heathrow Airport. It didn't matter. The stubby gun under his arm, with its single charge of heavy buckshot, would not only kill instantly but also totally destroy the face, the mirror of the soul, its victim had presented to the world.

'The mirror of the soul,' Flannigan mouthed to himself, relishing the expression he had never heard until Mr Connolly had used it three hours earlier. It added a religious flavour to the revenge he had been so suddenly summoned out of Ulster to take on his dead brother's behalf. Being a deeply religious man, he liked that. He almost crossed himself, but desisted before his hand had properly begun the movement because now was no time to do anything conspicuous. Mr Connolly had been very insistent about that.

'Don't do anything conspicuous and by that I don't mean waving a flag, I mean things like avoiding eye-contact with anybody including the target,' Mr Connolly had said. 'There are no prints on the gun or this smoke grenade, so keep it that way and drop them both when you've made the hit, then take your time getting out of there. There'll be five thousand quid in your pocket, your brother's love in your heart and God's blessing on your head.' Flannigan almost crossed himself again.

Mr Connolly had also explained other things. It had to be done before the murdering bastard was taken into custody, or put under police protection, or left the country. It had to be done when the two were within sight of each other for the punishment to have the maximum effect. It *had* to be done right if Flannigan wanted to avoid having his kneecaps disciplined. There had been no need for Mr Connolly to make that particular threat, but Flannigan hadn't resented it. He was used to the methods of the IRA and had occasionally implemented them himself. He took the front page of *The Sun* with Shaw's photograph on it from his pocket, looked at it quickly and put it away again. That hadn't been necessary either because he knew every line on the face, but it gave him enormous gratification. A moment later caution overcame gratification and he screwed the paper into a ball and put it into a litter bin because it would be suicidal to have it found on him.

There was no photograph of the girl. Mr Connolly had told him that there had been no time to take one, but that should cause him no trouble. 'Stunning woman, I'm told,' he had said. 'They don't grow on trees. Think of your favourite erotic dream, colour it black and that's her.' Flannigan looked around him. There were several black women in sight, but none was so much as pretty. He felt no concern. Shaw's flight arrival time was still forty minutes away.

A big articulated road vehicle had jack-knifed somewhere near the Hammersmith fly-over, the young policeman told Sarah Cheyney. Then he looked at the 'Doctor' card displayed on her windscreen and went to a lot of trouble gaining inches for her from the cars ahead and behind so that she could cross a short section of pavement into a side-road clear of the snarl of traffic. His actions made her smile, reminding her of the treatment she had received aboard Concorde, because she knew that it had been her looks and not the card which had motivated him. For all that, she was extremely grateful as she was twenty minutes late.

There had been a lot to do after darling Solly had told her of Harry's impending arrival at Heathrow and she hadn't been able to start doing it for the long minutes it had taken for the wild surge of soaring happiness she had experienced to subside sufficiently to allow her to think. When it had done so she had cancelled all those appointments with her patients for the following day it was safe to cancel and arranged for a locum to handle those it was not. That had left her with one case she had no choice but to deal with herself this morning and that had taken longer than she had hoped.

After that she had changed into street clothing, her choice of garments arresting, provocative. She wanted to gleam for him like a beacon signalling sanctuary, refuge from the forces which would still have a hold on his mind. It was the doctor dressing, not the woman, the doctor who knew a great deal about drugs and, even had she not, she had seen what they had done to William Townsend. Look at me, was her message. Think about me and forget everything else. I am the focus of your life until you are well again. Not that she expected him to be in anything like the condition to which Townsend had been reduced. The Americans would have been too expert to permit that, but it could still be bad.

Satisfied finally with the visual impact she had contrived she had gone to her car and driven west as fast as she dared because the time factor was becoming critical. Then had come the traffic jam which had made her bite her lip in frustration and intense anxiety until the heaven-sent policeman had guided her clear of it. Now she was hurtling towards Heathrow, passing car after car on the inner lanes, wondering which of the endless stream of planes approaching the airport was Harry's and praying that it would take him at least twenty minutes to clear immigration and customs.

Flannigan also bit his lip because the British Airways enquiry desk confirmed that Shaw's flight was on the ground and still he had seen nothing resembling an erotic dream in any colour. In another ten minutes or so he knew it would be too late and he didn't like the thought of having to explain that to Mr Connolly, or of being deprived of his prurient and sadistic pleasure, but only three of those minutes had gone by when she stalked through one of the automatic glass doors on to the concourse.

Whatever relief Flannigan might have expected to feel was drowned out by sexual arousal so violent that it dried his mouth, sharply increased his pulse rate and drove his hands into his trouser pockets to ease the tension there. As soon as Mr Connolly had given him his orders he had known it was going to be good, but not this good. 'Holy Mother of God,' he whispered to himself, then almost giggled aloud for she didn't look in the least like the Mother of God, or the mother of anybody else for that matter. Nor did she look remotely holy. From the cap tilted over her nose to the high heels of her tall boots she was encased in black leather which left only her shadowed eyes and the dark skin of her lower face with its scarlet slash of a mouth exposed. He watched, fascinated, as she moved across the concourse towards the arrivals barrier, highlights rippling on her coat, then dragged his gaze away from her to watch for Shaw.

It seemed an age to Flannigan, but it was only minutes before he saw him. Heart pounding now, arousal extreme, he walked to the girl in black, dropped the smoke grenade at her feet, then took the gun from under his jacket and pulled the trigger.

*

Shaw didn't notice the five Special Branch men who closed around him as he pushed the trolley loaded with the baggage somebody had packed for him in the States out of the Green Channel. He was wondering what he was going to do, wondering if he had either the strength or the courage to see Sarah Cheyney that day. Focusing his eyes was still giving him trouble and he got only a blurred impression of a dark pretty face before it blossomed like a flower, a terrible red flower surrounded by a corona of pink mist. His brain froze the image as though it were a flashlight photograph, froze the crowds of people, froze him for the appalling eternity of a second's fraction. Then the slam of the gunshot reached his ears with the screams of people, and everything was movement again.

Smoke jetting from some unknown source, spreading, his trolley thrust from him, careering, toppling, his legs driving him towards the barrier, strange sounds coming from his throat. A voice shouting, 'Brown plastic jacket moving left!' Misjudging the height of the barrier, his foot snagging its top, falling, knocking somebody aside, his head thudding down on to her booted thighs.

'Harry! Harry!'

The call ignored because professionalism had taken over at the sound of a controlled burst of Heckler & Koch automatic fire. Too familiar to mistake. They must have issued the things to Airport Security now, and they'd used them too late, too late, *too bloody late!* Professionalism swept aside by overwhelming grief.

'Let go, Shaw.'

Hands grasping his arms, breaking their encircling grip on her dead legs, lifting him, forcing him forward through the smoke at a stumbling run. A glimpse of men with guns standing round a prostrate figure in a brown plastic jacket pock-marked with bullet holes which reminded him of something, but he couldn't remember what. Ulster, was it? His mind not answering the unspoken question, but registering the shock of cold as they reached the open air. A car door opened and his head came into sharp contact with something as he was thrust inside. He was aware of somebody hurled in after him just before darkness closed in.

281

Voices. Voices heard faintly through the ululation in his inner ear.

'That was supposed to be me, wasn't it?'

'I'm afraid so. We covered the wrong target.'

'I was late.'

'You were lucky.'

'Perhaps we should emigrate.'

'That might be wise.'

The ululation identified as external, not in his head. Police siren? Ambulance? Fire appliance? Head hurting, so ambulance probably. Try to sit up and find out. Muscles tensing. Eyelids fluttering, but not ready to open yet.

'He's coming round.' The voice male and vaguely familiar. A finger on his throat checking his pulse. A thumb raising his eyelid. Both hands dropping to his shoulders, shaking him.

Close to his ear, Sarah Cheyney said, 'How *dare* you, Harry?'

He was dreaming. The drugs they'd pumped into him. The bang on the head. The ghost in his mind aboard the plane had spoken after all. A real ghost now. Better reply because its mean moods were dangerous.

'I'm so sorry. So very sorry. I might be able to explain in time if you'll let me. It was about Ulster and –'

A furious voice interrupting, saying, 'How *dare* you think I'd *ever* go about dressed as though I was into bondage? How *could* you? Are you some sort of kink? I –' A long indrawn breath and the fury gone from the voice. 'Oh God, that poor girl.' Arms sliding around his neck drawing his head to her. Softness, and the darkness again.

'I thought . . .'

'Hush, darling. It's all right. It's all right now. That was just nerves talking. Go to sleep.'

On the outskirts of London: 'Shouldn't we get him to a doctor, Sarge? He looked pretty bad to me.'

The man in the front passenger seat of the speeding car glanced over his shoulder. There wasn't much of Shaw to be seen. His face was buried in the front of the girls's flame-red dress and he understood why the police driver had used the past tense.

'He's already got one,' Detective Sergeant Fenner said.